the Uninvited

F. P. DORCHAK

Copyright 2013 by F. P. Dorchak
Published by Wailing Loon, 2013
Cover design by **Duvall Design**
Print formatting by **A Thirsty Mind Book Design**

ISBN-13: 978-0615906829
ISBN-10: 0615906826

**WAILING
LOON**

Also by F.P. Dorchak

Novels

Sleepwalkers (2001)
ERO (2013)

Anthologies

"Tail Gunner":
*The You Belong Collection–Writings and Illustrations
by Longmont Area Residents* (2012)

Extreme thanks goes to Rob Butts and Laurel Davies-Butts, Dr. Sydney Heflin, Ron Pehr, Esq., Moe Morris, Jan (C.J.) Jones, Eric A. Reyes, Esq., Karen Lundstrom, Paul Kahn and his historical adaptation, the Honorable Jane Looney, District Judge, the Honorable Anne McLauglin, Pat LoBrutto, Karen Lin, Madelon Rose Logue, Therese Byorick, Lynne Bliss, Dr. Lawrence Gilbert, of the University of Texas, Dr. Tim Xie, of CSU, Long Beach, Simon Ager, Luigi Krapji, Denise Little, Margrit Trenker, my cover artist, Karen Duvall of Duvall Design, my most patient and masterful formatter, Pam Headrick of A Thirsty Mind Book Design (and Lynda Hilburn for introducing me to her), Cherry Weiner, the Pikes Peak Writers Conference and its founder Jimmie Butler, to my wife, Laura, for her constant and unwavering support, and to all those who had *any* part in assisting me…

With the exception of the Urgench and Takashima characters, all *historical* figures presented in this work are *real*, and I did my best to present them honorably. I mean no disrespect to them, their people, or their memory.

FPD

To Those Who Have Passed…
and
Lord MacTavish du Lac
Cassie
Lucy

Chapter One

1

Sunset Harbor, Florida, the Gulf Coast
Safe Harbor Retirement Community
March 10th, 1:12 a.m.

Palm tree fronds rustled comfortably outside eighty-six-year-old Matty Jenkowicz's small manufactured home, one of fifty identical frame dwellings within the compact and still-under-construction Safe Harbor Retirement Community. The silver-haired occupant sat on one end of her yellow, vintage fifty's Soren Willadsen couch, bathed in the comforting and flickering glow of her ancient and loud Curtis Mathes television set. A partially finished crossword puzzle rested in her lap. Her husband (God rest his soul), Abner Ignatius III, used to sit at the other end of the worn sofa, simultaneously reading some Robert Ludlum novel, watching TV, and slowly working an ice-cold lemonade, which'd always sat on a portable TV tray that'd always butted up against the sofa arm. Tonight's cool semi-tropical breeze and the hollow haunting tolls of wind chimes wafted in from Matty's open, screened-in windows. She returned to her television and laughed at *The Andy Griffith Show* rerun. She reached for her delicate china cup of still-steaming tea and chuckled again.

Suddenly inspired Matty returned to her crossword, searching for the blocks in question: the Greek goddess of discord…where was that—oh, yes, seventy-nine across—"Eris." Matty triumphantly penciled in the letters. She knew she knew the answer…it just took a little time. Everything took a little longer at her age, but that was okay. She'd lived a good life. She'd wished her husband of sixty-five years was still around, but *Lymphoblastic lymphoma* had put an end to that two years ago. He hadn't suffered much, thank the Lord, it'd been a quick attack when it'd finally rallied its forces, but oh, how she *missed* him! She still talked to him, thought of him every day, every minute…even wrote herself letters that she mailed to herself and imagined came from him. But her friends, and the sunshine and beauty of south Florida all managed to help stem the pain when it got a little much to handle. Sometimes, more so recently, her anxieties kept her from sleeping and she got to thinking about death…and about how much closer she was to it than she had been eighty-six years ago.

How time flew.

The young never thought about that—and needn't have to. Life was meant to be lived, and that's just what she and Abner had done. Together. Her favorite cup of Earl Grey and television would help assuage the phantoms tonight, but one day…one day, she'd finally be with Abner again.

Andy and Opie went in for the night, but Matty waited patiently through the commercials—which she never really minded watching— for the next show, *Gomer Pyle, USMC*. This used to be one of Abner's favorites. She and Abner'd actually met Jim Nabors once up at Montana's Glacier Park International Airport, while vacationing years ago. He'd been such a nice man.

Her tea still warm, Matty returned to her crossword. Eleven down was "Disturb," she'd already had "the Northernmost trees around German City," which turned out to be "timberline," and the "Jeweled weight" of "carat."

"Ah-ha! '*Roil*'!" Matty again penciled in her entry, then looked up.

She grabbed the remote and muted the television. Listened. Wincing from arthritis she turned her head to one side, allowing her good ear a better angle. Slow to her feet (she hadn't done anything fast in over twenty years), she went to one of her open windows. The room she was in actually used to be a screened-in portico, but Abner, ever the handyman, had extended the home out and walled it in, making it a regular sitting room. Peering outside and inhaling the cool, floral breezes, she saw nothing. But that didn't say much for her eyesight, glasses or no. Her night vision had never been any good.

Matty sighed and returned to her couch, returning the television's volume to its more normal—well, to her anyway—loudness. As she set down the remote and lifted her cup of tea, her patio door slid open and in waltzed the shadowy form of a man. Matty let out a surprised puff of air from asthmatic lungs. Squinting and heart racing, she readjusted her glasses.

"*A-Abner?*"

The figure continued in, not too quickly, not too slowly, but as if it knew the person on the couch and was just coming in after a long night out on the town.

Before Matty could say anything else, she heard, from outside across the way, a sharp report. She looked away, back out the window, and as she did so the man raised an accusatory arm toward her. When Matty looked back, the man now stood directly before her, holding out something that smelled of oil and something else she couldn't quite identify. But, before she could complete that memory, the object flared and sent a rifled slug screaming directly through the center of her forehead, slamming her back against the couch. Brains and memories splattered out behind her, all over the faux-wood paneling Abner had put up not five years ago, and all while Sergeant Carter was busy chewing out Private Pyle during an in-ranks inspection.

The intruder fired another round into her chest, then dropped the weapon to the green shag carpet. Wasting no time, he lifted her up off the couch and took her outside to the screened-in carport, another Abner project fifteen years old. There the intruder lay her down at the end of a large throw rug already in place, duct-taped a plastic bag around the remains of Matty's head, and summarily rolled her up. Then he duct-taped the rolled-up rug, got back to his feet, and gave everything a final once-over. Satisfied, he grabbed the thirty-four-inch Rawlings baseball bat—and without further ado—began beating the living shit out of Matty Jenkowicz's fragile, arthritic body, as Gomer Pyle received yet another ass-chewing from Sergeant Carter back in the living room…

2

In the balmy, late-night humidity, the dull dead eyes of a security guard stared blankly up at the man called Tiger. The rest of the security guard's body lay cockeyed on the guard-shack floor in one of those crazy "corpse angles" that look so good in black-and-white movies and police photographs. Tiger never stopped, but continued on past the shack and the busted barricade arm; made his way into the Safe Harbor Retirement Community complex. A nasty wind kicked up through towering Slash Pine and several varieties of tastefully arranged palm trees, as well as through his long, scraggly and unkempt hair and beard. Tiger kept his head low and continued to kick and swipe at the hungry little *Solenopsis richteri Forel* and *Solenopsis invicta Buren*—fire ants—off his legs. He pulled his ratty overcoat tighter about him, tightening his grip on the object held hidden within one of his overcoat's pockets. The humidity was unbearable in his long coat, but he refused to discard it no matter how itchy and sweaty it made him. By God, he'd worn it this far, and he was gonna wear it clean through this business. But the sweat was making it hard to see, and those goddamned fire ants were vicious. He kept trying to shake them off as he shuffled along the Bahiagrass-lined culvert, occasionally swatting at those that had made it up his legs, but the little shits held on, pinching and biting all the goddammed way. Between them and the humidity and the sweat it was near impossible to continue. His ant wounds were painful and swelling and were making it increasingly difficult to focus. But...he was just being tested. He'd been through far worse, elsewhere...

One foot in front a th'other...one step at a time, he kept telling himself, and everything would fall into place. All would be avenged. Righted. Even-steven. All he had to do was *be* there, that's all, and everything would take care of itself. All markers called in. The last bell. Wall Street be closed for the week, my friend...

Tiger lifted his head to the scent of rain. Ah, the sweet, cleansing wash of rain. Lightning flashed in the distance. It was gonna let loose soon, and when it did, oh, boy, was it gonna pound down in sheets and torrents of hell and damnation for the wicked.

Hopefully it'd wash away tonight's sins.

Tiger winced as more ants dug their mandibles into his already tender and tortured flesh, then followed through with their take-this-you-son-of-a-bitch jab of their stingers. The old fire ant one-two. The little bastards were pissed, and he guessed they had every right to be. He was the one who came plowing on through *their* homes. They hadn't been looking for trouble. *He* had. They were just defending their territory, their right to live. And they're fast, he found, as he'd come tumbling down and landed onto that first mound upon entering town. Were they like bees, one sting and they blew their load? Dropped off and died? Doubted it. He could tell from their fury they were a tenacious bunch. But he had bigger fish to fry and was almost there. Tiger tried to take his mind off the pain...allowing the deafening roar of the wind and screams to consume him. The noise that had been in his head for years. The wind, hot, aching, and desiccating, it had become his friend, his only companion. He continued on…focused on *getting* there…on the *wind*…

As he made his way down el Prado Street, Tiger saw several other shadows crisscrossing the road ahead. Off to his left he spotted another up just a little farther, on the opposite side of the road.

An image flashed through his mind…a woman being beaten to death while rolled up in something…no, that wasn't quite right…she'd *already* been killed…

Tiger lowered his head and stayed true to his course, going where his legs blindly carried him. That had been how he'd found his way here, after the past, dimly remembered couple of months—or had it been years?

New York City.

And he saw no need to change things now. He was almost there, dammit, he could finally put all this insanity behind him. It was…the wind…not just those external Floridian gusts heralding the oncoming

(*Armageddon?*)

downpour, but the screaming, burning, aching blast *internal* to his head. That's what kept him going. The winds that just wouldn't goddamn stop. Let him go. The winds that had started years ago, gradually and sporadically at first, then had taken on full-force gale proportions. The very winds that had caused him to find himself where he was now, in a town he'd never heard of until tonight.

Tiger stumbled; brushed away more ants.

The pain was intense, his legs, hips, and lower torso all on fire…all growing numb…trying to…but what use did he have to feel his legs or any other part of his body for that matter?

Did people die from ant bites?

He supposed they did or could, if the pain was any indication. He was sure it could get worse, because it certainly wasn't getting any better. As long as his legs got him there—where else had he to go? But the pain kept him moving, he supposed, because he'd stumbled, and that simply wasn't tolerated. We must all pay for our transgressions, mustn't we? Dead or alive, zombie or not, he was going to get there and finish what'd been started, oh, so long ago. If anything positive could be made out of all this, those hungry little bastards kept him *moving…*

* * *

Espanola Street.

Tiger took a slow right onto it, each step an unparalleled experience in agony. The storm's wind, the external Floridian one, picked up. He was sure there was more moisture in the air on the way just begging for its angry release. On this road were the beginnings of the trailers, the homes, and he had to continue until he came upon his. There was more activity, here, among the wind-chimed and well-manicured lawns...

He had arrived. This was the place. It might not have been as expected, but it was finally making sense. *Everyone* was coming home.

As Tiger passed the home directly before his, he smelled smoke and saw and heard muffled activity inside.

Thumps.

Things breaking.

A cut-off, stifled scream.

Other images assaulted him. One person's throat cut. Another shot. Still others beaten beyond recognition.

Boiling water...*in a tub?*

He shook his head, tried to rid his mind of the images.

Had to remain focused on his own task.

Tiger stopped before his trailer. It was now a veritable battleground of thunder and lightning, flashing and exploding everywhere, allowing him to spot the backlit huddles of other shadowy forms all around him, similarly wandering the streets. Spits of rain began to slam down out of the angry, tormented night sky. He wasn't sure he wanted to see just how angry the sky really was, but he liked it back here, in the dark—no cars, and the ants seemed to have backed off. Here, the internal howling was the strongest, however. Tiger spit out the grit that filled his mouth, and turned, trudging up the lit carport alongside the trailer. Tightening his grip on the object still hidden within his overcoat, he continued, clumsily maneuvering past the Grand Marquis. He made for the screen door beyond it, opened it, but made sure he closed it behind him. Once inside the screened-in AstroTurf porch, he turned to the home's patio glass door and opened that. Good for him, it really was open, not that he'd thought about it; he'd just assumed they'd be waiting for him like they all had…for so long. He slid it open and sloughed up the two AstroTurfed steps. He closed that door behind him as well.

Mustn't let in the ants.

Streetlights shone in through partially opened curtains of the now-storm-dampened interior, otherwise the trailer was dark. He glanced outside, and saw another shadow shamble past the trailer. It was going to be a busy night, indeed. The shadow continued on down to the next home. Tiger returned to his task and entered the short, dark corridor, hand still in pocket. It was almost done. Just had to muscle through it and everything would be alright.

Finito.

Tiger passed the first door to his right and a second to his left. The first one opened into a darkened-but-empty room (he saw by filtered streetlight and flashes of lightening), and the second, on his left, was a night-light-illuminated bathroom, a small circle of light highlighting sea shells that filled a small glass container by the night-light. He continued on to the closed door ahead; grasped the handle and slowly twisted it open.

Entering the room, he closed the door behind him. You couldn't be too careful…had to close things up and be tidy, before, during, *and* after. He knew about tidy, though his present condition might well belie any such knowledge. He knew from a previous life. A life he didn't think much about, and, in all reality, couldn't. His memory wasn't as good as it used to be. It was all ancient history, now, anyway. Had been replaced by howling winds—and all that wailing and screaming—which had left little in their wake. All he remembered now was sand and wind…and horses…horses that thundered across wide open spaces, or wherever it was those charging beasts thundered across…*those* things, he remembered. But he'd get the job done, and the streetlights would help, the ants' welts would help, and so would the broken and jagged remains of a Chateau St. Michelle Chardonnay that at one time went so well with crab, poultry, and scallops, and which he now withdrew from his pocket. It didn't matter if they stayed asleep, but it would certainly help things along.

As he raised the broken bottle overhead, there was another explosive clap of thunder, and bright unnerving discharges of lightning chained across an angry night sky. Tiger had a momentary glimpse of the two aging lives he was about to take. They slept, hugging each other under their blankets and comforter. Like the ant bites, it made little impact on him—well, except for that tiny whimpering part, deep inside, still pleading for him to *not* do this—but he had to. Had no choice. The wind, the sand, and the tortured wailing all compelled him on…he had to make right what had been wronged, oh, so very long ago…

Chapter Two

1

Kacey Miller, tote bag, recorder, and notepad in tow, collected herself after clearing the stucco wall and landing in the *Brunfelsia pauciflora* and *Calliandra emarginata*, which surrounded the Safe Harbor Retirement Community, and spattered rain water remnants onto her face and clothes. As she looked back from where she'd come, she spotted a delivery truck driving past that declared "Guilty Pleasures!", a picture of a woman eating a pear on its side. Wincing, she anxiously made her way across the reflective, moisture-laden asphalt and through the deserted police cruisers, their silent, still-flashing lights painting surreal, patriotic colors everywhere. It was just after two in the morning, and haze obscured the streetlights, buildings, and trees in the fresh dampness that followed the storm that had just pummeled the area. People were supposed to be asleep…but not here. Here were all kinds of activity and flashing lights, and here Kacey Miller was trying to sneak an interview or two from those who had made it through some horrible massacre, the likes of which she was sure this sleepy little town had never seen before. Thank God for insomnia, Radio Shack, and cheap scanners. Kacey was almost shaking with anticipation as she continued to—unbelievably—thread her way closer and closer to the clubhouse. The scent of the recently passed thunder boomer remained strong in the air, lightning still flashed in the distance, and she thought, what a tragic dichotomy: the beautiful and cleansing power and smell of nature set against the backdrop of a heinous crime. If what she'd heard were true, this was big news, and she was first on the scene. *First.* The *Sunset Harbor Gazette* had to give her a job after this one…*had to.* Why, the sheer magnitude of it all…*who would do such a thing?* What was their motive? Where had they—

Two pairs of hands reached out from the darkness, and Kacey near jumped out of her skin. She found herself staring into the quite unimpressed faces of two of Sunset Harbor's finest.

"Well, aren't we quite the persistent ace-cub-reporter-wannabe?" came the voice from behind.

Grimacing, Kacey immediately slumped both her shoulders and her enthusiasm.

"Oh, come *on*, Fisher…" she said, rolling her eyes skyward.

Kacey turned to meet Detective Thomas Fisher, Sunset Harbor's Special Operations Bureau crime scene investigator. He always seemed to get in her way. Or something like that.

"You gotta let me in, *c'mon*. This is *big*. This could really make it for me—"

Detective Fisher nodded to the two officers, who released her and returned to their previous duty, shaking their heads as they made their way back toward the clubhouse. Fisher pulled Kacey off to the side.

"Look, we only just got here—don't you have anything better to do this time of night, for God's sake?"

Kacey looked up at him. "No."

"Yeah, well, knowing you, you're probably right. Ms. Miller…this is serious—it's a mess in there, and we haven't even gotten up the tape, yet—"

"So, it's true, then? Are there any survivors? Who did this?"

Fisher escorted her farther back into the shadows. "You know you're not even supposed to breathe the same air as me and my department, so will you back off a bit? Huh? Let us do our job? Then…then we'll see what I can give you? Okay?"

Kacey stared back at him. Of course not, but he didn't have to know.

"Okay."

Fisher looked away, exasperated, then stuck one end of his cell phone in her face.

"Look—you get caught, that's *it*—I can't keep helping you out any more. You're on your own—then onto your next town, got it?"

"Got it," she said, wincing, but pulling out her notepad.

Fisher let out a long sigh. "We really don't know what happened, okay?, we just got here. I got people all over this place, still pulling out suspects—or survivors—we can't quite tell them all apart, yet—and you keep my name out of this!"

Kacey nodded, scribbling furiously. Without missing a beat she crossed out Fisher's name, rapt attention focused on his every word.

Fisher expelled another sigh between clenched teeth.

"Shit. It appears as if a group of unknowns walked into this place then went on a no-holds-barred killing spree."

Fisher stared off into the darkness.

"It's like they're drugged or something…we're finding them just sitting or walking aimlessly about—confused."

"Confused?"

"Like they don't know where they are or what they did."

Fisher paused.

"Okay, that's it, get outta here—"

"What?"

"Don't push it, Miller, or I swear—"

"Are you telling me these people just walked in off the street and went house-to-house, killing everyone in a mass-murderous funk?"

Fisher stared at her long and hard.

"You don't seem to understand me. *I'm* not telling you *anything*."

Fisher made a move to leave, but Kacey grabbed him. When he turned back to her his look actually frightened her.

"I'm not kidding. This is serious—the biggest thing we've ever had to deal with around here—or anywhere else, for that matter—and now I have to find enough jail space to store all these creeps."

"They killed everyone in here, didn't they," she said more as a statement than a question.

Fisher turned away and disappeared back into the crime scene.

"Wow."

Kacey stood, stunned, looking after Fisher as he walked off into the darkness. Then she remembered why she was there and quickly went to her gear. She looked up just in time to see an elderly couple leave the clubhouse, arm in arm. Hitching her gear back up onto her shoulders, she hurriedly made her way toward them, but remained in the shadows. She really didn't want to piss off Fisher any more…at least, not so *soon*, anyway…

The air smelled clean and fresh. There was a gentle balmy breeze playing over the tops of Slash Pine, Coconut palms, and Desert Cassia, as Kacey tried to stay hidden in the shadows, skirting around the parking lot, tracking the couple. She also tried to avoid the cops that continued to pour into this tiny little community, a community that—until a few minutes ago—had always kept a low, quiet, profile. Kacey picked up her pace. If she didn't act soon, she was going to lose the pair into the darkness and presence of more Sunset Harbor Police and state troopers.

"Excuse me! *Excuse* me!" Kacey hailed, in a loud whisper. Reshuffling her gear, she emerged from the shadows, casting wary glances toward the cops. The couple stopped, turned, and the man immediately took up a defensive posture.

"Thank you," Kacey said, catching her breathe. "I-I'm sorry, I don't mean to alarm you, but I'm with the *Sunset Harbor Gazette*— would you mind if I had a word with you?"

The couple looked to each other. They had to easily be at least in their seventies, but Kacey was amazed at how fit they looked for their ages. Trim. These two were definitely not push-overs by any stretch. The man stood ramrod straight. He had a severe white crew cut capping a rough face. His wife, somewhat shorter, also stood straight, but she couldn't hide the fatigue as well as her husband and had nowhere near the fire in her eyes. The man's intensity unnerved Kacey as he sized her up.

What had those aging eyes seen over his lifetime?

The man's voice was weary, though authoritative.

"We saw you with the detective," he said. "Ma'am…we're really tired and have nothing more to say." They turned to leave.

"Sir—ma'am," Kacey insisted, appealing to the woman as she jumped directly into their path, hands upraised in a non-threatening— pleading—way. "I really don't mean to impose—I don't—and I know I can't *possibly* understand the magnitude of what you'd both just been through—"

Kacey stopped dead in her tracks. As she looked to the couple's shadowy and disheveled appearance, she realized that what appeared to be splotches of mud were actually blood.

"My God…are you two all right?"

At a loss for words, Kacey extended a hand toward them. They both backed away. Kacey then pointed across to the community's entranceway, toward the main street, where she'd parked her car.

"I-I'm…so sorry…would…would you like a ride to wherever you're going? My car's right over there—"

"We're fine, ma'am, really" the seventy-something-year-old-man said.

"Okay…look, I really don't mean to intrude, and promise not to take up much of your time…but this is the biggest thing this town has ever seen—and you two survived it. Are you planning on heading home?"

"Where else can we go?" the woman asked.

"You don't really want to spend the rest of the night, *here*, do you? Wouldn't you rather get away from all this for a little while?

"Look," Kacey said, dropping as much pretense as possible, "I understand you've been through a lot—let me take you away from here—just until you get your heads together."

There was a pause as the three sized up each other.

"Well," the woman finally said, looking to her husband, "the detective did say they were still going through our home."

Kacey could see it in her eyes; she felt the man could probably have done it—had probably already done plenty worse during his lifetime—but when he looked into his wife's eyes she saw him immediately cave.

"What do you have in mind?" he asked.

2

Kacey couldn't believe she'd actually had possibly the only surviving members of the Safe Harbor murders in her apartment. Before they'd even left the parking lot they'd introduced themselves as Jack and Hedda Hocker. Kacey'd had a couple beach towels in her trunk—never knew when the urge to stop at a beach would strike—and threw them over the seats for the couple to sit on, given their…condition. Though she drove what was quickly becoming known as a "beater" car, Kacey didn't really want to include blood stains on the car's list of characteristics. On the way home, Kacey'd discovered that Hedda had been a nurse during the Korean War, where she and Jack had met, had taken to raising their two kids once married, and was currently active in many community activities. Jack was a thirty-three-year Marine Corps Master Gunnery Sergeant veteran retired many years, now a gun shop owner. Kacey's dad had been Navy, and though she no longer remembered the details of the rank structure, knew "Gunny Sergeants" were pretty high up there.

Back at her apartment, at the Coral Gables Estates, Kacey helped the couple clean up and into some old sweats she'd had, and was amazed at the extent of their injuries, though, luckily, all were superficial. Jack Hocker had cuts and scrapes all along his arms, on his face, and was developing some nice purple-and-yellow bruising, but Hedda was none the worse for wear, having been spared any direct contact with the assailants. Jack and Hedda's clothes were also torn in places and covered with splotches of blood. Kacey had a scare—only once—when Hedda had been using her bathroom and she realized she was alone with Jack for the first time. She began to wonder if maybe, just maybe, she'd been wrong—and these two had actually been *part* of the murder spree—the only two who had gotten away by lying to police. Her fears, however, were quickly laid to rest once Hedda returned from her shower.

"Oh, this feels *so* much better—thank you, Kacey," Hedda said. "I don't know if I could have really done that, going back to our place just then. We really appreciate this."

Jack looked on lovingly to his wife, obviously pleased at her much revitalized demeanor. "You look wonderful, hon," he said.

"How about we all move into the living room—such as it is," Kacey suggested, directing them into the adjacent extension of her dining area, "and I'll bring in some coffee?"

Jack got up and took his wife's arm, while Kacey got the coffee and followed them in.

"Okay…do you mind if I were to now ask a couple questions?"

Both shook their heads.

Kacey looked down to her notes. As she picked up her pen she found herself trembling and hoped they didn't notice. Nerves, first-time jitters, or maybe just a realization of the magnitude of what had happened to this couple, it hit Kacey that this was no longer just some silly little game to get her name into print. This was real life and real people she was messing with. What she said, and how she said it, would probably affect this couple for the rest of their lives. She had to be mindful of that.

Calming herself, she inhaled and said, "Now, I realize what you've just been through was probably the most horrific event either of you've ever experienced, but could you please tell me what happened?"

Hedda sipped her coffee with both hands, casting her husband nervous glances. Kacey could still see the terror in her eyes. Without looking to his wife, Jack began.

"I think it was about one-fifteen—I'm a very light sleeper—when I heard this noise. As I'd lay in bed, I remembered looking to all the shadows in the bedroom—it's something I got used to doing while in the Corps, and it's just always stuck with me. Anyway, something didn't feel right—when I see these shadows enter our bedroom—just walk on in as if it were theirs. I tell ya, I've seen lots of things in my time in the Corps, but in all those instances you *knew* you were in harm's way…were *expectin* it…but I tell you, you're not expecting something like this once you're a civilian, to see figures enter your bedroom—your home—in the middle of the night, your wife beside you—"

"There was more than one?"

"Two, yes, ma'am. Walked right on into our bedroom as pretty as you please. Well, I hadn't experienced an adrenaline rush like that in years, but my instincts were still sharp, and I leapt out of bed and asked questions later—"

"You confronted them?"

"Yes, ma'am."

Kacey scribbled away, raising an eyebrow, and caught Hedda pulling her husband in closer as she stared down at the floor.

"It wasn't much subduing them, but when we turned the lights on and looked around, I saw and heard others out in the streets—out there in the park—and when I looked out into other homes, I saw and heard what sounded like other struggles. Screams. I knew we were in trouble. It was like I was back in the jungle all over again. I had Heddy get our Browning, and I grabbed my KA-BAR and .45—"

"That's a knife, isn't it, 'KA-BAR'?"

"Yes, ma'am. Marine Corps issue."

"And—sorry—'Browning' is…"

"One of our hunting rifles."

Kacey nodded, scribbling away.

Jack continued. "So I grabbed my gear and rushed outside, yelling to Heddy to call the cops and pick her targets. She's a crack shot," the Master Gunny Sergeant added, to which Hedda smiled and nodded, raising a hand into a mock pistol and dropping her thumb as the hammer.

"Jack went house to house, but didn't find—"

Hedda broke off in a surge of emotion Kacey saw surprised even Hedda herself.

Jack put his hand to her lap, finishing her thought. "I didn't find any survivors. At least not around us. It looked like a well-coordinated attack. Whoever they were had managed a complete and total ambush and wiped us out, at least our block, by the looks a things. I just hope there were survivors in other parts of the park," Jack said. He took a sip of coffee.

"Do you know?" Hedda asked Kacey.

"Sorry?"

"Do you know? How many other survivors there are?"

Kacey stared at the couple and thought about what Fisher had told her—well, more like what he *hadn't*. That it appeared as if the only survivors were sitting before her, right this moment, sipping coffee in her living room.

"Well, the detective I talked with said they were still arresting suspects and really didn't know anything, yet. That he couldn't tell survivors from suspects at this point."

Good God, his words had just sunk in—*really* sunk in.

The couple nodded. Again, the thought crossed her mind. What did she, or the police, for that matter, really know about this couple? All they had was their story, and, let's face it, couldn't they have also been in on the murders themselves, then cleverly saved ass by saying, "Hey, we're the *good* guys!"? Their home could have been a clever ruse, an "in" into the community. Kacey began to wonder if inviting them in had been such a good idea...

But they didn't seem the killer type.

They just didn't *feel* like the kind of people who'd murder innocent people in their sleep one moment, then calmly discuss it the next. They both seemed genuinely unnerved by the whole incident, though weirder things have been known to happen...

"So," Kacey continued, keeping her uneasiness to herself, while also noting she did have a clear shot to the door, a pen in hand, and pepper spray in her purse on the end table by the door, "you woke up to find intruders in your bedroom, took care of them, then went outside to help others—and called the police? Do you remember anything else?"

"That's about it," Hedda said.

"Well...there was one other...kinda weird...thing," Jack said.

"Go on."

"When I was outside, it was really odd...I mean, they fought back when I attacked, but otherwise...otherwise it was like they didn't care. Didn't seem to care I was there, that I saw them, walked among them, fought them."

"Excuse me?"

"Well, with those I fought, sure, they tried to fend me off, half-heartedly and all, but I had many others pass me by—literally—several times, when I was engaged with others. They simply *ignored* me. It was like I didn't matter, and they just walked right on past to their next target. If I intercepted them, they fought back, but, otherwise, they just let me fight who I was fighting and continued on to their next kill."

Kacey stared back in silence.

"And one other thing," he added, turning to his wife. "I just remembered something else—but in the midst of all this," he said, turning back to Kacey, "I thought I was gonna get trampled over by horses or something."

"*Horses?*"

"I coulda swore I heard and felt the thunder of..." Jack broke off laughing, "this might sound really stupid, but I swore I heard and felt the thunder of thousands of *horses* bearing down on us—on *me*. *Thousands* of them. I swore the ground trembled with their charge."

At that point Jack, though he never mentioned it and forever kept it to himself, had the fleeting image of him fighting in a kind of low-grade armor, wielding a sword and crude mace. He never spoke of it to Hedda or Kacey.

Kacey jotted down all of what the Hockers had said.

"Huh. Well, I thank you for your time, Mr. and Mrs. Hocker, and I'm so sorry—I can't begin to tell you how sorry I am for what's happened—and I just hope the police find out who did this and why. If you ever need anything, please, *please*, don't hesitate to call. You're free to stay the day, if you'd—"

"If it's all the same to you, ma'am," Jack said, getting to his feet, "I think we'll head back. Sooner or later we'll have to face things. Hopefully, they're done with our place by now."

Kacey nodded.

And, maybe, Kacey thought, she could sneak into a house or two...

3

Sarasota County's newest inmate, number 5943667, otherwise known as Susan Sibley, housewife and volunteer worker, always considered herself a strong woman, not just physically, but mentally and spiritually, as well. In her late forties, she'd already raised her three kids, Polly, Ben, and Wendy into well-adjusted members of society and the college scene. All were intelligent and none of them did drugs. They'd all written home, called home, and sent those special occasion cards and flowers on time. For what more could a mother ask? Susan had the perfect husband in Andrew Sibley, who was, admittedly, a bit on the workaholic side, but who paid her as much attention as possible, and frequently called from work, or left humorous, loving, text messages on her cell. They had a beautiful home, though it was now an empty nest, and Susan had gone back to school herself, studying art. She'd always been particularly interested in Dali, and had always wanted to study art ever since she'd discovered, with her first child, that she could, suddenly and unaccountably, paint. She was, however, drawn to barren landscapes...prairies, plains, and deserts...all things remote and desolate...which she couldn't explain—but no less ignore. It was just what emerged from *within*. She'd sought the help of other artists, entered therapy, and even consulted psychics to try to understand why it was her sketches and art work were all so sullen and barren. She never felt that way at home, or with Andrew—just in her art. All the Rorschach tests, all the psychoanalysis, and all the *Dr. Phil* and *Dr. Drew* shows had told her that she was, unequivocally, happy, and should, by all rights, be painting and sketching sunrises and sunsets, glorious seascapes, and fields of plenty and happiness...

So why all the artistic desolation?

She had no answer. She just chose to ignore it and went about life as she had for the past twenty years, painting what came to her, and living life to its fullest. She took up biking, weight training, even taught cardio classes—all in an effort to maybe, she and the professionals thought, release any possibly *unconscious*, pent-up, angst. Abandonment or lack-of-attention issues. She didn't have any, she insisted, but they (those darned professionals) insisted try it, it couldn't hurt, could it? Look at it this way, if there were any unconscious issues this might release their orneriness, and if not, look at what great shape she'd be in! She'd be so buff she and her hubby won't be able to keep their hands off each other (not that they did already). Well, who could resist that argument? Buff *and* more sex? *Woo-hoo, America...*

So, Susan made the gym and running her daily routine, and, indeed, created quite the conditioned physique. And, yes, the results were just as the professionals had envisioned...but still, there had been no "rage catharsis," no internal psychiatric purification, *because there just hadn't been any pent-up* anything.

No harm, no foul. Life goes on.

Then, what had come to be called "The Event," happened. A Beechcraft Bonanza, a sightseeing plane out of Teterboro, its pilot and three passengers, had all slammed directly into the thirty-seventh floor of the Pall Meadows building, on New York City's Park Avenue. The obvious comparisons were made, but it was nothing more than a fifty-four-year-old pilot having had a heart attack while taking the Beech in a lot closer than he should have in the first place. The plane would have crashed somewhere, no matter its altitude and heading, but it just so happened that on this day, given this set of circumstances, it had crashed into Pall Meadows, the very floor upon which Susan Sibley's only brother, Wallace Theodore Bryce, worked. They'd always been close, Wally and Susan, but on that fateful day he'd told her he'd *seen* it, seconds before it'd actually happened, in the reflection of a nearby building as he'd been daydreaming out his window. It had been a beautiful, clear day…he'd been sipping a double-mocha extra latte with a cinnamon twist…when he saw the unthinkable. "Saw" that plane plow straight into Pall Meadows like a replay of 9/11, and "felt" the shocking impact reverberate through the offices of Meyers Financial, past the legs of that hot new investment broker, Sonia McGrath, four cubes down, then "telegraphed" through his leather-back throne, as he had it swiveled toward the plate glass of his corner office windows. Yes, brother Wally had "seen" it, seen it all, all the fire, the smoke, the surreality, and, lucky for him, brother Wally had been quick to respond. Something deep within him had actually propelled him to his feet after that vision (double-mocha extra latte with a cinnamon twist splattered all over the carpet and portions of his leather highback, not to mention his slacks and shoes), and it was then that he actually *saw* the Beechcraft coming straight at them. The words came flying out his mouth before he knew what he was saying: *Oh my* God! *That plane! It's gonna* hit! *We have to get outta here!* Now!

Brother Wally had felt his legs grow wobbly, something he'd read about in books, but had never really and truly believed until this very moment, then quickly rediscovered locomotion, as he rushed out of his office into the reception area of Meyers Financial proper. Others were also up, milling about, pointing and commenting at the casual flybys of the sightseeing aircraft. They all looked at him, crazy like. *Crash?* It was just flying *around* them…but in no short order, things quickly changed from curiosity to dire concern, and when it happened, it happened *fast*.

But, to Wally, every moment was exquisitely drawn out.

They also all spilled their chais and lattes, and began screaming and yelling, just like him. Even beautiful Sonia was wailing strings of nouns, verbs, adjectives, and not to mention some rather choice expletives. So, brother Wally hurried everyone out and cleared the office, but, as he was the last one out, found himself staring—simply staring—at the suddenly empty office, the horror of what was about to happen still a smoking hole in his mind's eye, and a weird feeling in the pit of his gut.

Not to mention he could now *see* the wobbling, unsteady Beech coming straight for them, as he looked all the way through the now-deserted office space and out an office window on the opposite side. Not only wasn't this right, on this bright, beautiful Wednesday morning, at ten-forty-one, a.m., but he'd had his first distinct and wholly psychic event in his entire dull and droll life. In his mind's eye—as clear as the day was gorgeous—he'd pre-witnessed the stark and harsh contrast burning before him...office papers flickering down from the sky like so much confetti, shimmering in the early morning sun, and desks, filing cabinets and people blown out the exploded windows at the impact location.

Brother Wally was the last one to hear all the phones that were, even now, ringing; he was the last one to smell the coffee that was still brewing at various locations around the office, and the last one to see those rays of sunshine hitting the desks and potted plants just so. He was the last man on earth, at this moment, but he wouldn't last if he didn't get his ass out of there *now*.

So, out Wally rushed, and, adrenaline flushing his system, glanced at the Last-Man-On-Earth Time as he left the offices, which clocked in at ten-forty-two. He'd tried to take the elevator, but so was everyone else (which was a mistake), so he hoofed it down the stairwell with those not using the elevators. Thank God for his five-mile morning runs...

Well, not that Susan knew all of the exact, intimate details of the last moments of her brother's life, but she had talked with him ever so briefly on his cell phone after he'd evacuated. She still recalled hearing all the noise and screaming from the others around him, his labored breathing. In those few short seconds, Wally had told her what had happened, and what they were doing, and that was the last she—or anyone else—had ever heard from him. Over the past couple years since, Susan had had ample time and imagination to fill in all the holes she didn't know about her brother's escape, and what might have really happened up there. No one had ever found him after the crash, which had slammed precisely into the floors of the offices of Meyers Financial, at ten-forty-two that morning, and no one had been able to find his body—wholly or in parts—following the extensive relief efforts and hospital searches. Susan had done all she could, but despite her best efforts, had not turned up anything on her only brother. He was simply and succinctly listed as "missing." She had just chosen to fill in all the spaces by thinking and rethinking the scenario over and over in her mind. She doubted he'd perished in that building, preferring optimism to the alternative. To her, two facts remained: he *had* told her of his one and only premonition, and she—to this day—*felt* him still alive.

And that had been the single most defining moment of Susan Sibley's life—except for today. Here, during the early morning hours where she suddenly, inexplicably, found herself in a Gulf Coast Florida detention center cell for committing a series of murders of which she had plenty of blood and other DNA all over her, as well as a load of partial memories and screams and pleas still echoing in her head that could only be attributed to the actions of which she'd been accused. If ever there had been a time in which she might have had any kind of unconscious, pent-up rage, this would be it, but it appeared as if all her therapy and cures had come years early, years before the symptoms, and had all, long ago, fallen flat. Any problems she'd thought she'd had in the past of her short-but-sweet life had all been a joke. One huge, cosmic prank played upon a poor, meek soul that had actually proven to be more prophetic than anything else.

Close but no cigar.

Horrifyingly precognitive, at best.

Boy, was the joke ever on them, wasn't it boys! Susan's life up til now had been a walk in a rose garden, and no one could even appreciate it…except for her. Susan had had no problems…you wanna talk *problems?* Talk Sunset Harbor, Florida, one-twelve in the a.m., when she found herself fourteen-hundred miles from home, with a much-used pair of stained grass shears in her hands, bloody and dripping.

In *her* hands.

In someone else's bedroom. As she stood over two mutilated and quite dead bodies, still snuggled against each other in bed. Streetlight streaming in, the occasional thunder and lightning punctuating each act, of which she had little memory—even as she stood over the tell-tale corpses, her weapon of choice still hot with their unknown lives running off it and onto her slacks and shoes and soul. She'd then, mechanically, rolled the bodies up into two throw rugs, rolled them all up into rugs—why, she'd hadn't a fucking clue—then tied them up with electrical cords yanked from bedroom lamps, macramé, whatever, and stacked them atop tables, bookcases, and a refrigerator. Stared blankly at her handiwork, then left, actually left the homes, again in a haze, only to find herself suddenly standing before another bed, again with her True Value grass shears dripping with warm, unknown, blood on her Esprit pants, Mephisto shoes, and Lutheran soul. This time, her hands shaking, and defensive wounds covering her arms and face. Again, she left, in her now-trademark haze, but, yet again, found herself in yet *another* bedroom…until she found her face smashed down against the warm, familiar metal of a black-and-white Sunset Harbor police cruiser hood, flashing lights painting everything around her a blur of red, white, and blue, no longer that blinding white from the lightning, or those pleading screams tormenting her. Now, cuffs slapped on wrists already sore and cut up from pleas of mercy she'd ignored, hands covered in drying blood from people she didn't know…

Yes, these were the last memories Susan Sibley, wife of Andrew Sibley, and sister of unaccounted for Wallace T. Bryce had, as she screamed and screamed and screamed in her holding cell at three in the morning. Pain and hot winds blasted through her soul as she began to remove her blouse (they hadn't enough detention center jumpsuits to go around, she'd heard) in this tiny enclosure, after the officer had come in and again yelled at her to please shut the hell up. Vague images again blasted through her mind like hot sand as she deliberately began to tie her blouse sleeves in a knot, staring off into space. She may not have had pent-up rage in her life for the past twenty-odd years, but she certainly had pent-up something now, and she sure as heck wasn't going to go through all those years of whatever was going to surely happen to her next. Certainly "insanity" would somehow be tagged to it this time, given her history. Or at least something involving "life sentence," if spared the almost-certain capital punishment that awaited them all. So, Susan, having removed her blouse and holding it out before her, continued to stare ahead at her impersonal cell walls, and think how they so resembled much of her work on oil and canvas, and lifted the garment above her head, hanging it around her neck like a preppy college

(*Wendy! Polly! Ben!*)

co-ed's sweater. She grabbed the ends of her sleeves in each hand, and looked to them. Good thing for working out, she thought wryly, tightly gripping and digging in her knuckles for a firmer hold. She stood up, and felt anything but preppy now. She really did love her family and three kids and hoped they'd only remember the good parts, the 99.999% of her life they'd experienced firsthand. There was no way she was going to drag them through a bloody trial—there was no need for any more blood, and there was certainly no need for a trial. She'd done whatever they'd arrested her for, and that was that. Open and shut. She was tired of being labeled repressed, depressed, pent-up, or quietly suffering, and, most of goddamned all, she was *so* sorry for what she'd done.

Summoning all of her strength in one single explosive effort, Susan exhaled and did the only thing that needed be done to put everyone out of her misery and bring all those years of mis-diagnosed therapy to closure. She grasped a firm hold of her sleeve ends and yanked with the might and resolution of the insane, wrenching her blood-stained blouse quickly and brutally around her neck as she exhaled and crushed her own windpipe.

Her *coup d'grace* to all who'd helped her over the years.

Her final thoughts, as she spastically gasped for air and choked the life out of herself, were of Wendy, Polly, Ben, and Andrew.

I love you, my darlings...

Chapter Three

1

After Kacey dropped off the Hockers, and with her palms sweating just a little, she turned off her car's lights and pulled into the first empty carport, of the first deserted-looking retirement center home she came upon, instead of leaving the park like she told the officers she would. Switching off the engine she sat, nervously, listening to her breath and heartbeat, while watching for police. She removed a knotted and bunched-up bandanna and flashlight from her glove box, but continued to sit a few moments longer as she tried to build up the needed resolve to do what she was planning to do. She'd never done anything like this before, for all the grief she'd caused Fisher since moving into town four months ago. This was the first time she'd ever made it into a full-on restricted, cordoned-off area. Today, luck had been with her, and she hoped it'd remain so.

Kacey cautiously exited her car. She looked to her surroundings, wind tossing her hair about her face.

This was *totally* creepy.

Unnerving. Like a fake movie set.

She was caught in *in-between* time. A non-person in a non-Time event. The light and balmy breezes tossed about the Palm and Pepper trees, Bougainvillea, Heliconia, and other landscaping, and in the distance through the humid early morning haze, the thin, towering pines she thought looked so cool down here…but in each of the humble, silent residences she looked to, where she'd ordinarily never have given a thought as to whether or not these buildings were inhabited by sleeping or not-so-sleeping residents at this time of morning, she knew—*knew*—they were empty. Every one of them. Just like the deserted streets. Cars were parked in all the driveways and car ports; lawns were covered with the variety of knick-knacks seniors adorned upon them, some gently and casually spinning or rocking or clacking away; various flags, U.S., Florida, or otherwise, lightly fluttered and occasionally snapped in the breeze. But otherwise everything…everything was utterly quiet…*still*…in a hard to define way. It was like she was viewing a setting she wasn't meant to see. Her car, she realized, now fit in with every other prop on this set, and she wondered how the Hockers were doing…felt…upon returning home. Farther to the east she saw the glorious red slivers of a rising sun just beginning to poke its way up and between the strata of low-lying, deserting, storm clouds.

This had been quite a different place yesterday.

She inhaled the gentle, damp, floral breeze, and listened to the soothing sounds of lazy wind chimes, rustling palms, and awakening birdlife—when a stronger gust briefly kicked up, upsetting the wind chimes and palm trees. She had better hop to it before sun—or prying eyes—ratted her out.

Shuddering, Kacey hurried her way to the screened-in patio of her intended break in, where she undid her bandanna. Using the large handkerchief as a glove, she opened the screen door and entered the patio, thinking, *funny…this is where some of those very same murderers had also walked just hours ago.* Her next thoughts, however, were how sad it was that all those people had been murdered after having spent their entire lives building their nest eggs so they could find a decent, comfortable place to live out the twilight of their existences. What brings on something like this? From where had this nasty little contingent of killers come? And why, why, and *why?*

Kacey hastened through the unlocked patio door, sliding it shut behind her. Her initial nervous scan told her everything appeared normal enough, but as she switched on her mini flashlight, she glanced down to the floor and saw the ants. Tons of ants. *Thousands.* She again hurried across the dining area, keeping her light trained on them. They were goll-dang *everywhere.*

As Kacey sidestepped their legions, she allowed her flashlight to linger on them a little longer in muted fascination, but continued on to the rear of the manufactured home, toward the bedroom. She wasn't sure she really wanted to see this, but knew if she was going to do it *right*…she had to. No one else had this story yet, and she needed it to get her foot in the door. To survive. There was no way she could get turned away now, not with this story. She was it. First one in. No doubt when she left the park, she'd see the line of media setting up outside, but, for now, she was *it* and had to act quickly.

Kacey hurried down the short expanse of hallway toward the bedroom door. This was where the rubber met the road...where the deed was done. Bandanna in hand, she grabbed the doorknob, twisted it open, and braced herself as she entered the crime scene.

Upon first inspection, it looked just like any other standard bedroom—right down to the rumpled sheets and comforter, kitschy paintings, and plastic plants...until you saw the dark spatter sprayed across every wall, the headboard, furniture—ceiling. You could tell the whole story of a crime scene from the blood that *CSI* TV show forensics expert character, Grissom, had once said.

Now, wasn't that sad?

Any so-called knowledge she had of this stuff came from television. Some reporter she'd be. But, Lord in heaven, it was *everywhere*. The curtains...light fixtures...the carpet. And there were areas on the carpet where there were even heavier concentrations of blood that looked as if actual *butchery* had taken place...

And the *smell*.

Kacey looked behind her. Wrinkling her face, she raised a hand to her mouth and nose and gagged—spatter marks were also on the back of the door, smeared all over the doorknob. She was glad the lights weren't on—or that the sun wasn't yet fully up. There was the definite smell of death in here. *Angry*, pissed off, death.

Angry?

Kacey carefully directed her mini-light around the room, trying to stem her gag reflex. When the beam touched a dark stain, she quickly moved it away.

Man, maybe they were all right and she wouldn't make a good reporter. In this business, if she couldn't stand the sight of a little blood what good was she?

Kacey got hold of herself, exhaled, then slowly re-directed her light back over the stains. Good God, there were running trails of the stuff all over the place. Then, remembering how the ceiling had also been tainted, she uttered a short yelp and jigged about underneath it, until she saw she hadn't been under anything—dripping or not.

Continuing her examination of the room she found herself besieged with probable images of the attack, like a movie played out in her head: a couple, asleep in bed...killer (a woman) wanders in, broken bedpost in hand—and *crack-crack!* But, for some bizarro reason, that's not quite good enough for our assailant, oh, no—she has to do serious, egregious damage to their corpses before moving on to her next kill, and—

Kacey shut off the images.

Too much…too, too much. Maybe she was better suited to Sunday supplements and fluff reports. How did cops and coroners do it? No wonder they were so tough and cynical. If you had to deal with shit like this on any kind of a recurring basis it was bound to harden a soul.

As Kacey continued exploring the room she found other things she was sure most other bedrooms also didn't have: broken furniture, damaged bed frames, and shattered lamps.

And all these damned ants!

It was quite clear there had been a nasty struggle, here, death, then dismemberment, and she wondered in what order.

Kneeling bedside, Kacey shined her light under the bed, then between the bed and nightstand. Of course, maybe the broken lamp had just been from a spastic arm shot out during a dream—but it most certainly tended to look more like it had been from surprise at being accosted by his or her murderer. Like the line from that *Bladerunner* movie; Brion James's character had said, while attacking Harrison Ford's character on an noirish, future-LA street: "Wake up! *Time to die…*"

What a way to go. *Good night, Gracie.*

What could have caused these people to go berserk and wander into this place and start killing? Was it a random killing spree or premeditated? What could the people of this community have possibly done to have justified their total—brutal—annihilation?

Kacey got back to her feet, and, unsure if it had been all she'd just been through or that she'd perhaps just moved a little too fast, but felt instantly dizzy. She tried regaining her balance, but it was hard to stand. Kacey closed her eyes, and shot a hand out to the wall beside her, which, unknown to her, landed directly onto a drying spatter stain. She stayed that way for a long moment—when she also felt a hot blast of wind permeate the room—no, that couldn't be, all the windows were shut…it wasn't quite a *wind*…it was…the *sound* of wind, and it was…

(*inside her* head?)

…a dry, sucking, and aching bluster that raked its nails across the blackboard of her mind…

Kacey shot open her eyes and looked about her, her entire body electrified.

Someone was in the room with her!

But she was alone. There was no one, nothing else here…except for the ants.

Kacey spit. Out from her mouth and from between her teeth came (what appeared to be) grains of sand…

2

Chin gas…chin…gasss…

The words rang through attorney Harold Gordon like diarrhea through a dog. Harry stood in the middle of a darkened bedroom, squinting, hand to his head. Confused.

Chin gas? What the hell was *chin gas?*

But before he could try out an answer, a barrage of thundering horses surrounded him, and a shadow of a man, not on horseback, lurched at him. Harry had no time to sidestep the attack, and took it full in the gut.

Chin…*gaaas*…

More invisible horses thundered around him, and he found it hard to stand, like he stood at the epicenter of an earthquake, but in the darkness saw—nothing. Harry turned, and found his assailant behind him, kneeling on top of his bed and vigorously digging at something in the

(*sand*)

sheets. Sand sprayed up all around him from the shadow's frantic digging with a toy shovel that positively glowed a sky blue. Harry felt the grains hit his face. He spit out sand that'd gotten caught in his mouth. Harry moved closer, but still couldn't make out for what the figure was digging so furiously. He could just make out the wide scoop of a shovel, it was surely plastic, he figured, a bright *sky-blue* plastic, as it was rhythmically and quickly shoved into the sand, then whipped up and into the air over the figure's hunched and heaving shoulders. "Coco" was inscribed on the handle. Harry continued to be hit by sand, honking and spitting the stuff out of his mouth and nose. He was able to sidestep the onslaught until the shadowy sand-box digger shifted position, and again redirected his efforts at Harry, who also, for some perplexing reason, took extreme note of how the sand sprayed the walls and ceiling of the bedroom. There was something odd about it that utterly fascinated him.

Why was a sand box in his bedroom? In his bed?

Harry came up to the shadowy individual and tapped him on the shoulder.

"Excuse me, sir, but what are you doing?"

The man jerked to a rigid, taunt, stop. Harry couldn't take his eyes off the now-confirmed, plastic, sky-blue shovel, which the man held upright like a paused weapon. He could see it shaking. A particularly large scoop of sand had been flicked out of the shovel when he stopped him, and had fallen to Harry's feet.

"*What?*" the highly agitated figure asked. "Look what you've *done!*"

"I do apologize, but for what are you digging?"

"I'm digging for ants, is that okay with you? Good-fucking-Lord. Nasty fucking fire ants. You know bout them?"

"Yes."

"Then get the fuck away from me, so I can finish the goddammed job."

Harry took a closer look at where the man was digging.

"May I help?"

The man slowly lowered his shovel. Narrowed his gaze.

"Sure…be my guest," he said, and thrust the sky-blue shovel toward him. When Harry took the shovel, he had an instant's flash of a bright blue sky against a dun-colored landscape. So brilliant was the sky that it almost blinded him. The man slipped off the bed to the other side away from Harry. Stood watching.

Harry climbed up onto the bed, and, plastic shovel in hand, knelt before the sand mound in the sand box. Something just didn't feel right about this…about the sand. And the shovel felt kind of…*heavy*…

"Why is this shovel so heavy?" Harry asked, holding it out toward the guy, who continued to impatiently eyeball him.

"What, you a fucking pansy or sumthin?" The man made a grab for it, but Harry yanked it back before he could.

"*No.*"

"Then either help me, or get the fuck out of my way!" The man's words blasted through Harry like a sirocco.

Harry looked back to the mound. He couldn't make out what the shape was in the sand before him, but saw the dark, gaping hole already dug there. Tiny grains of sand were already starting to slide back down the steep, sloping, sides. And as he looked down into it, Harry saw movement, in fact, *lots* of movement, roiling within it…

"Hurry it up, asshole—they're starting to regroup!" the man shouted from the sidelines, anxiously peering over the edge of the bed and nervously shifting position.

Harry thrust the shovel into the hole, felt it hit something hard—hardpan, in a *sand box?*—and twisted it around before pulling it back out and flipping the sand, and, hopefully, ants, behind him.

"That's better, fuckhead! Keep going, that's *good!* That's *reeeal* good!"

Harry again thrust the shovel into the dark, damp hole, again twisted it, and again withdrew it, dumping the sand-ant mixture out behind him. He soon got into a rhythm, shoveling faster and faster—but the ant's numbers multiplied instead of diminished.

"Good! Keep going," the man continued to coach. "Don't stop! Move it! *Move* it!"

But the ant's numbers continued to multiply, and Harry felt a definite anxiety with their continued multiplication. They began to spread outward, toward his knees, and he began to widen his area of excavation.

Then he was bitten, and jumped.

"Don't stop, goddamn you, *don't you goddamn fucking stop!*" the bum shouted, eyes wide and mouth spitting froth. Veins popped in his beet-red neck and head.

But it was hard to keep shoveling as more ants crawled onto his knees and legs, gnawed at him, stung him. They were only little ants, for crying out loud, tiny, little *ravenous* bastards, but they were goddamned tearing him a new one.

Harry began swatting at them with the little blue shovel, when he noticed something else poured out of the deep hole before him. And it *smelled.* Like rotting…

"*Get the fuck outta my way, asshole!*" the bum yelled, and grabbed the shovel, roughly shouldering Harry off the bed and sending him crashing onto his shoulder. Harry felt a snap, crackle, pop, and tumbled along the floor, smacking up hard against a wall. He hit with his chin, then, as the rest of his body slammed into the wall—was the push *that* forceful?—he let out a loud load of flatulence that smelled just like what reeked from that hole.

Chin gas?

Harry pushed himself away from the wall just as the bum again began digging away, the sound of the shovel crisp and quick. *Ticht!* over the shoulder, *Ticht!* over the shoulder, *Ticht!* over the shoulder. Sand sprayed him furiously, and every time Harry went to get up, more sand flew into the air and landed in his face, hair, mouth, and nose.

"Goddammit, would you *stop*, already!" he shouted, but another clump landed in his face, and he'd just begun to inhale, so tiny grains of pulverized quartzite, feldspar, mica, and silica, along with ants, were sucked up into his sinuses. This sent him into a painful coughing and sneezing spat, but Harry, eyes watering, still managed to force himself to his feet, hands flailing and periodically bouncing off the wall from ill-conceived attempts at balance.

"Goddammit, what the hell are you *doing?*" Harry shouted, wobbling unsteadily on his feet and taking another clump smack-dab to the chest. Remembering the ants, he quickly brushed it off him.

"There!" the bum said, and, like a kid proud of his work, backed off the sand box to stand beside Harry, shovel in hand. "All done! It wasn't all that bad, now was it?" he asked, forcing the shovel back into Harry's hand. "Later, asshole!"

The man leapt off the sand box/bed and disappeared into the darkened recesses of the room.

Harry looked to the sand box, at the hole they'd dug, and saw that something still wasn't right about it. Sure, the hole was larger, and there were no longer any ants crawling out of it...but why the hell was there still something *wrong* with it? He leaned in and saw a piece of what looked like cloth sticking up out of the sand. He tugged at it, it yielded, and he grudgingly yanked it out of the sand until he had about a foot of it exposed. It looked like part of a shirt. A shirt tail. Harry dug his fingers around the base of the shirt tail, tugging at it, trying to shake it free, and exposed more of the shirt panel. Though afraid of what he might find, he couldn't stop, and frantically continued pulling and digging away. In no time he excavated a body, a body with a huge gaping hole in its chest. Out of the hole roared the sound of an ocean. He also smelled briny air exiting the wound.

"*No!*" Harry screamed, and spun around to find the bum standing directly behind him, another shovel in hand. Only it wasn't a shovel, but the business end of a jagged and broken wine bottle. Harry felt the slash across his chest and was thrown back onto the body he'd just unearthed. But it was gone.

He now was the body in the sand box, partially covered with sand, a gaping hole in *his* chest.

"God-fucking-*dammit*," the bum cursed, "if you want sumthin done right, you gotta do it your goddamn self!"

Before Harry knew it, the bum had jumped back up onto the sand box, straddling his now partially buried body, and continued digging out that large gaping hole in Harry's chest, out of which continued to scramble all manner of hungry little fire ants, to the sound and smell of a roaring ocean…

3

Harry Gordon awoke in a frenzy, wildly kicking and flailing arms and legs. He tried to push off that bum and wipe away the fire ants that hungrily crawled all over his body—and still came pouring out of his chest. He opened his eyes to find them all over the bed sheets and ceiling, and leapt out of bed, screaming. Bedside, he jumped about like a freaked-out junkie, when he realized…

A dream.

It had all been a dream, a fricking nightmare.

Harry collapsed against the wall, sliding down to the floor—when he again thought of the ants and quickly shot back to his feet. He switched on the light. Grabbing the bedside flashlight he directed it about him—the bed, the sheets, the floor. His body. Satisfied there really were no ants (he even apprehensively poked around inside his shorts), he let himself again collapse bedside, allowing the flashlight to fall away from his hands and roll to a stop against the wall.

"Good Lord," he panted, glancing at the clock on the nightstand, and closed his eyes. One-twelve a.m. was far too early to get up…

4

Kacey stared at her laptop in disbelief. Even loaded on caffeine, nothing about this crime made sense…a group of who-knew-how-many persons, from—what Jack had told her—all walks of life, just wandered on into the first retirement community that struck their fancy and begin hacking and slashing their way through its residents? What made all these people go crazy enough to kill off an entire retirement community? Why not any of the other handful of retirement communities surrounding it? Why *this* one—why was the killing entirely confined to only *this one place?*

Kacey hit the print button and sat back, taking another swig of coffee. She glanced at the clock. Had to get moving before any of the pro's got in before her. She grabbed her pocketbook and keys, already disconnecting her laptop from her printer, and the last sheet it printed.

She gave the article a quick once over, stuffed her notebooks and laptop into its case, and made for the door.

Kacey rushed into the *Sunset Harbor Gazette* building like she knew the place—which she kinda did. Knew *of*. She'd been trying to get on as a stringer for the past three months. No openings, they said, try again later. *Thank you!* So she'd go on down the road to Charlotte. Same thing. Punta Gorda, Venice…everywhere, the same response. No matter where she went, there were no Kacey Miller openings. She wrote great copy…okay, maybe not *great*, but pretty-darned-good-for-not-being-a-*professional*   copy…pretty-darned-good-to-get-her-foot-in-the-*door* copy, to get a job and then, then she could really prove herself. This was exactly what she needed. This would be her big break. No one had this story yet, *no one*. They couldn't turn her away.

Before Kacey got within ten feet of the editor's office, Connie Belleview, *Sunset Harbor Gazette's* editor-in-chief, saw her coming and smiled. Kacey strode confidently into her office.

"Well, good morning," Connie greeted, still smiling, "What have you for me today?"

Kacey entered the office and slammed her piece down on Connie's desk. Connie didn't move; just looked to the article.

"And this is—"

Connie read the headline and slowly picked up the article.

Entire Retirement Community Slaughtered.

"No one—*no one*—has this yet. Guar-un-*teed*. I am the *first*. None of your folks will ever get as close as I did. Hire me, dammit." Kacey sat down, confidently crossing her legs and settling in.

Connie looked between Kacey and the article. "Is this true? How'd you get this?"

"Does it matter? I was there. I got it all."

Kacey leaned forward.

"C'mon, Connie, you have to hire me—part time even, anything, on spec—this is hot and you know it. Give me a chance…that's all I need, just give me the *chance*."

Connie got to her feet still reading the article; walked around to the front of her desk. "This is…incredible." Connie looked back to Kacey. "You have the softcopy?"

Kacey danced the CD out before her, all smiles.

"How'd you get there so fast?" she asked, leaning back against the front of her desk.

"Let's just say I was in the neighborhood."

"And the marine and his wife?"

"Right place, right time."

"Okay. I'll tell ya what…since you did hit this one first—I'll take ya on—but on one condition."

"Anything."

"Find out who did it, why, and could it happen again. Where'd they come from? Why'd they kill everyone—that kind of thing." Connie glanced back to the article then back up. "Is this right? *Everyone?*"

Kacey nodded. "Except for the marine and his wife. That's—that's what I heard. They were still pulling out bodies when I wrote the story," she said, careful to not add *that's what the cop told me*. Fisher had made himself abundantly clear on that point.

Connie nodded. "Okay. Stay on this. Find out if anything like this has ever happened before, anywhere else—and…" Connie said, going back to her chair, "if you could interview a suspect or two, anyone with anything to do with this crime," she said, pensively tapping her nose and eyeing her.

"You got it."

Connie nodded, smiling.

Kacey got up, also smiling, and grabbed her gear. She turned to leave, when she again addressed her new boss, this time in a more appreciative tone.

"Thank you, ma'am. I really do appreciate being given this opportunity. I won't let you down."

Connie had already hit the intercom, nodding. "I know you won't."

5

Harry Gordon had spent the rest of the night sleeping on the couch, and when he finally got up for good, switched on the local news. What he heard screeched to a halt any morning rituals faster than a cold shower.

Upwards of seventy people murdered last night at a local retirement community…

Harry rushed back into the living room and sat on the edge of the coffee table, intently focused on the newscast. The commentator, local anchor, Hillary Brown, recapped:

"Sometime between midnight and two this morning what appears to have been a senseless, cult-like mass murder took place at the Safe Harbor Retirement Community—a small community composed of less than a hundred residents, on Tamiami Trail Boulevard. Details are sketchy, but police have arrested over thirty suspects allegedly involved in the murders…"

Harry's jaw dropped.

"…officials aren't saying much, but say they aren't yet discounting any cult or gang-related activity, though all suspects appear unrelated, which further baffles authorities…."

Harry's phone rang. "I'll bet," he mumbled as he picked up the cordless.

"Yeah?" he asked, still watching TV.

"Harry? You watching this?" Simon Stansfield asked, one of Florida's Sarasota Circuit Court prosecutors.

"If you're talking about the killings at Safe Harbor, I have the news on right now."

"That's the one. It's gonna be big."

"No doubt. We have anything on it?"

"Nope. But you can bet everyone's pretty upset about it. Especially the retirement community."

"Oh—yeah—now there's a surprise."

"I think because of the extreme nature of this case, they're going to wanna push to get this resolved ASAP, not to mention a change of venue. I mean, shit, it's pretty grisly."

Harry nodded. "Every person over the age of sixty is no doubt pissed or scared shitless. We'd be lucky to find a useable jury. Move to Tampa or Orlando? Fort Meyers?"

"Yup."

Harry again nodded. "Where are you?"

"On the way to the Sunset Harbor cop shop. I gotta see these people firsthand. I'm told they're everyday folk, Harry, just like you and me. People with *lives*. Can't figure it. Something in the water? Government experiment? Don't know, so I'm heading on over to see for myself."

"Great. Well, I'm gonna get going—"

"Yeah, and that's the other reason I called—sleeping in, again?"

Harry chuckled. "Yes and no. Had a killer nightmare last ni—"

"Same one?"

"Yeah."

"I told you you'd better get your head checked out—"

"Yeah, but you always tell me that. No, I don't need any shrinks to tell me I'm stressed. Xanax be my friend."

"I think it's a little more than that, buddy—but hey, it's no brain shoveled off my sidewalk—I just pulled into the parking lot. Gotta go!"

Harry recradled the phone.

Simon was right, but what Simon hadn't known was the extent of the dreams—the nightmares—he'd been having "lately." He'd been having them as long as he could remember, about horses and sand, wind and sea—combinations of each—but in the past month or so these dreams had been turning up virtually every night...and they'd grown in intensity. Were becoming more real. The other night he even *knew* he was dreaming while in the dream, and was still powerless to stop it. Initially it had only been something like going-out-to-eat-a-hamburger dream, but it's in the desert instead of the local drive-through, and he had to chase down his meal on the wind-swept plains of a deserted dreamscape. Or he's eating horse, rather than hamburger. But in the past month he'd had the ones like last night—not every night, but a couple times a week—in which a particularly nasty murder is committed. In this—and most of the others—he knew, or felt something bad was coming his way, but was always powerless to stop it. He knew something wasn't right in the dream, but couldn't control it, change it, and was always condemned into participating on the track the dream was headed. It was wearing him out. Normally an early riser, he'd taken to coming in later and later, depending on how much he was particularly affected by the current night's lack of sleep. Tonight's was the most real one he'd had so far. And they'd been growing increasingly angry and more violent as the weeks progressed. And as he began about the task of getting ready for work, he wondered, just wondered...had his dream foretold the crime that had just been committed in that retirement community?

And what the hell was chin gas?!

Chapter Four

1

Detective Fisher ducked under the yellow-and-black tape that stretched across the screened-in patio entrance, then stepped up the two steps to the sliding glass patio door that he slid open to enter the once-theoretically-happy, now-violated, home. This home's crime scene investigation was as complete as possible, his forensic army now gone on to one of the other fifty homes of this little community that was still under construction. The retirement business was good down here, despite all the increased hurricane activity a couple years ago. He examined the frame around the patio doors as he passed through it.

This town—all of Florida, no doubt—had never before seen anything of this magnitude. What had drawn people from all walks of life to stroll into this town, to this specific patch of earth, and begin to systematically, brutally, kill off all its residents? In each of the handful of homes he'd visited, he found nearly identical MOs—or groups of MOs—and one of the oddest things he found were that any guests— any *visitors* who didn't actually live in the park—had been totally, and unequivocally, spared.

Untouched.

Not one *of them had even been awoken during the attacks.*

Except for the Hockers, each of the survivors interviewed said they were either relatives or friends, and though some had had disturbing nightmares, not one person remembered hearing a thing during their slumber. Several of the survivors had even been sleeping in their host's *master* bedrooms while their hosts slept elsewhere, *and had still remained untouched.* This was an extremely deliberate, calculated, act. What could have possibly brought on such selective slaughter, and how could it have possibly been carried out so perfectly?

Fisher made his way down the short corridor toward the bedroom, and nudged open the partially opened door with a toe.

Why were so many of the bodies rolled up in carpets or other material, while others had been dismembered or otherwise left where they lay? And those in the carpets and tarps had all been placed atop tables, benches, and refrigerators.

What did rolling up victims in carpets signify?

In nearly all of the homes like this one, the vics had been "carpeted," as he'd come to call it. However and whenever they were actually dispatched would be determined by forensics, but the basic end-all was the roll-up into some kind of on-hand blanketing material. One person had been found rolled up in Saran wrap and tin foil. Others had plastic bags fastened over their heads while they'd been rolled up into their tarps or carpets. Many appeared to have been beaten while *in* their wraps. In one home, broken posts from a bed frame had been employed. The anger and strength that had been used to rip apart those posts was most disquieting. He'd seen whacked out perps on drugs, but there was something more to all this. The carpeted murders definitely fit under the heading of symbolic, or ritual, killings, but, once you got past the initial "why carpeted," then the flip-side reared its ugly head:

Why not *all* of them?

A mass murder of an entire community, but only some of which were ritualistic? Had the killers been rushed? Forgetful, once lost in the frenzied mêlée of murder? Or were some simply neat freaks?

Fisher walked over to the window where this residence's victim had been found. Stared at the floor where the rolled-up carpet had been shoved against the wall—atop a dresser—a bent golf club (a number 2 "wood") nearby. Others had been drowned in sinks, toilets—and there were two, perhaps the most bizarre of all, who'd been *boiled in their own bathtubs*. He'd never seen anything like it. Two tubs man-handled outside, leaving deep and ragged drag marks across the otherwise heavily manicured lawn. That had been some power. Some *rage*. Two couples actually boiled alive, fires packed underneath and around the base of their tubs—the only two homes with detached, "claw-foot" style tubs.

Jesus.

Others had been strangled with electrical cords or macramé. Socks. Some had been brutally thrown about and beaten to death, while another handful had been "pressed" to death by cinder blocks and refrigerators thrown atop them...and given their age and osteoporosis—well, that was still a brutal way to go. And there were, of course, those dispatched by the more traditional methods involving guns and knives.

Fisher'd grown up in Sunset Harbor, done a few years of Miami homicide, then returned for—what he'd hoped to be, but had now been summarily dashed—a more relaxed environment. Safe Harbor was a retirement community—a *safe harbor*, essentially—for those who'd come here to enjoy the breezy Gulf coast lifestyle and sea food, and live out the rest of their lives in as much peace and comfort as possible. To take it easy. He knew not everyone'd lived chaste, choir-boy-or-girl existences, but whatever they might have done, they were trying to make up for it, now, most of them, anyway, he liked to think. The rest were probably just trying to sneak out of this existence without getting caught, enjoying the home stretch. Apparently that just wasn't meant to be for this group.

But no matter the intermediary murderous actions, the usual, final act was that of being carpeted. Tarped. Tin foiled. You name it. Then placed atop some structure as if in offering to some deity.

It was stupefying.

But, more so, another thought nagged: how did the assailants get in without breaking a single door or window? Not one door nor window had been jimmied or smashed.

And how had they managed to kill only *residents?*

It looked as if everyone had just waltzed right on in, no locked doors to hinder their passage, and surgically exterminated specific targets, bystanders—except for the gate guard—totally untouched or awoken. The entire community might as well have hung out a sign that said, *Come on in, folks, we're all asleep, so you shouldn't have too much trouble taking us out!*

And how was it that all seventy-two residents had had their doors unlocked? How was that even *possible?* The elderly were typically more habitual about this area of home security than anyone else.

There are more things in heaven and earth, Horatio…

Fisher turned away from the window, glanced at the spatter stains on the head board and wall behind it, and left the room.

Once again in the living room, he looked to the entranceway and patio door. Damn—not a *touch* of a screwdriver or crowbar.

And what had brought all these people of diverse backgrounds and ways and means together for the common purpose of murder? Suspects who looked as if *they* had had families of their own and had never hurt a fly in their entire lives.

Good, God, how was any of this possible?

2

Tiger awoke groggily to a room full of white and machinery, tubes stuck in his arms, and an annoying beep-beeping somewhere around him. Images he couldn't quite make out pounded away in his head like a deep, throbbing, pulsing, migraine…screams, and cries…*blood*…

He couldn't move.

This one thing, above all else, terrified him most.

What had he done…where *was* he?

In a coma?

Is this what death was like?

No…he'd just opened his eyes…they were closed now, but he'd distinctly remembered *opening* them…seeing all the brightness and white…it was much better with them closed. He liked the dark…it was comforting…but what was…*where was he?* All that beeping…the white…the sheets hanging from above…

Tiger tried to raise an arm, but only managed a feeble, uninspired, twitch.

Ants.

Ants?

Ants!

Yelling, Tiger immediately attempted to bolt upright, but found that despite his best efforts, he was entirely restrained. His behavior, however, immediately elicited the response of a uniformed police officer, nightstick removed from his belt, and also sent that calmed beep-beeping around him into an electronic frenzy.

"What the hell?" the officer exclaimed, quickly forcing Tiger back down into the bed, nightstick pressed against Tiger's upper chest. Right behind him piled in a handful of men and women in white coats. An older lady, in graying sandy hair, came bedside and checked his restraints, while the officer kept Tiger pinned to his bed.

"Well, it appears you've had quite a nightmare, John Doe," the sandy-haired doctor said. "As well you should, considering what you're accused of." The doctor looked to the cop. "He's okay."

The cop slowly eased up and took a more relaxed stance—alert, but relaxed.

The doctor continued to examine Tiger. "I don't know how much you recall, but you're in a hospital…awaiting transport to the county jail when you're better, I might add, if that's anything to look forward to. You've been severely attacked by fire ants…some eighteen-hundred to be exact. Small consolation, if you ask me. You're lucky you're not allergic."

Tiger relaxed. He was physically and mentally exhausted. He searched his memory and found…images…visions he preferred to ignore…

"Where am…" Tiger started to say, but ended up choking on the last word.

The doctor soothed him, beckoning a nurse to bring water.

"You're in a *hospital*—"

Tiger raised a hand. "No…where *am* I…what…*state?*"

The medical staff and cop exchanged looks.

"Maybe I'm not the kind of doctor you need."

Tiger again asked the question, following a sip of water.

"You're in PC—Port Charlotte—Memorial, in Port Charlotte, Florida."

But Tiger wasn't listening any more…at least not to the doctor. There came the winds again…the hot, dry blast of that damned incessant gale, and something else modulated onto the sound of wind. He heard it a lot lately. It was the sound of water…rushing water, incredible amounts of angry, rushing *water*…

Tiger didn't just close his eyes, this time, he closed his mind…

He liked the dark.

3

Nora Stoker, fifty-five, paused, her pen hovering just above her note pad. "Is that it? Anything else to add?"

"No, that is all," the psychically channeled Enoch personality replied, speaking through Nora's sixty-three-year-old husband, Howard.

A light breeze filtered in through the windows, gently stirring the pages of a nearby newspaper. Nora relaxed, reaching for, and taking a sip from, her wine.

"Wait…give us a moment," Enoch/Howard added, in his rather high-pitched, flat, tone.

Nora put down her wine and went back to her note pad. There was silence for a moment as another breeze wafted on in through the house, only this one wasn't as pleasant. It was, surprisingly, stifling. Hot. And riding upon the breeze came a distant sound of thunder. It startled Nora so that after uncomfortably squirming she dropped her notepad and uttered a surprised "Oh, my!" She stood, looking toward the windows.

"What was *that?*" she asked.

"My apologies," Enoch/Howard said. "It was not my intent to startle you. In fact, I am quite amused at the intensity of the image's delivery—and your perception of it."

Nora retrieved her pen and paper. "What was it?"

"It was...my attempt at a different *form* of delivery. We have progressed much over the years, and are learning at an accelerated rate. I endeavored to try a new approach with you two, tonight. Give us a moment...."

Nora got up and again walked to the windows. She looked outside into the balmy Fort Meyers evening. There was, once more, that familiar, cool, evening breeze that drifted back in.

"What you experienced," Enoch/Howard said, with Nora quickly returning to her seat, "was a new method of delivery. I wanted to try to present data in a new way, and am surprised at the intensity of its...manifestation...and that so much made its way through to you. Again, my apologies."

Enoch/Howard got to his feet and began to pace.

"Your husband—Howard—will be involved...in a very different kind of case in—in your terms—the near future. This case will both shock and enlighten...expand awareness...of all involved. It will also involve an energy personality essence of such intensity that it could not be contained within one earthly body. In fact, three of them existed in the same time period, with one killed early in his life."

Nora hastily continued her speedwriting. "Can you elaborate?"

"I am carefully choosing my words, here, in order to not...adversely affect...the situation. Your husband is inadvertently blocking me on this one...."

Enoch/Howard sat back down and closed his eyes.

"He's worried," Enoch/Howard continued, "for reasons he does not entirely comprehend—or, more to that point...does not want to. He does not wish to upset his current comfort zone."

"I see. Anything more you can tell us?"

"This trial will have far-reaching implications that no one in your world could ever have predicted…perhaps not immediately—except for those involved. The trial will be convened uncharacteristically quickly, due to the energies involved. I will not say more, given your husband's worrisome attitude on the matter, and his laudable efforts at trying to remain objective."

Enoch/Howard opened his eyes.

"More will be forthcoming. You may remove these notes from his view, for the time period specified, if you wish. I know he dislikes it when I predict his caseload!

"Do you wish to have another break, or discontinue for the evening?"

Nora looked to the clock, which read 11:37 p.m. She flexed her hand, which was growing tired. "I think we'll call it a night, Enoch."

"Then, a good evening to you both…and do not be worried about this new material…it will be most beneficial to all involved, though it will take *all* personalities out of their comfort zones. My fondest wishes for an enjoyable evening!"

"Night."

Before Nora finished writing, her husband was staring at her as her husband again.

"How was it?," Howard asked. "We do good?"

Nora finished her notes before looking up. "Yeah…we have some really good information…but a really weird thing happened that'd never happened before."

"Really?" Howard stood and stretched. Clearing his throat, he took a sip from his wine glass. He turned to the window and said, "I see images…*thousands* of horses…thundering across a great plain."

Howard finished stretching, still staring out the windows, then turned to his wife.

"And a really uncomfortable heat…*oppressiveness.*

"Wow. That's weird," he continued, "It feels familiar…but very uncomfortable—*oppressive.*"

"That's exactly what'd happened! A blast of heat and the sound of thunder—horses, I guess it could be, charging."

As Nora talked, she spirited away the last page of notes discussing the impending trial.

"Well, honey, feel free to read the notes, but I'm tired, so I'm off to bed. Have an early day tomorrow."

Howard again stared out the windows. "Very interesting.…"

Nora came up behind Howard, sliding her arms around him, and placed her head onto his back, eyes closed. "I love you," she whispered, sighing.

Howard smiled, and twisted around into her. He kissed her on her forehead. "Love you, too."

Nora left for bed, Howard looking after her, smiling.

4

Howard B. Stoker III read over the session's notes for the evening. Wasn't it incredible how life worked itself out? If someone had told him about a judge who claimed to channel "energy personality essences," not only would he had moved to disbar the freak, but he would have also moved to have had a battery of psychoanalysis performed on the individual's state of mind. Yet here he was, one of Florida's Twentieth Judicial Circuit Judges for twenty-five years, channeling an "EPE" that called itself "Enoch."

Snatching up a refreshed glass of wine, he entered the study and sat beneath the lone floor lamp. He readjusted the light to its lowest setting and sat in his high-back chair, notes and wine in hand. He took a sip, set the glass on the end table, placed the notes in his lap, and closed his eyes.

Peace. Quiet.

Two relatively unknown concepts any more.

Everything had to be extreme these days, fast paced. Everyone wanted a piece of you, either through voice mail, e-mail, or snail mail. Facebook. Cell phones. Twitter. Telephones or court appearances. Faxes, television, or hallway meetings. Let's do lunch, drop me a line, *stop on by!* Traffic tickets, arrest warrants, search warrants, and summonses. It was neverending! And this didn't even begin to factor in whatever surveillance equipment was out there, all that high-tech gadgetry orbiting high, and not-so-high—drones!—above everyone, or in the form of department-store or traffic-light cameras. PIs. Good Lord, it boggled the mind! Now throw in beings like EPEs, and one really had to wonder—were we ever, *really*, alone?

Howard opened his eyes and looked to the notes. He still couldn't believe it. Had fought it. But, in the end…it just simply…*was*. It had, as these things normally do, initially manifested itself in childhood. His parents thought he was simply doing what all kids his age did…playing with an imaginary friend. But his never went away as he'd grown up, and his gave him information that couldn't possibly have been made up. Like when his grandmother across the country was dying, and little Howie told his parents how her "limp nodes" were being "eaten away." Or, back in the seventies, when a friend of his was being let go, young-man Howie steered the man toward another job that involved "tiny cities" that everyone would eventually have in their homes, connected by some kind of an "Interstate."

His parents had tried to "breed" it out of him, but the little voices and inclinations merely hibernated—and Howard found that he had begun to unconsciously use his incredible insight in very useful ways...and when a friend suggested that he change his degree program to law and become a judge, well, that just clicked.

Howard B. Stoker III had found his calling.

But Howard had also found that he just simply "knew things." Information just seemed to keep popping into his head. He had an incredible propensity for knowing when someone was lying, but also realized, very early on, that just "knowing" wasn't enough—especially in the eyes of the law. This country needed—and rightly so—the burden of proof. "Beyond a reasonable doubt," the directive went, and with good reason. Howard thought wouldn't it be neat to have a type of person who could be a kind of "Truth Seer"? Like the medical or clerical profession this person would exist solely to help seek out the truth in the world. They would be like Holy Men and Women, who's character and morality were above reproach, and would be used not only in law enforcement, but on a global scale to seek out untruths and wrongs, and set people straight about it.

Real-life *Jedi*.

Of course, life being what it was they would also exercise *extreme* good judgment, knowing when would be the proper time and place to tell all. Some secrets were better kept as secrets. But imagine the possibilities! Judges and lawyers no longer worrying if they'd made the right decision! Truth in advertising! And politics—whoa, there was a thought! No longer could people hide behind lies. Of course, it would bring about a whole new life paradigm, and he wasn't quite sure how ready the world was to live so openly and honestly. How ready *he* was. As Friedrich Nietzsche had once said, *that which does not kill you, makes you stronger.*

So, Howard picked up the notes, and began to read what words had come out of his mouth without any conscious knowledge on his part…

5

Allan George sat on the floor, back in the corner of his cell, hunched over and huddled about his knees, hands occasionally clamped over his ears, trying to shut out the wailing from that girl at the end of the cell block. She'd scream, stop, then start up screaming again. The images just wouldn't go away…and all that *blood*…where had it come from? What had he *done?*—why was he—

A person in the cell next to him was again making those damned thudding sounds…sounds Allan also desperately tried to shut out. He didn't want to think what he or she was doing. He'd had enough screaming and wailing going around inside his own head. Didn't want to think of…it was just too much. Please, make it stop!

Make it all just go *away*…

Allan looked up, slowly removing his hands from his ears.

The screamer had stopped. He hoped she'd be all right. But always, he came back to the same question…why the hell was he locked up in jail? What the hell—

Then the wind started up again…that howling, wailing, desolate raking of his mind…that internal cry of anguish that had only just begun to take over his life about a year ago. And the horses and blood, all the *blood*…just wouldn't go away. On his clothes. In his mind. But it was the *wind* that was the worst that was always there, loud or faint, in the background of his psyche, in the background of *everything*…

Allan looked to his hands. They still shook. Good Lord, the last time he'd looked to them, they'd been covered in a dark, sticky, substance. And he'd held a small hand scythe, something he'd picked up on his way here—he no longer remembered where, Oklahoma, Tennessee…what difference did it matter, now? He'd be in jail for the rest of his life, barring capital punishment—did Florida have the death penalty? He'd find out soon enough. And, apparently, he'd earned it—fair and square. There were cuts and bruises all over his arms and hands, still raw and sore. He couldn't even clench a fist into a ball for any length of time before it spasmed out. Jesus Christ, he wanted all those evil memories to be a dream—a nightmare—he wasn't a *murderer*.

He was a family man with three kids and a wife back in Idaho. How the hell had he found his way down here? He didn't even *like* Florida.

Allan kept his head down low, eyes closed. He tried to keep out all the other mumbling and sobbing from the other cells, but closing his eyes only made things worse. He didn't want to open them, because then he was faced with the grim reality. He missed Liz and the kids. Missed Ranger, their Golden Retriever, and—he couldn't believe he was saying this—but he also missed his *job*. He missed his home, his friends, his state. He missed everything about, what was quickly forever becoming…a former life.

Well, get used to stir, bra, cause this be your last stompin grounds. Oh, and by the way, d'you remember how you stomped that eighty-year-old man's head into the floor?

"*No!*" Allan said, shooting to his feet. "No-no-no-no-*no*…," he continued to chant as he again took to pacing his cell. "No-no-no-no-*no*…."

Yeah, Allan, bay-bee, that was after you removed his throat with that little tool you'd been carrying around for a half-dozen states…he wouldn't stop pumping his life's blood up all over you—guess he had a stronger heart than you'd imagined, huh?—so you rolled him over and tried to stop the madness by crunching in his little, nearly hairless and age-spotted, head…

"*Nooooooo!* I didn't do that…I did *not* do that! I *WOULDN'T* do that!"

Oooh, but you did, Allan, that's the beauty of it, see?…you did, but you don't believe you did…which is perfect! Don't you see where this is headed (get it? "headed"!)?

"*Shut up! Shut* up! Get out of my *HEAD!*"

Now it was Al's turn to pick up the slack in cell block "D." Now, no one was talking except for him, no one was wailing and yelling, but for him. He was the one all the others were now focused on, all the others were momentarily extending their hearts out to, feeling sorry for a brief respite from their own madnesses. Even Thumper in the next cell had stopped thumping and was listening and feeling for him. Crying for him, because they were all similarly fucked, awaiting the same fate. Before this day, none of these people had ever killed a soul…before one-twelve a.m., none of these people had ever even met each other, and now they were all awaiting trial together.

Misery loved company.

Pleased to meet you, I'm Allan George, and I killed Mr. And Mrs. Jim Dandy and their neighbors. What're you in for?

Oh, so nice to meet you, Mr. George. My wife, Gina, and I did in the Robertsons, Kings, and Farnsworthies. Small world, ain't it? What'd you use?

Allan had never smoked a joint, never hit his wife or kids or dog (though he had slapped Ranger once, kinda hard, across the rump when he'd run across the road and not come back when called); never cheated on any of his girlfriends, or, once married, his wife…and now it seemed for such a perfect life lived he was getting it all in one fell swoop. Hell, he even did all the required reading for raising children. Attended every offered management class and actually listened to his coworkers and subordinates…

Why was all this happening to *him?*

Why had that faint wind he'd heard every now and then, and which his doctors had conveniently labeled tinnitus, decided to grow into a full-out wailer and possessed his life? Seduced him into leaving his family? Forced him to travel cross-country to a state he didn't even like? To steal a tool from a farmer's barn and pocket it all this way, only to imbed it into the throats of a bunch of elderly people he didn't even *know?*

None of this added up…*none* of it. Maybe he should have gone to church more…idle minds, you know…maybe he shouldn't have had those thoughts about Monica, in QA…maybe…maybe, he should just…just…

Put himself out of his misery.

Allan George began to, slowly, at first, tap his head against the cell wall. He picked up the rhythm a bit and increased the force of contact…but the winds were still there…the charge of the horses…their snorting…their *hooves*, pounding and *pounding* away at the imaginary earth with their thunderous imaginary passage….

Chapter Five

1

Kacey Miller didn't just wake up one morning and decide, *Gee, I think I'm going to leave my husband and child, and strike it out on my own*—no, it had actually been more of a gradual thing.

Wilmington, Delaware hadn't so much been a bad place, as it had just been where she'd ended up. Originally from Alexandria, Virginia, Kacey had grown up an adventurous spirit, her father in the Navy, her mother a travel journalist. When Kacey had graduated high school, she'd tried college—for two-and-a-half years—but kept getting into trouble, which, invariably, lead to trouble keeping her grade point average up. She just wasn't cut out for academics. She'd had enough of school and yearned for excitement; traveled the world as a Flight Attendant and worked on dive boats in Hawai'i and Australia. Experienced skydiving, base jumping, and bungee jumping (she'd also picked up some part-time work hang gliding and surfing). Then, when she'd returned home to visit her parents, she'd met Mark and they just clicked. He wasn't into everything she was, but was a private pilot (had his instrument rating), skydived, and was also a cave-diving scuba instructor at a local dive shop. Where Kacey was the "screamer," Mark was the quiet adventurer.

But that wasn't the problem.

What was the problem was that once they'd married and had had their first and only child Mark had turned, well, there was no use sugarcoating it: *soft*.

Domesticated.

Had stopped all skydiving and poking around in submerged caves and anything else that involved risk. He'd gotten a "real" job as a techie IT supervisor with a utility company, and settled down into a life of boredom and complacency—well, according to Kacey, anyway.

Though he was still tremendously interested and in love with her, *she* was no longer interested in *him*.

That was the problem.

Kacey felt as if her entire life was screaming down the tubes…and she didn't want to get tied down to a boring bit-nerd husband who never did anything, never went anywhere. But the other thing was that everything revolved around "*The Kid*," and that, frankly, scared the crap out of her. Kacey, as much as she loved Emily, simply couldn't stand it. She still had so much to do, so much to see, and so much yet to experience. She'd originally thought, hey, how cool! Now, we can raise the ultimate extremer! Introduce her to skiing, bungee jumping, skydiving, you name it, and at such an early age that she could become a truly physical phenom, and possibly even make a name for herself!

But what a mistake that had been.

Kacey thought about taking Emily with her, then thought better of it. Mark had become the perfect dad…dull and boring…so why not let him continue to do what he did best? Raising Emily. Kacey'd often thought she'd been born into the wrong skin…wasn't this what *men* were supposed to do? Feel trapped…stifled? Flee commitment? She could no longer look at herself in the mirror. She'd screwed things up royal, and now that involved a child—her own flesh-and-blood—and she couldn't stomach that. She should never have married, and never have had a child, as much as it pained her to even think the thought. As much as she loved Emily, she knew it would be far better for all involved if she just…left.

So, that's what she did. One day, she said she was going off on another ten-mile run…

And simply never returned.

She'd planned to start off "small," taking her summarized suitcase-of-her-life with her to Dover and stay at a Days Inn. She'd only stayed one night, agonizing over her choice, when she decided it was time to either cut bait and bolt, or return home. So, the next day, Kacey decided to make a clean break of it and headed across Chesapeake Bay into Norfolk, where she'd intended to hop a flight to LA and stay with some friends she knew from the airline business.

It was also there that she'd met Sheila.

2

The funny thing about airports are all the distractions.

You can buy just about anything. Airports are their own little microcosms, and it was easy to lose yourself in their world of transit make-believe. It was extremely seductive, at least to Kacey. She loved travel, loved airports. You could buy a ticket to *anywhere*. Buy a book or magazine about anything. Or a great (well, pretty good, anyway) dinner. Heck, you could buy just about any kind of food or drink and meet people from the farthest-flung corners of the globe. Kacey bought her ticket, one that would take her to the other end of the country (in a mere handful of hours!), and decided to get a little looped before her flight, which was in three hours—not smashed, but just pleasantly "happy" enough to take off some of the sting—and found an all-but-empty lounge just outside the metal detectors. She'd begun her drinking at the bar, watching *NNC*, or the National News Center, out of New York City, when she noticed a businesswoman take a seat two stools down. She felt intruded upon, sure, this was her bar, *her* bartender, and she wasn't in the mood for sharing, let alone with some uppity-looking bitch in a business suit.

But was she *really* here? Was she *really* about to leave her husband and child for the great unknown? This wasn't *her*. All her jewelry, her clothes, her extreme sports gear, were all still at home.

Home.

Her favorite coffee mug. Still felt the comfort of her favorite chair in the living room. The comforting feel of their Black Lab, Boomer. And she still had the dishes to do, the laundry to finish—she'd thrown a load of wash into the dryer just before leaving—*and she'd actually left her husband and toddler playing on the living-room floor none the wiser.*

What kind of creep did something like that?

How could she just up and leave her family? What must they be thinking? Man, she hadn't even left a note—just to let them know she was okay—*okay*? And how was she any *definition* of the word? Sure, she wasn't murdered, at least not yet (where'd that come from?), she was alive—*but she had just up and left her family.*

How was any of that *"okay"*?

That was when the question had hit her. Ain't it funny how life worked?

"Excuse me, but are you okay?"

That had come from the businesswoman soon-to-be-known-as-Sheila sitting two stools down, in that Norfolk International bar.

Kacey looked over to her and realized she must have appeared quite the sight. She hadn't realized she was hunched over the bar, drink in one hand, the other shoved up and under cascading hair, supporting a brooding forehead in that universal "I've hit rock bottom" repose.

"*Do I know you?*" businesswoman Sheila asked, eyeing her.

"I get that a lot," Kacey said. She turned to directly address this person who dared interrupt her self-loathing.

"But it's just all so *absurd*, isn't it? Life, the universe—everything!"

Kacey looked to the woman as she smoothed her hair away from her face, then looked away.

"Excuse me?" businesswoman Sheila asked.

"Sorry; I don't mean to offend, but—"

Then a weird thing happened when Kacey again looked up to this woman and into her eyes for the first time. There *was* something intensely familiar about her, so intense, in fact, as to actually border upon the emotional. It not only surprised her, but actually frightened her, significantly toning down her mirth.

"Do...*do* I know you?" Kacey asked, swallowing nervously. She suddenly felt very, very, warm.

The woman looked to Kacey. "No...no, I think I was mistaken...."

Kacey choked out a couple nervous chuckles, but was soon laughing deep belly laughs, laughs which felt surprisingly good. The bartender eyed her. Kacey raised a hand.

"I'm so sorry, it's just that my life has suddenly gone to hell in a bucket—and here you come," she continued laughing, "asking if I'm all right!"

Kacey buried her face in her hands, trying to muffle her amusement.

"I-I'm sorry to have bothered you," the businesswoman said, collecting her things and getting up to leave, when Kacey leaned over and touched her.

"No, please—don't go," she said, "I didn't mean to embarrass you...it's just, well, I don't know if you really want to get involved in all this, but I just left my husband—yesterday—and I'm drowning my guilt in cheap booze." She briefly eyed the bartender eying her.

Kacey choked off her laughing and stuck out a hand. Grimaced.

"My apologies. I'm Kacey."

Sheila looked to her hand. Reshouldering her purse and laptop carry case, she managed a smile. "Sheila."

As Sheila and Kacey shook hands and looked to each other, Kacey narrowed her gaze. Images of a wide open and barren plain filled her mind.

"Are you sure we've never met? You really do seem awfully familiar."

Still holding Kacey's hand, Sheila said, "It does seem like we've met. I travel a lot."

Kacey shrugged her shoulders; they released their handshake. Sheila placed her purse and laptop back on the stool between them and shifted back onto the stool.

"Are you all right—stupid question, of course not. Wanna talk about it?"

Kacey returned to her drink. "What's to talk about? You married?"

"Used to be."

Kacey stared at her. "Oh. One of those hubbies who didn't pay enough attention to ya? That kind of thing? Always at work, doin the office bitch?"

"Noooo, we had other issues—look, Kacey, not all men are pigs. Sometimes things just…just don't work out, even with the best intentions. People *change*. There's no accounting for what happens, sometimes, you know? What happened with you, if I may ask?"

Kacey silently played with her glass and as she did so felt an unaccountable…attraction…to this woman who just showed up in her life, on a bar stool in the Wonderland that was Norfolk International. Out of nowhere she blurted, "Hungry? Want some…chili…or something?"

Again that barren-plain imagery…*wind* in her hair…

"No…I'm fine."

"Okay. Well…*I* messed things up. He didn't really do anything wrong, I guess you could say—it was all me. It's just that I married this guy, active and adventurous like me, and when we had Emily, weeelll…he changed. He stopped skydiving, stopped scuba diving, became this full time *bore*."

Kacey turned to her new friend.

"Oh, don't get me wrong—he's a great father and all—always there for the both of us, always doing the right thing—heck, he even loves changing Emily's poopy diapers! You know, the Hershey-squirty ones? *I'm* the one who gags. It seems like nothing bothers him about parenthood. *I* was the problem. I kept seeing my life flash before me…no more trips, no more *fun*."

Kacey fell silent, staring into her empty glass, out of which she tried to suck another sip.

"Beertender!"

The bartender came over and eyed her for a good, hard, moment. "This is your last," he said, pouring only half a glass.

"Everyone's a critic."

"So," Sheila began, "what do you really want out of life? Why'd you marry?"

"Ooh, now that's the fiddy-cent question, ain't it!"

3

Nothing in Tiger's head made sense. It all ran together…the last thing he remembered was something about being beaten about the head and shoulders by a cop after he was told he was in a hospital—

Was that right?

He mentally searched about himself to see if he'd really been beaten, but found that hard to corroborate. There were all these other images…screaming people, ants, fire, explosions, more ants, sand, roaring water…and that godforsaken *wind*. Lots and lots of scathing wind. Wind and sand.

Where the hell was he?

Tiger decided to just grab onto one of the threads screaming through his head and hold on tight. As the wind and sand blew through him, he grabbed onto the ants that crawled along the grass…followed them along their trodden paths through Bahiagrass, past Ti plants, bougainvilleas, and citrus trees. Along buildings and over dead squirrels and rabbits and goats. They seemed very determined to get where they were going…possessed an incredible sense of

Urgenc…

Urgency.

Amused, Tiger went along for the ride. Up ahead he sensed-before-seeing their mound. Children were playing nearby, and a portion of the ants momentarily diverted toward the closest child who wasn't paying attention to where she was straying. As one of those ants, Tiger crawled over her unshod foot. The child jerked, and Tiger bit into her. The child shrieked, and he, and most of the others, were tossed off.

Tiger and company continued on their journey toward the mound, as the child fled, screaming for mommy.

Funneling in and scurrying down, down into the earth, Tiger was fascinated by the interior tunneling. He'd never owned an ant farm, had seen plenty of pictures, but it was quite something else to actually be running down inside one yourself. It was comforting, *cozy*. Tiger felt the call of the Queen and immediately diverted toward her. The column raced down and toward her and entered her chamber. Swarms of other ants surrounded her, and there were images again flooding his mind. Urgency, there was another sense of

(*Urgen...*)

urgency. Suddenly he was, once again, racing downward, him and the entire column of ants. Down, down...ever...

They were no longer scurrying through well-formed tunnels, but now tunneling through hardpacked dirt, which eventually gave way to looser soil. After what seemed an eternity, they broke through the surface and exploded out onto desert sand in a torrent of ant bodies gysering out of the earth. Tiger and his fellow ants hit the ground running, sprinting across hot sand. It felt cathartic, just running and running and not knowing where he was or why. He just followed the others...when it soon became apparent something wasn't right. There was a smell to the air. Rot and decay. It was a smell that wove its way into his little ant sensors.

Did ants smell?

He never really thought about it, but it didn't matter because he was smelling something wicked horrible up ahead whether or not he was supposed to.

The flowing mass of chitinous exoskeletons continued their forward rampage, when loud, crashing sounds washed over them (could ants *hear?*). It sounded like waves, crashing against a shore...but that reek grew stronger. Tiger found it hard to breathe, but also found he couldn't stop. He was driven inexorably on...there was still something ahead, and as much as he grew increasingly sickened by it, couldn't stop. They were of one mindset, these ants, and he was a part of them. But they were almost there, he knew, and if he could just get past that horrendous *stench*...

As Tiger continued on with the rest of the swarm, he found they now climbed over bumps—obstacles—in their path. Obstacles meant nothing; they merely swarmed over whatever was in their way, but the interruptions quickly became more frequent until he found that, now, that's *all* there was. And the stench had grown unbearable. Tiger gagged, though he knew his little ant body was continuing on like a good little trooper, and when he was able to have the presence of mind to look down at what they traveled over, he experienced horror like never before.

They scurried over, past, around and *through* human remains and body parts.

Millions of them. *Trillions.* Everywhere. Arms and legs. Hands and feet. Torsos. Heads.

Bloodied, *all* of it.

Tiger tried to stop, to will himself out of there and back into his bed. This was supposed to be a dream, but he was beginning to wonder...maybe the dream part was him back in that odd, white, room, in that bed...attached to that weird, beeping, dream equipment, and *maybe*...

Screaming, he tried to quit the swarm, to turn around and head back—but his little ant body just wasn't cooperating. It didn't even twitch. He was a helpless prisoner. And the sound of the ocean was quickly getting closer. That smell that reek from hell was only getting worse, and Tiger could have sworn his brain was bleeding, melting. Tiger began to weep as he continued to swarm throughout the body parts, all sticky and fresh from whatever had caused this carnage. The wholesale, pandemic, prevalence of it all was unfathomable. It went on for as far as his little ant sensors could discern.

But he continued onward, *ever* onward...

Finally...a crashing of waves just up ahead. He'd long ago given up that the smell would lessen and had consoled himself to drowning in its breakers. That would surely end his misery, though the imagery, he was sure, would carry with him into any next life an ant might have.

Oh, please, God, God of Ants and All That Is, let me die! he pleaded, *I can't take this anymore!*

Tiger grew dizzy. If ants bled, he was certain he was doing so now...his little ant brain melting from the horror he waded through. He found he'd just run into the gaping mouth of a severed head, only to exit through a messy and jagged fracture out the back of it.

When would it end!

The waves...they were just up ahead...it couldn't be much longer. When he should have been smelling sand and surf, instead he gagged.

He felt the actual pounding of the surf, reverberating across the mangled bodies. He was almost there…he could just keep running, run straight into the sea…drown himself and forever be rid of the horrible smell, the unspeakable imagery…put himself out of his misery…the sea, the stinking, rancid sea…his only hope.

Tiger increased his pace, forced his little ant legs faster, faster, until he began to outdistance the rest of the swarm and felt his little ant lungs (if they had them) burn. He grew dizzier, so much so he was unable to focus on his efforts, and was unable to continue in a straight ant line. The breakers not far ahead, Tiger just pointed himself in the direction of the sea and hunkered down. It wasn't much farther…if he could just hold out, he didn't want to die among this decaying butchery. He wanted to be free of it when he exploded from all his disgust…

The breakers were deafening, and Tiger was unable to focus. He felt the warm spray on his little ant face, but the smell was no better. In fact, he felt himself actually beginning to rot for the intensity of the odor, from the horror of it all—but he forced himself *onward*…

He'd made it! Was finally there!

He could die in peace, now, because he certainly wasn't able to turn back and make his way all the way back across this hell. No, he was here to stay, here to die, here it would all end.

Tiger met the breakers and made one last-ditch effort to look up and welcome the warm ocean waters he would allow to overcome him—when his heart sank. No longer able to hold himself up, and with the rest of the colony fading away and decaying along with him on those bloody shores, he met his fate head on, in an apocalyptic hail of tears and sorrow. Tiger's little ant legs give out, and he collapsed in his tracks as the breakers that weren't breakers, for the sea that wasn't a sea, fell over him and swept him away. Tiger died in the churning surf of a million-trillion severed and bloodied, mutilated body parts that washed over him in its disgusting foam of frothing, churning, *roiling*, blood….

4

Detective Fisher stood incredulous in the Sunset Harbor detention center, hands on hips, staring down the length of aisle. He listened to the sobbing and thumping that echoed from the cells around him. Cells filled with people who'd all just participated in a mass murder in his sleepy little town. People to which he swore none—or most of them, anyway—would've ever have hurt a fly.

Yet they were all locked up in cells, banging their heads against his walls, sobbing and professing their innocence—their disbelief. Praying for forgiveness.

What the hell had happened?

After talking with several, he still had even less of a picture than he'd hoped. Housewives and husbands. Sons and daughters. All of them overloaded his jails. He had suspects scattered across two counties.

Detective Fisher shook his head and left for his office.

Fisher's office was a ten-by-ten meager enclosure consisting of a desk, chair, and about half-a-dozen stacked bookcases, and what had once been wall space, but was now plastered with hundreds of crime-scene notes, photos, a whiteboard and a couple plaques, and various assorted bulletins. His desk was surrounded by and under books, files, and paperwork. Sunset Harbor wasn't exactly brimming with funds— nor crime—but there was enough to keep him employed. Most transgressions involved petty thievery of some kind. Stolen cars, bikes, or stereos—a domestic disturbance here and there—so the current task definitely stirred things up a bit. Fisher sat in his chair and stared at his whiteboard, where he'd written leads to an earlier, already solved, pawn store break-in.

So, what'd he have? He had an attacked retirement center. A murdered gate guard and residents. All the *residents*, key point, here. None of those who'd been visiting—*who hadn't actually* lived *there*—had been touched—even as they slept in the master bedrooms of some of those homes. It was as if the killers knew exactly who was who, and *where*. Only one resident couple had survived. Many homes had been unoccupied and some were still being built, and were, therefore, left untouched by the murderers. Additionally, all the murder scenes appeared to have been crimes of passion, and when their deeds were done, the perps all wandered about aimlessly, as if they had no idea what they'd just done, until confronted…the evidence on their clothes, their hands…their souls. They hadn't even *fled*. It appeared to have the trappings of a cult murder—yet not quite. Or it was just their way of trying to throw him and the rest of the police force off. Were they done? Were there more of them? What had been their motive? There was just something downright *creepy* about it all.

Fisher went to his whiteboard, wiped off a large section of it, and wrote down what he had. Then he sat down and stared at what he'd written.

Stared at it some more.

Then picked up the phone and dialed Dr. Kimberly Preston, clinical and forensic psychologist for the Sunset Harbor police department.

Chapter Six

1

Jack and Hedda Hocker headed for the Exit 189 on-ramp, destination: Tampa. Loaded in the back of their "Marine Green," as Jack referred to the truck's color, Ford were all of their important bits and pieces from their Safe Harbor existence, including, in the extra-cab, their pet cat, "KA-BAR," curled up in his cat-carrier. They just weren't going to stay there any longer. There was no longer anything remotely "safe" about Safe Harbor after last night, Hedda decided, and she wanted out. They were headed to see their son in Tampa, after just having left some friends in East Venice, and were headed out as fast as the speed limit-plus-five would allow. Jack was at the wheel, Hedda in the passenger seat, a folded newspaper in her lap. She held her face, eyes closed, toward the warm, late-morning sun, radiating in through her window and onto her face. Jack looked to her lovingly, reliving the moment they first met over sixty years ago, in that MASH unit in Korea. He'd had a shoulder wound and she'd been his nurse. He couldn't believe they'd been together all this time, through a handful of wars and "conflicts." He'd spent most of his life defending a way of life for people he'd never meet, but had found a woman he loved more than life itself. Through thick and thin they'd remained together, and, he could honestly say, their love was greater today than it had been sixty-one years ago—which had been love at first sight. She hadn't admitted it until after they'd married, not wanting to appear "easy," but never had there been any doubt. They married a year after they'd met. She'd put up with a lot from him and his tours of duty, but it was their deep and unwavering love and devotion that'd kept them together. And now, as he looked to her, the morning sun warming her calm face, he still felt that love like an unbreakable chain binding them together.

Hedda opened her eyes.

"Well, let's see what the paper says about last night," she said, looking to him. "Hey—what's wrong?"

Hedda reached over and wiped away a tear from the corner of Jack's eye.

"Nuthin."

"'Nuthin' my ass." She narrowed her gaze. "Spill it, Marine."

Jack didn't immediately pony up, and Hedda playfully shook her head, returning to the paper.

"I almost lost you back there," he finally said, jaw set.

Hedda looked up from the paper and smiled. Again reached out to him.

"We'll always be together, honey. In life *or* death, I firmly believe this—and I ain't afraid of going, you know that—"

"—me neither. I just don't want to go on living if you ever left me, is all. But, I'd *hate* it if I went first. Couldn't bear the thought of you—"

"Oh, stop it," she said, swatting him. "I promise to go first, how's that?"

Jack chuckled, though he felt oddly nervous. "Let's just look to the road ahead, and get the hell outta Dodge!"

"Agreed!"

Hedda continued to unfold and snap the paper into position. "Oh, boy," she said, reading the headline, "here it is. And, it's by that lady reporter!"

"What's it say?"

Hedda scanned the article, reading the important parts.

"'Sometime after one this morning, an inexplicable band of killers entered the Safe Harbor Retirement Community and systematically slaughtered all its residents—except for one fortunate couple. Jack and Hedda Hocker...'"

Hedda looked up to Jack, smiling nervously.

"'...he a retired Marine Master Gunnery Sergeant of thirty-three years and gun shop owner of nearly three decades, and she an ex-Army nurse, housewife, and retired realtor took on the attackers single handedly. Reported retired MGYSgt Hocker, 79, 'I was awoken by a presence in our bedroom and sprang into action. It was good to see I still had what it takes.' Together the Hockers managed to prevent their murder by going on the offensive, which is all the more remarkable, given their ages....'"

Again, Hedda looked to Jack, smirking. "We're getting old, Jack."

"Eh, what are you gonna do?"

Hedda continued.

"Retired MGYSgt Hocker, KA-BAR knife and .45 in hand, took the fight out into the early-morning streets of Safe Harbor, once dispatching their own threat. Hedda Hocker, also 79, immediately called police and took up position with her husband's Browning hunting rifle. Together the couple managed to survive until police arrived, but sadly, many had not been so lucky...."

Hedda stopped reading, scanning the rest of the piece.

"How sad," she said. "It just goes on to say that there's something like forty suspects scattered between two county jails...and some seventy victims."

Hedda lay the paper down on her lap, and stared out the window.

"I don't know, Jack...I don't get a good feeling about this...it's like, I don't know...like there's still something...something *bad*...still out there. Unfinished." She paused. "I just get a feeling it's not over. Yet."

"Hey—what's this?" Jack said, leaning forward and peering off to the side of the Interstate.

Up ahead, on their side of the Interstate as they approached the Exit 191 overpass, a man stumbled his way over the guardrail of a grassy embankment. He then teetered unsteadily on the shoulder alongside.

"I don't know about this, Jack. After *yesterday?*"

Jack was already slowing down, hitting the hazards.

"Just be wary, hon, okay? Dial 911 into the cell," he said, handing Hedda the cell phone, "ready to send."

Hedda took the phone and dialed in the number without sending. Then she eyed her husband as he slowed down the Ford and brought it onto the shoulder.

Jack and Hedda looked to each other. Hedda reached over and gave Jack's hand another squeeze before exiting. Not knowing it, both thought to the other *I love you.*

Vehicle still running and leaving both truck doors open, Jack and Hedda exited the truck and cautiously approached the man, who had now stumbled back to the overpass guardrail and leaned against it. He held a hand to his head, as if cradling a wound. Traffic screamed past behind the three at dizzying rates.

"Be careful, babe," Jack again warned his wife, in a low, cautious tone above the din of traffic. "Sir!" he then called out to the man, "Are you all right? *Sir?*"

The man muttered unintelligibly, as he continued to lean against the guardrail. He broke off into bursts of further incoherent babble, which neither Jack nor Hedda could make out. Hedda advanced a little quicker toward the man, concerned about the head wound. Jack eyed the surrounding terrain and embankment from where the man had come.

"*Be careful, hon*," Jack again urged, as he came to the embankment near the man—keeping an eye on both his wife and the stranger. Jack peered over the side, then diverted back toward the man who continued to babble and rant.

"Sir! Are you all right?" Hedda asked, her finger still poised on the cell phone's "Send" button. She then cast a wary glance back to her husband. An eighteen wheeler blew past, tugging at the air around Hedda. She cast a nervous look behind her.

As Jack and Hedda came within arm's length of the guy, they stopped. What at first appeared to be ratty attire and destitution now took on a more sinister, unnerving appearance. Both noticed that what they initially mistook for rags and hardship was a man covered in dried blood and dirt. The perception of ratty street clothes gave way to a tattered and abused high-end suit and heavily scuffed leather shoes. Jack and Hedda shot each other looks.

The man mumbled something about "chin gas."

"I don't like the feel of this...," Jack said, "not at all...this is all wrong, all..."

It was like the old days in the bush. That sick-to-your-stomach-we're-*surrounded* feeling. All the tiny hairs on Jack's neck shot to attention as he cried out to Hedda and attempted to sprint toward her. But his age and body betrayed him, and he was a lifetime too short.

As Hedda reached out to the man, who was now just beginning to look up at them, she also had a sudden flash of intuition. Damaged looking as he was, Hedda also saw him in another, quite different way. A way she couldn't put her finger on, like the finger that still rested on her cell phone's "Send" button, but which tugged at portions of a memory that didn't seem possible. She noticed the man was well-manicured, yet extremely scraped and cut up, gashes all over his exposed skin, especially his face. One eye was somewhat puffy and swollen, actually closed up on itself. She also saw, as he lifted his head to look directly into her eyes, that it looked as if he were missing teeth. But it was in this instant when this damaged, mumbling man looked up and into Hedda's eyes that something snapped, and a look of dreaded recognition crossed his face. Hedda also recognized what was about to happen, but a bit slower than her husband had, which was already far too late. Hedda hit "Send" as the man lurched up and bolted for her, still screaming his unknown tongue.

The man, his face a mixture of all manner of rage and hatred, bolted directly for Hedda.

He slammed into her, and with an angry drawn-out grunt lifted her up off the pavement and into the air like a sack of potatoes. He continued yelling as he charged with her, braked to an abrupt halt—then launched Hedda out into the blast of Interstate traffic. As Jack watched in utter sickened, horror-struck helplessness, arms outstretched toward his wife, a passing semi caught Hedda square in its front grill. The last thing Hedda saw was the stunned and incredulous look on her husband's face, as he stood powerless and watched her connect with the front end of a Freightliner, whisked away in a barrage of noisy air brakes, screeching tires, and skipping thuds.

The sickening introduction of his wife against 90-mph metal hit Jack just as hard, and all time slowed. He watched as the cell phone Hedda had held was knocked from her hands like a spent tooth during a boxing match, smashing on the shoulder of the Interstate at his feet. Jack's knees wobbled and his breath grew thick and short, as if some incredible weight had just been dropped square on his chest. All of Jack's experience in the jungles and deserts of the world meant shit. He, sluggishly (it felt), turned to the attacker and saw that the man was now making his crazed advance toward him, and for a moment—just the quickest of moments—Jack didn't see the attacker he *expected* to see, but saw a very different man, a very different...*face*. A face that was now dirtied and angry and weary, but determined. Dirt covering it in patches, and the eyes...so much *hatred*. Jack never knew a person could contain so much hatred in one look. He couldn't make out everything about this new...point of view...but knew the man he was looking at was quite different than the one they'd stopped to help—*yet the very same man*.

But all this was brought back into cohesive perspective by the force of the man's attack, as he slammed into him, bowling him over.

Time shifted back into present-tense mode, and Jack found himself under a raging attack by Mister Tattered Hugo Boss Suit, who screamed unintelligible garble and raked and pummeled his body with his bare, damaged, hands. Cars and trucks continued to slam into each other from the collision of his wife with the Freightliner and its subsequent jack-knifing behind him. Jack felt stones and other debris strike his body as he fell to the shoulder. He thought about how Hedda'd probably slid from the truck's grill as it decelerated, fell to the concrete, and how the thump-thump-thumping of the jack-knifing semi was probably the truck's eighteen wheels plowing over her dead body as it continued to charge forward, before finally skidding to its gory conclusion. His eyes also caught sight of their still-running truck, and he thought about KA-BAR, curled up in his cat-carrier.

Seconds.

Seconds can change a life *forever.*

It was at this point that all of Jack's fighting instincts finally kicked in. Hugo Boss had gone crazy and was not only beating the shit out of him, but was also alternately scraping up dirt and gravel and flinging it into his face. Spitting on him, even vomited once. Never in all his years had Jack ever experienced such an attack. This was like no hand-to-hand he'd ever been trained for, or been a part of.

Finally able to get a hold on his enemy, Jack flung the man, who seemed to be *two* men, off him, and against the guardrail. Reeling from his age, a possible broken bone or two, and the nausea of just having seen his wife splattered all over Florida Interstate, and that all his efforts from last night, not to mention his adult-life for that matter, had been for naught, Jack shakily got to his knees. As much as he was mentally ready for action, as much adrenaline was coursing through his body, and as much experience as he had had in hand-to-hand combat, Jack's body was no longer as willing a participant as it used to be. His mind raced with ingrained responses, but his body continually denied him the speed and power in which to wield it. He was just barely getting a foot underneath himself, when he was again bowled over onto the concrete, his face and shoulder mixing with Interstate debris. As he hit and slid along the road's shoulder, his eyes locked onto a familiar sight he'd seen plenty of in his lifetime, a sight that all but took the fight out of him.

A thick discharge of blood.

He'd seen plenty of blood across the world, but what took all the fight out of him was that it had come from his *wife*, from her precise moment of impact with the Freightliner's grill.

Jack lay on the debris-laden shoulder staring at the dark pool, and in a moment that seemed an eternity, asked himself the worth of it all. All his years of covert and not-so-covert defense. All his experience at saving his country from external aggressors, from training others to do the same…from an at-once finely honed and tuned body that saw every human as a potential target—to look where he was now. Look where his wife was now, strewn who knew how far down the road, amid a pile of still screaming Interstate carnage.

Where had all his training gone when he needed it most?

He'd served his country and served well, kept it free from aggressors, but couldn't do shit for the one person he loved most…the one person he was, consciously and unconsciously, fighting for his entire life. If he couldn't save her, what did it matter if he survived?

Marine.

That term echoed hollowly in his head.

Semper fi.

What good was any of that to him—or Hedda—now? Jack felt the once-polished shoes of Mr. Hugo Boss Suit repeatedly slam into him—his stomach, groin, and back—and felt no need to respond.

What the hell did anything matter?

He'd done his time and he'd *still* lost his wife. The love of his life, his reason for living *and* fighting.

It just didn't fucking matter.

And Mr. Hugo Boss Suit was more than happy to oblige, as his once-polished shoes came crashing down upon Mr. *Semper Fi's* head. Again and again and…

Mr. Hugo Boss Suit unsteadily backed away from his handiwork, wildly panting and foaming at the mouth and leaning forward and bracing himself on his knees. The current spate of vehicles slamming into each other seemed to bring him out of his rage.

He looked up.

Shocked by what he saw, he slipped and collapsed to the ground.

"Oh, nooooo…no-no-*NO!*" Mr. Hugo Boss Suit whined, "Not *again!* What have I *done!*"

He fell into explosive sobbing.

There were shouts down the Interstate, along the wreckage, and they were coming his way. Scrambling to his knees Mr. Hugo Boss Suit looked to the thrashed and lifeless body of the man he'd just murdered, and the carnage on the Interstate before him.

No, this wasn't happening.

An image crossed his mind. There had been a woman…there had been something about a *woman*…

Several scraped-up and dirtied hands grappled him, and Mr. Hugo Boss Suit found himself lifted bodily from the shoulder of the Interstate. All their cursing and yelling fell on deaf ears. Mr. Hugo Boss Suit looked to them dumbly as he was angrily jostled about.

It didn't matter.

None of it did.

He had to put an end to it. Couldn't let it happen again. Mr. Hugo Boss Suit jerked rearward, freeing himself from the tangle of angry citizens, slamming them into each other, then made a run for it. The mob pursued, but wouldn't get to him in time.

And what *was* time, Mr. Hugo Boss Suit wondered?

Did anything really matter? No jail time for him—at least not in the conventional sense. Whatever waited for him, he would gladly meet, but on his own terms. He was more than willing to meet his Maker.

And with that, Mr. Hugo Boss Suit never looked back as he launched himself up and over the I-75 guardrail and into the cool Florida-morning air of Exit 191, arms and legs windmilling.

Just before he hit U.S. 41, some thirty feet below, he wondered, would this be what it felt like to slam into the grill of an on-coming eighteen wheeler?

Chapter Seven

1

Harry Gordon dumped his briefcase onto his second-floor Florida Circuit Court of Sarasota desk, glanced at the messages Libby Pointner, Administrator, had left, and made for his morning ritual of coffee and Danish. Returning to his desk, he plopped into his chair and immediately dropped his face into his hands.

Was it still there?

Yes…always drifting in and out of the cluttered babble of his mind…it was always there…that grainy mind-itch he'd been living with for ten years. No one'd been able to tell him what it was—no doctors in white jackets, no diviners, no psychics—no one.

Stress.

The usual diagnosis, Xanax or Prozac the prescribed treatment. The affliction had just popped into his head out of the blue, one day…the sound of an ocean, its breakers hitting a beach—sometimes faint and infrequent, sometimes loud and all-consuming. The thought was he'd had tinnitus, but he soon discovered that wasn't exactly the case. As the years progressed, so had his symptoms. But they'd always been manageable…until three weeks ago. Every night, the same or similar dream…and such *anger*. Intensity.

A sandbox—in the middle of his bedroom?

Ants?

And every time he had that dream, it was like the first time…like it'd never happened before, and he had to act out the entire dream in exactly the same sequence. It was like mentally he knew he was doing it over and over, but physically (in the dream, anyway) he had to plod mindlessly along, unable to stop the madness. Could people really control their dreams? He hadn't been able to. Not once.

Harry sipped his coffee. His gaze fell upon an ornamental urn positioned upon a black-lacquered pedestal across the room from him by the door. It stood before a framed reproduction of the 13th century *Moko shurai ekotoba* scrolls he'd purchased several years ago, about an attack on a Japanese island. He took another sip. That almost made everything better—the coffee. He took a bite of Danish. Power breakfasts for power hitters. Sugar and caffeine—was there any better way to start one's day? No, your Honor, there ain't. Comfort food in an uncomfortable world.

Harry's intercom buzzed.

"Mr. Stansfield's here. Five minutes. In the conference room."

"Thanks—"

"And Mr. Banner just arrived."

"Show him in."

Private Investigator Moses Banner, big, badass, and black, in his fifties, filled the doorway. He stayed just inside the door, chewing on a toothpick.

"Morning."

Banner nodded, staying put.

"Take it you heard?"

Banner again nodded. "S'pose you want me to nose around."

"I would."

Banner nodded. Harry looked down to his desk; when he looked back up, Banner was gone. Harry grabbed his paperwork and left for his morning meeting.

2

Moses Banner surveyed the Safe Harbor retirement community from across Tamiami Trail Boulevard, also known as U.S. Highway 41, as he flicked yet another toothpick out the beautifully restored '67 Camaro's window. There was no way Sunset Harbor's finest was going to be able to keep an eye on every square inch of crime scene real estate, even with all the county and state support.

Banner slowly maneuvered the Camaro around the back of the empty office park and shut it off. He exited the car and made his way back around to the front of the deserted building, then just kept walking. He crossed Tamiami Trail and headed into the palm trees, Saw palmetto, and myrtle bushes of the undeveloped lot that bordered the retirement community. A low, stucco wall was hidden on the other side of the bushes. Fisher was more than likely more concerned over the one-and-only entrance in and out of the place—not a great way to plan a development in this P.I.'s not-so-humble opinion—and had the rest of his already-stretched-thin force keeping the evidence as sterile as possible. There were a lot of homes to cover. He'd lost a friend in there, and the thought of him being murdered by a roving band of cowards really pissed him off. He'd hoped Garrett's place was still untouched, which was out on the back edge of the park, along yet another undeveloped expanse of field.

Banner ducked into the lazily-breeze-tossed Coconut palms and Saw palmetto, hunching along the vegetation-lined wall. Overhead, hawks and kestrels circled. He squeezed in between the brush and wall, flattening himself against the stucco structure, collecting scratches and a small wall-rash along the way. Senses heightened, he shot down the length of the barricade about a hundred feet before stopping. Bird and insect life chirped and buzzed busily about him in the rising humidity. He peeked over the wall. He saw he was along a length of open and as-yet undeveloped lot on the inside of the retirement community. Grapefruit and tangelo trees dotted the backyards of the completed homes. Still no cops.

Banner continued until he reached a stretch of homes another fifty feet down, and again stopped. Flushing out an egret that had been standing near-motionless in an eerily deserted backyard, Banner hid behind a Pepper tree. He again slowly poked his head over the wall. Using the Pepper tree's branches to shield his face, he continued scanning the area.

Everyone of these residents had been killed—except for that one couple, and those who'd been lucky enough to have been visitors. It was highly implausible that all the friends and relatives could have been in on the murders—but was it any more impossible than the scenario that currently existed? Were humans getting more fucked up with each generation? Wars and terrorism were bad enough, but this was so much more…seemed so much more…*personal*. One on one. Hand-to-hand. These people had lived their lives for their kids, their companies, and had made their meager fortunes. They'd no-doubt wanted to do what *they* wanted for a change in their waning years—no kids nor corporations to any more dictate their lives. Tennis, poker, and restaurants. Good friends. That's all Garrett Stiller wanted, a retired homicide detective from New York City. How had he managed to get surprised? Taken out?

What a goddamned waste.

The coast clear, Banner hefted his muscular six-foot-four frame up and over the wall and disappeared between the homes.

3

Kaccy Miller awoke reluctantly. Having been up all night listening to her scanner, interviewing the Hockers, and punching out that article after her emotionally horrifying in-her-face adventure—her breaking and entering—had worn her out. She wished the Hockers well, and hoped they'd indeed left this town for Tampa and their son. What a horrendous thing to have happen to you in the first place, but to single out a entire *community*? A *retirement* community?

Kacey swung out of bed and entered her combination living-room and kitchenette. She pulled out a carton of orange juice from the refrigerator, took a sip, and took it with her to her door. Outside, on her doorstep, was her issue of the *Gazette*.

Hers.

This was it—the shining moment for which she'd been working. She was actually shaking. Her byline—not someone else's—*hers*. She quickly opened the door and snatched it from the AstroTurfed landing. Ducking back inside, she plopped down onto the couch, spilling juice, and opened the paper.

She'd never thought about it before, but not only was it her byline, not only was it front page news, but it was *headline* news. Big, bold type on the front page. Top center. She looked to the byline.

Kacey Miller.

Good God, that's what it said, all right. It really did. *Kacey Fucking Miller.*

She closed her eyes, allowing the emotion to well up inside. She'd just wished it had been under far-less-horrific circumstances. But that's the trade. Bad news made for good news, the worse the better.

Entire Retirement Community Slaughtered, it read. "*Sometime after one this morning....*"

Giddy, Kacey put down the paper and looked to her hands. Trembling, she was still trembling. Everyone in town was reading her words this morning—*her words*—not just those who made it to page three, lower inside gutter, but everyone who just picked up, or even cast a glance toward it would see it. *Front page headline news!*

She again picked up her paper and mentally compared each word in the story with each word she'd written. With minor edits, it was all there. Every disturbingly gruesome detail. Her article scared her, so she could only imagine what affect it would have upon the community...the senior citizenry.

Kacey took the article with her into the kitchen, took out a pair of scissors, and snipped it out. She tacked it up on the cork board beside her laptop, stood back and stared at it. Yes, she'd come a long way from...

Sheila.

Kacey sat at her table, buried her head into crossed arms, and let out a huge sigh, as she leaned forward and stretched.

Sheila.

There had been one huge mistake.

Why couldn't she shake her? And could she really call her a *mistake?* Running away from her family—*that* had been a mistake—but could what had happened with Sheila be termed one? Sheila had been understanding, supportive, and, well...loving. There was nothing wrong with that, was there? Sheila'd also been needy herself...understandable, given her situation. They both had been. There was no real right or wrong assigned to them...things had just been...*what they were...*

How Kacey had ended up in a hotel room on her way to her flight that was to have taken her away from her family she couldn't recall, but she had been a *wee*-bit tipsy from all the alcohol from that bar, and probably, no doubt, from all the guilt screaming around inside her head like a steroid-sucking wasp. But she now found herself sitting on the edge of a bed, hand to her head and tears wet on her face. As if a breeze had begun to blow apart her fog, she anxiously realized *she wasn't alone.* The sound of running water filtered in through her mental fog—a bathroom?—and there was also a shadow that moved about in there...

Think hard...where *was* she...had Mark found her? Dragged her here? Where was Emily? Were they on vacation? Good God, why couldn't she remember anything—and why was the room *spinning?*

"I hope this helps a little," the woman said, who exited the bathroom holding a glass of water, aspirin, and a towel draped over an arm. She stood before her suddenly, in a business suit and skirt, her jacket removed, which, Kacey observed, lay at the end of the bed.

"This should help loosen up that headache."

Kacey looked up to her in a mixture of pain and relief. Oh, yeah, she did have a headache, but there was also something far worse breaking her apart like a creaking and groaning, fracturing ice floe.

A *heart*ache…

The woman sat on the bed beside her, holding out the glass of water and aspirin, placing the damp towel on a pantyhosed thigh. Kacey noticed (with surprising clarity) how the bed gently gave way to this other woman's slight weight, and how this, in turn, caused her to lean *into* this woman…how her perfume—a light, clean musky scent—was incredibly and unnervingly intoxicating…and, most surprisingly of all, how she swore she felt the woman's radiation of body heat into her side.

This was wrong…all *wrong*…

Kacey placed her hands on the bed to steady herself when another bout of headache mercilessly pounded at a different part of her head. Groaning, Kacey brought a hand back to her throbbing noggin.

"I guess I really do need these."

Sheila smiled. "Of course you do; you've been through a lot."

Sheila placed an open hand before Kacey, two aspirin nestled comfortably in her upraised, rosy, palm. Kacey took the aspirin and water and again swore she felt her—what was her name? Sheila?—body heat radiate from her hot-water-warmed palms. Finishing her water and aspirin, she handed Sheila the empty glass. She'd meant to ask how they'd found their way up here—but, oops, hey, wouldya look at the time? Gotta go!—when Sheila suddenly wrapped the warm towel around her head. As if incontinent, Kacey melted and collapsed back onto the bed.

"Better?" Sheila asked, gently assisting her head to the pillow.

"*Yeeesss.…*"

"Just relax, honey. Take a load off. You've been through a lot," Sheila said, smoothing out Kacey's hair and wiping away tears. "Believe me, I've been there. You just have to work through the pain…the emotion. It takes time…you can't rush it."

Kacey said nothing. She closed her eyes like she had a choice. That helped a great deal from all the spinning, but didn't help with the inner turmoil. She now remembered what had brought her here, what they'd been talking about.

Family. *Her* family.

Her husband and daughter back in Delaware. And why? Because he loved changing *diapers?* Was that it? Because he loved being *married?*

A whole new emotional torrent overtook Kacey, but Sheila was right there, wiping away her tears as she cried and heaved and wailed.

"It's okay...it's *okay*...let it all out," Sheila coached, gently stroking her face and hair with the back of her hand. Sheila tenderly brought Kacey up to her shoulder, cradling her.

"What am I *doing?*" Kacey exploded, leaving the shoulder. "How could I leave my *family?*"

"You left for a reason, didn't you?"

"I left because I was *bored!* Scared! Those aren't *reasons!*"

"Of course they are," Sheila said, gently bringing Kacey back to her shoulder, "why would a beautiful, intelligent woman like yourself just up and leave her family? You had to be bored and scared for a reason."

Kacey continued to disintegrate into Sheila's shoulder, ashamed that she was intentionally inhaling deeply of her scent—was that *Dolce and Gabbana?*—all while Sheila continued to stroke her hair and shoulders, soothing her with soft, comforting, *whispers*...

"You said you'd lost interest in your marriage...that Mark had become boring. Was no longer fun and exciting...."

This time as Sheila stroked her hair and cheeks, she looked to her, wiping away the tears and tracing a finger to Kacey's lips—which she quickly withdrew.

"Am I missing something?" Sheila whispered. "It's not easy doing what you did. It takes guts...lots of guts. Resolve. Most people stay in unhappy marriages, unhappy lives...don't have the wherewithal to do anything about it. *You* did. That says a lot about you. I wasn't as strong as you...not at first."

Sheila looked off into the distance.

"I wasn't sure, like you, that I needed to leave," Sheila continued. "I knew there were...differences...but still loved my husband. It wasn't until he found us that events took on their own momentum."

Kacey looked up to Sheila with her tear-streaked face. "I guess we're both really messed up, aren't we?"

Sheila smiled wistfully. "Guess we are."

Sheila again wiped away Kacey's tears. Wiped away the wetness at the corners of her mouth.

"You know, you really do look familiar."

Kacey allowed a tiny, choked, chuckle.

"That's better," Sheila said, smiling.

Kacey was suddenly quite uncomfortable leaning against Sheila's warm, very warm, breathing, alive—*very* alive—body. Attempting to resituate, she pulled away from Sheila and straightened herself out.

"Let me get you some Kleenex."

Sheila returned to the bathroom and Kacey found herself watching her, in her smartly outfitted business skirt and blouse. Found herself noticing what a great figure she had. Found herself—

Shakily, Kacey swung out of bed and to her feet, smoothing out her own attire and wiping her sniffling face.

"Here," Sheila said, suddenly again before her, "use this." She handed her the tissue. Kacey blew her nose.

"Thank you."

"Better?"

Kacey nodded. "I'm still a bit woozy, but I really should be going—"

"You think that's such a good idea? I mean with what you've had at the bar and all?"

Kacey shot a look to the clock, moving just a little too fast for her condition, and wobbled unsteadily.

"*Damn*, I missed my—"

Sheila reached out and grabbed Kacey, cradling her close to her, their faces inches apart.

"Well, there you go. Now, what are you going to do?"

Kacey again felt very warm.

4

Banner carefully worked his way around the retirement center's homes, Ti plants, and palm trees. He kept an eye on the investigation teams that also worked their way through the complex. Feeling a sudden pin-prick of fire at his lower shin, he jerked. He looked down to see he stood on a fire-ant mound. Several other fiery pin pricks followed, and he quickly swatted and stomped at them, cursing and backing away from the mound. Lifting up his pants legs, he made sure he'd gotten them all, brushed both his shins and pants, and returned to business.

810 La Paloma.

Two nights ago was the last he'd seen of Garrett Stiller after their weekly poker game. Him, Fred, Bernie, and Hoosier, whose real name was William Tucker, recently retired from Omaha, Nebraska. But, now, no more Garrett.

Moses made his way through the back yards and up against the rear of Garrett's home. It looked as he'd last seen it. Banner headed for the screened-in window in the back of the manufactured house. Garrett had loved the active, balmy breezes of south Florida, which was why he moved here in the first place. Didn't have that up in the Big Apple, that Big Rotten Apple, he used to say when he talked about the more crappier aspects of the job. New York had a lot going for it, but he'd just seen too much of its asshole and armpits and had to move somewhere he knew nothing about.

Banner felt another pin prick, and again swiped at his legs, but continued to weave his way between the grapefruit and orange trees he and Garrett had planted. He came around to the screened-in window and found it open, propped that way with one of those cheap, collapsible screens. He removed the screen and crawled in.

Garrett had been an interesting gent. In his late-sixties, he'd been born and bred in NYC, and had started his career by walking a beat. He'd risen to the rank of Lieutenant after many harrowing cop adventures, but, after having been shot in the hip while assisting another officer, he'd figured enough was enough, and retired. His retirement interests had been pretty basic: beer, babes (he'd married twice, but had long-since divorced both), and poker. The occasional trip—but never outside the country, except for a stint in the Army and Vietnam. Not even Canada or Mexico. For some reason, he never quite answered to anyone's satisfaction including his own, Garrett had an aversion to most things foreign—except for certain pieces of Oriental art. Yes, at times, Garrett was an odd bird. This, he admitted, even baffled the hell out of him. Except for Vietnam, Garrett'd never been to anything remotely Asian, never had any interest to, but for some ungodly reason found himself collecting certain objects d'art that struck a chord in him, and they usually involved warriors or battle. He said there was something about the "way of the warrior" that he loved to emulate in his own life. He used to joke about the possibility of having lived another life as a Samurai, perhaps a *ronin* (of course).

Banner surveyed the bedroom. Everything was certainly all still there…including those Jap vases depicting horses trampling enemies to death, or the swordplay bestowed upon soon-to-be-headless foe, or pikes at the ready preparing for charges across ancient fields. Of course, as he continued to survey the bedroom, Banner also noticed the blood-spattered floor, walls, and ceiling. The other pieces of broken and destroyed artwork. The viciously torn apart bed. The overturned nightstands and lamps. Fractured bedposts. The smell of death. Oh, yeah, there had been one helluva fight in here, but in the end, *Garrett* had been the one at the end of those pikes, blades, or hooves, hadn't he?

Banner stared at a vase Garrett had made a point in showing to him. He'd been mildly amused by it. It was of a ronin warrior (Garrett liked to think), taking care of business. Garrett had told him that this piece particularly grabbed him, because he'd had dreams of this scene throughout his life. When he'd seen it at a pawn shop, his blood froze, and he felt as if he were standing not only in the present, but also on the depicted battlefield. He simply had to have it.

But, in the end, all of Garrett's "way of the warrior" hadn't been able to save him when he needed it most, had it? About the only saving grace, in all this, if Banner knew his friend, was that he was probably wherever he was, thinking, *you know, at least I died a* warrior's *death. I died...in* battle.

5

As Kacey lay in that hotel bed, head still pounding, arms loosely wrapped around Sheila—who also had her arms wrapped around her, but much more passionately—she wondered, *how the hell had they found themselves* kissing?

Sheila was a wonderful kisser, lips soft, supple, and hungry—and she managed to maintain quite the effort of restraint. If Kacey kept her eyes closed and didn't think about who she was kissing, it didn't seem all that bad...did it really bother her she was kissing a woman? Was that such an evil thing? Apparently not, but her spinning head only spun more when she tried to wrap her arms around *that*. She did find, however, that when she relaxed and just went along with the flow of things, things felt, well...great. Exciting. Here she was, wife and mother, had just left her family, and was holed up in a nondescript hotel room near an airport in the dead of night, in bed with, not another man—but a *woman*. A woman full of passion and desire...something she hadn't felt in a long, *long* time.

And how had she found herself here in the first place?

All the world was still a haze, but the excitement of this new experience seemed to take some of the sting out of her predicament—the fact that she had had just a little too much to drink and hurt inside like a jackhammer had been mercilessly taken to her heart…well, things suddenly seemed a lot less urgent. Sheila's tenderness and passion were salve to her soul.

And she really was a great kisser.

Kacey allowed herself to be consumed within Sheila's passion, which, she could tell, was increasing like a smoldering fire in a stiff breeze. She took in the subtle sound of Sheila's mouth as it gently worked and explored hers. The sound of her own excited and panting breaths, the feel of her warm, flushed skin against hers. How Sheila ran her hands along her body…how she simply drank in all that was Kacey Miller. How Sheila was now atop her, sexy, pantyhosed legs straddling her, business heels deposited on the floor beside the bed—one upright, the other knocked over…

Kacey looked into Sheila's eyes. The restrained passion that bore back into her (and this was hard to admit to herself) *excited* her. Kacey was being a bad, bad girl, and she knew it, and admitting this to herself only further excited her. She'd never done anything remotely like this before and began to wonder—why the hell not? If all lesbians were like Sheila, she might be able to get into this from time to time…

Kacey closed her eyes and inhaled deeply, sucking Sheila's breath from her mouth. Boy, there was just something *about* her…

"*Did you like that?*" Sheila whispered, moist lips glistening in the low light, dark eyes passionate and burning from behind loosened tresses.

To Kacey's inebriated surprise she replied a lazily drawn out, "*Yesss.…*"

Sheila smiled, began slowly undoing Kacey's blouse—to which Kacey did not object, her chest rising and falling nervously beneath Sheila's busy (if slightly nervous?) fingers. Sheila, her dark hair cascading about her face, slowly, deliberately, undid Kacey's brassiere, removed it, and Kacey heard her sigh unlike any she'd ever heard before, because it came from a *woman* strained with passion and desire. A *woman's* passionate desire for *her.* One who'd just removed her brassiere and was contemplative of what now lay exposed.

Kacey swam in a mixture of confusion and excitement as Sheila gently and lovingly kissed and teased Kacey's exposed flesh. Kacey, gritting her teeth, grew dizzy. *This* felt different to her. She moaned, not quietly but loudly, and spread apart her legs. She pulled Sheila into her, forcing their bodies together. Sheila wove her hands around and inside the back of Kacey's opened blouse, and when she opened wide on an exposed breast Kacey never protested. When Sheila'd lifted her trembling body off the bed and made love with her now highly sensitized nipples…Kacey never objected. But when Sheila made her way down her stomach to make a play for…*deep south*…well, that's when Kacey saw Mark and Emily. That's when Mark flooded her mind…of the last time *he'd* been down there…of their daughter…still back in Wilmington…of their wedding day…the day they met…of making love with a *man*…her *husband*. And when Shelia began to unzip Kacey, Kacey, torn between her urgency to fulfill a growing and recently unfulfilled need, and the images of her family and what she was presently doing, reached down and gently removed Sheila's hand.

"*No*," she whispered firmly.

Without missing a beat, Sheila quietly worked her way back up Kacey's flexing and heaving and clenching body. Then she lifted her mouth from Kacey's warm, inviting, flesh, and carefully repositioned herself over Kacey's pelvis. Holding her gaze, Sheila began removing her own blouse.

"What are you doing?" Kacey whispered nervously, breathlessly.

Sheila eyed her with unnerving hunger, undoing her own brassiere but stopping at her skirt. "*You have such a beautiful body*," she whispered.

Kacey found herself strangely—uncomfortably so—excited at seeing Sheila's own nakedness atop her. Seeing Sheila's own well-formed and firm though not large breasts. The position of her legs straddling her, and how her skirt fell upon not only Sheila's legs, but upon her own body, as well. And when Sheila slowly came back down to Kacey's lips and they both wrapped their arms around each other in the most passionate kiss she'd had in a long, long, time, Sheila's naked, warm skin pressed into her own exposed, flushed, and quite warm flesh, Kacey gave in to the passion without guilt, without holding anything back, and without any thought given to tomorrow.…

Chapter Eight

1

Kacey lay on her apartment's couch staring at the ceiling, newspaper cast on the floor beside her.

Did making out with a woman a lesbian make?

The question had haunted her ever since Sheila. Her "experience" with her had been—well, there was no lying to herself—*extraordinary*. No matter what Kacey may have thought about kissing women before her, she had done a complete one-eighty since. Sheila had left her her number (no last names, that had been the unspoken rule), but Kacey had left her with nothing—except for one really good, absolutely *crazy* one-night stand. Well, actually, it had just been more of a make-out session, since Kacey hadn't allowed anything else to advance, but Kacey had never called her, thanked her, nor did whatever it was you were supposed to do after your first lesbian encounter. And after having left Sheila, Kacey had tried "it" once again, yes she had tried to relive the experience to see if there really had been anything to doing it with your own kind. She'd done it again only once, in California, but it just hadn't been the same. There had been no (and she found this strangely curious when she actually clarified her feelings on the matter)...*spark*. Kacey had even touched herself to Sheila's memories, which still brought on intense orgasms, but when she tried it with other women...it just wasn't happening. It was nothing short of embarrassing—even if only she knew.

But, still, she had done it with *Sheila*. So, what had it meant?

Did it have to mean anything?

Again: *Did making out with a woman a lesbian* make?

Kacey didn't think so, but had done no real research into the matter. Did feelings, honest feelings, *need* research? How could she return to her husband and family—if she were ever to do so—without resolving what had happened in that hotel room?

And this said nothing about why she'd left Mark and Emily in the first place.

But every time she got up and looked at herself in a mirror, or passed a store window, she couldn't bring herself to look directly into her own eyes for any length of time. *She'd left her family. Made out with another woman.* Left her three-month-old daughter, her husband of almost two years. Left the clothes in the dryer and told them she'd gone out for a *run.*

A frigging *run.*

Who does something like that?

No one, that's who, and that's what kept her from leaving her Florida apartment and heading north. Emily would be fifteen months, now. How would her leaving have affected her—how would her *return?* Would it do more harm than good? Was there even a chance of reconciliation, and would Mark even acknowledge her existence?

Kacey closed her eyes. She'd really screwed things up this time, perhaps irreparably—

The phone rang. Kacey wiped her eyes. Answered it.

"Kacey?"

"Yes?" Kacey cleared her throat.

"This is Connie—Connie Belleview, from the *Gazette?*"

"Hi, Connie."

"There's been another murder—"

"No—"

"You may want to sit down." Connie paused. "It's Jack and Hedda."

"Oh, no—*no-no-no*—"

"I'm so sorry. Authorities found them this morning on the Interstate. Exit 191."

"Oh, dear God, this can't be…how'd…how'd it happen—are you *sure?*"

Kacey collapsed to the floor.

"Details are sketchy, but I want you on this. There was some kind of roadside altercation. The guy who killed them took his own life."

"My God…."

"Look, this is pretty hot, and, well, it's *your* follow-up. Want it?"

"Of course."

Kacey was amazed at how calm she was able to portray herself. Guess it came from leaving your family and having lesbian sex.

"You got it. Get me some news by ten this morning, okay?"

"Ten. Sure. Thanks."

"Kacey?"

"Yes?"

"I'm so sorry. Sometimes…sometimes bad things just happen to good people."

2

Kacey, hair tossed about in the early morning Floridian breeze, had parked beneath I-75's Exit 191 overpass, on the shoulder of U.S. 41. She knelt before the still marked and stained grease spot that was where the suspect had taken his concrete digger. She looked up to the overpass, contemplating what it must have taken to take that leap…then back down to the spot before her.

Somebody had *died* here.

Hit the concrete with the full force of their body from a height of what had to be at least thirty or forty feet. But, nothing stood out to her, not that she'd necessarily know what would or wouldn't. Her journalistic and investigative experience consisted of six-year-old academic college courses, a lucky break yesterday morning, and television cop shows. As she got back to her feet, she stared into the hazy treetops, and wondered, good Lord, *what in hell was she doing here?* This was the big time, Missy, people actually lost their *lives* out here, and back in your comfy apartment you'd just thrown together a pile of words telling others *about* it. You just happened to be roadside, because you couldn't sleep and had been up listening to a cheap scanner. You were in the right place at the right time, was all—you was *damned* lucky, seester—and now you gotta prove yourself. Produce on demand…to a timeline, an editor—*the public*. Would have others constantly and mercilessly peering over your shoulder. Judging you.

Could she find a lead?

Follow it up—*write* it up—this time with the whole state of Florida watching, perhaps the whole U.S. of A.?

This was big news…murder on this scale, except for wars—had it ever happened before? She was the nation's front line, and that was the unnerving truth of it all. It made questions like *did making out with a woman a lesbian make?* childishly trivial.

But, still…where was Sheila, and what was she doing right now?

"Hey!" a voice called on down from the overpass above, "can I help you?"

Kacey looked up to see a Florida Highway Patrol Trooper peering down at her. She shouted back over the din of passing traffic.

"I'm Kacey Miller—from," she said, fumbling for her press badge and holding it up to the trooper in the balmy Floridian breeze, "from the Gazette Harbor—I mean, the *Sunset Harbor Gazette!* Can I ask you a few questions?"

The trooper paused, looked around, then shouted back, "Come on up." Left the guardrail.

Not quite expecting his reaction, Kacey flinched.

"Thank you!"

Kacey began her way up the same embankment, the same route the killer must also have taken. After several minutes of struggling up the steep, grassy slope, she found an outstretched hand of a sergeant in the Florida Highway Patrol awaiting her.

By the time Kacey arrived at I-75's Exit 191 overpass, most everything had been picked clean by investigators. All that remained were tiny chunks of broken windshield safety glass, miscellaneous shards of metal, and some pieces of black-and-yellow tape caught around guardrail posts, flapping in the breeze. Up the Interstate a couple hundred feet, however, were the still-flashing lights of state patrol vehicles where troopers continued to mop up the spoils of the multiple-car pileup that had resulted from the Freightliner's stunning capture of Mrs. Hedda Hocker's frail, osteoporotic body. Traffic continued at a slowed and measured pace through this stretch of roadway.

"You know," the sergeant said, dryly, reaching out to her, "you could've driven." Smiling, the trooper indicated behind her to the on-ramp.

Kacey looked.

"But, that's against traffic—"

"I think I could have bent the rules a little for a member of the press. What can I do for you, Miss *Sunset Harbor Gazette?* Sergeant Gil Parker."

They shook hands.

"Is there anything you can tell me about the crime scene?"

"Well, it appears—"

"Mind if I tape?"

"Yes, actually, I do."

Kacey nodded, stuffing the recorder back into her bag and resorting to "old school": notepad and pen.

"It appears the suspect negotiated the same embankment as you, up onto the shoulder, here," he said, directing to a section of embankment, "and the Hockers stopped, perhaps thinking they were providing roadside assistance. For whatever reason the suspect attacked, which caused the massive traffic foul up we're still managing."

"How'd the traffic get so messed up?"

"Witnesses saw the suspect throw Mrs. Hocker out into traffic."

Kacey had fully meant to respond to the officer's comment, but the words had gotten chocked off by a huge knot in her throat.

Sergeant Parker nodded grimly. "Charged her, lifted her bodily into the air, then tossed her out into traffic, where witnesses say she connected with the business end of a Freightliner."

"'Freightliner'?"

"An eighteen wheeler."

Kacey's face drained of all color.

"Ma'am? Come, sit over here," Parker offered, guiding her to the guardrail.

"I-I'll be okay. T-thank you. I really liked them, the Hockers. C-can't believe...."

Trooper Parker crossed and uncrossed his arms.

"You knew them?"

"I interviewed them in my first article."

"Sorry, ma'am. Sometimes bad things happen to good people."

Kacey shot him a look.

"Look, I have to get back up there. I was giving this a once-over before wrapping things up. You gonna be okay?"

Kacey nodded. "I will be. Thanks. Mind if I look around?"

"Go right ahead," he said, sizing things up, hands on his hips. "We're all done, here. If you need assistance back down that embankment, ma'am, let me know, and I'll drive you down," he said, giving her a reassuring smile and checking out her worn-out wedge pumps.

Kacey looked back down the embankment. "I might take you up on that."

The trooper headed back toward the eighteen-wheeler wreck.

Kacey closed her eyes, stunned at the affect the Hockers' death had had on her. It wasn't like she really knew them, but they'd affected her more than she'd expected. Part of it, she guessed, was just the fact that she'd met and talked with these people, and, now…how they *died*. It was unspeakable.

They were meant to die.

As she sat there, trying to collect herself, she ran the heel of her shoe along the shoulder in the dirt and uprooted a tiny object just as a hot gust of wind kicked up. The tiny object glittered in the sunlight. She picked it up.

A ring?

Together…

We will be together…

Kacey looked around, then to Sergeant Parker. She could have sworn she heard…

Casually secretive, she hid her find from view as she examined it. The ring was quite worn and scratched, but she could tell someone had taken great care in its creation. Gold in color, and, by its heft and feel, probably *solid*, she pressed it into the edge of the guardrail. It marred easily. Scratching at the ring's indentation with a fingernail, as if trying to appease a wound, she turned it over, wiped away dirt, and found worn, engraved characters on the inside she couldn't make out. On a whim, she placed the ring partway up her ring finger, when, without another thought, all the way on.

A perfect fit.

There was something unnervingly familiar about this ring…something *more* than right as it rested on her finger.

Take thissss…

Reeememmmber meee…

Kacey glanced back to the trooper, who continued toward the other accident scene.

She didn't want to get into any trouble, holding back on possibly valuable evidence at a crime scene…

But a little old *ring*?

How could a little ring have any pivotal affect in the investigation? Heck, they'd already picked clean the scene, according to the sergeant, so maybe it was only just recently deposited from a passing car…

"Sergeant!"

The trooper turned.

"Could I get that ride?"

3

Beneath the overpass, Kacey sat in her car for a long, hard, moment. Stared at the ring, which presently occupied a position on which another piece of jewelry used to reside.

Wedding plans and marriage vows. Family. Love. *Til death do us part.*

Mark and Emily.

Kacey fingered the ring, reluctantly removed it, then placed it on the dash.

Reeememmmber meee…

Reaching into her pocketbook, she fished out a tightly wadded little package and unwrapped it.

Memories of another life.

Happier times, when both thought they could take on the world and win. Together forever. Create an *über* race of extreme sportsters. Kacey stared at the other ring. Mark had gotten her a simple gold band. It wasn't that he was cheap, he just felt having a more ostentatious setting would get damaged with all their activities. He also just hadn't the cash for anything extravagant. Mark had never told her the second reason, but she knew, just like she knew so much else about him. She knew that had been a big factor, extreme sports or not. You just knew people after a while. Like how she knew he loved dolphins, loved to watch clouds, loved to listen to her talk, to take long autumn walks in the leaf-strewn parks of Delaware, and, most of all, knew how he feared commitment—at least until he'd met her. She knew how he joked that all those years of commitment issues just meant he'd been waiting for her to show up, because once she had, all his fear had been obliterated in that instant. He thought that had been just about the weirdest thing to ever happen to him, and it just proved they were meant to be. He hadn't been afraid of sky or scuba diving, but had been afraid of settling down.

Until her.

But could he be with a lesbian?

Someone who up and walked out on their family?

And could she live with a man who lost the identity she'd grown to love? Who, really, was the one afraid of commitment? Remember who up and left *who.* Not to reduce the entire subject to trite discussion, but maybe thoughts of lesbianism were not so much real as *wannabe?* Maybe she was just a wannabe lesbo, so she could have an easy out to all her problems. Certainly makes it easier, doesn't it, saying, "I love women." Also removes the guilt trip from your husband; now he didn't have to think it was something *he* did. "Oh, my wife left me for…a *woman*." Of course, maybe she hadn't thought it through far enough, either, because now his guilt trip could very well be *"Did I do something to turn her?"*

Right. People didn't *turn* to lesbianism out of spite.

But riddle me this, Batgirl, if you really were lesbian, then why hadn't you gone all the way with Sheila—or the California chick? Why'd you stop at the lips (and we are talking *upper* lips, ma'am)—and don't tell the world because you just wanted to practice safe sex—we both know that was as far away from the case as China is from Florida.

Kacey slipped her wedding band onto her finger.

I will be with you…

It still fit—of course it would—and she felt her stomach knot up into another burst of twisted emotion. She had to stop this or was surely headed for the funny farm. And an ulcer.

Clutching the steering wheel, Kacey choked out a cry and closed her eyes. She loved Mark, still did, goddammit, but something kept her from returning. From their life together. With Emily, her beautiful daughter, now fifteen months old—a daughter without a mother. How was *that* fair?

Oh, hadn't thought that through, either, had we, Supergirl? Sure, we were leaving our husband, boring husband, but did we also consider we were also leaving our child? And when we were sucking face with those gorgeous gals, were we even for an instant considering what our daughter would think of us? "Hey, honey, don't worry about Mommy, she swings both ways, and lesbians only swing girl-girl. I've got everything under control; no more girl-girl for Mommy—well, except for Lisa, who Mommy met while standing in line at the Post Office, or Rachel, who Mommy met while shopping, or—

"*Shut up!*" Kacey shouted, pummeling the steering wheel. "Shut up, shut up, shut *up*…." Kacey dropped her head onto the wheel.

Mark Burnett.

Just a phone call away. Cell phone to home phone. Kacey sat back up, removing her cell from her handbag. Without wiping away her tears, she dialed his number, hands shaking. Would he be there? This was the first time she'd dialed those numbers since leaving, and she stared at them in her cell's window like a starving person at a buffet. All she had to do was hit "Send." Just that one little button at the lower right, and *poof!*, off her little request would go on its merry way.

Home.

She lay back in her seat, dropping her hand and cell phone into her lap. Did she really want this? Was she ready for it?

Was he?

Kacey hit send, and nervously brought the phone to an ear. Her hand shook. She heard that blank, in-between electronic pause, then a click, as the connection was made. The first ring hit with such a jarring force that it actually caused her to jump. She ran a trembling hand through her hair and sat up straight, clearing her throat. Staring straight ahead, she steadied herself for the blow of an answer at the other end. What would she say? What would be her first words in over a year? "Hi, honey, it's me!"? Or how about "You know, despite what you may have heard, I'm really *not* into women...." Or maybe, "Hello, Mark. I know you probably don't want to talk with me, right now, but I'm sorry...so very, very, goddammed, *unbelievably* sorry for having left you and Emily. We can seek therapy, in fact I *insist* upon it, but I really, *really* want to try to make things work...."

The ringing stopped.

There was a delay as the phone at the other end was raised from cradle to another ear. Then came the sound of a male voice for which no amount of preparation prepared her.

"Hello?"

Kacey froze.

How could one simple, friendly word strike such fear?

Her mouth hung open, primed for operation, and she really wanted to say *something*, anything, like how's the weather? Your parents ok? How's Emily?—but froze. Nothing came out, not even an exhale.

"*Hello?* Is anyone there? Rod? Hello?"

Again, Kacey tried to respond. Willed herself to, but nothing came out. Her entire body trembled uncontrollably.

Is this what you really want? Sheila's voice asked, suddenly popping into her head. *I thought we had something special, you and me...that we connected. You still have my number, don't you? Call me...let's talk this out before doing anything rash...*

Mommy? Is that you? Emily's voice chimed in. *I've soooo missed you, Mommy! Why'd you leave? Was it something I did? I'm so sorry, I promise to be better this time...won't poop my dipees as much as I used to—I won't, you'll see...come back, Mommy, I really want my Mommy...*

"*Kacey?*" Pause. "Is that y—"

Kacey hit "End" and exploded into tears.

Chapter Nine

1

Detective Fisher stood before the detention center cell. Inmate Peter John Cooper sat in the far corner of his confinement, head down, hands cradling the crown of his head like a crazed "Thinker." Fisher nodded to the uniformed officer, who unlocked the cell. Cooper nervously shot to his feet.

"Morning, Mr. Cooper," Fisher greeted, entering the cell.

Cooper stared at him. "What can I do for you."

"Same thing I asked yesterday. Why'd you do it."

"I ain't done *nuthin!*" Cooper shouted, charging toward Fisher, only to stop halfway. The officer began to quickly unlock the door, but Fisher raised a hand.

"Sit down," Fisher said. "Take a load off; relax."

Fisher moved to Cooper's cot, leaning against it. Cooper didn't move.

"I mean it—sit your ass down or I'll make you relax."

Warily eyeing Fisher, Cooper sat, returning his attention to the floor.

"Are you telling me," Fisher began, "that you're claiming you didn't kill anyone?"

"I ain't sayin nuthin," he said, running a nervous hand through long, stringy, hair.

"What do you do for a living when you're not killing?"

"Mechanic. Foreign cars."

"Foreign jobs, huh? Don't like American?"

Cooper shrugged. "I dunno. I just do em; it's a job."

"I see. Like travel? See sights?"

Cooper looked up to Fisher, hands clenched. "Not particularly. Don't like foreigners."

"Yet you work on their cars. Don't see the irony?"

"Cars ain't people."

"True. Yet foreigners make the cars upon which you work."

Cooper looked back to the floor. "Fuck em. Money's money. Like I said—it's just a job."

"Hate old folks?"

"I know what you're doin, so just—"

"Just answer the question. Quicker you cooperate, quicker I'm outta your face. Hate old folk?"

Cooper glared at him. "Got nuttin gainst em."

"Yet you're pretty handy with a wrench, aren't you—"

Cooper again shot to his feet.

Lunged at Fisher.

Fisher sidestepped and deflected him back against his cot, where he tumbled onto the mattress. The officer who'd been monitoring the exchange entered the cell, taser extended.

"Jesus Christ, what the fuck you want me to say!"

"I want you to tell me why the hell you waltzed into my life and killed off a handful of *my* citizenry, that's what I want."

"I didn't *do* it—"

"We have your murder weapon, your fingerprints, and enough evidence spattered across your clothes and body to convict you for three lifetimes. Why deny it? Who organized this and why?"

Cooper rolled over in his cot, covering his face with an arm. The uniformed officer hovered nearby.

"I don't *remember*...."

"Now, how am I supposed to believe that?"

"Aren't I supposed to have a lawyer or something? I don't fucking remember any of it, *okay*? Goddammit, you think I wanna spent the rest of my life behind bars? Or get the chair—or whatever it is Florida has? *Shit*." Cooper rolled onto his back, a tear running down the side of his face. He quickly and forcefully wiped it away.

Fisher removed a small notepad from his pocket and began reading from it. "You don't remember smashing in Mr. and Mrs. Scovelli's skulls? Or the Green's? Beating Fran and Herbert Kirchen's faces into their beautiful green shag carpet?"

Fisher turned away from Cooper and the uniformed officer.

"Shit, Cooper, there's no way we'll get all their blood and brains out of those carpets for the next residents—"

Cooper spun around in the cot and leapt up off it at Fisher. This time the uniformed officer rammed the taser into Cooper's intercostals. There were several seconds of arcing electricity, spastic grunting, and Cooper collapsed, moaning and balling up into a tight fetal position. The officer came alongside Fisher.

"It's like he really believes it. He really seems to think he didn't do anything."

Fisher stared at Cooper. "Funny thing is…I'm beginning to believe him."

2

Dr. Kimberly Preston reviewed the facts. Thirty-seven suspects (minus the suicides and the Hocker's efforts) left twenty-eight who had killed seventy-two retirement-home patrons…the lot of them—minus the visitors, which was also perplexing. Only a fraction of the suspects admitted their guilt, while another handful had taken their own lives upon incarceration. All suspects appeared unrelated, all appeared repentant, and most had retreated deep into themselves. Her assignment…interview them and find out just what the heck happened, and, more importantly, *were they mentally fit to stand trial.*

No tall order.

Dr. Preston shivered. There was something distinctly unnerving about this case. Good God, the magnitude of the crime was *unthinkable.* And in such a small, backwater town. Something wasn't right, and she got the distinct impression she was going to find out what…but that she also wasn't so sure she was going to like what she found.

She scanned down the list of names. No place like the top to get started. Better reserve those interrogation rooms….

3

Howard Stoker III stood before the dream tribunal. He knew he was dreaming, but that didn't make things any less real. Enoch's presence was beside him, yet it wasn't really there. *Invisible.* There, but not there, the way things like this always happened in dreams.

"What do you think?" Enoch asked.

Howard looked around. He couldn't quite make out the faces. They were fuzzy, angry. Always in motion. There was also this blast of warm wind from time to time, and a lot of noise, white noise, everywhere, riding the oppressive air blast.

"Well," Howard responded, "I guess so. Looks like an interesting case. Won't be easy, will it?"

Enoch said, "Not in the conventional sense."

Howard examined the jurors. They all wore some kind of armor, he was finally able to make out, though not very well. Helmets? In the background came a thunderous advance of horses...

"Thanks for doing this. Only you can take this case," Jack Hocker said.

"You're the only one," Hedda added. Another blast of hot air tossed about Hedda's hair.

Howard reassessed his surroundings. He now stood on the shoulder of I-75. No cars, no traffic. Jack's body was at his feet, a smashed-in head still freshly oozing gore. He looked up the road to see (even though he knew he shouldn't be able to see any detail at this distance), Hedda's pulverized and mangled remains as if he stood directly before her.

A ravaged Hedda sat up, angled off from them slightly. She looked off into the hazy distance. "You *have* to do this," she insisted. Howard heard her plea as if she'd spoken it directly into his ear.

"For everyone," Jack added, beside him. Jack also sat upright on the Interstate, dislodged brains slowly creeping down the side of his road-rashed face.

Howard, heart heavy, nodded. "I will. It doesn't have to be like this you know...."

Jack looked down to the shoulder of the road, then to his wife, who now stared at them. "I think we know that...now. I guess...I guess...."

"We didn't know any better," Hedda chimed in, again sounding as if she stood beside Howard.

"Eh," Jack said, "it was time to go, anyway. It was okay. We left together. I was the first to go last time and promised I wouldn't do that again."

"It was fitting to our lives," added Hedda. "We both liked a little action. Go out with a bang and all."

Hedda chuckled, and bloody internal matter issued from her mouth and various other ruptured areas of her body. "Oops," she said, embarrassed, hand to mouth.

"I miss you," Jack said. He struggled to his feet and stood before Howard, who helped support him. "I gotta go. Want to be with my

Heddy."

Howard nodded.

Jack made a few steps toward Hedda and was instantly there. Howard watched Jack kneel down to his wife and encircle her with his arms. They hugged. Howard closed his eyes…

Howard stood on a windswept desert. The sound of horses thundered behind and among the great dunes surrounding him; a bright white hospital bed stood behind him.

"So…you're this 'Tiger' I've heard so much about," Howard said.

Tiger lay in bed; looked up to him. "I am." He spit out a mouthful of ants. "Why do these damned things follow me everywhere I go!"

Howard smiled.

"I'm in trouble, aren't I? *Big* trouble."

The judge nodded, the sound of horses still echoing crazily in and around the dunes.

"I had it coming, huh?"

"Well," Howard said, as he stared off into the dunes, "we all have our challenges…some just chose to handle them differently."

"I'm sorry, so very sorry" Tiger said. "I'm having a hard time with everything—"

"I understand—"

"You're no saint, either, from what I hear."

Howard grunted.

"I wish I could do it all over again—I mean, I wish I could do things differently."

"You are."

"I'm still so very sorry."

"Learn from it."

Tiger smiled. "I—"

He started to say something, when a sirocco of sand and hooves blasted through Tiger and Howard, trampling over Tiger and his white, bright white and radiant bed. Howard watched everything before him obliterated. When it all passed, Howard found one ant left rooting around in the sand. The sound of the horses faded. Howard stooped, extended a finger, and let the ant climb on up. Returning upright, he watched it crawl about the ridges of his skin just before it bit him.…

* * *

What do you think? Enoch thought.

This is going to be one helluva case, Howard returned in thought.

Enoch smiled. *It'll keep you on your toes!*

I like that. A little grit, Howard said, spitting out particles of sand, *never hurt anyone…*

Howard bolt upright in bed, wide awake. It was 2:03 a.m., Nora fast asleep beside him.

4

Banner entered Harry Gordon's Sarasota Circuit Court office. Harry met him, hand outstretched.

"Find anything?" Harry asked.

"There's something weird about the whole thing."

Harry wrinkled his face. "What do you mean?"

Banner pulled out his notebook. "I got into a couple homes, and it was pretty much all the same. Attacks were mainly in the bedroom, where there were marked signs of struggles, and in some cases, quite a wake of carnage."

"Like?"

"Blood…everywhere. Broken furniture and windows. Slashed and smashed beds. It all looked…fanatical. These weren't random attacks. There's motive behind these murders; we just have to find it."

"And…Garrett's place?"

Banner held his gaze. "Same. Signs of an intense struggle. He put up a good fight."

"I'm sorry," Harry said. "I've also been to the detention center— *they don't know each other*, that's the weirdest part," Harry said. "Many don't even recall what it was they *did*. Some'd even taken their own lives."

Banner grunted. "How're your headaches?"

"Still there. From time to time."

Banner nodded, pensively. "Well, there you go."

Harry saw him to the door. "Keep me posted."

"It's what you pay me for."

As Banner exited, he caught sight of the urn.

"Don't remember this…"

"A client gave it to me as payment last week. Said it was valuable. I had it appraised at a tidy sum. It was made during the 1700s, about an invasion of some Japanese island. Kyushu. I was never much interested in Oriental art, but when she showed it to me…I just took it."

"Huh," Banner said. "Garrett had one just like it."

"Huh," Harry said. "Hey—what about that reporter?"

"Headin there, now," he said with a casual wave of a hand, not looking back.

5

"Kacey Miller?" Banner asked, standing before a tiny and cramped desk at the absolute rear of the *Sunset Harbor Gazette* offices.

Kacey looked up. "Yes?"

Banner extended a hand.

"Moses Banner. I work for the prosecution. We're investigating the Safe Harbor murders. Read your article."

Banner flashed his credentials.

"Oh," she said, getting to her feet and tucking loose strands of hair behind an ear. She shook his hand; rough and calloused. Muscular. "Pleased to meet you. Have a seat."

Kacey scrambled to make room for his huge frame in her little corner of the world by the storage closet. Banner pulled out a chair from another desk and sat.

Her first, honest-to-God private investigator—coming to talk to her—*about an article* she'd *written.*

"Good scoop."

"Thanks," she began, "I hadn't been sleeping very well that night so I'd been driving around, listening to scanners. Looking for work."

"Appears you found some."

"Yeah. So…what can I do for you?"

"There anything you can tell me that you hadn't written up?"

"No…I pretty much wrote up everything I learned."

Banner nodded. "How'd you get in with the Hockers?"

"I was there, is all. In the right place at the right time."

"Inside the crime scene?"

"Yes—well…"

"So you know someone."

Kacey paused, smiling. "Might."

Banner nodded. "Guess you're already aware of the Hockers' Fate?"

The smile drained from Kacey's face.

"I...I visited that scene, too. It was quite upsetting...."

Kacey looked away, briefly, unconsciously, rubbing the ring she'd found there and now wore.

"Understandable."

Banner eyed the ring.

"Find anything?"

Kacey stopped rubbing the ring and folded her hands in her lap out of sight. "No."

"No keys, glasses...jewelry?"

Will be together...

"Nope." Kacey cleared her throat, avoiding eye contact. Again touched her hair.

"See any skid marks? Blood? Anything unusual—"

"It was all pretty much picked clean by the time I got there, and I really wouldn't know 'unusual' if it bit me."

"There anything you found, or saw, which might be of use to us—at the original scene? I mean, you come out of nowhere, get a gig like this—"

"Look, Mr. Banner—I wish I could be of more assistance, I really do—but I'm just beginning my investigation. I really just happened to be in the right place at the right time, that's all there is to it...I really have no special insight into any of it...no special privileges you don't already have. I'm just a simple girl trying to make a

(lesbian)

"living. If I do think of anything—or find anything remotely of interest—I'm more than willing to share, as long as you let me print it first. You have to believe me on this. I'm really at a loss.

"So—if you'll excuse me—I need to get back to my work—just as I'm sure you do."

Kacey stood up, extending her hand.

"I don't mean to be rude...but I really do have a lot to do."

Banner slowly got to his feet. "Thank you for your time, Mrs. Miller."

"That's 'Miss,'" she said, shaking his hand.

Banner eyed the ring. "Miss."

Chapter Ten

1

Harry sighed and closed his eyes.

"So, same dream," Dr. Richard Arnot said, scribbling on a note pad. He eyed his camcorder. "Okay…Harry, I'd like to try something different, if you don't mind."

Harry lay back in a comfortable recliner, eyes closed. Without opening them, he said, "Anything."

"As you know, hypnosis has been used for centuries—"

"Oh, no, you're not telling me you believe in that stuff," Harry said, opening his eyes and sitting back up.

Raising a cautionary hand, Arnot said, "Now, Harry…all hypnosis is, is focused, relaxed concentration. Every one of us do it every day when we're so tuned in to whatever it is we're doing to the exclusion of our spouse's questions, the noise outside our offices…whatever. What I'd like to try, with your permission, is a clinical version of it. I'm not going to tick-tock you out, or anything like that, but I am going to ask you to relax, then we're going to play a mind game of sorts—a free association. You'll have total control over it—if you don't want to play, you can stop at any time. Up for it?"

"You mean I just kick back and say whatever comes to mind?"

"Exactly. And don't worry if it's right or wrong or feels made up."

Harry paused for a moment. "Alright."

"Okay, I'd like you to relax…just think of a relaxing scene that's pleasing to you. Tell me when you have one."

Harry didn't immediately reply, but soon found himself enjoying an almost immediate sense of a deep, relaxing calm. He sat along a beach, eyes closed, and allowed the soothing sound of the breakers to wash over him.

"Okay…I have one…I'm on a beach, listening to the waves…."

"Good, good…now just follow the deep, relaxing sounds of those waves," Arnot coached. "Enjoy the rhythmic sounds of the ocean, the birds screeching above, the wind in your hair…you inhale deeply of ocean air…hold it—then let it out."

Harry did as instructed.

"Now, do this a couple more times…at your own pace."

Dr. Arnot waited patiently for Harry to complete several more cycles before continuing.

"Harry," he said, his voice taking on more authority, "I want you to blank out your mind. You're still sitting on that beach, but I want you to close your eyes and not think about the breakers any longer…I want you to drift inward…to be at home and at ease in the warm, comfortable blackness of your mind…it's a secure, restful, place…just drift about, not consciously trying to think about anything in particular…you'll shortly see shapes and colors gradually forming out of the darkness…passing by and through you…all kinds of shapes and colors…."

Harry did see shapes and colors and allowed them to emerge and fly past, when an image of a squat Oriental structure flashed through his mind.

"Now…what is the first image that comes to mind…no need to rush—"

"I see an Oriental structure. A house of some kind. Low and flat."

"A house?"

"Atop a mountain…by a cliff."

"What else can you tell me…look around, *turn* around."

"Well…and this is kind of weird—*am I making this up?*"

"Doesn't matter, Harry, we're playing a game, remember? Go with it."

"Well, I don't so much as 'see' as *feel* things. Does that make sense?"

Arnot nodded. "Just go with it, Harry. Do you see yourself?"

"I seem to have visual images without the images, is the only way to describe it, though sometimes I do seem to actually *see* something." Harry chuckled. "I feel like I'm this—a warrior-philosopher—enjoying a sunrise. He—*me*—stands on an overlook looking out over what appears to be Mount Fuji…there's a beautiful sunrise…I feel at one with myself and life…calm yet powerful…."

"How old are you?"

"Thirty-three comes to mind."

"What year is it?"

"I'm unconcerned with time, the year...it's...a non-issue...I'm here on a mission."

Amused, Arnot quietly continued to scribble notes and checked the camcorder.

"What are you wearing?"

Harry again paused. Internally, without seeing, he "looked" down to himself.

"I'm wearing a heavy, stiff—I can actually *feel* the stiffness of it—overgarment, over white undergarments."

"What else can you tell me?"

"Why are you asking me these questions? Can't you come up with something more important...more constructive to the session? My clothing—the time—simply aren't important...."

Arnot raised an eyebrow, jotting down the observation.

"...my garment is brown. On the upper portions of it is a gold sash that crosses from the shoulders to the waist. The entire outfit is ornate, the gold...embroidered...."

Arnot sat quietly, amused, scribbling on his pad and again checked the camcorder. "*Amazing....*"

"I'm wearing wooden sandals. I have a sword...my hair...is black...ponytailed, but only shoulder length or so..."

"I'm powerful and confident...a good fighter, but don't like fighting. I became a warrior out of need. I consider myself...a philosopher-*teacher*. I have much to teach, and learn, and were I to...publicly...come out with my views, I'd be put to death—"

"What views?"

"—so I became a warrior...and take to solitude and travel...I'm very good at being a warrior. I've done this many times before *and* since...."

"You have a name?"

"Kioshu."

"*Incredible...*," Dr. Arnot again said to himself, continuing to scribble madly.

"I consider myself...journeying—that wherever I am I'm just visiting—philosophically...physically—journeying through life. This is but a stop for me. I live alone in that meager dwelling. Behind it, where I'm standing, are colorful flowers and other vegetation. There's a dirt and stone path leading back to the house...as I stand with my back to the cliff and face the house, off to my right, is an incline into lush, heavily vegetated mountains, which I find beautiful and soothing. There's no real path, though, but I, and others, have walked it so frequently there's a worn trail. In the distance are high mountains with low cloud cover. It's spiritually dense, here…I *love* it…."

"Where does the path lead?"

"I take to this incline and walk with only the clothes I'm wearing, my sword…I feel it's my mission to help those who seek me out—but also for me to learn…I just go where my journeys take me…."

"What's the next important incident that comes of walking this path?"

"I come to an ancient temple hidden just off the trail. I feel this is one of the reasons I've come to live here…it's extremely secluded, this temple, which is tall and very narrow—or it's the façade of whatever's left of this temple. It's abandoned. I stand before it and smile. Amused. I think: good effort…for children. I understand why the temple was built…I feel that those who built this, as do all people, make their best attempts at understanding life, however misguided, and that it is the intent toward *understanding* and the bettering of life that counts. I do not agree with the belief systems of my time…and feel it is my chosen…my chosen 'task'…to help others understand…and that being a warrior is…a 'necessary compromise'…to better serve this end.

"I continue along this path and have images of conflict and battle—but do not engage in any. I am a teacher, to teach whoever'll listen and ask of my help—I teach whatever they come to learn—it's different with each traveler. But *I* also learn…."

"What lesson do you feel you've learned in your life as Kioshu?"

"Sanctity of life. That, as I stated, I had to make certain…'agreements'…to kill…so the 'greater good' could also come across to those I wouldn't normally have interacted with and who most need the teaching. I also," Harry said, and here he smiled, "there is something about the feel of physical objects, a sword—though not in using it to kill—but in its inherent *feel*, its use in practice—*kendo*. There's a certain…*heft*…to steel and sword. I draw a metaphor between the sword and life: both are double-edged. It is the intent of the wielder to make each what it is."

"Are you still okay, in this life?" Arnot asked.

"Ask what you want."

Arnot again raised an eyebrow.

"I'd like for you to jump ahead in time…to the next significant event in your life—"

"I'm thirty-five…confronting bandits. Two of them. I'm protecting peasants in a field…I have extreme…conflicting…emotions…."

"I…" Harry began, but his voice grew thick, his face strained and contorted in pain.

"I'm ambivalent about helping these peasants and those I will soon dispatch. I'm frustrated these men are doing what they do!

"A third man is behind them, on a large horse with bow and arrow—he's dressed as me. Watches us. I'm extremely angered…these bandits, their *greed*…but if they continue, then fine, they'll die…and I kill them—"

"All of them?"

"Only the two before me.

"I look to the horseman and sense he wants to kill me…but for some reason does not. He says nothing and calmly turns away without ever looking back…

"I'm greatly saddened. These people—including the peasants—only see the exterior manifestations and do not realize I have not really killed anyone. They will not understand the greater philosophical ramifications…and I am a teacher, a—a…*Kyoshi*…it is my *passion* to teach. I grow weary with killing, but continue on my path, because there are still lessons to learn. Don't know why I choose *not* to fight—except that there is still…a 'greater good,' something I have not learned…that seems in the best interest, yet…."

"Okay," Arnot said, "I'm bringing you back…you're no longer in that field…you're back in this room, with me, in the present…slowly returning…returning…you are now Harry Gordon, prosecutor for the state of Florida, in the town of Sunset Harbor…coming back…when I count to one, you will be back, alert, and conscious of all that occurred…three…two…*one*."

Harry opened his eyes. For a moment he said nothing, trying to coax his face awake, widening his eyes and stretching open his mouth. He cleared his throat.

"*Wow*…that was, uh…*incredible*.

"Got a cigarette?"

Arnot chuckled and jotted his final notes.

"I…I can't believe that. There's no way any of that could be real—"

"It's as real as you choose it to be," Arnot said.

"But it felt like I was making it up the entire time."

"That's okay," Arnot reemphasized, leaning back, and again

scribbling on his note pad. "All I was trying to do was get past your daily filter and see what the big, underlying issue you might have had lurking about beneath your consciousness...I never expected any of that."

"Come on—how could any of that be for *real*—"

"Why not? Because it felt 'made up'? Don't worry so much about whether or not it's fake—for now. Just realize that for some reason, this...'other you,' for lack of a better term, this *Kioshu*...surfaced. Made himself known—"

"But I'm not even a fan of Asian culture! Nothing against it, I've just never been all that interested in it."

"Try to understand what this information might mean *symbolically*. It doesn't have to be a literal interpretation. For example, it might just symbolize an internal struggle going on within...as we already seem to feel there is. The Asian theme might have come from something you saw—or heard—earlier."

"Well...I was talking with an associate about an Oriental urn a client had given me."

"There you go. Just give it some thought. The mind is extremely creative...as you just experienced. Don't judge it...just try to understand it...what it might mean on other levels. Give it time."

Harry nodded, pensively.

2

The police undid Tiger's handcuffs and turned him loose inside Port Charlotte's city lock-up. He'd been traded one cell for another, though, in here, Tiger mused, he doubted whether anyone really gave a shit about a whacked out, injured, alleged murderer. Those days were over, he was pretty certain. He rubbed his wrists and shook his head. The wind was still there, whistling around in his messed-up psyche, though subdued and still somewhat drugged, and his skin still itched like crazy. Eighteen hundred fire ants had nibbled at his flesh and injected their poison. Pretty impressive for a homeless guy.

Damn, how it itched, though.

He raked away at his stomach and arms and legs as he approached his cell-door's viewport. An empty hallway with other similar cells lining the rest of the detention center. As he left the cell door, he heard a subtle, scratching, sound. He followed it to one of his walls and placed an ear against it. Scratching? Rubbing? Someone next door must be busy. He shrugged it off, and returned his attention to his new home. At least now he had a roof over his head...and for the rest of his life.

So, he had that going for him.

The cop who'd escorted him in kept joking that he'd better enjoy his stay while he had it. Life was short—shorter for convicted killers. Everyone's a comic. They knew nothing. Nothing about him...or what'd actually happened. Not that *he* knew exactly what'd happened, but he knew a damned-sight more than they thought they did.

Tiger threw himself down on his new bed and a forearm across his face (vigorously scratching at areas of itchy ant attack wounds).

What the hell had he done?

What the hell had become of his life? From the high-rises of New York City...to *this*? He used to think life was funny...but this wasn't. Funny was rags-to-riches-to-rags...*not* funny was riches-to-rags-to-*murder*. People used to pay him well for his advice, now he couldn't get a dime for the time of day. And he'd brought it all on himself.

He'd run away.

Disappeared from society.

Nowhere to run, nowhere to hide. Nailed. He was stuck in his ten-by-twelve rent-controlled, heavily fortified, apartment. Awaiting death. Just like the rest of the mob who'd also wandered into that sleepy little retirement home and also began to whack away at the residents, one, by one, by...

Why?

What the hell had possessed them...did they all have that same storm raging about inside them...that same hellish noise screaming around inside *their* souls? The evil nightmares and images that just wouldn't go away—that remained with you even when you opened your eyes? Did the others taste sand in their teeth and tremble to the thunder of unseen hooves?

Death was ever so welcomed.

Tiger stared at the solemn gray jail-cell door. He'd wished he'd been able to OD while at the hospital, but he'd been too weak, and too, well, *guarded*. Round the clock. Suicide watch. Shit, why not just let him do it and save the taxpayers a hit? But that wasn't how civilized folk did things, was it? We needed drama. Something to make us feel important, something with which to compare our dull, daily, existences against. Due process, we called it. He figured it was more akin to the old Roman gladiators…only more civilized…refined. And lawyers, judges, and the media all needed their cut. Bored humans needed something to do while alive and kicking about on this lump of dirt, flying through lonely, empty space. Watch the condemned man (or woman!) kick in their final moments to give those *not* in their shoes a sense of safety. Superiority! That no matter how bad a day *ours* was, no matter how bad *our* lives were, they weren't nearly as bad as the poor schmuck now being paraded about in front of them, in this new, civilized arena we called the courtroom….

3

If nothing else, Tiger was eternally grateful for the lack of fire ants. The hungry little bastards that just hadn't stopped biting. He was pretty sure they shouldn't be able to get at him from here…almost sure. He didn't know if anything was for certain any more. All bets were off on just about anything, as far as he was concerned. Was the sun coming up tomorrow? Wasn't placing any odds. He never would have placed himself in a jail cell even a year ago, though he definitely would have placed himself on the streets. But a few years before that was when his world began to fall apart, his mental landscape slowly, methodically, peeled away like a rancid onion. He began hearing wind, lots of it—*yet there was none*. Or felt hot during the dead of winter. Tasted sand in the streets of New York. Yes…that was when his life began to take a turn for the worst…and he thought foraging for food out of dumpsters had been bad…

…the streets of New York were many things to many people. To some it represented excitement and culture, to others loneliness and despair. To still others…both. On one frigid December morning, Tiger slept beneath the Manhattan Bridge, between Chinatown and the East River. He'd been homesteading there for the past couple months, hidden within a city he'd long since lost interest in. Curled up within spent cardboard boxes and other pieces of rubbish, with the remains of moth-eaten blankets, an Army field jacket, and other ragged and decaying trappings he'd been carrying about in his shopping cart— which also doubled for one side of his makeshift home. He'd lead a fairly simple, nondescript existence. He came as he wanted, left as he needed. Sure, it'd made other aspects of life difficult…like entertaining, finding food, booze, and a warm pair of anything, but, hey, that's what he'd chosen, right? He'd left his previous existence for this; it had been his choice—no one else was to blame. And maybe that was the problem…too much blame. "Tiger," was as he'd come to be called one day early on, after having put up quite a fight when cornered by several homeless attackers who'd decided they'd needed his rather fine threads more than he did. He ended up keeping them then, but they, like everything else in his new world, eventually decayed and fell away, and he found himself curled up in a disgusting trash heap in a back alley of New York City, trying to keep from getting additional frostbite. He couldn't feel his ears any longer, his fingers, nor (for that matter) his pride. And the fact that it was snowing like a son-of-a-bitch didn't much help matters. Life just fucking sucked, and he'd accepted the need to die…to languish away into another troubled sleep and secretly expire alone and in obscurity among the other street refuse. He'd picked his life, and he'd pick his death. It was all right, he reassured himself, as he shivered among the cardboard and newspapers like just another piece of refuse. You just did the best you could until you couldn't any more, that's all. Until you reached the end of your road. There was no harm in picking the time of your passing. He'd tried his best.

So the new-him called Tiger closed his eyes and tried not to let the shivering bother him much. If he could just keep his mind off the cold, maybe the cold would take him away from all his other worries…

But, like the street, there was no easy way out of anything. That's when he, sometime later (time meant little, except that he still had *some*), was jerked awake. Not in the way of hypothermia, but in that something, or someone, was pulling on him, one of his feet, and bitterly yanking him back to full wakefulness. He'd found shadows hunched and huddled over him, pulling at his boots. No sooner had he tried to, groggily, arise from his welcomed death slumber, when another shadow flew past, and he saw stars and experienced a heavy crack to the head. He flailed at his attackers, kicked wildly, when suddenly both his boots slipped free from his frozen feet. Still conscious, he renewed his attack, while at the same time experienced additional painful attacks about his body. Kicking wildly, he felt some of his blows land solidly into soft matter and saw through his clubbed haze that the shadows were finally retreating. As he fumbled about in the loose trash for a hold, the shadows again attacked. He was now able to make out that they were, indeed, men—of course—as they beat and pummeled the shit out of him with a busted-up two-by-four, but before he could gain an upright position, they split. He heard them trample their noisy, flailing way out of the alley, leaving his socked feet bootless, one sock pulled completely off, the other half-way. Bleeding and dizzy from the thumping, Tiger staggered to his feet and peered after his assailants under a quickly swelling lump over one eye. He spit out blood and a tooth or two from swollen and cut lips, which quickly froze over.

And still it snowed.

Whether it be from pure attitude or the incoherency that came with approaching death, Tiger followed his attackers out into the snowy, freezing streets of a dark, forgotten part of the city. His attackers were long gone, as was his life. He didn't need no stinkin shoes no more, because, he realized, he didn't need no stinkin life, no more, neither.

What the fuck, right?

He was already frozen and useless—why not add shoeless? Why fight it? Take it like the man he used to be. Take responsibility for your actions. Confront it head on. No flinching.

The snow still made its way down, but away from the confines of the alley he found wind, bitter and cutting, also slicing through the urban canyons called streets. The streetlights bathed everything in their eerie, snowy, glow. Perfect way to go, he thought, cozy and alone, staggering on one socked, and one unsocked, foot. Tiger made his way out to meet his Maker. He may not die with his boots on, but he'd die standing up, confronting it head on.

Stumbling and sliding on cold, snow-packed streets, he watched the snowflakes alight on the ground before him and smiled. He remembered the days he'd spent as a kid out in his backyard watching it snow. Sometimes he'd lay down in the snow and just watch it all fall down directly on him—then his mother'd find him and yell at him to get up off of the ground—*what, did he want to catch his death of cold?* No, ma, he'd respond back, struggling up in his bulky snow suit, brushing himself off. But, for just a moment there, when all was hushed, and he could actually *hear* the snow land on the ground, he felt all was right with the world, and always would be…

And that was how Tiger felt, now, collapsed onto the snow-packed streets of New York City, feeling the snow alight upon his face. He could even hear it hitting the ground. He smiled. He was about to close his eyes one last time, when something else startled him. Something dark and swift. Something that actually reengaged his mind back into action. Angling his head into better position, he craned his neck to see…a horse. And rider. Positioning his body a little more, he was able to get a better perspective and saw the cop. He smiled. Go ahead, ticket him. This was one fine he wasn't ever going to collect, and closed his eyes…

But something about the rider wouldn't stay still in his mind and Tiger again opened his eyes. There seemed to be…renewed energy…seeping into his weary limbs, his weary mind, and he found himself able to, surprisingly, push himself upright. Through his incoherency and the ever continuing heavy blanket of falling snow, he again focused on the rider.

It wasn't a cop.

The rider sat silent and motionless, seemingly unaffected by the cold and snow, as the horse snorted and stomped about, whinnying huge fountains of vapor into the air. The rider turned slightly to its right, and pointed its pike—*pike?*—down to street level.

Tiger looked in the direction beckoned.

Again, another surge of renewed energy coursed through, not only his body, but his *soul*. He had no choice but *to* stand.

Slowly, painfully, he got to his feet.

Bent over and staggering against wind and snow, he felt impelled toward the direction of the pike. Going against the wind, he dragged himself to where the rider directed and found the pike pointing to a steam vent at the entrance to another alley. Tiger hurried to the vent and collapsed atop it, allowing…*willing*…the warmth to penetrate his ice-enshrouded mind and body. He curled up into the fetal position, drawing up his feet over the vent. He didn't know how long he lay there, but gradually and now, even painfully, physical sensation returned. And when he again looked up, the rider was still there, only this time down inside the alley. The horse continued to snort and stomp, but, now, at its hooves, lay a bundle of rags. Loathing at having to leave the warmth of his vent Tiger was again made to move…and as he approached the rider and bit-chomping horse, saw the bundle was actually a body—a frozen body. A dead man with boots and an overcoat.

His boots.

Wasting no time, Tiger frantically stripped the corpse of its boots and socks, and the thick overcoat he'd no longer be needing, and returned to his vent. It was then, as everything warmed up, and he lay,

finally feeling human again and having a desire to remain that way—
alive—that the *other* wind began its assault. Another wind blast, not of
this blizzard, seared through him...his consciousness. As he huddled,
eyes closed, he heard the mount again stomp and snort, the rattling of
the rider's accouterments cutting through the blizzard. He looked up to
find horse and rider rearing, the horse's fore hooves freewheeling high
into the air above him—and saw them charge.

The thunder of its hooves was deafening. Tiger couldn't move out
of the way fast enough. His mind and body just weren't that
quick...but it didn't matter, because as he awaited the single-horse
stampede, the rider and mount vanished...while the sound of its
thundering hooves continued on deep into his head.

As Tiger squirmed and wiggled, trying to avoid the phantom
stampede of a thousand horses from nowhere, he was also besieged by
powerful images of battle and screaming and death. He tried to shut
them out, to shout above them...but they only grew louder, more
violent. Somehow, he witnessed unspeakable acts of carnage...

And it was all gone, just as quickly as it had arrived.

Once again, he was alone...huddle over his steam vent on an
empty New York City street, except for the wind...not the December
blizzard...but the screaming, blistering tempest that would now,
forever, be a part of him....

4

As usual, Mark Burnett more played with his daughter, Emily, than
got her ready for day care in the morning. It didn't help that it was late
morning after having spent an extra-late night at work yesterday. It was
just something about being a fifteen-month-old that made changes in
diapers and clothes, or getting fed, not a high priority. Daddy was
up...that meant *play* time! So, Mark sat in the middle of the living-room
floor, while *NNC* presented Buster Harris, in New York City, relating
all the news that's fit to report, as Emily went chasing after a ball he'd
tossed. She charged across the room in mock toy-soldier, pseudo-
marching fashion, rocking her shoulders up and down, when her
attention was suddenly and mercilessly diverted by a *Sesame Street* noise
maker the ball had grazed upon it's cross-living-room trip. Emily
immediately plopped down on the floor and began banging on the toy,
composed of Oscar, Elmo, Ernie, and the Cookie Monster. She

especially liked the *I love trash—and anything dirty or dingy—or* dusty! noise she kept making issue from it. Mark watched in amusement, as Buster Harris related a mass murder in some small Florida town, the exact name of which Mark missed. Something Harbor. Propping his arms behind him, he leaned back and half-heartedly watched the news, casting loving, smiling, glances to his daughter. Buster talked about a sleepy retirement community that had been inexplicably decimated yesterday by a horde some labeled as cultist. That only one couple had survived, only to be, in a bizarre twist of Fate, killed this morning—by a man who'd also taken his own life. Police speculated the man had been involved in the previous night's activities. The report also went on to say that just as inexplicably, only the actual *residents* of the community had been murdered—all visitors and visiting family had been spared.

Mark shook his head. "What is this world coming to—"

Just then Emily bolted across the floor, in her wobbly way, and bodily dumped into his lap, giggling wildly.

"Oh, you think *so?*" Mark said, laughing, lifting her off her feet, "you think *so?*"

Emily continued giggling and Mark slowly rose to his feet, lifting her upside down.

"You think you're funny, do you? Well, I'll show *you* funny!"

Upside down and giggling madly, Emily lazily swung by her suspended feet, her little hands and fingers dangling just above the carpet. She clenched and unclenched her tiny hands toward the floor.

"Jolly Green Giants *know* what to do with delicious little morsels like *you!*" Mark roared.

Emily giggled and giggled as Mark tickled her feet, her shins, and down her legs to her arm pits. When he thought she could no longer stand it, he gently lowered her back to the floor.

"Okay, kiddo, time to eat!"

"*Eet!*" Emily repeated, stretching out on the floor.

"And what do we do before eating?"

"Ans!"

Now it was Mark's turn to chuckle. "That's right," he said, "we wash our hands! Let's go!"

Emily got to her feet, quickly waddled her short, hurried strides across the living room into the kitchen, and stepped up on the plastic step stool before the sink, "Emily" marked on it in black, permanent marker.

"Good girl!" Mark exclaimed. He reached across the sink and turned on the water, making sure it wasn't too hot, then directed the faucet over Emily's outstretched hands, as she already made preparatory washing motions in the air before it. Emily had a big smile on her face and gleefully rubbed her hands together under the water. Mark took the liquid *Winnie-the-Pooh* soap dispenser from the sink and squirted a drop into her hands.

"We have to wash them good," Mark said. He made sure her hands were properly washed before turning off the water.

"Now, what do we do?"

Emily stared at Mark, unable to say the word "dry."

Mark again smiled, "Aw, that's okay, honey!"

Emily turned around on her "Emily" step, and held out her dripping hands before her over the floor like a soggy sleepwalker. Mark pulled a clean dish towel from the kitchen drawer and draped it over her hands. He began to dry them, when she again called out in protest.

Smiling, Mark let her have control, supervising as she did a fine job in drying her own hands. Emily handed over the damp dish towel.

"Great job!"

Mark scooped her up off her stoop and soared her through the air, over her highchair, by the table.

"Now, we eat!"

"*Eet!*" Emily mimicked, another huge smile consuming her sweet, chubby little face. "Eet! *Eet!*"

As Mark buckled her in, Emily again grew fussy. Rather than fight her, he supervised Emily's searching for the buckles, and, again, backed off to let her buckle herself in. Or try to, anyway. It was then the phone rang, but Mark let the message machine pick it up. It was Rodney, from work. There was a corrupted LAN server. He let him leave a message as he had to help buckle in Emily's twenty-three-pound body to the highchair.

Mark finished fastening Emily in, who was happily giggling and making "laddle-laddle-laddle" sounds, looking out the kitchen window, and went to the phone to return the call, when it again rang.

"Hello?"

But, this time, there was no answer.

"Is anyone there? *Rod?* Hello?"

Silence, dead silence. Well, not totally. Emily was still making her "laddle-laddle-laddle" sounds, fine little bubbles forming on her tiny, ruddy lips, while happily banging about on her tray, but Mark heard the faintest sound of breathing over the phone—or, to be more specific, a sudden inhalation of air—masked by the muffled sound of traffic. Then, a strange thing happened. As Mark stood there, empty phone pressed against his ear, he had that distinct feeling only a husband and wife knew. That feeling that the other was *there*, even though they didn't speak…or that they were thinking of each other, miles apart. Mark felt a chill sweep through him and looked down to the caller ID box. It wasn't a number he recognized, but had, instead, the phone company "Verizon" listed. Mark felt his legs go noodley and no sooner had he realized said noodley legs, when he collapsed, reaching out to the counter to break his fall. His heart had jammed itself up into his throat in fine sledgehammer fashion and his mouth went dry and dumb. The hair on the back of his neck stood on end. He tried to say something, anything, to hang on to this moment—his wife was on the other end, and he *knew* it.

She'd finally called.

Was she—maybe—*finally* ready to talk? Work things out? Explain what the hell had happened?

Images of her beautiful, smiling face filled his mind. Of their wedding…bike rides and hikes, and—

"Kacey? Is that *you*…."

But the phone had already gone dead.

"Kacey? *Kacey!*"

No response. No sounds of breathing.

Trying to restrain himself, but not doing a very good job of it, he half slid, half slammed the phone along the kitchen's tiled floor. He sat there, listening to it as it glanced off a leg of a chair and the kitchen table, then spun around into the wall at the opposite end of the room. He watched as the phone did a couple of rebounded, confused spins, then came to a stop, like some angry spin-the-bottle game, its stubby antenna pointing, accusatorily, to Emily. The crunching and hollow plastic cracking sounds didn't bode well. Then he looked to Emily, now silent and staring at daddy, her mouth open in a tiny "oh," wide-eyed and confused, unsure of what to do next, hands poised in mid-air. Choosing the lesser of evils, Emily let out a strained wail, cut short—looking to him as if in confirmation to either stop or continue. Then she let out another one, dropping her hands to the tray, her little face suddenly, horribly contorted, flushed a fine bright red.

"Oh, it's okay, *Em*, everything's all right…."

But things were far from okay.

Otherwise, why had his wife—the love of his life—run off a year ago? Go out for her daily run, only to never be heard from again? He'd thought her kidnapped, murdered—something terrible—but never had he thought she'd actually *run away on her own*—

But was that true—really?

No…he'd seen her frustration after having Emily. He had to admit he'd been quite surprised that she'd even conceded to having a child…she'd always been the wild one, the adventurous one, and had been adamantly opposed to anything that would have tied her down…even getting a house had been a huge deal for her. A new car. She'd wanted nothing that even *implied* permanence. Stability. Ties. So when she'd found herself pregnant and decided to keep their baby, he was as impressed as could be. Felt his wife was definitely growing. Sure, she hadn't been happy about the weight gain, but on her well-developed, fit frame she hardly showed her pregnancy, and was, of course, the envy of pregnant women everywhere. She hadn't gained much weight—not even in her face, her pregnancy had been a breeze.

Labor?

Not even an hour. Out popped their bouncing baby girl, and almost as immediately, off melted the baby weight. In no time, she was the same old Kacey—running marathons, teaching Zumba classes, hefting weights…

Though she had had moments of occasional depression and self doubt.

She attacked all the old sports with a renewed and, yes, *scary-crazy* recklessness. Rock climbing, skydiving, mountain biking. Bungee jumping. He was seeing a side of her that was troubling, and she just kept brushing him off matter-of-factly about it. Kept needling at him to go with her—but he had new responsibilities, now, they both did, and Emily had to come first, foremost, and all-consuming. Diapers had to be changed, formula made. Early morning feedings and wailing. He had a real job, now. Attention of the most intense and loving kind had to now be directed toward *another*…

Emily started to cry. Wiping away tears, he sprang back into action.

"Hey, Buckaroo…there's no need to cry," he said, still wiping away tears. He lowered his voice in a soothing tone, and a foot crunched down on broken plastic parts that used to be cordless phone as he approached her. "There-there…how about some breakfast, huh?"

Mark checked Emily's straps and smoothed aside wisps of her light blonde hair. "How about some applesauce? Huh? Does that sound like a plan?"

Emily stopped crying and looked at him. Such all-consuming total *focused* concentration. Mark took her face into both hands and kissed her. As he looked into her deep, beautiful, watery blue eyes, he wondered what Kacey was doing right this minute.

Was *she* crying?

Missing them?

Considering a return?

"Well, my love," he said, "that was your mommy. She's still having problems, but, I think...," he began to say, choked off by emotion, "I think...she may be finally willing to work things out. And we're going to be there for her, aren't we, my sweet, little, pumpkin, because..." he again choked off, "because...we're a family, and that's what families *do*...."

Chapter Eleven

1

Harry recradled his phone and stared at the Japanese urn sitting atop the pedestal across the room from him. Yet another call from a family member of one of the murdered Safe Harbor tenants. This wasn't going to be just another small-town trial. Hell, it'd made it onto *NNC*, and there was talk of *NNC's* producers actually showing up.

Their story now belonged to the world.

Pencil in hand, Harry leaned back in his chair and strayed back to his visit with Dr. Arnot. The funniest thing (besides him giving the time of day to his so-called "Japanese experience") was that, for the first time in years, he'd had absolutely *no* nightmares. All his logic told him that what had happened the other day had been the product of a highly stressed imagination—of which, curiously, he never really thought he'd had much. He didn't believe in other lives. The soap opera had it right. All we had was one life to live. That was it.

Uno.

Whatever happened after we died…was, well, better left to philosophers and theologians. Schmucks like him, stuck in the down and dirty of society's worst didn't have the time nor luxury to ponder such useless notions. If we lived other lives, then why hadn't we learn from them? Why were there so many criminals to prosecute? To jail? To *execute?* If there really were other lives, what a goddamned waste of time *and* energy. We keep living and remaking mistakes—murder, rape, burglaries? *Jesus!* And Mr. Harry fricking Gordon was turning *Japanese?*

I don't *think* so.

But—what the hell, let's consider this for a bit; consider the evidence of the past few days—not a big effort, mind you, didn't want the bar or profession to catch wind of one of their finest dabbling around in such metaphysical nonsense—but he had done some quick and dirty Internet research. What he'd found was a wealth of information on the subject—even *support* groups—out there.

With the eraser tip of his pencil, he scooched toward him the hastily scrawled list he'd penciled, pulling it out from under his paperwork as if he were a teenager sneaking a peak at nudie pictures hidden under school work. On his list were such titles as ...*To Be Continued: Reincarnation and the Purpose of Our Lives; Other Lives, Other Selves; You've Been Here Before, Passport to Past Lives: The Evidence*, and *Mystery of Reincarnation: The Evidence & Analysis of Rebirth*. And there were plenty of books on children remembering their so-called past lives: *Return From Heaven, Children's Past Lives, Old Souls*, and *Soul Survivor: The Reincarnation of a World War II Fighter Pilot*.

There were all kinds of fictional work on the subject. The novels of M. J. Rose and L. E. Waters. Films like the old *Reincarnation of Peter Proud*, from 1975 (even George C. Scott's riveting 1970 film, *Patton*, involved reincarnation—General Patton, himself, believed his was reincarnated), *Living with the Dead* and *Yesterday's Children*, not to mention those *Medium* and *Ghost Whisperer* reruns, and the more recent *The Fountain* and *Cloud Atlas*. There were many Japanese and Indian films, like 2005's *Reincarnation* and 2012's *Dangerous Ishhq*. And stuff from psychics (or so-called psychics, Harry's jury was far from out on such things, but he was suddenly a bit more open on the matter). People who just seemed to have this stuff come pouring out of them, like Edgar Cayce, Jane Roberts, and a quiet, little-known early 1900's Midwest osteopath, named Riblet B. Hout.

How did stuff like this happen?

Given any of it was real, why'd it happen to some and not others? Perhaps that was a question for another time, but on the "evidence" of it all, there did appear to be a fair amount of circumstantial data. Lots of people *claimed* experiences, but did a lot of people claiming anything make anything real? Proof of existence beyond the grave? Many claim visitations from the Virgin Mary or Christ Himself, but there's no *proof* for any of that, either.

Has any archeological evidence—*hard, irrefutable evidence*—ever been found to prove the existence of Christ? A person and personality literally touched by the Hand of God that *something* should have survived? A transference of divinity from spirit to the physical?

Barring the controversial Shroud of Turin, has anything ever turned up, say, a tablet written from His hand, a lock of hair, a shred of His clothing? Maybe a goblet from which He'd sipped? A sandal?

No.

All of his existence has been based upon a book written by imperfect Man and all His filters (substitute "Woman" and "Her," it doesn't matter), and something called *faith*. And don't even bring in those *Da Vinci Code* books. So, what hard evidence was there for past lives? Define "hard," and define "evidence."

Harry grunted. He remembered a prime time news magazine show he'd watched about a-then-two-year-old James Leininger (the name he found from the *Soul Survivor* book search) who "remembered" a past life as a WWII aviator, and another about an English woman, Jenny Cockell, who'd claimed she'd lived in Ireland from 1898 to 1930, as Mary Sutton. Harry'd also found four books Jenny Cockell had written (and *Yesterday's Children* was the made-for-TV movie of Cockell's accounts). According to Mrs. Cockell, as Mary, she'd been married to a rather nasty fisherman in this small coastal town and they'd had something like eight kids. From what he remembered, her life had been hard, and her husband had been far from nurturing, which had, ultimately, resulted in her death. To make a long story short, the present-day Mrs. Cockell'd been sketching images of that past life since early childhood, and had finally made the trip to corroborate her images, with her present-life's (God, this sounded so *ridiculous!*) son and husband. She found things exactly as she'd envisioned—*and all without ever having set foot there in her* current *life*. She even tracked down the hidden, overgrown remains of the past-life house she'd lived in, which wasn't visible from the road that went past it—and the clincher?—*she'd found several of her surviving past-life children. Still living, though well into their sixties and seventies.*

Harry shivered. "I can't believe I'm giving serious consideration to any of this!"

How could any of this be? If none of this was true, how had this Mrs. Cockell'd been able to track everything down? How could her childhood scrawlings corroborate her adult discovery? *Had* she ever been there? Everyone who knew her swore she hadn't, yet the argument could be made that she'd researched it without anyone's knowledge—but how had she known about events in the lives of those surviving elderly? Things only a *mother* would know? When Jenny had been a young child, she'd started drawing all this stuff—*this* was known—just like the fact that she'd never been out of the country. She still had many of the sketches. But were the seventy year olds simply *wanting* it to happen, making it all up with her? A product of senility?

Empathy? It's always a possibility, but think about this: given what we know of the mind, is it any less amazing that things like this *could* happen? If we attributed so much "poppycock" to the imagination—that our minds have this incredible capacity toward the imagined—why not also presuppose that maybe—*just frigging maybe*—some of it might be true? How much of a leap would it be, really, from our minds making us believe things that are false…to our minds simply releasing—*remembering*—real, past-life memories?

Memories.

Which was more far-fetched?

If what we were asking for was to remember a past life, isn't this exactly how it might happen?

Why deny it? And if what we base reality upon is what Most People agree upon as What's Real and What's Not, by the ability to distinguish, on a mass level, that basically the same thing one sees is the same thing others see, than wouldn't that also apply?

Every lawyer knows that no one person sees exactly the same thing as another, even if both are handed the same object, each standing before each other, or witness to the same event firsthand—but certain basics always hold true, such as time, space, ground, sky, etc. This has been proven countless times in courtrooms across the globe and throughout time.

Jesus—has it always been that obvious?

Has it been there all along, right under our own noses, but we've simply been too close to the evidence, too *disbelieving*, to notice?

Harry got up and came to the Japanese urn. Touched and traced it's smooth surface. Looked to the framed *ekotoba* scrolls on the wall behind it.

Shit…no two people can perfectly describe a single object or event in the same precise detail as another (and why was that, anyway, if facts were facts?)…hell, even Harry's own perceptions were different from those of witnesses he'd dealt with over the years…but if we used the judgment that what Most People Agreed Upon *is* reality…what *about* all those claims of past lives? The Civil War, Nazi death camps, the Titanic, you name it—and even little children are documented as having said such things as *my* other *mommy's hair was curly*, or *I died at this intersection* before. One of the books Harry'd hyperlinked to on the Internet talked about a man fraught with insomnia had recalled a life as a marshal in a western town…how a sexually frigid woman remembered a life as a slave girl—how another suffered from an inexplicable fear of heights, only to recall a violent death from a high fall during the Middle Ages. Do people just make this stuff up for their own amusement, or are deep, buried memories actually, slowly, fizzling into conscious and full-on awareness? It's like UFOs...if so many people are coming up with this stuff, must there be *some* truth to it?

Harry picked up the urn and stared into its polished surface.

And a lawyer, from Sunset Harbor, Florida, suddenly recalled a past life as a Japanese ronin on a cliffside dwelling overlooking Mount Fuji...

"Harry, you have another call—hey, are you all right?" Libby Pointer asked, poking her head into his office, "I've been beeping you for the past ten minutes."

Harry stared at her blankly.

"Oh...sorry," he said, returning the urn to its pedestal. "I'll take the call—thanks, Lib."

2

Mark and Emily walked the aisles of Food Mart, Emily comfortably wedged into the seat of the shopping cart. Mark scanned the seemingly endless shelves of baby food, looking for something different. Whether or not Emily felt a need for newness in her diet, *he* felt the need for it. He scooped up a couple jars of blendered beef, turkey, and assorted vegetables and fruit into the cart, as Emily busily *laddle-laddle-laddled* to herself, playing with her tongue and the foamy bubbles she made with her lips. Mark was sure other children were probably able to do the same thing with their tongues as did Emily, but he never saw it, so pretended it was just another "sweet little thing" only his talented little daughter did. Emily was able to turn her tongue sideways ninety degrees while making it into a U-shape. Mark smiled absentmindedly...

Kacey.

Ever on his mind, but since what had to have been her first phone call to them since she'd left, she was even more there. Not that he had ever gotten over her desertion. After all, sooner or later, you just had to move on. For the longest time, he'd been a wreck...had even filed a missing persons report, but nothing'd surfaced. Then he'd found the smoking gun.

Her diary.

The book with all its damning evidence.

Oh, yeah.

It reminded him of that old Bread song from the early seventies. About the guy reading his girlfriend's diary, thinking all this time her musings about love and longing had been about him...only to discover that it had actually been for another.

Well, similar situation, folks, only these musings had been about being *strangled*.

Yup, that had been the word, along with "held back" and "suffocated." All those words and more had been written down in handwriting he recognized and had loved as his wife's—but not about another, no, these words, unfortunately, had all been about *him* and *their* life together. About—

"Oh, what a *darling* girl!" a woman, her son also stuffed into her cart before her, declared, suddenly standing beside Mark and Emily.

Startled by her loud and sudden presence, Mark gave the obligatory Baby-mill response, "Thanks. Fifteen months."

"Oh, isn't she just *adorable!*" the attractive and somewhat overly dramatic and well-dressed woman continued to exclaim. She hunched over Emily like a cuckooed aunt. Emily continued being her cute little self, *laddle-laddle-laddling*, with her tongue and lip foam. "What's her name?"

"Emily."

"Oh, my, what a *darling* name! Hello, *Emily!*"

"What's your boy's name?" Mark asked.

"Timothy," the woman responded.

He really wasn't in the mood for this, but such was the responsibility parents took on in public with adorable children, "in the baby mill"...and Hot Mommy was easy on the eyes. And wasn't it curious that nearly all of the Beautiful Mommies had the same shoulder-length bob cut? He'd learned early on (again through the baby mill) that moms wore bobs because their children kept pulling at their hair. Okay, whatever. It looked good on them and that was all that mattered from a guy point of view.

And there was another thing. The mommy attraction factor. He'd been without spouse for a year, and it really bothered him that he was finding all these mommies more and more attractive. Part of being a mommy was, usually, the *married* part...and part of his interaction with them was his *Emily* part...all a result of the *Kacey* part.

But Kacey wasn't here, was she?

"Well, have a nice day," Gorgeous Mommy proclaimed, in that

usual High-On-Life manner all the young, preppy, Baby-Mill Mommies did. The Mommy Mafia. He waved and nodded good-bye and Emily gave her usual *laddle-laddle-laddle* good-bye, her lip foam spilling down a corner of her mouth. As Mark wiped it away, he watched the young mommy's slim, fit form (yeah, she Zumbas…weight trains…) depart, pushing along young Timothy and groceries onto her next Baby-Mill greeting.

Mark shook it off, for but an instant wondered what a lingering, passionate kiss from her was like, the touch of her skin…then instantly chastised himself.

But it was the diary. The diary that had brought it all home in stark, brutal clarity. What had gotten him to thinking, and, over time, to looking at other kids' mothers.

She'd wanted out.

Pure and simple. Kacey. His wife, Emily's own Gorgeous Mommy (who also did Zumba classes and weight training). Mark's love of *his* life—

Emily blurted out protests of inactivity at no longer being the focus of attention. Mark pushed their cart forward. He still had a list of groceries to fulfill. Done with the baby food row, Mark continued into the next aisle.

Kacey had lamented how her life had been running away from her…without her.

That her once-exciting husband had turned corporate. How he'd lost his taste for adventure. Romance. For just about anything they used to do. How he worked too long, slept too little, and playtime? Ha! Nonexistent—unless it involved Emily. There were diapers to change, Emily to focus upon, and overtime to work. Broken servers to mend, corrupt files to correct, and hackers to thwart. All his scuba gear gathered dust in the spare room and he'd sold his jumping rig when he'd given up skydiving with Emily's birth…

He tossed a couple frozen dinners into the cart.

Why had she *had* Emily, then?

That had burned in his mind—and continued to do so—since her departure. She told him she'd love to have a child, love to raise a kid as an extreme sports god or goddess…yet everything seemed to do an about face following Emily's grand entrance.

He'd found his answer not long after he found her diary.

She'd just been…*surprised*, was as good a word as any…at the level of effort involved in growing a human.

She'd had no real concept of how totally *life-consuming* it was. There was no down time...no "me" time. It was all child time, *period*. No longer long blocks of time to sleep...to take a run...or take that far-flung trip. No...all that was on hold until eighteen years later when, hopefully, you'd done a good-enough job in raising Arizona that they were ready to fly the coup and begin their *own* life.

Eighteen years. If you were *lucky*.

She couldn't wait that long. And, Mark surmised, after having all this time to think about it, he was sure that that one thought had begun to fester and fester and fester until that was *all* she could see—

"Oh, hello, again!" exclaimed Beautiful Mommy, as they passed each other down the paper-products aisle. "Hello, Emily!" The woman waved to Emily like an excited circus clown.

Emily was still blowing bubbles and doing digital gymnastics with her tiny little hands.

Laddle-laddle-laddle...

Eighteen years...and the loss of her life, as she'd called it. Of her husband...to a little (and this was the most damning—the one word that had affected Mark the most, in all that he'd read in that cursed, little

(laddle-laddle)

diary: *Monster*.

A Monster.

Yes, there it was. In her own handwriting...in black and white...his wife had written that their child—the product of their union, their love and raging hormones—was now, in her eyes—*A Monster*.

Good Lord—how could she have even *thought* such a thing?

How could the woman he loved—the mother of their child and who had carried Emily for nine months and brought her into this world—have put such a thought to paper?

Was she really his wife?

Maybe (he'd tried to reason) Kacey was only trying to help out a friend and had taken a *friend's* diary in hopes of better understanding what this "friend" of hers was going through?

So hopeful in this train of thought was he that he'd actually pulled out some of their love letters to each other to compare handwriting...when his heart sank, and his soon-to-burgeon internal affair of thinking about other Beautiful Mommies began. It was her, all right, no mistake about it. His wife thought of their child as *A Monster*, and of him and their life together as "suffocating."

Men and women across the world find each other, fall in love, and sometimes (the ugliness goes) fall out of love…that was a given…that was something he could deal with (or so he thought), but to have his wife refer to their own progeny as *A Monster*…well, that was a horse of a different color…and it got under his skin and remained there. In fact, until her call he'd almost—*almost*—forgotten about it.

Mark looked to his list, determined he'd gotten everything, and began to head to the checkout lines, again spotting Beautiful Mommy and Timothy, up ahead, already in line.

The thought had festered in him since he'd read it, until he'd seen a doctor about it. That's when terms like *Postpartum Depression, posttraumatic stress disorder, and hormone-induced lifestyle changes* became known to him. *Interpersonal psychotherapy.* The doctors had told him that in a certain percentage of the female population something happens to a woman that can totally change her personality. Some women have suddenly turned into gifted, world-class artists without ever having written a word. Or painting a bowl of fruit. Some have turned into pillars of the community, while having been hermits prior to giving birth. There was no accounting for what happened to these women, but it was clear in all the "negative" cases, where the women took on radically different personalities, that counseling—and sometimes drug therapy—were needed.

Mark pulled Emily into line, right up behind Beautiful Mommy, much to his divided dismay. Yes, she definitely looked good in her skirt and nylons…but he looked away to the newspapers, magazines, and candy, surrounding them. He wondered if they might even know each other, this Beautiful Mommy and Kacey…maybe even had taken the same cardio classes? Trained in the same gym?

Beautiful Mommy looked back to him, smiling, as she shuffled up to the cashier. She turned sideways and began depositing items on the conveyor belt. Timothy just stared at him, as if to accuse: *You have your own mommy, mister…stay away from mine. I can't help it if she ran away…but mine's still here, and I don't want her running away with anyone…*

Mark looked away, smile fading. As he scanned the papers, one named something like the *Star-Herald-Weirdly*, had as their lead story, the "truth" about the Safe Harbor, Florida murders…that they'd all been possessed by Satan. *Mass possessions*, it went on to say, *could it happen again? Had Hitler also been possessed by Satan?*

Intrigued, but not enough to buy the rag, he looked to see what local papers said about the tragedy. There were a handful left.

Authorities Baffled! one headline declared. Folding it in half, he tossed the publication into his basket. He failed to see Beautiful Mommy looking back to him—not Emily—for a few moments, as he repositioned groceries in his cart.

Mark looked down to Emily, who was now giving him a huge smile, when she opened wide her tiny little mouth like a baby bird ready to receive mommy (or daddy)-bird's offerings of worms and grubs. Mark smiled and brought his face down to hers. Rubbed noses. Emily winced, giggling joyfully. They weren't called little angels for nothing.

As he looked back up, Beautiful Mommy was collecting her receipt, and said, "Bye, Emily!" waving to her as she collected her checkbook and five-hundred keys from the check-writing counter. Emily heard her name and tried to turn, but couldn't make it all the way around. Mark smiled and waved good-bye to Beautiful Mommy, who began to walk away, still waving to Emily. Now Emily could see her, and let loose a huge smile for the departing lady, from whom Mark found he just couldn't look away. Just before Beautiful Mommy forever turned away from his life, she cast Mark a deliberate look and a smile—just for him...a look that Mark caught and knew meant *Yes, I am attracted to you...but, hey, we're both married to different people...so, well, have a nice life...okay?*

Mark looked back to their groceries and the cashier.

You have your own mommy, mister...stay away from mine...

But where the hell *was* his?

3

Moses Banner listened to the hum of a streetlight as he gave a shadowy passer-by wide birth in his journey along the main drag of Tamiami Trail Boulevard. He'd been walking for hours, it seemed, trying to figure out why or how something like the retirement home's murders could have happened. Tonight was to have been the night they all were to have gotten together at Garrett's for poker and beer. Good times. No more of that...ever. He stared down at the dirt. Up ahead was Safe Harbor...in his mind's eye he could see it still taped off, its damaged gate area barricaded from casual entry. He wasn't sure why he'd come out here, tonight, except that it was what he'd done for the past handful of years. He didn't want to miss it. Perhaps he wanted to honor it—and fallen comrades. Garrett and the others...but Garrett and he had been close...drinking buddies, poker buddies, backyard grilling buddies, fishing buddies...and the loss gnawed at him more than he cared to admit. Some tough guy...

But just what the hell had brought all those people down here to kill?

Banner bumped against a passer-by he hadn't noticed, but which had startled him into almost decking the man.

"Hey, brother, can ya spare a buck?" the homeless man asked between coughs, hand outstretched, eyes wild, weird, and uncomfortably red.

Banner looked to him, jammed his hands deeper into his pockets, and said nothing.

Shouldered past.

Poker and beer...with Garrett, Fred, Bernie, and Hoosier. Well, Mikey wasn't much into cards, but he liked the company—and usually brought good beer. What might Garrett be up to, now, wherever he was? He doubted he was in hell, if there really was such a place, but he certainly might be in whatever passed for Purgatory. Garrett was the first to admit it, he hadn't lived the perfect life, but had always tried to do his best. If he did have to burn off a few sins, he hoped he didn't have too much soul to singe.

Unnerved that he had come so close to a homeless guy without noticing it (*no* one sneaks up on him, goddammit), Banner lifted his head—only to see another shamble past. The guy looked to him, but said nothing.

All the years he'd lived here, he'd never noticed so many wandering roadside street folk. This was a retirement community, for chrissakes, not inner city New York.

A warrior's death, that's what Garrett'd wanted.

All that Japanese Zen stuff. He'd been into it. He'd tried to live his life like a warrior while on the force, but retirement had softened him a little, which was probably his undoing, as it does with most that age. Why'd you have to remain tough when no one was out to get you—or so you thought. Case in point. As much as Garrett had loved being a cop, all the excitement, the power, the living on the edge...he found he also loved retirement. Felt he'd earned it...had his own war wounds, and plenty of them...shin splints, brawl-and-knife-fight scars, two divorces, high blood pressure, and his ever-present cynical attitude. Yeah, he'd earned his life, he said, every nick and bruise of it, but none of it—*none of it*—mattered any more. On the good side, Garrett had three kids, a pension and medical benefits, a beautiful new home in the subtropics, and great friends.

Poker and beer. Weekly. What else mattered?

Knife-wielding murderers, that's what.

You'd never been completely safe, had you, my friend? You tried—did your damnedest—but they still found you. Hunted you down. Just like everybody else in that place.

All those residents thought they'd given up the stress and strain of their working lives…only to have a murderous horde invade their privacy, steal their *lives*…

Banner sidestepped another wandering indigent. This one, a woman, stared back at him with deep, dark, eyes. There was something creepy about her—all of them. As he shouldered past the woman, she, also a little too close for his liking, teetered on tiny, bundled feet, performing an unstable dance for balance, while tracking him with an outstretched hand.

Too fucking weird…

He hurried past, keeping her at glaring distance. Scanned the street before him.

What was the afterlife of a warrior? He certainly hoped there was something for everyone after all the hell we all went through during our existences—some more than others. He wasn't a praying man, nor a church-going one, but believed there had to be something better. Nature comes and it goes, so it had to come and go *somewhere*…there had to be *something* or Someone driving it all…that much he felt to be true. Most cultures believed in an afterlife…the very thoughts themselves had to originate from somewhere. This was all too grand a plan to not have divine, logistical, support backing things up.

"*What are ya thinkin?*" another homeless person asked. The raggedy man stood directly before him. Banner almost rammed into him.

"C-can you spare a dime, buddy?" the guy asked.

"What'd you just ask me?"

Where were these guys coming from?

"Can you spare a quarter."

"That's not what you—"

The homeless man wiped his nose. "Fiddy cents?"

Banner stared at him.

"Look mister, I'm just asking for a dollar, is all. One dollar…can ya spare one?"

Banner grudgingly fished out a quarter and flicked it to the man. Continued past.

Then Banner thought better of it and spun around.

Froze in his tracks.

Positioned roughly in a straight line out from him no longer stood the bum, or any of the other homeless he'd *thought* he'd passed...but instead were dark and shadowy snorting mounts and their riders that looked just a little bit too large, distorted, for what they were.

Silhouettes of four riders.

Each held a spear, or some kind of pike, upright in their possession, and that was about all he could make out. He also got the distinct impression they meant business.

Banner backed up a step...looked to see if anyone else took notice of four horsemen with pikes along Tamiami Trail Boulevard. A glow radiated from behind them, though he knew there was no such light source. Instead of running, Banner held his ground. They seemed to be wearing helmets and possessed a bulky look, as if they also wore some kind of armor.

The horses shifted, stomping and snorting, rattling their and their riders' gear, exhaling a hellish-looking vapor. They reminded him of a *Molly Hatchet* album cover.

The Four Horsemen.

Death.

Banner heard a distant, rising wind...saw images of blowing sand and barren steppes...

(*swords*)

(*battles*)

flashed before him. The distant clang of metal on metal echoed around him...cries and shouts...death and destruction...*a shrill scream raining down from the skies...*

Banner looked into the night sky. Brought his hands to his head; tried to shut out the madness. Looked to the horsemen, their steeds anxious and jostling.

What do they want?

Who were *they?*

The closest horsemen directed his pike to Banner's left. The others followed suit, their mounts continuing to protest the needlessly imposed inactivity.

Banner discovered he stood only yards away from Safe Harbor.

The wind and cacophony of an advancing horde was all around

him, filled his mind.

The crash of battle.

Trembling ground.

The stink of death…foreign lands…

Banner crouched, arms unsteadily stretched out before him. Couldn't see straight.

No one. *Nothing.*

Why didn't these guys stop traffic? Didn't anyone else *see* them? What the hell was—

A horse reared.

Banner shot a look back to the four riders. None had moved, but he couldn't shake the images…one part of him experienced the cries and horror of battle, while the other saw unmoving horsemen on a dark, lonely, city boulevard…

Banner again shook his head…it all became painful…grew in intensity…he lowered closer to the ground…

Groaned. Twisted in agony, as if his head were in a vise.

He looked back up to the horsemen and found he could no longer focus…they wavered, warped…their mounts breathing fire and destruction…*death*…

He felt his body *doing* things he couldn't possibly be doing…running, attacking, *destroying*…

Banner shot back to an upright position just as one of the horsemen did or didn't attack.

Screaming out as if he'd just been disemboweled, Banner fled.

The four horsemen disappeared, yet their stomping, snorting, and gear rattling commotion continued to momentarily hang in the air like vaporized steam….

Chapter Twelve

1

Pretty, demure, quiet, homely, and bookish. Charming. All these terms had been used at one time or the other in describing twenty-three-year-old Ronda Ettbauer, one-time Elementary schoolteacher from West Cheyenne Middle School. Except Ronda could no longer return to her Cheyenne, Wyoming position, because she'd been caught elbow-deep in the Safe Harbor Slaughterfest with the rest of the twenty-eight remaining suspects. And, like the others, Ronda had also had no idea what had brought her to beautiful Gulf Coast Florida only to commit so foul a deed, but she did know you didn't have to go to college to know that given the evidence covering her petite frame—the coils of blood-stained rope in her rope-burned hands from hauling cinder blocks onto her victims, which she'd only remembered once incarcerated—she'd done the crime. Yours truly, single and freshly teacher-certified, in the middle of a murder spree. Not even a full year teaching, and look at the mess she'd gotten herself into. Principle Wright wouldn't be bailing her out of this one.

Ronda huddled in the corner of her Punta Gorda Detention Center confinement, away from the direct line of sight of the view port into her cell, and rocked back and forth, arms wrapped tightly about her midsection. Her hands and arms still smarted only because she'd continued to reopen her wounds to remind her of her transgressions. She still needed to remember the pain, now, more than ever, and just like all the other pain she'd endured throughout her young life, she'd grit her teeth and bear it. Her bookish glasses were cast along the floor up against the opposite wall. Her long, dark curls hung exhaustedly about her down-turned, tear-and-sweat-stained, dour face. A face that used to smile politely at everyone she met. A pretty face, she'd heard the mothers of her children say. Well, she didn't feel pretty any more.

Her end was predefined, and it would be anything but pretty, demure, *or* charming.

Ronda muttered, crying in spurts, pleading with God...*how could she have* done *such a thing? Why had she done such a thing?* Her entire life had been lived in the most wholesome and upstanding of manners, as her parents had taught her.

Well, except for that time with James. Her first year of college.

But she'd chastised herself plenty for that and was still working out her own, personal, self-prescribed penance for their fornication. Penance which she'd lumped on top of that which her church and parents had already prescribed...four years ago. The church's penance had been too easy. But the hot baths and showers, the disinfectant soap, the scrubbing and the prayers...*that* was what penance was all about. The lashings she'd asked her father to provide, every day for a month, once she'd broken down and told her parents; all three had sat down and calmly, intelligently, decided upon her punishment, as they quietly and tenderly soothed their distraught daughter, stroking her hair and drying her tears with their kisses; they still loved her, they assured, but we must all be held accountable for our actions—each and every one of them...yes, *that's* penance. Her parents had been extremely proud of her for coming clean with God, and had even bragged about her to their congregation. It had been a good thing. Never once did they look down at their wonderful daughter for her transgressions, but we must all pay the piper when we sin...and the Lord has set up punishment for each and every sinful act. It took a strong soul to admit they'd faltered...but a stronger one still to take their medicine. Ronda was the strongest soul Mr. and Mrs. Ettbauer had ever seen, they cried, as Mr. Ettbauer stripped away portions of his daughter's smooth, naked back with his whip in the barn that night, the strongest, indeed. And God would not forget that, no He wouldn't, Mrs. Ettbauer lamented, standing behind her husband as he vigorously administered Ronda's penance. He would give her the strength she needed to get past the pain, to take her medicine, and to learn and to *grow* from her transgression. For their God was a forgiving God...a tough and demanding one, to be sure, but *forgiving.* As were her parents, God bless em.

So, most-penitent Ronda had allowed herself to be tied to the posts she'd been tied to many times over her then nineteen years, and did what she always did when punished. As the blood and tears flowed, she begged the Lord for strength and forgiveness, and prayed her little heart out. She never prayed for *unconsciousness*, nor to dull the pain, because that wouldn't have been fair...she needed to experience her punishment in all its fine and just excruciating detail. That was what strong souls did. Face up and take their medicine, like Jesus did for all of us. Your reward shall be in Heaven, when you stand before your Lord and Savior, then and only then, would there be no more pain, no more suffering. Our physical lives were meant to be hard and unforgiving—transitory—that was the way of the *Lord*...

So, Ronda knew, when it again came time for her to take her medicine, she would know what to do, and would take it full-on, staring it square in the eyes.

Because she was a Strong Soul and that's what Strong Souls *did*.

But, now, in her current time of need, before whatever punishment the Lord saw fit to dispose upon her...she needed to understand why she had done so wrong. Why had she strayed from the Righteous Path...*again?* What had caused her to kill...and not just once, but multiple times? How had she—again—invited Satan into her soul? She had been so good at keeping things under control...so good at only thinking *good* thoughts...she didn't understand this, it made no *sense*...

Ronda's mind hurt. Even she knew one had to rest the mind during penance, so that one could think clearly about what it was one had done...to properly and *clearly* atone.

Ronda slowly got to her feet and paced her cell, still hunched over and cradling her midsection. She needed to feel like a teacher one last time. Maybe teach herself something in the process...

She came to a cream-colored cinder block wall and extended a trembling finger. Began to outline invisible tick-tack-toe grids...flowers...Eastern Orthodox crosses. Horses. A tiger. A big tiger, with large, menacing teeth...

Teaching children had been her life, and she needed to relive that again, once more, if but for the short while she had left.

Ronda looked about her cell. To her glasses on the concrete floor across the room from her. To the cell door. Something then brought her gaze to her cot. She stared at it. Slowly turned her head. The whispers and winds, previously in their quiescent mode, once again grew in intensity. Hunched over and hugging herself, she approached the cot. The noises grew.

She lifted an end of the mattress from its frame.

There, nestled back in a little way, were hidden a handful of black, super-sized, permanent markers. Ronda pulled one out. Grasping it like a holy relic, she pulled off the cap and inhaled deeply of its scent and released memories, closing her eyes…

A teacher should never be separated from their tools.

Tears exploding from her eyes. Ronda turned, marker extended before her, and approached a cell wall. Savored the remembered feel of her previous teacher life. The sharp, defined edges, the smooth, slick feel of the writing instrument that felt like nothing else on earth. She remembered the whiteboard upon which she used to write…the infectious laughter and giggling of the children behind her. Yes, now, she could continue her work, as the wind and whispers taught her something. One last thing she could pass on to her students before she had to go. Eyes closed, and more tears running copious and unchecked down her face and off the end of her nose, she reverently touched the marker to the blank wall. Slowly a smile formed upon her thin sullen and quivering lips…bringing back the old look of that once pretty and demure woman she'd been described as having been. Slowly, deliberately she danced the marker across her whiteboard.

Class was in session.

2

Kacey Miller stood on a vast and barren plain amid howling wind. River narrows gurgled nearby, along which grew wild pear and onion. A gray hawk fluttered against the wind as it ripped apart what looked like a black (and now bloody) pheasant along the river bank. The wind gusted through Kacey's hair and hollered past her ears, carrying with it an earthy scent. She looked down the length of the river into the dusty distance. Hazy hills and rock outcroppings. Indistinct and spotty tree growth. Scattered and grazing livestock.

Kacey looked behind her. A large, round tent. Not a circus tent, but a smaller dirty structure with internal framing that only modestly buckled against the gale. Its loose fabric and ropes flapped wildly in the rapidly intensifying tempest.

Kacey entered the tent.

Ducking through the heavy flap that closed behind her, she rose back to her full height to find herself

Inside a house.

Her Wilmington, Delaware home.

Kacey inhaled sharply.

MONSTER!

The word *MONSTER* was scrawled in what looked like blood across every wall. Looking to the ceiling, she quickly sidestepped. There, too, was the accusation.

A television was on in the living room. Scenes of scuba diving, skydiving, and bungee jumping played across its screen. Then the screen switched to a *Monster.com* commercial. Kacey absentmindedly continued into the room, but came to a stop behind the couch in front of the TV. Looking to her hands, she held a heavy heap of dirty diapers. Kacey looked back to the door from which she'd just entered. She could still hear the wind's sorrowful wailing, but also what sounded like something pelting the house.

Sand?

Someone gingerly stepped down the stairs behind her. She turned.

Sheila.

In one of Sheila's hands she clutched a bloodied butcher knife.

"Honey—what are ya doin with those?" Sheila asked. "Didn't I ask you to throw them away—like everything else in your life?"

From out of nowhere laughter filled the room, like a disturbingly ghostly laugh track to a television sitcom.

Stunned, Kacey dropped the now-bloodied diapers to the living-room floor, backing away. Blood seeped out from the diapers, staining the rug.

"What are you—" Kacey asked, "*Where* am I?"

Sheila picked up the diapers.

"Why can't you do as I ask? It's so simple. It's things like this that make me want to rip off your head and shit down your neck."

More laughter filled the room. Kacey looked around, wrinkling her brow.

"What...what the heck is going on—what are you doing with that knife?"

Sheila absentmindedly wiped the blade on the diapers, staring off into space.

"What? Sorry!" Sheila said, "Well, I had to put the kids to bed, now, didn't I?"

The invisible ghostly laugh track again went wild.

"*Kids?*"

Kacey looked to a crib that now appeared by the couch and TV. Emily and Mark were asleep inside it.

The front door suddenly flew open and in barged Jack and Hedda

Hocker. Jack stood ramrod straight, a fire in his eyes smoldering out from underneath a severe white crew cut and rough face. Hedda was at his side, her white hair unkempt, her appearance tousled and unruly.

"We heard screams," Hedda said.

The laugh track again erupted.

Scowling, Jack closed the door.

From the kitchen, Tom Fisher also entered the living room. He carried a briefcase, assorted instructional teaching aids, and a tripod and whiteboard. Several "*Monsters, Inc.*" stickers plastered his briefcase. Just as he entered the room, Sheila pegged the bloody diapers at him, just missing his face. Fisher shot Sheila a nasty look.

The laugh track was off da hook.

"What are you doing here?" Fisher asked Jack and Hedda. Fisher gave Jack a forlorn look and immediately went about setting up his tripod and whiteboard.

"Look, if you're going to kill," Fisher continued, "you have to do it right. Murder's a *privilege*—not a right."

More ghostly laughter.

Jack took a seat in a recliner, eyeing Kacey and Fisher.

"You look familiar," Jack said to Fisher.

"The sooner I get started, the quicker this whole mess can get under way," Fisher said.

"Hurry up, I got itchy fingers!" Jack said.

"Oh, shut up, Jack!" Hedda said.

"*You* shut up!"

Hedda's face immediately bloated like a feeding mosquito. "*I swear, one of these days someone's gonna gut you while you're still breathing, then feed you your own* dick!"

The laugh track went *crazy*.

A look of annoyed disgust filled Jack's face. "You don't even know the *meaning* of the word, you stupid bitch...."

"Oh, I know! I know all right! *It means I cut open your fucking stomach and yank out your guts, you big fat sonofabitch* that's *what it means! I'll goddamned kill you one of these days—I will! I fucking SWEAR! I'll show you what it means, all right, I'll—*"

Fisher shot across the room, knocking a still-stunned Kacey back against the stairway banister on his way to Hedda. Kacey looked incredulously at the word "MONSTER" on all the walls, as if seeing them for the first time. The word physically crawled across everything as she looked on.

Sheila joined in on the brawl. Fisher threw himself between Hedda and Jack as Hedda made a play for Jack, then Sheila intercepted Hedda and held her arms behind her back, pinning them there.

Kacey's legs gave out and she collapsed into a chair that was just *there*. She looked to it, but found she was actually sitting on the couch between Sheila and Hedda—who was simply beside herself, positively *seething*.

"Okay, now this is important," Fisher instructed, "if you're gonna cut open a person, you need a sharp knife...."

Fisher looked to everyone to make sure they were paying attention.

"Okay," Fischer continued, "class question: when do you *not* want to use a sharp knife? Anyone? Anyone?"

"When I'm doin Hedda!" Jack shouted, frantically waving a hand in the air, "I want her to feel *all* the pain and *twice* the rip-n-tear!"

The laugh track went off.

"That's exactly right!"

A commotion erupted upstairs, followed by incoherent shouting. It sounded as if something extremely heavy was being dragged across the upstairs floor. Kacey turned in the direction of the noise. A man emerged at the head of the stairs. All by himself he vigorously and fervently dragged a cast-iron claw-footed bathtub down the stairs, cursing and shouting and spitting the entire way.

Kacey looked to everyone, but no one seemed to take note of the man and all his red, swollen anger. The man continued to drag the tub—with one hand—down the stairs. She heard steps snap and crack from the weight of the claw-footed tub. The man then took a right at the base of the stairs and dragged the tub behind everyone out into the kitchen. He then continued screaming and spitting his way right on out the back door.

Kacey shot to her feet.

"*What is going on here!* This is *crazy*—insane! All *wrong!*"

Sheila and Hedda reached out to Kacey and tried lowering her back into her seat, but Kacey swatted away their hands and followed after the Angry Man with her eyes.

"Why did you leave?" Jack asked Kacey.

"*What?*" Kacey turned to Jack.

"Hey, Jack, don't talk to my wife like that!" Sheila said.

"I'll talk to anyone I want, *however* I want, you prissy little dyke!"

Sheila cast Jack a hateful glare, reached between the couch cushions and withdrew a large, ugly knife...

Angry Man was now outside, still yelling and ranting on at the top of his lungs. Kacey continued toward the kitchen. As she departed the living room, only a distant part of her registered that the living-room situation had degraded into full-on yelling match. She exited the kitchen, following after the angry man.

Kacey stood on a lawn—at night. She crossed her arms before her, shivering. Blinking, she found herself on a street before a residence at the Safe Harbor retirement community. From all around her screams, shouts, and the sounds of intense struggles issued from every home. Shadows stalked the streets and grounds.

Kacey now stood before one of those residences…its front door wide open. An inside light was on and she heard shouts from the angry man inside. It sounded like he was still dragging around that claw-footed tub.

Kacey looked back from where she came, saw the kitchen

And was suddenly there. Back inside the house.

As if never having left, she opened the refrigerator, also covered in "MONSTER" graffiti, and rummaged about inside. No more yelling issued from the living room, only muffled pleas and disgusting sounds of ripping and tearing…

Kacey removed a carton of milk from the refrigerator. "MOTHER" was boldly printed on all four sides of the carton. Kacey took a swig. Milk overflowed out her mouth and ran down her face and chest onto the floor, pooling at her feet. There was far more milk than container.

Sheila entered the kitchen, bloody, her hair and clothes disheveled.

"Honey—what's the matter?" she asked, smoothing out her hair and clothes, "You've simply not been yourself, these days."

Kacey removed the carton from her mouth, but the milk continued to flow unabated onto the floor.

"This whole dream is seriously *fucked!*" Kacey said.

Back outside on that nocturnal lawn, the Kacey *there* shook her head in confusion.

How can I be in two dreams at once?

Back inside the kitchen, the Kacey *there* stared at Sheila. Sheila extended a bloodied hand out to Kacey's chest. Blood from Sheila's hand, and the spilled milk on Kacey's chest, mixed.

"I know what'll cheer you up. *Let's go upstairs*," Sheila said, running her bloody hand down Kacey's front.

The invisible laugh track erupted in surprise.

Kacey pushed Sheila away. Looked to her bloodied hand and appearance.

Back outside, shouting and cursing, Angry Man crashed through that other house and out the doorway, dragging his claw-footed tub with him. Splinters and wood chunks exploded from the smashed doorway as he forced the tub through the opening.

Angry Man dragged the tub across the lawn, gouging out deep channels. He stopped directly in front of Kacey. She again blinked. When she opened her eyes all kinds of wood and other consumables were now packed beneath the tub.

"I'll show you!" Angry Man shouted at the top of his lungs, *"I'll FUCKING SHOW YOU!"*

Kacey took a step back.

Angry Man now had a roaring fire raging beneath the tub, the tub's water boiling. The heat was stifling. Kacey looked back to the residence's open door. Two body-sized bundles were tied up there in front of the door. Angry Man continued ranting and raving.

One of the bundles jerked back and forth like a Mexican Jumping Bean. Angry Man saw that and charged the door, yanking the old man wrapped inside the writhing bundle to his feet. Grunting and growling he viciously slapped him around.

"I'LL SHOW YOU WHAT IT'S LIKE!" Angry Man shouted, *"I'LL GODDAMN SHOW YOU BOTH!"*

Angry Man savagely punched the old man in the head until all struggle ceased. Angry Man stuffed the old man under his arm like a newspaper, then also grabbed the man's wife by her hair and charged the tub, spitting froth.

"I'LL FUCKING SHOW YOU, YOU FUCKING BABY KILLERS! I'LL SHOW YOU WHAT IT'S LIKE, ALL RIGHT!"

Once at the tub and without missing a beat, the Angry Man chucked the old man into the boiling tub feet first. The man awakened, screaming and struggling to get out of the water, but Angry Man forced him back under with a bare hand, still clenching his wife by her hair. Rabidly frothing at the mouth, Angry Man's head swelled grotesquely, his veins popping out the sides of his head and neck in thick ropes.

In tears, horrified, but still unable to move, all Kacey could do was watch…the old woman, who was in severe pain and sobbing, her scalp hideously torn and bloody, was trying to find her husband, who had finally gone silent among the roiling water.

Back in the kitchen Kacey backed away from a now naked and

bloodied Sheila, who offhandedly tossed her knife over her shoulder. It stuck into a wall, in the middle of one of those still dripping "Monster" words that continued to grow and crawl across the walls, floor, and ceiling.

Sheila was in mid conversation when Kacey had focused back in on their kitchen scene.

"...nuthin...or we could just do it right here, while everyone else is in the next room...."

"None of this is right," Kacey said, "this whole thing is *wrong*...."

Back outside, on that Safe Harbor residence's lawn, a sickened Kacey went to the old lady who lay on the lawn, but Angry Man wasn't having any of that and quickly shot between them, grabbing the old lady.

"No!" Kacey shouted, straining against incapable action.

"*You fucking bitch!*" Angry Man shouted to the old lady, "You want him? Go—*go* to your fucking commander!"

Angry Man hefted the wiggling and struggling woman above his head and heaved her at the tub. Her head hit the edge of it, snapping her neck, and she tumbled lifelessly into the boiling water.

"*No!*" Angry Man wailed.

The old woman bobbed about, unmoving in the boiling water with her husband.

Angry Man's shoulders slumped. "That won't happen again," he said, sighing.

He stared at the tub a moment longer, before turning and purposely striding across the lawn and street into another home. Kacey turned away—and *bolted*.

Back inside the house, the Kacey there also ran from the kitchen, back into the living room. Fisher was holding a writhing and bound-and-gagged Jack on the floor, while Hedda was busily fishing out Jack's intestines from his slit-open stomach. Hedda turned to Kacey and grinned.

"Oh, my God...," Kacey said.

Naked, one hand behind her back, Sheila came up behind Kacey. Sheila's entire body was smeared in blood and milk.

"Oh, come on, honey...get with the program! We all just wanna help!"

The laugh track erupted.

Kacey again turned to run, but Sheila brought her hand out from behind her back revealing the large-bladed knife that morphed into an exaggerated KA-BAR. She took a stab at Kacey, but Kacey knocked the knife from her grip. Kacey again tried to flee, but now Fisher and Jack are there, Jack with his intestines dangling out his belly. Jack and Fisher pinned Kacey, as Sheila calmly picked up her knife and handed it (handle first) to Hedda. Sheila came up to Kacey and planted a big wet one on her, seductively grinding her body into Kacey's. She then backed away, gaze demurely lowered. Hedda came up to Kacey, brandishing the KA-BAR.

"I'm sorry, dear," Hedda said, "but it's for your own good, you deserting little *bitch*."

Hedda rammed the blade deep into Kacey's abdomen while maintaining eye contact, and, using all her body weight, yanked it brutally across her belly. She looked to Fisher.

"This how it's done?"

"Sure…if you wanna take all the fun out of it," Fisher said.

The ghostly laugh track went off.

"No-no-no-*no*…." Kacey said, life ebbing from her.

Pleading and in tears, everything began to gray—then black—out, Kacey felt her body jerk and jerk and…

The last thing Kacey heard were the two of them calmly and rationally discussing the proper way to gut a person, like so much venison…

3

Kacey bolted upright, sweating. Her heart pounded and her hands clutched the blankets to the point of cramping as she tried to control a severe coughing fit. Leaning across the bed, she grabbed a small plastic cup filled with water and took a sip. Slowly regaining her composure, she laid back down, staring into the ceiling. Glanced to the clock. One-thirty-two a.m.

The same, basic, dream she'd been having for the past year, yet now there was a different, horrifying new episode, with a new cast of characters.

And where had all the anger and violence come from?

Never had the dream been so violent, so *angry*…and now Fisher and Jack and Hedda had been added, and in such nasty, *terrible* ways…

And *Sheila*.

A blast from the past.

If she never met her again, it'd be too soon. She was sure she was a nice person, but was eternally embarrassed at her behavior in such an exquisite moment of weakness—and the fact that Sheila had actually taken advantage of her...*that* got her even more. The emotions, the stress...the *booze*. She hadn't known what she was doing...what she wanted, and was eternally thankful that they hadn't gone any further. She was sure she'd never have been able to again look herself in the mirror if they hadn't *stopped*...

But she had been taken advantage of, that was what really haunted her...Sheila, as sensitive as she may have behaved, had still taken *advantage* of her.

But you put yourself there, her little voice cried.

I may have, but I was messed up. She *wasn't—or at least, didn't appear to be.*

Are you writing her script, now? How do you know what was or wasn't going on in her head?

I don't.

All right, then. Maybe she's not as evil as you're making her out to be, ever think of that?

No.

Maybe you're also not the lesbian you're making yourself out to be...

Kacey cast a look to the ring she'd found, there beside her wedding band on the nightstand. She rolled over, away from the light of the nightstand clock, pulling her blankets up over her.

She'd run away from her husband, her child, her life, had full-on made out with a *woman*—and was now living alive and not-so-well in sunny south Florida, working as a stringer for a local rag, covering a heinous mass murder.

Strangled. Suffocated.

If it wasn't one thing, it was another.

Could life *get* any better?

4

Dr. Kimberly Preston sat at the table across from Margrit Malotki in the Punta Gorda, Florida, interrogation room, quietly tapping a pencil against her notepad. Miss Malotki sat handcuffed to a bar set into the concrete floor. Her hands were folded before her in her lap. She stared down at the table, tears in her eyes; sniffling.

"Miss Malotki...you're telling me that you've been having these images all your life? Then what made you all of a sudden walk into homes and start killing?"

Dr. Preston intently focused on every move of the woman before her.

Margrit looked up and replied in her thick German accent.

"I do not know. Maybe...maybe, I think, they got more violent...more intense. It's hard to talk about, umm...*describe*. The most recent Träume...um-um dreams...had a tiger in them. Stalking streets...city streets. It would end up at that...Platz...the, um, place—*Harbor?*"

"The Safe Harbor Retirement Community."

"Ja...that place. But...but...."

Dr. Preston put down her pencil and folded her hands before her on the table. She waited, but Miss Malotki was not forthcoming.

"But what, Miss Malotki? What are you trying to say?"

Margrit squirmed in her chair, grimacing. "Ich weiß *nicht*...."

"In English, please."

"I don't know how to say this! It's very confusing!"

Dr. Preston softened her tone. "Just try to express what you're feeling. Is there an image you'd like to draw, perhaps?"

Margrit Malotki continued to squirm.

"Ich habe Kopfschmerzen...in my head...it's all in my *head!*" she said, bringing up cuffed hands as far as she could. "It's like...like...I'm not really *here*...."

Preston straightened up, raising an eyebrow.

"Excuse me?"

"It's like I'm not actually *here*. There are times...many times...none of this feels *real*. I feel...feel like I'm in a dream...*all of this*...like I don't belong here."

Dr. Preston looked up from her note taking. "Well, then, where do you feel you belong?"

"I don't know...just...not...*here*. Not in this...*time*."

Chapter Thirteen

Banner wove his way through the hallways at the *Sunset Harbor Gazette* newsroom, sipping coffee from a Styrofoam cup. As much as he tried to will his hands from shaking, he wasn't very successful. The last time he'd been so driven to the shakes was way back in the early days—in the jungle. Banner passed a men's room, paused, then decided to duck inside. The restroom empty, he entered the far handicapped stall, braced himself against a stall wall with his free hand, and closed his eyes. He again tried to will himself to stop shaking like a damned leaf, but the screams, the horses, the horrific battle imagery were all still there...in every corner of his mind...

He was getting too old for all this.

And there had been something about sitting atop a *box?* A tall, large box...after a *battle?*

He'd just started seeing that image after his Tamiami Trail incident. The four horsemen. He tried substituting images from his own life in an effort to drown out the other ones, but that didn't work. He tried mentally erasing them, as a psychologist had once instructed, to acknowledge the images for what they were, then allow them to fade away into the darkness on their own accord, and this, with some concentration, kinda worked. It got his hands to stop shaking, though an occasional tremor did, spasmodically, resurface. Focusing on his hands instead of the images themselves, he was finally able to command them silent.

Incontinence was for the old and infirm.

Breathing a heavy sigh of relief, Banner left the men's room and continued on to Kacey Miller. As practical a man as he was, he was certain his experience—and what Miss Miller might know or had experienced herself—might somehow be tied together. He was a stone's throw from her desk when he saw her hastily cover something up before turning around.

"Morning," Banner said, taking another sip from his coffee.

"Morning," Kacey replied, turning away from her desk, clearly surprised by his presence. "To what do I owe this audience?"

Banner removed the same chair as last time from a nearby desk and again sat beside her. As he sat, his knees buckled for an instant. He hoped she hadn't seen that.

"Um—Mr. Banner is it?—what can I do for you?" Kacey asked, returning to her desk. "I've had kind of a rough night last night," she said, uselessly rearranging items on her desk.

"Maybe we both did," Banner said, eyeing her. "How's that story of yours coming along?"

"Fine. Look, I don't mind helping you…but, as you can see, I'm kinda busy…deadlines—"

"We're all busy, ma'am. I'm won't take up much of your time. I have a quick question, then I'm outta here."

Damn the body—he could still feel the tremors niggling, taunting. He again tried to mentally shunt their imagery, tried to focus only on the woman before him. His voice had actually wavered a touch—not much, just a little—but enough, this time, he was certain even Miss Miller might have noticed. She stopped her needless rearrangement.

"Are you all right?" Kacey asked, suddenly looking at him, *really* looking at him. "What's the matter?"

Banner reached across her and set down his coffee directly in front of her. His hand, muscular and crisscrossed with veins and scars, trembled.

She looked up from his hands…to his eyes.

What had his *eyes seen over* his *lifetime?*

"See that?"

Kacey actually blinked, coming back to the present.

"Too much coffee?"

"I saw something last night. I'm not easily shaken."

Kacey studied him; his hands.

"Miss Miller…you don't know me, but the first and last time I was ever so shaken was my first night firefight in a VC jungle. I've seen all kinds of horror, but what I saw last night I've *never* seen before."

Kacey paused, quietly reaching for the pocket where she'd hidden her new

You are ours *now…*

ring. It was still there.

"What'd you see?"

Banner grabbed his coffee and sat back. Checked to see no one was within earshot.

"I saw," he said, clearing his throat, "Ghosts. Four of them."

"*Ghosts?*"

"Alongside Tamiami Trail. There was plenty of traffic, but, apparently, only I saw anything."

"How do you know this?"

"It was right on the boulevard, Miss Miller. Cars kept driving past, yet no one stopped or looked my way. *Nothing.*"

"Mind if I take notes?"

Banner shook his head, inhaled deeply, and took another sip of coffee. Set it down before continuing.

"I don't know how else to explain this, but I saw—in my head—*images*…visions, while I was there, standing before these…ghosts. Warriors of some kind."

"How did you know this?"

"There were four of them, all on horseback. Dressed up in some kind of armor I couldn't make out, carrying pikes. They never said a word, never moved—except for their horses, which seemed very impatient, snorting and stomping—but as I stood before them, I had these…visions…of horses and battle and death…and had the most terrifying feeling they were coming for me. *All* of us. I know this sounds stupid, but it's what I experienced…*felt*. I felt like…I was actually *there*, wherever 'there' was. Wherever those battles *were*. It was hard to focus…to breathe…do anything, so I—and you have to understand this isn't easy for me to admit—I fled."

Kacey stared at Banner.

(deserter!)

(loser!)

(*lesbian!*)

Kacey nodded pensively, intently focused on Banner. "W-where'd this happen?"

"In front of the retirement home. Between midnight and twelve-fifteen."

"Why were you there in the first place?"

Banner didn't respond at first, staring straight ahead.

"I'd lost a friend to there. For the past six years, last night was to have been poker night. I've been walking that stretch on our poker nights since all this happened."

"Oh," Kacey said reaching out to Banner, "I'm sorry."

"Shit happens. People die. We move on."

"Why tell me this?"

"I think—somehow—it all has something to do with this story of yours. I *was* by the retirement center. Too coincidental."

"Why do you think that?"

"While I was watching these guys—it lasted several minutes, or felt like it did, anyway—one of them pointed to the retirement home."

"*Really?*"

"With his pike."

"A *pike?*"

"A pike."

"Okay—weird."

"The whole damned thing is weird."

"Yeah…why the ghosts, and why point to the retirement home? We already know what happened there. Have any idea how you think they might relate?"

Banner shook his head. Took another sip of coffee, and found his hands had finally stopped shaking, though now, he was definitely chilled. He sat quietly; drank his coffee. Trying not to be obvious about it, Kacey again felt for the ring she'd found on the Interstate.

Together…

It was still there. After a several moments of silence, Banner resumed.

"How's your research?"

"Great…great. Well, okay…not really. I'm having a hard time focusing, to tell the truth." Kacey leaned across her desk and plopped her face into her hands, groaning.

"Why?"

"I don't *know!*" she blurted. "I've been after this job for *months*, you know?, and I finally get it, and it's like…I don't know…."

Kacey pushed away from her desk.

"I don't know if it's because of the death of the Hockers, the grisliness and details of this whole, freaky, story, but I just can't seem to get into things. Is it a case of the grass is always greener?" she asked, throwing her hands up into the air. "I don't know—I guess I just have a lot on my mind."

"I'm not a reporter," Banner began, "but what I know is good reporters report, no matter what. No matter how they feel at the moment. They do their job, period. Like any other professional."

Kacey sighed. "Maybe I'm not professional grade. I don't know—I keep trying to get in to talk with the suspects, but no one'll give me the time of day—"

"Has anything weird happened to you?"

Kacey stared at him.

"W-why do you ask?"

"Just a leap, I guess. If something weird happened to me, maybe something's also happened to you. I mean, after the police, you were first on scene—"

"I told you…I was listening to scanners and had trouble sleeping, that's a—"

"I'm not insinuating anything."

"Look," Kacey began, "I've been having…nightmares…okay?"

Kacey started to say something else, then thought better of it. She stared at him a moment, debating about whether or not to continue.

"Fair's fair. I have nightmares about being in a house on a TV sitcom—complete with a disturbing, ghostly laugh track—but with people from this investigation…Fisher, Jack and Hedda…and something about a *bath* tub…"

Kacey again paused.

"Okay, I can't believe I'm really gonna tell someone this, but, the long and the short of it is that weird, horrible—*disgusting*—things happen in these dreams—but there's still a laugh track, along with, I don't know, an *aura* of funniness—though it's very dark and nasty. Very black humor."

"Give me an example."

"Last night's dream had Fisher come in and teach a class on how to kill."

Banner nodded.

"And it got really, really…explicit. Sickening. There's a lot of anger in these dreams—in one scene Hedda disemboweled Jack—while he was alive. In front of all of us."

Banner again said nothing.

"And, dammit, there was something about that bath tub I just can't seem to remember…I get shivers just thinking about it, but can't seem to force the memory out—screams? I don't know…."

Kacey got to her feet; paced back and forth. "I don't know…maybe it *is* this case—some of the imagery is pretty obvious, I know…but I haven't been able to really dig into anything…and the cops won't let me see any of the suspects—"

"I thought you knew someone on the force?"

Kacey grimaced. "I don't really *know* him—them—that well,

really." Kacey flushed. "Actually, I'm more of an annoyance," she said grimacing. "I'd always tried to get in at crime scenes, so I could write a story to get this job—"

"You appear to have gotten it, so it should be easier to talk to them, now, right?"

"Well, you'd think, but I've made calls and've been told they're off limits to everyone but their lawyers—"

"I can get you in."

Kacey stared at Banner as if seeing him for the first time.

"Of course—you work for those lawyers! The—the…."

"Prosecutors. I'm on retainer. But, let's get back to your story."

Kacey sat.

"I have them every night. It's only been recently that the dreams have turned so dark."

"And you're telling me you haven't been able to find out anything through your research?"

"No," she sighed. "Maybe I'm just new, but nothing short of there's a lots of crazies out there. There're probably better than a hundred known cases of serial killers across the world, with unthinkable numbers like Luis Garavito, convicted of killing about 140 people, but thought to have actually killed over 400. And Henry Lee Lucas and Ottis Toole thought to have killed more than two hundred people…uh, Pedro…what's his name…."

Kacey shuffled through piles of paper.

"Alonso Lopez, out of Peru, sorry. He killed over three hundred young girls in Columbia. And of course, there's Hitler, and more recent events, if you chose to throw those in there. But nowhere did I find anything about a bunch of unrelated people walking in off a street and just start killing people off like this."

Banner again paused, mulling over their conversation.

"You able to go now?"

"Now? Really? Well, *ye-ah.*"

Kacey quickly snatched up her gear, stuffing her tape recorder, press card (she was still amazed she actually had one), and notepads into her handbag.

"Thanks, I really appreciate this!" Kacey added.

As she and Banner made their way out of the newsroom, Connie, her editor, spotted her. Connie was talking with a group of business people in expensive suits just outside her office.

"Kacey!" Connie called out, excitedly waving her over her way.

"Come here! I have someone I'd like you to meet!"

Kacey excused herself from Banner, who marked time by continuing to sip his coffee and reading the office bulletin board. A poster on that board proclaimed *"Don't put the cart before the horse—invest FIRST!"*

"Yes, Connie?" Kacey asked, reshouldering her handbag and smoothing out her appearance. Behind Connie stood several suits, men and women talking excitedly among each other.

Connie leaned in to her, and said, "we have all kinds of interest generated from your piece, and have *NNC* right here—behind me— wanting to talk with *you*. How's that for a first assignment, huh? Girl, I wish I was in your shoes!"

Connie smiled, then turned and lightly touched the shoulder of a female executive to whom she then addressed. The woman turned.

"Kacey," Connie said, excitedly, "meet Sheila Petrova, *NNC* producer!"

Kacey's world dropped out from under her.

Chapter Fourteen

1

Dr. Kimberly Preston and detective Fisher stood before the one-way mirror, observing Evelyn Roberts, in the Sunset Harbor Police Department's interrogation room. Mrs. Roberts, however, was in a child-like, withdrawn state, sketching on a large sheet of butcher paper without blinking. She drew slightly-better-than-stick-figure people and horses and blood and battle scenes. Tears glistened off an otherwise emotionless face.

"Whatever's happened to her," Preston said, "she really doesn't want to talk about it. She wasn't the least bit receptive to hypnosis. On a hunch, I gave her paper and pencil...and here you see—"

"I thought anyone could be hypnotized," Fisher said.

"Yes...and no. In Mrs. Roberts case, she didn't even talk with me. Not even an 'hello.' I tried a couple different methods of trying to break through to her, but nothing worked—until this, which really *is* a form of hypnosis. Whatever'd happened, she's so far gone, so in denial, she's effectively blocked herself off from the world. Reality. Interacting with other people. But...I've found that many—when given the opportunity—readily pick up a pen or pencil and doodle. It's a basic instinct—to communicate. To release what's pent up inside. You could even say it's an unconscious drive making itself known."

"As much as I've seen over the years, it still amazes me how complex the human mind is. How messed up we can get. I mean, it's such a thin line, isn't it, between insanity and reality?"

Preston nodded. "It *is*."

"It's so unnerving that this woman, who'd been a wife and mother, a successful realtor, is also a cold-blooded killer."

"Until proven guilty, detective?"

"Until proven guilty," he said, nodding. But my money's on her blood-soaked clothing, scars, and bruising—and that when we found her, she was still tightening the knot she'd made around her last victim's throat. With the belt from a bathrobe."

As they left the one-way window, Preston entered the room to better observe Mrs. Roberts and her sketches. As she studied Evelyn, Preston took a closer look at her pictures of horses and warriors. How her rudimentary figures trampled and decapitated their rudimentary enemy. Noticed the copious use of red in her childlike pictorials. As Mrs. Roberts colored in some of her victims, Preston also observed how she kept diverting to another sketch she'd started but not finished in a different corner of the paper. She'd only do a line or two, every so often, but soon began devoting more and more attention to it, until she finally stayed with that part of the drawing, completing it. Preston tilted her head in curiosity. This new figure looked out of place among the horses and people, and, Preston saw, she drew radiating lines from this figure out to several others she'd already drawn on her page. To the victims of the battle scenes. Her lines were incomplete and jagged, some of them actually ripping through the paper from the force she applied to her pencils—breaking lots of lead—but she'd just reach for another pencil and continue. The figure she connected to all these others was an animal. A lion, or, maybe…

A tiger.

2

White as the proverbial sheet, Kacey's smile faded like water down a drain as she extended her hand zombie-like to Sheila Petrova, who, make no mistake about it, looked just as surprised, though not as upset. Sheila shook Kacey's hand.

"Pleased to meet you, Miss Miller," Sheila said, smiling, holding Kacey's gaze. "Great story you have here."

"Why…uh—"

"Kacey, are you all right?" Connie asked.

"I'm, uh—"

"Oh," Sheila kicked in, "I'm sure she's just a little overcome by big, bad *NNC* talking to *her*. Isn't that right, Miss Miller?" Sheila released Kacey's hand.

Kacey brought her hand to her ashen face; smoothed away strands of hair with nervous fingers.

Was absolutely sick to her stomach.

"Yes...I...I-I'm sorry. I'm not used to, um—will you excuse me?"

"Certainly," Connie said, amused.

"Pleasure meeting you, Kacey," Sheila added, clasping her hands before her and continuing to beam.

Kacey hastily departed the crowd and blew past Banner—who'd observed everything.

Kacey flew into the Ladies Room, immediately plunging into a stall, and latched it closed. She plopped down onto the toilet, throwing her hands to her head, and burned her gaze into the floor below before her.

Oh, my God...*this can*not *be happening! Of all the*
(lesbian)
one-nighters I had to have, I had to have one with a top *executive of a* top *news agency?*

Kacey closed her eyes and bent over, moaning.

This was absolutely insane. Had to be a dream. Her first lesbian fling had to be with some big-wig, hot-shot producer, rather than *any* other no-name, misunderstood, club-hopping party chick, housewife, or businesswoman?—*and* she had to come back to haunt her...remind her of their past transgression...after she got the job she'd been lobbying for, for *months*. After she'd been trying to get her *life* back in order...

How was any of this fair?

Her throat constricted and her thoughts spun so heavily inside her that her head feel like a thumping, unbalanced washing machine.

Oh, no analogy *there.*

Mark and Emily.

This simply couldn't *be*...it all had to be some terrible, horrible nightmare—

The restroom door opened.

Kacey sucked in her breath.

Someone entered the room.

The woman entered slowly...deliberately...her heels clapping tile floor as she crossed the empty room...and stopped before her stall. Kacey inhaled subtle, musky, perfume.

Dolce and Gabbana.

"*Kacey?*" came the soft, concerned voice.

The voice of insanity.

Madness.

Kacey didn't answer, found herself unable to speak, breathe.

"Kacey…it's me, Sheila—I know…I know I'm the last person you ever expected to see, and you certainly have every right to feel the way you do…but I had to see if you were okay. I mean it. I really didn't expect you to be…well, *you*…I didn't. I had no idea…I'm sure neither of us ever expected to see the other again…."

Sheila paused, and Kacey heard her quietly reposition outside the stall.

"Look, I honestly came out here to track and investigate the story…I'm sorry, really, really, sorry for what…happened…*really*, I am. I never meant to take advantage of you…."

Kacey heard her sigh as she again paused.

"Well, okay…maybe just a little—but I *am* sorry for what I did, for what happened. I'm quite embarrassed. I've grown a lot since we'd last met. I promise not to make your life a living hell while here, and I will limit my activity around you as much as I can."

Kacey remained silent, eyes shut as tightly as possible.

"Okay, then…."

Sheila turned to leave, again paused, and returned to the stall.

"I know it's trite, but, we really can be friends if you're interested. I mean this. I still think you're a wonderful person…and I hope…*hope* things are finally working out for you."

Sheila turned and left.

Eyes still closed, Kacey rested her forehead on one hand, elbow propped on a knee…and just sat there.

When she finally exited the Ladies Room, Kacey found Banner patiently waiting, leaning against a wall, tapping his now-spent coffee cup against a leg. He stopped tapping with her approach.

"You okay?" Banner tossed the cup into the trash.

Kacey smoothed out her clothes. "Sorry about all that. Guess it all just took me by surprise."

Kacey glanced around the newsroom then gave him a sidelong glance.

"They're in Connie's office," he said.

Kacey nodded, smiling nervously, repositioning an errant strand of hair behind an ear.

"She seems like a nice
(*lesbian!*)

"person, that producer," Banner said, glancing toward Connie's office. "You still up for this?"

Kacey's eyes strayed to the "*Don't put the cart before the horse—INVEST FIRST*" poster, and stared at it. Cart. Horse.

"Let's get outta here."

3

Fisher and Banner led Kacey through the Sunset Harbor Police Department, to the rear, into the holding cells.

"I'm sorry about you getting turned away, Miss Miller," Fisher said, "but I hadn't been made aware you'd contacted us. I was actually surprised you hadn't shown your face sooner, to be honest."

Kacey grunted. "I'm just glad you're helping out, now. Thanks, Detective."

Fisher raised an eyebrow. "Oh, so it's 'detective,' now?"

Kacey smiled wanly, and said, "What can I say? I'm growing up."

"Well, I think you'll find Mr. Williams not your normal, run-of-the-mill suspect—if you've ever met any before," he said, looking to her. They stopped just before the detention center entrance.

"I wouldn't know the difference, I promise you. This is my first time."

"That *you* know. Take it from me, they come in all shapes and sizes—motives—but this crew...there's something decidedly creepy about them, this whole damned thing. It's the most baffling case I've ever come across—we even have them undergoing psychiatric analysis—each and every one."

"Really?"

"We have a psychologist assessing them, checking for cult mindsets, insanity, that kind of thing. We should know more later this week."

Fisher lead them through the door and to the glassed-in front desk.

"Please deposit anything that could be used against you as a weapon...knives, mace, nail files...anything similar. Banner, you know the drill."

Banner casually deposited his Glock 9mm, a rather large lockblade pocketknife, and a lock-pick kit. Kacey eyed him.

"You always carry that?"

"Tools of the trade."

Kacey turned to the man on the other side of the glass. "I have nothing so interesting, but this purse and my

(*ring…*)

"keys." She began to unload her pockets into the slot, but quickly removed the two rings she'd inadvertently deposited in her pile for the officer.

The cop smiled, "We don't need everything in your pocket, ma'am. Just potential weaponry."

Kacey cast Banner another sideways glance, but said nothing. When she put the rings back into her pocket, she noticed that the one she'd found felt…*funny*. Images of barren plains…winds, *lots* of wind, and wide, open spaces…

As long as there is the sun and the wind…

As long as *what?*

"Okay, we're going to speak with a Mr. Billy Williams—and yes, that is his real name," Fisher said, leading them into the detention center. "He's twenty-eight, and is—was—a software engineer out of Huntsville, Alabama. Military space programs. Now, there's a waste of good DNA."

"Okay," Kacey said, nervously. "I've never been inside one of these, before."

Fisher smiled and cast a grin to Banner. "We should hope not, Miss Miller. Just keep to yourself and don't get too close to him. Try to keep one of us between you and him at all times. You never know what he might do, though we'll keep him cuffed. So far, as I'm sure Banner's told you, we've had no trouble with them, short of a suicide or two…here, and with those we also have locked up in Port Charlotte and Punta Gorda. This one's one of the most tame of the lot."

Kacey nodded. "That isn't normal, is it?"

Fisher grunted. "No, and me letting you in like this is not normal, either. I'm just trying to help you out, is all—and maybe find out a little more, myself, in the process to all this insanity. Maybe he'll open up to you."

"Wow," Kacey said, "I'm calling you 'detective' and you're being helpful. Armageddon?"

As they passed through the detention center proper, they entered an entirely different world. The uniformed police officer silently tagged along behind. The jail, otherwise dubbed a "detention center," was drab and oppressive, and lent a distinct dullness to her senses. She didn't know if that was because of its intended construction, or just her impression of the place, but there was a definite "solemnity" to the atmosphere. Kacey heard muted noises from behind some of the cell doors...mumbling and scratching...bumping and other, unknown, activity. Each cell had its own steel door, into which was cut one small viewport and a food slot.

"Is everyone in here a suspect from the murders?" Kacey asked.

"For the time being, yes," Fisher replied, "we'd moved our regular lovelies' elsewhere. We don't usually get much crime, here." Fisher shook his head. "I've really never seen anything like this before."

They stopped before one of the cells and Fisher stepped aside, allowing the uniformed officer to unlock the door. Inside, Kacey saw a continuation of the same dreary, drab confines. Painted cinderblock walls, concrete flooring. Only the bare necessities were here: a cot, a toilet, and a sink. Billy sat on the cot, staring down at his hands. The uniformed officer went in first, handcuffing Billy.

"Okay, let's go—" Fisher said.

"We're actually going *in?*" Kacey said.

Fisher and Banner smiled.

"That's where he is."

"But I thought...there was some kind of, I don't know—*interview room?*"

"There is, but it's in use right now by our psychologist. Small town, small budgets. We'll be okay; Banner and I'll be in there with you, and Junior, here'll, be right outside." "Junior" sneered at Fisher. "And he's cuffed. See?"

Kacey peeked into the cell. Fisher and Banner entered. Kacey tentatively entered the cell, once the uniformed officer stepped back outside. After she entered the cell, the officer locked the door behind her. She looked back to the door, then to the inmate, or whatever they were called.

Billy Williams.

That's what he was called. His name was Billy Williams.

And somewhere...he had a father and a mother...and whatever else of a family he'd grown up with...

Billy sat on the edge of his cot, staring down at the floor, hands cuffed and clasped before him.

"Billy," Fisher said, "this is Kacey Miller. She's a reporter. She'd like to ask a few questions."

Billy looked up. When Kacey saw his face, she felt suddenly, inexplicably, emotional. Though brooding, the guy, who was quite

handsome, looked normal enough—*except that he'd* killed *people.*
Murdered.

Kacey felt something strange inside. A certain…*familiarity?*

"Reporter, huh," Billy said, sullenly.

Kacey found it hard to speak, her new-found emotional knots constricting her throat and chest. It was one thing to write about these people, but quite another to meet them face to face.

"Yes…I, uh, wrote a story on…"

Here, Kacey found her usual byline no longer all that glamorous, actually embarrassing, as she encountered one of her stories' real, flesh-and-blood suspects.

"I wrote an article about, uh…"

"Us murderers," Billy finished.

Kacey looked away, ashamed. "Yes." Some Big Time Reporter she was turning out to be. "Yes…I did."

"Well, somebody should." He looked to his handcuffs, flexing its short chain several times.

Intrigued, Kacey found herself walking around to the front of Billy, and crouched down before him. Fisher and Banner split up to either side of them.

"Billy…I have to admit…seeing you, here…I don't get the feeling—"

"I'm a killer? That we all are?"

Kacey swallowed hard. "What happened, if I may ask? How'd it start?" And how *could* you?, she thought. *What would your mother—*

Billy rubbed his hands together and Kacey could see he was—*was he actually fighting back tears?*

"Christ, *I don't know!* One moment, I'm this software geek, developing integrated system architectures for the government, and the next I'm…."

Kacey could see he was trying his best to not cry, but his entire body shuddered.

"I have these damned *noises* in my head!" he blurted out, jumping to his feet and blowing past Kacey, knocking her off balance. Banner and Fisher made a start for Billy, but when they saw him go to the opposite end of the cell and just pace—talking to himself—backed off.

"You okay?" Fisher asked Kacey, still eyeing Billy.

Regaining her balance, she looked back to the cell door, then back to Billy.

"I'm fine."

"Maybe this wasn't such a—"

"I'm fine, really," Kacey said, a hand up to Fisher. "I've dived with sharks and jumped off bridges." Straightening herself out, she pulled out her tape recorder. Pressed "Play."

"Billy," Kacey continued, her voice full of a new—almost defiant—confidence that even surprised her, "you mind if I ta—"

"Don't know when it all started...only that somehow, some day, I started hearing all this...*wind*...and it never went away—in fact it's there now—I can hear it, *feel* it...hollow, wailing, *torturous*...the only consolation is that you're all in here with me. Behind bars. So nothing'll happen...."

Billy continued pacing, staring at the floor.

"No...no, I don't mind," he added. "Others need to know.

"At first...it was mild amusement...walking around like I constantly had this conch shell to my head...then it began to grow...the sound...it always sounded like there was a storm raging just outside my window, or something—but it was in my *head*, see?—do you get it, really *get* it?" he asked, turning to the three of them, emphasizing with clenched and cuffed fists.

"God! I'd gone to all *kinds* of specialists, psychiatrists, psychologists...no one helped. Not one. My hearing constantly checked out perfectly, sometimes even better than perfect, and everyone began to think it *was* all in my head," he said, chuckling, and angrily rapping the first two fingers of one hand to the side of his head. "Of *course* it was, for Chrissake! The last test I had, had me hearing stuff theoretically only a *dog* could hear. Now, how do you account for that?"

Kacey realized Billy was no longer talking to them.

"The wind...you hear it as it builds up outside your imaginary, inconsequential walls. Pummels your life like the crashing waves of the surf...and each time it crashes against your mind, it gets a little louder, a little closer...always hypnotic...until your curiosity gets the better of you, and you...foolishly," he said, chuckling madly, "because you think you're safe behind your imaginary walls, try to *listen* to it. Venture into and explore its rhythmic, mesmerizing seductiveness...try to see what it is it's trying to *tell* you...as if what it's trying to tell you is a *good* thing...."

Billy braced himself against a wall. Stared into its painted cinderblocks.

"Then...as if I actually stood on the steppes of some distant land...I hear them," Billy said, growing silent, more agitated. He picked at the wall. "That damned thundering charge…off in the distance…like the buffalo must have sounded like. The ground quakes, vibrates into my very *soul*…

"Thousands of them… all charging through my head… closer… louder, every day… and with them come the cries, the shrieks, the *carnage*. There were—*are*—battles being waged inside me I have *no* idea…."

Billy flinched several times, jerking, as if the stampede were charging all around him this very moment. Kacey, Banner, and Fisher exchanged looks.

"*Do you hear the stampede now, Billy?*" Kacey asked, whispering.

Banner and Fisher hovered closer. Billy never looked up, but periodically flinched as he continued picking at the wall.

"*Yes*…."

He left the wall and continued pacing, rubbing his hands together slowly, painfully.

"They're always there…trying to get out…their flying hooves, their charging cavalry, the screaming bodies—all of it…all trying to tear their way out of me and into…."

"What?" Kacey asked, when Billy didn't finish his sentence.

Kacey felt a sudden chill and looked to Banner and Fisher, who also appeared anxious. Banner gave her a look that commanded: *watch yourself.*

"The wind…."

Billy trailed off into silence, but this time, he walked right up to a wall and placed his forehead against it. He didn't beat it against the wall, but just leaned there, like a man exhausted from life, alternating between mumbling and silence.

Kacey slowly came up behind him, tape recorder in hand. Banner and Fisher followed.

"Miss Miller, be careful…," Fisher warned.

"Billy…*are they gone?*" she said, whispering.

"*No,*" he whispered back, eyes still closed. "*They never leave*…."

"Did *they* kill those people? Are *they* the ones responsible?"

Billy turned to her. Tears from red, terrified and bloodshot eyes, streaked his face.

"Ms. Miller…*I* killed those people…*I'm* the one responsible," he said jabbing a thumb toward his chest.

The two of them stared at each other.

You have it, don't you.

"*What?*" Kacey asked, startled. "*What'd you*—"

Kacey was no longer in that room. She stood in the middle of a deserted plain, wind and grit pummeling her.

"*Billy?*"

She spun around wildly, confused, shielding her eyes and face.

She was without Fisher and Banner. Without the comfort of four jail cell walls, a floor, and a ceiling. Without her purse, tape recorder, or anything else familiar. Just a bitter sand storm beating down on her.

"Billy! *Billy!*"

The wind howled and pummeled, and was now so thick with stirred dirt and sand Kacey could barely see her hand in front of her. It was like billions of tiny knives carved her into tiny, desiccated pieces to be scattered to the four corners of the globe. She squinted, catching a glimpse of her arms…but they weren't the normal, smooth and near-hairless arms she knew, but the tanned, sinewy, and weirdly muscular arms of another—a woman, dressed in loose, flapping garments unfamiliar to her.

Kacey shrieked, frantically scraping away at skin that wasn't hers.

"*Chim-a du tere baiig-a bije degen?*" shouted Billy above the storm, standing before her, clad in what looked like leather armor. He was the same him she knew from the cell, though something was entirely different about his face. Angry, battle scarred.

"*You have it, don't you?*" Billy again asked. "*Alib, bi üjey-e,*" he demanded in this strange language Kacey seemed to understand.

"*Yüü?*" she asked back.

"The ring! You have it. I can *feel* it. Let me see it!"

Something inside Kacey *clicked*.

Kacey forgot about her sinewy, tawny arms; reached inside the folds of her loose garments and removed the new, polished—now *shiny*—ring. Held it out before her.

"How did you know?" she screamed back, shaking the ring before her, accusatorially. "*How did you know about this?*"

Billy-as-warrior came to her; stared at the ring, mesmerized.

Stand to fight!

You are ours *now…*

"The ring…" he muttered. "Let me have it.…"

Kacey backed away from Billy-as-warrior. Billy stared at her with an insane, evil look, and slowly withdrew a sword from his scabbard.

"Billy," she cried, retracting the ring. She also held her own sword out before her. She continued backing away. "*What's happening!*" she shouted, into the sand storm.

"*Give me that ring!*" he demanded, advancing on her.

Both were surrounded by the sound of charging horses.

Billy-as-warrior continued to advance.

Kacey held her weapon before her—but was unafraid. She felt different…*excited* at what was to come.

An *adrenaline rush*.

Thousands upon thousands of horses and their riders charged directly for them, from behind Billy-as-warrior and surrounding sand storm—

Kacey was back in the cell.

Banner and Fisher, and an inmate, named Billy Williams, stared at her, only now, Billy looked as if he'd had an epiphany.

Kacey collapsed.

As she fought to remain conscious, the last thing she heard was Billy Williams whispering—in her head—*chi medene…chi medene…*

You know….

Chapter Fifteen

1

All there was…was black.

Deep black, utter black, all consuming *quiet* black…

Wind.

Creaking and groaning…*wood?* Rocking back and forth…a restrained shuddering and rattling of tackle…

Light.

Kacey Miller stood before a lonely and flapping tent…out on barren plain amid howling wind. A river gurgled nearby. A goat drank from its waters. Looked up to her.

Wind…caressed her face, tossed her hair…

The earthy smell of musky land.

In the distance…hills…grazing livestock.

A tent…dirty, round. Loose ropes and fabric flapped against its side. She watched the rope…it lifted up in the wind…fluttered its little jig, then fell back against the tent. Again up into the air it went, but not as high—only to catch a sudden gust and whip higher—flip back on itself, then fall back against the tent wall, to begin anew, yet another trip into the air…

Kacey entered the tent.

The word "MONSTER," smeared across all the interior walls, greeted her inside her dimly lit home.

She blinked.

She's seated on the couch, one of her hands stuffed down the front of her slacks. Sheila played with Mark and Emily on the floor before her. Embarrassed, Kacey pulled her hand from her pants.

"Oh, God…."

The ghostly laugh track kicked on.

Kacey shot to her feet. Sheila looked up to her. Mark and Emily continued to play with their toys on the floor before the TV. *Monsters, Inc.* played on the television screen.

"What's the matter?" Sheila asked, "Everything all right?"

Kacey looked around. Outside she heard wind, but it seemed to quickly fade into the background...

Kacey said, "No, not again...."

Sheila picked up bloodied diapers from the floor before the couch.

"Honey, you can talk to me...let it all out...."

Still playing, Mark and Emily looked to Kacey. They stacked tape recorders like Legos.

"Oh, God, I'm back again! This has to be a *dream*...."

Sheila got up and sat on the couch beside her.

One by one, Mark and Emily individually smashed all the tape recorders with miniature baseball bats. Kacey winched and jumped, pieces flying off her face, and legs, and Sheila...

"Of course it's not a dream, silly," Sheila said, "you're back *here*, with us—your family! Isn't she, children? It's that *other* stuff that's a *dream*."

The insane omnipresent ghost laughter again went off.

"Kids?"

Mark and Emily sat on the floor, staring at Kacey. Kacey looked to the TV. On the now-dark screen were the words, "YOU LEFT US!" written in thick black letters. Filling the screen in subtle, dark letters all around those words were CART BEFORE THE HORSE, CART BEFORE THE HORSE, *CART BEFORE THE HORSE*...

Kacey looked back to Mark and Emily. They now sat in a pool of blood, scribbling weird words on the floor using permanent markers.

Sand blew past, got in their hair and clothes.

"Honey," Sheila said, "if something's the matter we can certainly leave, just like *you* did...."

Again, with the laughter.

Kacey backed away—when Sheila reached out and grabbed her by the hand—but her grip slid off, and with it Kacey's wedding ring. Kacey watched the ring slowly drop to the floor.

"That'll leave a Mark," Sheila said.

The laugh track went *crazy* wild!

"The ring! Where's the *ring?*" Kacey shouted.

"Here it is, Mom!" Emily said.

More laughter.

Incredulously, Kacey grabbed the ring; looked to Emily.

"You can't talk—not like that—you're only…."

Sheila helped Kacey back down onto the couch.

"Okay," Sheila said, "let's talk about this, shall we?"

Kacey slid the ring back onto her finger, but instead quickly pulled it off—in pain.

"*Damn!* What *was* that?" Kacey said.

Kacey turned the ring over; looked inside it.

"What's the matter, honey?" Sheila asked.

"There's something wrong with it—something *inside*…."

"Let's have a look."

Kacey continued examining the ring beside Sheila. Sheila leaned over and gave Kacey a big, wet, open-mouthed kiss. Wiped her mouth. Sat back and eyed Kacey.

"What was that for?" Kacey asked without looking up, still inspecting the band.

"I love you."

Kacey handed the ring to Sheila.

"There's something written inside," Kacey said.

"Wow…and it doesn't say *forevermore*."

More laughter.

"Can you read it?"

"No. Can you?"

"No, but I know what it says. It says—"

2

Kacey awoke, startled, the acrid scent of ammonia waved back and forth beneath her nostrils. Banner stood before her, Fisher down on one knee beside her, performing the ammonia passes. Kacey lay limp on the floor, still in the police station. She felt like Dorothy, in *The Wizard of Oz*.

And you were there, and you were there…

"You all right?" Fisher asked, removing the ammonia.

Kacey shot to an upright sitting position, but Banner caught her. "Easy does it," he said, easing her back down to the floor, and the folded blanket beneath her head.

Kacey mumbled a few words, then sat up more slowly, bringing a hand to her head. "What…happened?"

"You fainted," Fisher said.

"You seem to be having a bit of a rough day, Ms. Miller," Banner said.

But Kacey was still trying to hold on to the images screaming through her head. Something about a ring...

Together forever...

Kacey shot a hand to her pocket.

Both were still there.

She closed her eyes, felt an intense vertigo, and let the dead weight of her body sink into the floor.

Mark...Emily—*Sheila*...

"I think," she said, exhausted and weary, "I'd better get home."

3

Kacey closed her apartment door behind her and collapsed onto her couch. It'd been nice of Banner to drop her off, but it had been a quiet, awkward ride back. Some days it just didn't pay to get out of bed. She felt beat...like she'd not only been run over by a steamroller, but backed over with it.

And there was the lesbian.

Her past had come back to bite her. Embarrassment, guilt, and pleasure all wrapped up into one, anything-but-tidy, little package. Throw in a hefty appetite of leaving your husband and daughter, and you have the makings of either a gone-platinum country ballad or a made-for-TV movie. When it rained it fucking poured.

Twang.

But why had things felt so good with Sheila, so unaccountably *right* when she currently felt so much hellish guilt? She'd gone over it a million times since their encounter and still felt that they'd never met before their little airport introduction.

Yet felt as if they *had*.

Somewhere. And, now, heh-heh—Life could be so goddamned funny sometimes—here they were, cozily working together on the same story.

And they'd kissed on the lips.

Fooled around *naked*-like.

How would she ever be able to look at herself in a mirror again?

Go back to her husband?

She *couldn't* be lesbian—she'd never felt that way with any other woman before or since—so why Sheila? What made Sheila so goddamned special? The depression? The alcohol? The entire stressed-out, angst-ridden on-the-run flight from *commitment?*

Sheila was the lesbo—not her.

Sheila'd been the one who'd made the play for *her*...so maybe there had been a somewhat stacked deck against her, pardon the pun, but that didn't make her...

But, was there really anything wrong with what she'd done? All they'd done, really, was kiss and be kissed...nothing more. Okay, it had been with a *woman*, and okay, she was *married*, and, yes, there had been *exposed body parts*...

She just couldn't shake that one part...that it had been with a *woman*.

Kacey removed the rings from her pocketbook and set the one she'd found on the Interstate on the coffee table. She held the other one—her wedding band—out before her.

To have and to hold.

Til death do us part.

I do.

Good Lord, there it was, the instant replay in super slo-mo.

I do.

Two of the most legal and emotional words ever spoken by anyone *to* anyone.

It's not the complicated that impacts people's lives the most, no ma'am, it's the simple. The basic. Things only get complicated when we try to go against the grain. She'd found a wonderful man, one who'd wanted to spend the rest of his life with her—*her*, no one else—and together they'd created a child. And what had been his biggest fault? His only crime? That he loved changing his daughter's poopy, smelly diapers? That he gave up sky and scuba diving? That he got a real job to support his family and became attentive to *them* instead of his past, self-involved, life? That he tried his damnedest to create a life with his wife and child, one with which they could be *proud?*

Yeah, guilty as charged.

Hang em high, and let em kick in the wind, sheriff.

And what had she brought to the table?

Selfishness? Fear? Abandonment—*lesbianism?*

Mommy had a child, then ran away to become a lesbo...

And a lesbian who seemed to have tracked her down and was about to make her life a miserable hell all over again.

Well, okay, maybe she hadn't exactly tracked her down. There was absolutely no way she could have known where and who she was. She, herself, hadn't even known what she was going to do with her new on-the-run life when she met Sheila. All they exchanged, besides some spit and nipple, were shared misery and first names. No, this was just one of life's little coincidences. But, what comes around always, *always*, sweet Charlotte, without a doubt, *goes* around. She'd screwed up, that was that, and now she was having to learn and grow from it. Face her mistakes…take responsibility and move on.

Kacey put her wedding band back on and returned to the couch, staring at the other ring…

4

Oh, God, Sheila Petrova lamented, as she collapsed onto her hotel couch. She sipped wine and listened to the sound of her hot bath running in the bathroom. She kicked her nyloned feet up on the coffee table. Nice little "run" there.

Could things get any worse?

First off their flight had been bumped. Then getting through security had taken longer than usual, because some nut job had been arguing with one of the TSA agents at airport security. Then the plane was loaded, and the first-class passenger in the seat before her had had the worst case of gas she'd *ever* had to endure in a confined area—and, like all planes since September 11, there was nowhere to move, because they were packed in like frigging sardines. Then her rental had been given away to another (reminding her of that *Seinfeld* episode…).

Then she'd run her nylons.

And finally, to top everything off, she runs into none other than Kacey Miller, super-stringer for a local paper and glorious one-night-stand.

All in a day's work.

All she now wanted to do was to take a nice long—*hot*—bath and forget about the nastiness of the world for an hour or so.

How long had it been since she'd first met Kacey?

Twelve months, two days, and seven hours.

And what had frigging possessed her to be so uncharacteristically aggressive that night? She'd never behaved so irresponsibly in her entire life. She'd run that night over and over in her head, and always,

always, the same conclusion: nothing about it made sense.

But there had been something about her, this Miller woman. Something about Kacey that had so irresponsibly drawn her to her like air into lungs. She knew what she'd done was wrong, careless, and stupidly rash, but she hadn't been able to help herself. She knew it from the moment she'd turned to her at that bar and looked into her deep, dark—hurting—eyes. From that moment on she couldn't get close enough, fast enough. At that moment, her entire life, her very *soul*, depended upon her getting as close as possible to this person. It wasn't her beauty, though she certainly had plenty of that…it was some other factor she couldn't put a finger on. Were past-life connections for real? Because, if they were, that was what she wondered must have been at work. What else could it be? She couldn't explain the sudden, powerful, attraction any other way. Ever since she'd been a child, she'd felt as if she'd lived before. But this was the first time she'd ever come God's honest face-to-face with the concept in such a concrete, real-life, *emotional*, way…

It had to be something else…didn't it? Something entirely different? Sometimes you just hit it off with people, and sometimes you didn't, and there was no real rhyme or reason either way, right? Pheromones? Body language? Who knew. She'd have to do a program on it someday, but for now…for now, she had to come to terms with her behavior *that* day, and its consequences *today*.

Man, sometimes, in a word, life just really *sucked*.

Kacey lay her head back in her bubble bath, and sighed.

Such sweet relief!

Baths were the cure-all for all the world's ills, her grandmother used to say. A few candles, relaxing music, and mounds of bubbles. Only thing missing was

(*Mark*)

(*Sheila!*)

a male body in the tub with her.

No, that wasn't even true…she just wanted to be left alone. No distractions. Not even fantasies…

She again sighed, and felt all her worries drain out of her and into this tub of hot

(*boiling…*)

water. She looked over to the vanity, where the rings were.

What was it about that thing?

Why couldn't she just shove it in a dresser drawer and be done with it? Maybe she should do a little research...contact some universities, see what she could dig up.

Kacey again closed her eyes. She allowed her mind to drift...thought of the lazy Florida palm trees swaying about in balmy breezes...about the myriad of bird life that soared effortlessly overhead...of the sea and shore and waves that pounded the beaches...of vast grasslands...hills and mountains ...water—streams and rivers—a couple traveling alone across those grasslands...one on horseback, the other in a horse-driven cart...only recently married...returning to the man's tribe...

But what were those three on horseback about, hurriedly riding toward them?

And...and the newlywed husband galloping off into the distance, alone, the three riders close behind...

Sheila exploded out of the water.

Grasped the sides of the tub.

Wiping her face, she tried holding onto the images. She'd just dozed off (not a good thing in all that water, for sure), when she saw images of an attack by three riders upon a newly married couple in a distant grassland...

Sheila splashed more water on her face then smoothed her hands down the rest of her body.

Riders and a marriage?

A ring?

Looking to her watch, she noted she'd been in the tub just over an hour. Stretching, she slowly made her way out of the tub, and toweled off, all the while experiencing the weirdest, most heart-retching and unaccountable sense of *longing*....

Chapter Sixteen

(TEAR-STAINED, SMUDGED, AND HANDWRITTEN LETTER)

May 2

Dear Mark and Emily:

I have no idea where to begin, so I might as well just start writing and see where it takes me.

Emily, you probably don't even remember me, and that will be my punishment til the day I die, but I hope, in time, you'll find it in your heart to forgive your very confused mother <u>who really does still love you</u>. There are no words that can ever adequately convey the sorrow and regret I feel in deserting you—sometimes grown-ups just do stupid things, and when it comes time to correct these stupid things, it's not nearly as easy to fix them as it was to do them. Just know that I do love you, and will <u>always</u> love you.

Mark…what can I say? I never planned on running off and leaving you and Emily behind, though you might pointedly disagree with me on that. I really tried to make things work (at least in my own mind), but something inside me just snapped, I guess, is the nearest I can figure. And I don't think it had anything to do with either of you. It was something to do with me. In <u>me</u>. I had, and still do, things burning away inside. Questions I still don't have answers to. Feelings and confusion I still don't even have <u>questions</u> for. I'm really messed up, and I can't come back until I find out what's the matter. I'm just sending this letter so you won't worry—if you even still are. I've got a job, an apartment—I'm living alone, Mark, so don't you worry about me having left you for someone else—that was <u>never</u> the case and still isn't—and am doing about as well as I can, all things considered. So, please, <u>don't come looking for me</u> (and ignore the postmark on this envelope; I gave it to another to mail for me in another state). When I'm ready to return, only then can I come back to you and Emily, because I don't want to have anything like this ever happen again. I mean it—<u>please don't try to find me</u>. When I'm ready, I'll return—if you'll have me. I know that sounds selfish, but it's the best I can do for now. Please try to understand, because <u>I'm</u> having a hard time understanding it myself.

I'm sure Emily is growing up into a fine young girl, and though I am joyous of this, I am also deeply saddened. <u>I should be there</u>. Forever. But I'm not, and this, I'm finding, much to my surprise, is tearing me apart. I never thought I'd feel this way about children, but I do. I'm more the mother than I ever thought, yet less than I should be. If and when I ever get things straightened out, I promise this will never happen again. But I can't ask for you to wait for me, because I don't know how long this'll take—it's simply not fair for you to wait on your screwed-up wife to return. As hard as this is for me to say…if you want a divorce, you have every right to one and I won't fight you over it. But since I'm not going to tell you where I am, you can use this letter for the lawyers, to give them my approval for you to proceed—if you feel the need to. I hope you don't, I really do, but will understand if you do. This is my official approval to let you file for a divorce—if you feel the need. But, please…don't.

Why did I leave? I'm not really sure. I think it might have had something to do with feeling trapped. That's the closest I can come to any kind of an answer. It had nothing to do with any other men, as I've already said. I think it mainly comes from feeling that my life was running away from me, leaving me behind. I wasn't ready to become a mother, with a child, diapers, feedings, and laundry. To live in one place. I still felt the need to do so much—and still do, I guess. To slap the world in the face and yell "This is <u>me</u>, world!" I didn't feel like I could do that any longer. And to have a place of my own, called a <u>home</u>?! Wow, that, too, was a permanence I just wasn't prepared for.

And then there you were, giving up your fun life—for diapers, no less. You seemed to have lost your edge, your drive for doing anything remotely "fun." It was like I saw you afraid to take chances any more, now that we (<u>you</u>) had a kid. I just couldn't do it. I needed to be <u>free</u>.

And this brings me to the next thing, which I can't believe I'm actually going to tell you. Whew—are you ready for this? Sitting down? The night I left you and Emily, I got held up in the airport. I had…a little too much to drink, I missed my flight…and I met someone—like I said, this still has nothing to do with <u>men</u>. Boy, I can't believe I'm actually going to put this into words and tell you (and I'm not really all that sure I'm actually going to mail this, either). We spent the night together. There it is. Out on paper. This bothers me a <u>great</u> deal. We didn't do anything "bad"…but did enough to leave me with enough guilt to carry around for the rest of my life. I just need to be totally honest with you, if I'm to get through all this shit and come home (if THAT'S still even an option). I never planned on doing anything with this woman, but I'd had a bit too much to drink, and well, I'd just run out on my family, you know? As much as I don't think so, I don't know if I'm interested in women, but my actions that night pain me a great deal each and every day. I should never have left—but would things have been any better if I'd stayed? Would we have divorced by now? Would Emily have witnessed fights and anger? So I really don't know which is better. Since I'm here, where I am now, I just have to make the best of it. Sort out all my demons and try to get beyond everything. But know this: I am <u>so</u> sorry for all I've done…for leaving—and the "airport thing." I hope you can forgive me some day, some year—some life. You <u>and</u> Emily. And please, <u>please</u>, don't <u>ever</u> tell her about what I did at the airport—it would kill me, and serve absolutely no purpose. I'd kill myself if she ever found out. Of course, you're probably not thinking that's a problem about now, but just try to think of our daughter's future and not about me on this one. I've given it a lot of thought, believe me.

God, what is <u>wrong</u> with me?

Know that I still love you, Mark, and you, too, Emily, my dear, sweet, girl, and that I hope to be coming back to you both, soon—if you'll still have me.

Love,
Kacey

Chapter Seventeen

1

The Circuit Court of Sarasota Building
August 1st, 9:53 p.m.

Harry Gordon looked down to the paperwork before him. This was it. Time to go. Tomorrow was the big day…the Safe Harbor murder trial, the Honorable Judge Howard Stoker III presiding. The time of reckoning for a group of unrelated people who journeyed from all across the world to the sleepy little town of Sunset Harbor, Florida, to do one thing and one thing only—murder the entire resident population of a sleepy retirement complex. Seventy-two people. No apparent motive, no single M.O…and many who continued to dispute their own part in it regardless of the evidence. Some had even been apprehended with murder weapons still in hand, bodies at their feet. Months of investigation, and not one, corroborative, linking clue could be applied across each and every defendant. They'd simply hit a dead-end. And the speediness of getting to trial? Unheard of.

None of this was real.

However he'd prepared to argue in court, he wasn't sure he was really going to buy the outcome. There was something unnatural at work, here, he could feel it…like that damned past-life regression (translation: *fantasy?*)…it ate away at him with hungry little razor-sharp teeth. Whether or not he could prove any of this (of course he could—the evidence was all there), the more vexing problem was *why*. All those people descended upon this unsuspecting south Florida retirement community to slaughter residents—while leaving and ignoring any visitors who'd stayed at some of these homes—some even sleeping in the residents' *master* bedrooms. Many of the residents' pets—cats, dogs, and goldfish—had even been slaughtered, while those of the visitors had not. *Not one family member nor visitor had ever been touched—nor* awoken *during the murder spree.*

Explain that. *Any* of it.

It had clearly been an emotionally charged crime, a crime of passion, the rage was clear in the gruesome, unspeakable aftermath. Two sets of residents had been placed in *tubs of boiling water*, the only residents with the old-style claw-foot tubs. And what about the "carpeted" victims? Craziness didn't begin to explain it. Most were killed before being rolled up into carpets, then further wailed upon.

Whatever motive there might be, whatever tie however illusive, all felt curiously irrelevant. Twenty-eight surviving suspects had committed murder most foul, and it was his job to prove that and convict them…in a fair trial. Which he could…short of a motive. Motives didn't always matter, but actions did. The long and the short of it was that each of the defendants had killed every last resident in that community. Period. End of story. And *that* he could prove.

So, how could he actually feel any kind of sorrow for the suspects—which, dammit, he did. He'd read the transcripts and personally visited each of them. He'd never admitted it until now, but he honestly felt sorry that they'd probably never find out what motivated any of them, because he sincerely doubted *they* knew. It was all surreal—a freakish nightmare had taken over and brought everyone here, to this one moment, this one physical coordinate point in time and space.

But how do you prove any of it in a court of law?

They came, they murdered, they got caught—and now they were going to pay. They'd gone in together, and they were all going to go out together—and the sad part of it was that no one would probably ever find out what had driven them to do what they'd done. In the U.S. legal system, all that mattered was the end result. Crime and punishment. And which side had the most convincing argument.

Tomorrow. All this was going to be put to the test. Tomorrow.

But what about yesterday?

2

Howard Stoker sat in his study, pen paused above paper, beneath a small, illuminating desk lamp. It was nine-fifty-five p.m. Howard stared straight ahead unblinkingly at the richly paneled walls of his home office, his mind a jumbled blankness—but his pen continued to rapidly scrawl ancient characters across the sheet of paper before him. His pen, under unconscious direction, raced deftly across the paper until it had written all it had come to write.

Still entranced, Howard deliberately placed his pen down, picked up the sheets of paper, folded them neatly in half, then stapled them together. He got up from his desk, strode purposefully out of the study through the darkened interior of his home and into one of several guest rooms, where he went directly to a hanging oil depicting a Gulf Coast sunset his wife had painted. He lifted the painting away from the wall then tucked the miniature manuscript into the paper pouch on the back of it. He exited to his study, but was in the doorway when a mental switch suddenly clicked back on—and not losing a beat—exclaimed, "Ah-ha!—*there's* my tea!" He retrieved it from his desk, taking a sip.

"Huh—cold. That was quick," he said, curiously, looking to the tea and feeling the outside of the mug.

Howard returned to his highback leather chair and sat; took another sip of tea, then set it down on the table alongside him. He stared out across the study again, this time conscious of his actions.

What had he just been doing?

He felt he'd momentarily lost track of something…but, no matter. He had to get his mind prepared for tomorrow. The trial. The murder trial from up north. Thirty-seven people walked into a retirement community and killed all its residents. Some took their own lives. He was supposed to keep an open mind—innocent until proven guilty, a jury of peers, and all that—but his feelings said otherwise…he knew they did it, and that was the unsettling part. There was so much more to this trial. He tried not to tune into the crime, but kept catching threads of it. This one was very different. There was a metaphysical density, a weight to it he could feel in his marrow and had never before felt in any of his other proceedings over the years—but which he'd felt he'd been waiting for his entire life…and it upset him.

Howard took a final sip of cold tea, got up, and made his way to bed. Weary, feeling lifetimes older than his sixty-three years, he made his way toward the stairs and the bedroom. Something was very wrong…bizarre…and hung about this case like Scrooge's undigested morsel.

Howard shuffled down the unlit hallway toward the stairs. As he approached the steps, he came to focus on his ticking Grandfather clock, which stood against the wall at the base of the stairs. Its ticking seemed louder, more *concentrated*. In fact, the entire house actually felt *thicker*. Like the house *became* each tick and tock. As he stared at the clock, what at first appeared to be a trick of light and shadow quickly took on a life of its own...he could have sworn the clock's shadow appeared heavier...*darker*. As he focused on the clock and its shadow, he swore the shadow—was the clock's shadow actually *expanding?*

Howard backed up a step or two; watched as the clock's shadow indeed expanded, its ticking more pronounced...multidimensional. Felt his entire home and life waver in and out of reality. As the clock's shadow expanded, a portion of it—a sliver—split away from the clock and stood off by itself.

Was he imagining this?

A blast of wind then shot through him, carrying with it the musty scent of grasslands and cattle, and before his eyes that sliver of shadow took form.

Howard found himself standing on those distant and barren grasslands...

3

"Tiger," Dr. Preston began, sitting before Tiger in the Port Charlotte jail, "I'd like to ask you something off-subject for a moment." It was late and she was exhausted.

Tiger kept shading in his picture without looking up. Preston had been continually impressed with the professional quality of his artwork, something that had always struck her as unusual for a homeless person.

"Tiger...you appear...you sound and handle yourself as if you've not been a street person forever. Your artwork. Your vocabulary. What happened? What brought you to where you are now?"

Tiger didn't respond; didn't look up nor stop drawing.

"What are you running away from? Are you a war veteran?"

Tiger ignored her. Preston thought she'd try the question one last time, but her query met with the same silence each and every time attempted. She just thought sooner or later he might drop his guard. But that hadn't happened, and looked like it never would.

"Last attempt...what drove you to kill?"

Tiger fidgeted in his shackles at the table before Preston. Both his hands and feet were bound by the hardened case-steel restrictions. He shrugged, staring down at his drawings.

"The wind," he said without looking up. "My answer hasn't changed from the last hundred times you've asked. Believe me, I wish it had."

"But, how can wind make you kill?"

He sighed, again shrugging. "Don't know, it's just *wind*...always there, in my head. Sometimes there're voices, sometimes it's just wind, but usually it's a combination of both...whispering, *screaming*...."

"What do the voices tell you?"

"It's not so much what they're saying—which I can't really make out, anyway—as how they're saying it."

Tiger picked up a different pencil and added more shading to his pictures. Preston was absolutely dumbfounded by his artistic ability. His work should be properly viewed in a gallery, not a police interrogation center.

"What do you mean?"

Tiger shook his head. "I don't know how to define it, ma'am, we've been over and over this...emotional...lots of *anger*...."

Tiger remained focused on his ant drawing, then began scribbling a picture of a horse-drawn cart and rider alongside another rider on horseback. Preston homed in on the sketch.

"What are you drawing?"

"Something in my head."

"What else do you see?"

"Riders. Coming for this woman," he said, tapping the pencil point on the figure on the cart.

Preston stared at the picture. "You know," she began, reaching down to the portfolio at her feet and removing several sheets of the same kind of drawing paper Tiger was using, "I have another drawing just like this one. A couple, actually."

Finding what she was looking for, she laid one out on the table before them. It showed, in rudimentary stick-figure fashion, a wagon with a rider, another rider on horseback beside the wagon—three other riders on horses rode toward the two.

"It's the same," Tiger said.

"How do you know?"

"The same way I hear what I hear."

"Did the wind tell you?"

"Yes."

"Just like it told you to kill those others?"

"It didn't tell me to *kill* anyone—"

"But—"

"It merely…I *hear* things…battles…death…screams and wailing…."

"Then what drove you to—"

"I don't *know*…it was just…an urge. It's hard to put into words…."

"*Try.* Your life depends on it."

Tiger paused and looked up, not to Dr. Preston, but into space.

"Dr. Preston…what do you think happens when we die?"

Surprised, Preston paused. "Well, there are many trains of thought—"

"I don't want any 'train of thought,' doctor—I want *your* belief."

"This isn't about me or my beliefs."

"Isn't it? How is it not?"

"I didn't kill anyone."

"Do you know that? Do you remember all your past lives—your future ones?"

"You're going to invoke an insanity plea—"

"I'm not invoking *anything.* I'm trying to understand what's happened to me…to *all* of us. Nothing is ever isolated, dear doctor…it's all related. You and me…we're related to each other. At the very least, in your clinical opinion, by this investigation of my supposedly deranged mind. I'm related to one Detective Tom Fisher by my having taken a few lives. But…but what if things ran *deeper.* What if…what if we had past lives together…you and me, me and Fisher, me and those I slaughtered—*that's* what I'm asking. What would 'murder' mean under those circumstances? Wouldn't it change how we viewed things—the world?"

Tiger put down his pencil and looked directly to Preston.

"What do *you* believe, doctor, because it's going to be based on what we all believe, ultimately, isn't it? I mean, if you don't believe in something, you're not going to give it the time of day…you're going to ignore it…and, in this case, that might be the very wrong thing to do. A trial should involve *all* the evidence, don't you think?

"What do *you* believe?"

4

Banner sat at The Rusty Anchor staring into his half-drained beer. This case had been the freakiest he'd ever dealt with. It was almost as if the crime itself was going to pale in comparison to the aftereffects of the trial: all these people murdered, no motive, they're from different parts of the world...that reporter has disturbing dreams and his Four Horsemen?

There just weren't any answers.

Just months of disturbing dreams and crazy visions. They were going to trial in the morning, and no one had a clue about what had driven those people to do what they did. But they were going to prove in a court of law that, by God, they *did* it, and for that they were going to burn in hell. And rightly so.

Banner took another sip.

But, it wasn't just the Four Horsemen. He'd seen...heard...other things. Like that Billy Williams character, as they'd rushed to Kacey's aid when she'd gone catatonic. He'd seen, in his mind's eye—*felt*—the thundering approach of *horses and warriors*, goddammit. Just like that Four Horsemen thing. *Smelled* them, this time, for chrissakes, like they'd actually charged in and around them. *Felt the floor beneath his feet tremble with their hallucinatory charge.*

All in a Florida county detention center cell.

How the hell does something like that happen? He never said anything, but had looked to Fisher and saw the same look in his eyes...that same confusion, that same *terror*.

He knew he'd experienced the very same thing. Maybe not everything he'd seen and felt and smelled, but something so similar, so unbelievable, it'd put the fear of God into his world, too.

And when he'd taken Kacey home, those same images continued to assail him. Volunteering to take her home hadn't been so much chivalric, as it had been something to get him the hell out of there. He couldn't get those images out of his head...which brought him to where he presently found himself. Drowning his fear in his favorite brew. Not much scared him, but the images had grown worse over the passing months. He wasn't sure how much more his psyche could handle. He'd be glad when it was all over. Something wasn't right, and this trial was just going to make things worse.

"Want another one?" a voice in front asked. Banner looked up—

and jumped.

"Whoa, Banner, you okay, buddy?" the bartender asked. "Think you've had enough, big guy—"

Banner looked to the bartender, Rick, whom he'd known for years. Grunted a "sorry."

"Want some coffee?"

"You know coffee don't do a damned bit a good—why you guys ask that?"

Rick shrugged. "They do it in the movies."

Rick smiled, then took away Banner's empty glass and swiped his damp rag over where the glass had been.

"Hey," he added, as Banner fished out the necessary change and tip, "good luck, huh! You'll nail them bastards. Nuthin's been right these days. Whole world's going to hell in a handbasket."

Banner slid off the stool, nodded, and made his exit.

There it was again...he couldn't get away from it. When he'd looked up from his beer at the sound of Rick's voice he could have sworn he'd seen an angry, indistinct, *battle-scarred face* before him. It was just one more creepy thing to add to a long list of creepy...he didn't need to make out the face to know it had been another warrior. He simply *knew*.

This case was *seriously* fucked.

Chapter Eighteen

1

Mark lay back on the couch and flipped on the TV, turned it to *NNC*, then snatched up the newspaper from the coffee table. Emily was fed, changed, and asleep upstairs, and he could now unwind before also heading off to bed himself. He had a long day ahead of him tomorrow.

Shaking out the paper, the headlines immediately grabbed his attention: *Bizarre Florida Mass Murder Trial Underway*. Throwing his feet up on the coffee table, he periodically glanced to *NNC* as he read the syndicated article:

August 2nd

In the early morning hours of March 10th, thirty-seven people from around the globe walked into small-town Sunset Harbor, Florida and systematically murdered each and every sleeping resident of the Safe Harbor Retirement Community. No explanation has been offered by authorities, however unnamed sources cite total befuddlement. Special Operations Bureau crime scene investigator, Detective Thomas Fisher, of the Sunset Harbor Police Department, declined comment only to say that "it'll all come out in the trial."

Opening statements were made today as the trial began in Fort Meyers, Florida. A change in venue was necessary, says Sunset Harbor prosecutor, Harry Gordon, because of the "backyard nature" of the crime in the town's large retirement population. The prosecution is proceeding under the notion that the murders were cult motivated, under leadership of a man known only as "Tiger." Testimony turned gruesome early on, as descriptions of dismemberment, suffocation, and other bizarre acts filled the court room—including two couples who'd been boiled in their own bathtubs—and the many victims who'd been duct-taped inside large throw rugs, then beaten with baseball bats or broken bed posts. "This expects to be a long, protracted trial," said Mr. Gordon. "It's one of the most shocking cases I've ever handled, or heard about…certainly the most bizarre."

What was this world coming to?
Mark's gaze fell to the byline. Two words.
Kacey. Miller.
He bolted upright.
Sat back down.
Stood.
Kacey?
There it was in half-toned black and white: *Kacey Miller.* Of the *Sunset Harbor Gazette.*
Mark's hands shook uncontrollably.
After all his searching? All his anguish? Here she *was?*
Kacey Miller.
He'd finally found her, and, true to form, in the midst of some kind of out-of-the-ordinary, off-the-wall, escapade. Using her maiden name, no less. How totally like her. Always getting herself into one jam or the other, always the thrill seeker. In kind of a sad way it was comforting to know that some things never changed. He guessed she'd found herself in a good one, this time. A cultish mass murder, no less. And who've thought she'd be writing an article the whole country was reading? Guess she finally put that journalism degree to good use.
How goddamned good for her.
Left her family in the boring town of Wilmington, Delaware for the seductive life of the crime-scene reporter in sunny south Florida.
Fuckin A.
Mark threw down the paper and crossed his arms, fuming.
All she needed now was a little face time on *NNC*, and she'd be set for life.
"…and if you've been following recent events," Janelle Forte

reported from *NNC*, "you know that the small town of Sunset Harbor, Florida has been the site of the grisly slaughter of seventy-two residents many are speculating to be cult motivated. Our own Sheila Petrova is in Fort Meyers, where the trial was underway. Sheila, what can you tell us?"

Mark shot for the Digital Video Recorder remote and started it. Sheila Petrova's face filled the television screen, her hair blown about by balmy Gulf Coast breezes.

"Well, Janelle, things are definitely getting quite interesting down here in Fort Meyers, Florida, known more for Spring Breaks than murder trials. Emotions have been running high among the Florida retirement communities, especially in Sunset Harbor, an hour north of here—which lends a bit of irony to this whole thing: not only in the name of the small town, with a population of less than 16,000, but also in the community where the crime took place: the Safe Harbor Retirement Community. Janelle, it's almost too horrible to imagine," Sheila continued, her face no longer on screen, as she voiced-over shots of the retirement home, its March crime scene, and surrounding town film footage.

"Every single resident in this retirement community had been systematically murdered. Safe Harbor is set among the channels and inlets of small-town Sunset Harbor (more file footage). A small community by comparison, the Safe Harbor Retirement Community only boasted about seventy residents in the community, and was in the process of expansion when the murder spree hit. It was a well-orchestrated attack, military in its precision and ruthless in its efficiency."

Sheila returned to the screen.

"One couple managed to survive the initial onslaught, only to have been murdered the following day in a twist that further impressed just how bizarre this case truly is. Jack and Hedda Hocker (pictures of the couple flashed on-screen), both 79, had managed to overcome their attackers, call police, and," Sheila said, in disbelief, shaking her head, "took the fight *to* the attackers. Hedda Hocker, as told by one reporter, here, used their hunting rifle, while husband, Jack, a retired and highly decorated Marine Corps veteran and gun shop owner, rushed outside with his…."

Here Sheila glanced down to her notes, before continuing.

"…KA-BAR, Marine Corps-issued knife, and .45 automatic, and began picking off attackers as he found them. But, I'm sad to say,

Janelle, that the Hockers were killed the very next day, when they stopped to help what they thought had been an injured hitchhiker. The hitchhiker turned out to be the only one of the contingent of killers in the retirement community murderers who'd gotten away. Both of the Hockers were tragically murdered alongside I-75, northwest of Sunset Harbor. Their attacker then took his own life, leaping off the Exit 191 overpass."

Janelle Forte was now also in view, as *NNC* split the screen for both journalists.

"Wow, Sheila," Janelle said, with a look of disbelief, "thanks for that rather disturbing report."

"You're welcome. We'll keep you posted as the trial progresses."

"Wow," Janelle again said, shaking her head. "In other news...."

Mark hit the DVR's stop and replayed the recording. The *NNC* newscast started up again, but this time Mark wasn't listening to the two reporters, but was studying the screen. The scenes from Florida, where his wife was now, apparently, living, breathing, and writing AP newswires. He soaked up everything about the report and its scenes. Freezing one of the frames on his big screen, Mark came right up before it. He burned a hole into his TV set as he examined one of its images. It had to be her—*had* to be.

There, among a gaggle of reporters standing outside the court steps in Fort Meyers, in one of the earlier-shot sequences, had to be none other than Kacey Miller, aka, Kacey *Burnett*. It was fuzzy and indistinct, but he knew in his bones...this was his wife.

Emily's mother.

2

Kacey Miller, sans Burnett, typed at her *Sunset Harbor Gazette* desk beneath a lone desk lamp. A small TV, set to *NNC*, droned on in the background behind her. She was tired and confused, not a good combination. Tired from the long hours she'd been putting in on this story, the long drive back from Fort Meyers this evening, and confused with everything from Mark and Emily, to Sheila Petrova and the evil humans do. But, she had new meaning to her life, it was exciting, and she was getting paid.

What more could a girl want?

"Hey," a voice called out behind her. Kacey jumped.

"Jesus—*shit!* You're not in the jungle anymore, okay, Banner?"

"Here," he said, smiling, and tossed a folded-up *USA Today* into her lap.

She picked it up.

Kacey looked at the article. Not only was she somewhat of a local celebrity, but now she'd put Sunset Harbor on the map, and everyone coast to coast, north and south, was reading her words. Banner leaned on the edge of a desk, arms crossed. Eyed her.

Kacey scanned the article—then the byline.

"Oh, God…."

"What's the matter?"

"Oh, my God…" she repeated. "…oh, no-no-no…."

Banner studied her.

"My *name*." she said, tapping the paper. "Oh, my God—my *name*."

Banner eyed her. "You're a reporter. You report. Get a byline. Part of the deal."

"*Shit*," she again said, shooting out of her chair, newspaper falling to the floor. She nervously ran her hands through her hair. Stared to the paper now on the floor.

"There something you wanna tell me?" Banner asked, picking up the paper. Kacey turned to him, opened her mouth…and turned away. Looked to the clock.

"*Shit.*"

Kacey reached for her bag, which she missed on her first attempt, but snagged on the second. She darted away from her desk, stopped, then spun around. Brought a hand to her head. Pulled hair away from her weary face, and said, "I, ah…just…just…oh, never mind."

Banner watched Kacey spin back around and beat it out the door.

Kacey floored it to the post office. Of course it wasn't open, but she had to mail that letter. Now. She hadn't been able to bring herself to do it when she'd first written it, but now had no choice. She pulled up beside the 24-hour drop box, and looked at the times. Ten-thirty a.m. was the earliest.

Double shit!

What had she expected this time of night? She wouldn't have time to deal with it tomorrow. She put the car in park and brought out the battered and folded-in-half envelope. Unfolded it. Smoothed it out. Looked to the address. *Mark and Emily Burnett.* She exhaled long and nervous, smoothing over the Forever Stamp to make sure it was really on there, and stroked the envelope. Then she extended her arm out the open window. Watched as she held the letter just in front of the open, narrow slot of no return. You drop it in, and leave it—if you try to get it back, you can find Federal charges levied your way, so you better be wholly sure this is what you really, *really*, wanna do, Little Missy.

Closing her eyes like a suicidal jumper, Kacey flicked the battered little package through the slot, and into postal service control. In about four days, they should have it. And they'd know. They already might know where she was, that little syndicated piece saw to that—why the hell hadn't she thought of that? Just another strike against her being journalist material. She had to let them know she wasn't quite ready to return. Not yet. No, that would take a little longer—and she might have to again move if they tried to come after her. Which would suck. She'd finally found a niche for herself, and she'd hate to have to pull up stakes again.

But hadn't Mark and her also found a niche for themselves, once?

One person's niche is another's ledge....

Kacey sat in her car, parked in her apartment complex's parking lot, her driver's side window stuck in the down position.

Well, that hadn't been real smart, had it? Couldn't she had made up a totally different name? Now Mark would see that and know where she was, *and* come looking for her. Just great. She'd set herself up wonderfully, this time. Tell me, girl, do you even use that God-given brain of yours? Now what was she going to do? Go back? Make up?

Could she?

No...she just wasn't ready...still had too many issues pinging around inside her head. It just didn't feel right, going back, now, as evil as that sounded. If she went back now, what was to keep her from doing the same thing again? She had to get right in her head, first, because when and if she ever did return, it had to be forever. No turning back ever again. In it for life. Raising a *child* and a loving family. A *husband*...

Kacey dumped her head into her hands and began to quietly sob. All her life she'd tried to be true to herself and what she'd wanted. She'd never wanted to desert her family...never, never in a million years would that have ever crossed her mind...yet she'd done just exactly that. It was a part of her now. Her legacy. There would always be some speck of doubt in Mark's—hell, *Emily's*—mind, now. Would she ever do it again? Did she really love them? She'd tried her best—but would her best good enough? Was she cut out to be a wife and mother? To be...*tied down?* As much as she thought she wanted to return to Mark and Emily, as much as what she'd just written Mark and Emily—*did she?* She still had so many oats of her own to sow. So many things and places she wanted to do and see, preferably with another who wanted the same—but bringing a child into the picture?, well, that about changed *everything.*

Was supposed to.

No going back. For the next eighteen years your life was solely devoted to another other than yourself—and maybe that was at the core of the issue: selfishness. She wanted what *she* wanted. She didn't like answering to anyone other than herself. Children were for *other* people...not her. Some were built to be parents, and she didn't count herself in among that crowd.

But, apparently, Mark did.

She still needed adventure and adrenaline...did Mark? It looked like he'd already sold out to the family and corporate world. He got a real job and had given up his old life. Traded adventure for diapers and *Sesame Street* toys. How did she really feel about that? Could she live with it?

That, she found, she really didn't have an answer for.

Enter Sheila.

If she was totally honest with what had happened, alcohol or not, she'd *wanted* to do it—oh, yeah, she had. The booze and Sheila's aggressiveness had just been convenient catalysts. How could she love Mark (and did she really?) and Emily, yet hop into bed with another—man or woman? What the hell was wrong with her?

Does one night with a woman a lesbian make?

Yes, she'd wanted Sheila that night, and when she'd seen her again in the newsroom the feelings from that night had resurfaced, and *that's* what had frightened her, what had sent her scurrying to the ladies room. She was afraid of what she might reveal by her presence, eye contact. That she might, again, show whatever interest had attracted them together in the first place, and was flat-out frightened. It had been hard avoiding her since, but there was just something about Sheila, something about her touch, her—

"*Kacey?* Oh, my God, it *is* you...."

Kacey jumped.

There, standing outside her car in the dark, and staring in at her with a look of grave concern, stood none other than Sheila Petrova.

"Are you all right?" Sheila asked.

"What—"

"Are you all right?" Sheila again asked. "I was taking a walk, over there," she motioned, "and, well, heard you—"

Kacey wiped away her tears, embarrassed. "I'm fine."

"I don't know about you, but where I come from, 'fine' doesn't look anything like…." Sheila put a hand to the door, peering in more intently. "Wanna talk?"

"What are you doing here? Why aren't you—"

"In Fort Meyers?"

Kacey wiped away more tears, sniffling and trying to get herself back under control.

Sheila looked away, then back. "I was, oh…I had some business to attend to, and—"

"What are you doing *here?* At my apartments?"

"Your apartments?"

Sheila stared at her.

"To be honest, I didn't know you lived here…I'm staying just across from you, over there," she said, pointing. "Isn't this a surprise," she said, giving a strained smile, and nervously crossing her arms.

Kacey stared at the Pelican Palms hotel across the parking lot, to where she'd pointed. "Wonderful. Now you're stalking me."

Sheila took up a more defensive posture. "No—that's not what I'm doing. Look, can we talk—I mean, without this car between us?"

"Oh, what, like alone and up in my apartment?"

Sheila looked away, hurt. "I'm sorry to keep bothering you," she said, and turned to leave.

Kacey sighed, then shot out a hand to her.

She paused; collected herself.

"No…*I'm* sorry. Again. I had no right to bite off your head like that. I apologize. It's just…I've been through a lot lately."

Kacey took another deep breath.

"Sure, let's talk. I think we really need to."

Kacey brought Sheila a cup of hot Chamomile tea, then sat on the couch beside her. The patio door was open, allowing in the cool, night, gulf breezes. Palm trees gently rustled outside beneath security lights.

Kacey settled in beside her, stirring honey into her own cup. They both sat in silence.

"How are you doing?" Sheila finally asked, in a low, concerned, voice. "I mean…really?"

"I've had better lives."

Both set down their teas.

"Why don't you tell me some of your story," Kacey said. "You know all about me…what brought *you* here. What brought about…your life decision."

Sheila waffled. "Well, I don't know if I know *all* about you—"

"You know enough. What brought on your decision to leave your family?"

Sheila straightened up.

"It's not much different than your own, really. When I left Jeff I was also confused. We'd had a great life together, plenty of money, powerful positions—he's also an executive in the industry—but toward the end that spark seemed to be missing. When we'd married I really did love him, more than life itself, but something happened along the way and I couldn't put my finger on it. Short of questioning my orientation. People—lesbians and gays—say it isn't something they so much as decided, as who they *are*. I don't know…I can't honestly say I'd felt trapped within my sexuality, but I'd always wondered about it. Experimented in college. It was a source of surprisingly great curiosity for me. I just thought everyone was as curious. I've since found that isn't exactly the case."

Sheila took a sip of tea.

"When I began to realize the propensity of my curiosity, I bought a *Playboy* to see if I really was attracted to my sex, and, to make a long story short, found I couldn't throw the thing away.

"I'd had my first *relationship* with someone from work. We'd been working late at the office, not unheard of in this business, as I'm sure you're discovering, one thing lead to another, and I'd had my first affair—with a *woman*. To say I was riddled with guilt was like saying what happened at Safe Harbor was a polite misunderstanding. I tried to keep it from Jeff—not to mention myself. Kept trivializing it by saying I'd been with a *woman*, so it hadn't really been an affair…but of course it had been. Full-on."

Sheila didn't look at Kacey.

"It was much more than what we did, or what I did *to* you."

Kacey looked down to her tea and took another, nervous, sip.

"And for which I'm eternally sorry—really I am," Sheila said, looking up to Kacey. "I hope to one day convince you of that."

"Anyway, I found I really couldn't keep my mind off this woman. It became a regular thing, and, of course, Jeff found out. Actually," Sheila said, growing fidgety, "he'd walked in on us."

Sheila cleared her throat, nodding. Her hands trembled and she took another sip of tea. Her face began to swell with emotion, but Kacey saw she quickly got herself back under control.

"He took it rather well for finding his wife in an affair…maybe it was the 'guy thing' of two girls going at it…I don't know. I had to give him credit, though, because he tried to understand it—*me*—but, eventually, we just unraveled and fell apart. It wasn't pretty."

Unable to hold back the emotion any longer, Sheila finally gave in to the tears. Kacey gave her her napkin.

"He even to letting me continue on…with this other woman…that he still *loved* me," she said, dabbing her tears, "but I realized I no longer loved *him*. Not in that way. I couldn't stay with him—I mean, how could I? So, I left."

Sheila let out a huge sigh.

"Fast forward to you, me—and here I am, today, one powerful lesbo in a male-oriented world."

The two sat quietly.

"Have you been with anyone else since—besides—me?" Kacey asked.

Sheila snickered. "You know, that's where this all falls apart. After I left Jeff and my first fling, I'd been with a handful of others…some of whom I even tried to make work…but none of them ever did. In none of them—not one—did I ever feel what I felt…when I met you."

Sheila turned to Kacey, giving her full eye contact. Holding her hands close in to herself, she continued.

"You and I are meant to be. I *know* this—"

Kacey shot to her feet.

"*Dammit* Sheila! I did *not* leave my husband because I'm lesbian!"

"I *know!*" Sheila said, also getting to her feet and holding her hands helplessly before her, "That's the problem. It's not like we're even on the same page! When I met you that night in the airport, something inside just…"

Don't say it…please don't say it…

"clicked. I don't know how else to describe it. Before or since, no one has ever affected me like you affected me. *Affect* me."

Kacey turned and faced her. Good God, if ever there was a moment they were having one now, Kacey thought. The two of them…in her apartment, late at night—no one would ever know—she could just go to her. Wrap their arms around each other and plant pure sweet love on each other's lips. Let the night, the moment, forever take them away. This is where Kacey could, once and for all, put herself to the test. Put herself out of her misery and find out, once and for all, was she,

(*one rendezvous did not a…*)

or was she not? Did she have a thing for women? For *this* one? Well, here she was, standing before her, hers for the taking, begging her with all that was her soul, for her to find out.

Sheila continued to stare at her, unaccusatorily, arms crossed loosely before her. She quietly sat back down, but this time in a chair adjacent to the couch. Her knees pressed tightly together. She stared down at the coffee table.

"I was *furious* at you," Kacey'd finally said. "You'd taken advantage of me…got me drunk, lured me up to that hotel room—"

"I know. I did. I'm so, so *very* sorry—"

Kacey closed her eyes, splaying her hands out before her. "No…you *didn't. I* let you do it. *All* of it."

Sheila was ready to say something, but just stared at her.

Kacey opened her eyes.

"I…I don't know what had gotten into me…I've never experimented with other women, I've always known myself to be totally and unequivocally hetero…and I've been with a fair amount of men in my lifetime before Mark, but something happened when I saw you that I'd been trying to deny ever since—I've been questioning whether or not I can ever return to my family. Would doing so be me living yet another lie? I left Mark and Emily because I was confused, trapped—couldn't handle settling down—but things have grown since then…questions have…*matured*…but I still don't have any answers."

Sheila again looked to her nestled hands. "So, basically, I've added another level of complication to your life."

"It's not so much *you*, don't you see?" Kacey said, kneeling beside Sheila. "It's not so much *you*…or whether or not you're a woman and I'm attracted to you…I feel that there's something much deeper here…but I can't put my finger on it. I don't know…."

Kacey got back to her feet.

"Maybe I'm just a reporter in the most superficial sense, but I feel a need to investigate this more...find out what it is that's bothering me. I'm not saying we have to have sex to find our answers—I'm not all that sure that's what I really want with you, but I'm willing to explore *us*...our *relationship*...if that's what you want to call it. I just don't know at what price. Do you understand? Can you live with that? I'm not saying I love you...but I definitely have deep feelings that seem to be somehow centered *around* you."

Sheila nodded.

"Does any of this make *any* kind of sense?"

Kacey sat back down.

"I can't believe I've blurted all this out to you...but I can't go on like this. I just found out today that my syndicated story is in *USA Today*—with my name plastered all over it. I don't know why I never thought about it before—maybe, with everything on my mind...I don't know."

Sheila looked confused.

"Oh—Mark and Emily!"

"Yes," Kacey nodded. "Now they know where I am. Then in walks *you*. So not only am I still trying to figure out why I left my family, now I have to figure out why I can't go back just yet! I was almost there, can you grasp that, Sheila, almost *there*. Except for one thing—*you*—or whatever all this is about surrounding you. But don't blame yourself, *please* don't, because it's so much more. There's something else at work, here, I don't know if you can feel it, but ever since I took on this gig, I've felt—and had—weird things happen. Others have felt it, too. There's something bringing us all together, and I feel it's coming to a conclusion with this trial. And it's precisely for this reason I can't return home. Not yet. I need to find out what's going on, not only with this story, but with you and me.

"That's why you found me crying—and that's why I'm spilling my guts to you...I need to face things head on, Sheila. No more running away. Which is why I wrote Mark and Emily. Trying to bring out whatever's directing us all together like this, and I have to do it *now*, so I can get my life back on track. For my husband, my daughter, my sake—and yours. We need to get on with our lives. And then I have to testify at this trial. How did my life get so messed up?"

Sheila shook her head. "Wow."

Kacey let her head fall back against the couch-back and wall. "God, I'm so screwed up." She sat back up. "What time is it?"

"One a.m."

"Great. Look…if you want…and don't read anything into this, but if you *want*…you can stay here, tonight. On the couch."

Unflinching, Sheila responded, "Okay. Thanks."

"I'll set the alarm for five, and we can grab a bite to eat on the way down? McDonald's or something?"

"Okay."

"Let me get you some bedding."

Kacey got up, rummaged around in the back a bit, before bringing out some blankets and a pillow. She set them on the couch.

"I've also put out a washcloth and some towels for you in the bathroom," Kacey said, "feel free to use anything in the apartment you need."

There was a long pause.

"Um, *nooo*, that's not what I meant—"

"I know," Sheila, said, smiling uncomfortably.

Kacey looked away, slightly embarrassed, conceded and nodded. "Yeah, well, okay. Anyway…we can stop by your hotel on the way out—"

"You okay?"

Kacey nodded, her face a mixture of exhaustion and confusion. Then she turned and left for her bedroom without another word.

Sheila looked longingly after her as she disappeared, alone, behind her bedroom door.

Chapter Nineteen

1

Kacey was having no luck as she fiddled with her car window, waiting for Sheila to return from her hotel with her change of clothes and gear. The driver's side window just wouldn't budge. She cursed to herself, as Sheila pulled up alongside in her rented Buick. Sheila exited her car.

"No luck, huh?" she asked.

"Nope."

"Well…what do you wanna do?"

Kacey sighed. "I'm just gonna have to leave it here, I guess. Is rain in the forecast?"

"It's supposed to be just another gorgeous day in paradise. Low nineties, or whatever it usually gets to around here. I just caught the tail end of the report on the radio. Have anything valuable in there?"

Kacey again sighed. "No…." She did a quick once over, checking her glove box and between the seats. "Nope—but I think I actually had some duct tape somewhere," she said, getting out of the car. In the trunk, she pulled out a battered half-roll of the gray friction tape, holding it up triumphantly. "*Ha!*"

"Hey," Sheila said, "and I think…I have something you could use to cover that opening with. I think I still have those plastic mats in the car."

Sheila opened the rear passenger side door and pulled out the folded up floor mats. "Here we go! We're set!"

Together they taped up the open window. When done, they both hopped into Sheila's car and made their way south, to Fort Meyers.

* * *

"You know," Sheila said, breaking the silence first, several miles south of Punta Gorda, "I kinda lied."

Kacey looked to her.

"Last night when I'd said I'd had business that'd brought me back here…I'd actually overheard you tell someone you were returning. I'd wanted to see you…talk with you…that's why I returned to Sunset Harbor."

Kacey nodded, pensively. "I see."

"Mad?"

Kacey emitted a short chuckle, then a long sigh. She turned back to her passenger-side window. "Nooo…I guess not. I'm really finding it hard to be mad—let alone stay mad—at you."

Sheila repositioned her hands on the wheel. "I was really afraid you'd be angry, but I had to tell you." Sheila paused. "Thanks for not being angry with me. I don't want any replays of that hotel. I want to be honest with you."

Kacey nodded, smiling. "I appreciate your honesty. Thank you."

Kacey looked to Sheila long and hard. She then did something she couldn't believe she did—and had she actually *thought* about it instead of just mindlessly acting, she probably wouldn't have done it.

Kacey reached out and took hold of Sheila's hand.

Squeezed it.

Sheila shot Kacey a surprised look, momentarily causing the car to swerve. Both continued to steal disbelieving glances to each other that ended up in smiles. Sheila regripped Kacey's hand. Kacey smiled and returned her attention back out her window.

Kacey couldn't explain any of this…but there was something about this woman beside her, with whom she was holding hands, that stirred an unknown, emotional whirlpool within her.

Why fight it?

Should she?

Just go on down and drown in the unaccountable attraction she felt toward her…

Closing her eyes, Kacey leaned back in her seat. Images about that traveling couple split up by those three marauders on that deserted plain filled her head…

As Kacey continued to hold Sheila's hand, she realized it really didn't feel much different from holding Mark's—or any other guy's, for that matter—except it wasn't as rough. Soft, warm. It kinda turned her on. Not only was she still one confused girl…but she was also

playing the bad girl.
Again.

2

Mark awoke abruptly and leapt out of bed.

He rushed into Emily's room, but found her peaceful and asleep, curled up on her stomach. Her tiny little fingers calmly clutched and unclutched air.

Quietly, he hurried downstairs and flicked on *NNC*. A spot on Yellowstone wolf relocation was just finishing up, when the newscaster filled the screen, babbling on about world and domestic events. That wasn't what he wanted to hear, dammit, they knew what he needed. But after a few minutes, when it became apparent that there wasn't going to be any Florida trial update, he turned on the DVR and replayed yesterday's recording. Of course there wasn't going to be any news…nothing happened overnight. The trial would start up in the morning, and he could check out *HLN's In Session* court television coverage and catch the whole thing live. But for now, he played the recording up to the spot where Kacey was in-frame. Paused it.

Tears immediately filled his eyes.

He brought up the scrap piece of paper where he'd written down the *Sunset Harbor Gazette* number he'd found over the Internet. No picture, but, sure enough, she was listed on their roster, along with her extension and e-mail. He'd tried the e-mail a couple times, but it kept coming back with destination rejects. For some reason he felt there was little time. That he had to get hold of her, now—*soon*—or something was going to go terribly wrong. Yeah, he was pissed at her for having left, was enraged actually, and that surprised him. He thought he'd been dealing with it fairly well, but when he saw her name…her *image* on TV, for chrissakes…he just lost it.

Why hadn't she called?

Written a letter?

Anything to let them know she was at least alive and *okay*. *Thinking* about things. Was she that heartless? Was the woman he'd married that changed? That spiteful?

And he had a deep and troubling sense that things were going…*weird*…that he hadn't much time to bring her back—if that's what he really wanted. That if he didn't do something *now* he was going to lose her *forever…*

But he had her number. Her extension at the *Gazette*, and that was something. He could leave a message, and if she was still any kind of thorough (which she used to be), she'd check her messages. She couldn't have changed that much.

Yet she *had* left.

Mark hit "Stop," put down the remote, and went for the phone. Dialed her number. He got that automated menu dialing service. He worked his way through the menu and punched in her three-digit extension.

His hands shook and his mouth had gone dry.

For someone who'd run out on *him*, *he* was the apprehensive one. Scared. Angry.

Mark got the generic voice-mail, the beep, then he spoke.

"I hope I got the right number, but, Kacey…."

Instead of all the anger he'd been feeling, he suddenly felt shaky and chilled.

He hadn't spoken to his wife *in seventeen months.*

Almost a year and a half.

What the hell was he going to say? *Should* he say?

Could he keep it together?

You only had one chance at a first impression. What was his going to be?

Mark inhaled deeply.

"Kacey…this is Mark. I, uh, know you obviously didn't want to be found…but I found ya. I, um, I'm not rushing to get together, or anything—or maybe I am—God, honey, I miss you—we just wanna know how you are. Are you *okay?*"

Mark composed himself. Man up! Stop sounding needy!

Taking on a more confident timbre, he continued.

"All right…look, could you call us? We miss you."

And then he said it:

"*We still love you.*"

Damn it!

He couldn't hold it in any longer. Mark squeezed his eyes shut, but it did no good. His voice began to waver and his knees buckled.

He simply couldn't do it. He just couldn't go on pretending he was all tough and stuff, when it came to emotional shit.

Mark pressed the phone against his shoulder and lost it. Here he was—Mr. Grown Man, Mr. Nerves Of Steel Spelunking Cave Diver—

yet he was behaving no better then his twenty-month-old daughter.

Mark hung up.

Good, Lord, why hadn't she *called?* Why hadn't she sent one goddamned letter? Did she really hate them that much? What the hell had happened to her that she had turned so callus...to him...their sweet, darling, daughter?

And why had he this sudden, overwhelming feeling that he was almost too late?

3

Tiger lay in his cot flitting between slight consciousness and deep dreamstate. But as he lay there, he felt he also lay somewhere else...some *time* else...there had been a battle...brutal and swift. He'd lain on

(*his back?*)

the ground...there was some kind of loud "white noise" somewhere...approaching...trembling the ground...and there was nothing he could do about it...

(*ants*)

Tiger bolt upright in his cot. He was sweating...profusely sweating...shivering. Blinking tearing eyes, he wiped at them with shaking hands.

He was going to die—he knew this—and not from old age.

How was one supposed to behave with that kind of knowledge? Was he supposed to feel content? At peace? Or just plain old fucking scared?

He got up off the cot and went over to the cell door's tiny view port. Peered out into the aisle. There was nobody there...at least, not currently patrolling the detention center. But there were other cells, behind other closed doors, and in those cells, others like him...he could *feel* them. Knew they were all there, and they were all in the same boat. Had all been involved on that same, fateful, day. That day they'd all gone crazy, and none of them had had a clue as to why. What had possessed them—for he was certain of that, as much as he never used to believe in such things. They'd all been possessed, had to have been. How else could you explain such atrocities? He didn't know the others, not one of them, but he damned-well *knew* he wasn't a murderer, just as he was sure the others also weren't murderers. Okay, maybe he'd

BBQ'd some flies under a magnifying glass as a kid, but that didn't make him a *killer*.

Was this supposed to be some kind of Karmic repayment?

Tiger left the door.

What the hell were they all going to do? Plead insanity? Yeah, sure, that made no sense, since they'd already all been checked out by that court-appointed shrink…even to his semi-muddled way of thinking, he figured what would probably happen was they'd try to pick one of them as the ring leader and turn it into a cult thing. Like Manson. There was no religious zealotry involved, he guessed—at least not on his part, and if he wasn't one, he was sure others weren't, either—no, they'd try to pin it on a cult-leader figure, and do a Manson rerun.

And Tiger was getting the most unsettling feeling that he was their man Manson.

4

Fort Meyers Judge's Chambers
August 3rd, 7:56 a.m.

Howard Stoker sat behind his desk in his Judge's Chamber. He had nineteen minutes before the trial, and there was something uneasy gnawing at him. He felt extremely edgy…apprehensive. Something was hovering about the edges of his consciousness, trying to punch its way through. "Tuning in" just before a trial wasn't good, threw his concentration off. He didn't have much time. Looking to the clock, he set his watch alarm for ten minutes, placed it on his desk, then grabbed a clean sheet of paper and a pen. Put them on the desk before him.

His hands immediately went into motion.

Jerking, sporadic action across the page produced what looked like a poor attempt at chicken scratch. He looked to it dispassionately. This wasn't right…there *was* a presence. A huge one. As large and vast and deep as an ocean—but it wasn't quite making its way through to him. There was some kind of difficulty in…translating…the information…

Stoker stared at the paper…then balled it up and tossed it away into the trash.

He rubbed his eyes, then closed them behind his palms and leaned over on his desk.

Then bolt upright.

He'd been standing in some distant land…a grassland of some kind—God, how could he had *forgotten* that?

Or had it just been a dream?

But he'd been there—wherever "there" was, and however he'd "been" there—and had felt what he felt now…that same extraordinary, mind-boggling presence.

Something big was coming, and it was *incredibly* powerful…

Eight-fifteen found Stoker confidently striding through the passageway into the court room, on day two of the trial. The bailiff announced his entry.

"*All rise, the Honorable Howard Stoker III, presiding.*"

Stoker took his position at the bench, busily arranging documents before him, while also subtly taking stock of the atmosphere. It was packed. *HLN* cameras were positioned everywhere. Both counsels awaited his go ahead, and the homeless defendant, Tiger, sat beside his counsel, Ms. District Attorney, Frenchie Benét. And still…that persistent presence continued to hover about him. He looked to the jury. The head juror nodded they were ready. For a moment—just a moment—they all looked…different. Angry…*dirty*…

"The state of Florida and Lee County are ready to begin. Counsel?"

"Your Honor," Prosecutor Harry Gordon, announced, approaching the bench, "we request Kacey Miller be brought to the stand."

Stoker nodded.

Kacey Miller arose from the gallery and made her way to the stand. Sworn in, she took her seat. A box of tissues awaited use on the banister before her.

"Miss Miller," Harry began, "for the record, would you please state your full name and occupation for the court?"

Kacey nodded, her hands twitching nervously below view inside the witness box. She was glad she'd mailed that letter now, because with her syndication and now *HLN*, there was no longer anywhere to hide.

"Um, yes, Kacey Kelly *Burnett*," she said, leaning into the microphone.

"There's no need to lean into the mike, Miss Burnett," Harry said, smiling.

"I work at the *Sunset Harbor Gazette,* as a special reporter on this case. I'm, ah, separated from my husband at the moment, and have been using my maiden name of 'Miller.'"

Harry nodded. "I see. How do you prefer to be addressed?"

Kacey paused. Boy, surprises abounded. Her answer came out totally without thought. "'Burnett' would be fine for the purposes of this trial."

"Thank you, Mrs. Burnett. Now, could you please tell us how you happened to be at the scene of the crime, on March 10, at the ungodly hour of one-fifty in the morning?"

Kacey shifted in her seat, and oddly enough, memory of one of her nightmares flashed before her. The one with Fisher instructing everyone on the fine art of evisceration.

"I was driving the streets of Sunset Harbor scanning police bands. Ever since I moved here, I'd been trying to find a job, and thought I'd try my hand at reporting. Anyway, on this day, I guess I was in the right place at the right time, so to speak—no disrespect to the families intended, your Honor," she said, addressing Judge Stoker.

"None taken, Mrs. Burnett."

"Well, I picked up the call not far from the retirement home, actually. I was coming back from the direction of Port Charlotte, and walked on in—"

"You walked into a crime scene?" Harry interjected.

Guiltily, she realized her mistake. "Ah, yes, I'm sorry," she said, casting Fisher a quick look, who sat in the gallery, "but I had to get the story, I was the first one there."

"What did you do then?"

"Well, I searched out—"

Kacey paused. She wasn't supposed to tell anyone about her contact with Detective Fisher, but didn't think that applied here. She looked to Fisher, who nodded to her to continue.

"So I searched out someone I knew."

"And whom would that be?"

"Detective Thomas Fisher."

"And how do you know him?"

"Well, I've been quite a burr in his side, actually, since I moved here, trying to find stories."

"So, it's fair to say, then, that both your paths had crossed more than once?"

Kacey nodded, again leaning into the mike. "Yes."

"Okay."

"Anyway, when we spoke, he told me to stay out of the way, but also that he couldn't tell me much about what'd happened. He gave me the impression that whatever had happened, was pretty grisly—something this town had never seen before."

"And what did he do next?"

"He left, but I pursued an interview with a couple—"

"Jack and Hedda Hocker?"

Kacey suddenly found herself swelling with emotion.

Jack and Hedda. *Murdered.*

Dead and gone.

Married *sixty-one years*; met in Korea, he the Marine, she the nurse. It was unfathomable that they were gone after having been so full of life. The whole entirety of their lives, snuffed out in an instant. She tried to respond, but her words had grown thick in her throat.

"Mrs. Burnett," Harry asked, "are you all right?"

Kacey shook her head, bringing a hand to her face, which had suddenly grown hot and red. Harry requested water be brought to her.

"No, I'm not. They were wonderful people and a lovely couple, and now they're dead—they're all dead."

A bailiff set a glass of water down before her. Kacey paused, took a sip, then grabbed several tissues from the Kleenex box.

"Take your time, ma'am."

Kacey blew her nose, then continued: "Yes. Jack and Hedda Hocker."

"And what can you tell us about them—your contact with them?"

"They were—initially—the only survivors from the attack—"

"Objection!" Benét said, coming to her feet. "Innocent until proven guilty."

Kacey nodded. "Sorry. I meant until the suspects entered this…place…and allegedly did what we are, here, trying to prove or disprove."

Benét nodded.

"Continue," Harry said.

"Anyway, I managed to get the Hockers away from there after they'd talked with police, and I figured, would I want to go back to my home after having been attacked in it?—no—so I brought them back to my apartment. Gave them some safety, warmth, and coffee. And we talked.

"Pretty gutsy move, not knowing them from Adam. What'd you talk about?"

"Everything. How they met, their history together, the incident."

"And what did they tell you, about the incident in question?"

"That they'd been in bed, had been awoken, and that Mr. Hocker—Jack—had confronted the assailants, killing them."

"He did? He killed them?"

"Yes—two of them. Jack was a thirty-three-year retired Marine. A Master Gunnery Sergeant. I don't think he ran away from too many things.

(*unlike me*)

"He was amazingly fit at 79, they both were."

"I see. And what did they proceed to do, then?"

Kacey found a chuckle had escaped from her.

"Well…Hedda'd grabbed the phone and their hunting rifle, and Jack had grabbed a knife and a .45, and he charged outside to meet the alleged assailants, I guess you'd call them."

"Charged outside?"

"Yes. That's what he said. He took out the ones attacking them, then charged outside to help others. He said he took out a few before the police arrived."

"Impressive," Harry said, raising an eyebrow.

"They were both impressive people."

"Fast forward to the next day. What can you tell us about what happened then?"

Kacey again hit an emotional vapor lock.

"I'd heard," she said clearing her throat, "I'd heard there'd been an accident…out on the Interstate. Got a call from my editor who had told me that the Hocker's had been murdered. I rushed to the scene and found a multi-car pileup, but all three bodies had already been removed, two of which were Jack and Hedda."

"And the third?"

"After he'd done his business, their assailant had taken his own life. He'd jumped off the overpass. The killer did. One of those overpass bridges."

Kacey took another sip of water and grabbed another couple tissues.

"And is there anything else you can tell us about what you found

(*the ring*)

"at the crime scene?"

"No."

"Thank you. You may step down."

Kacey nodded and stepped down, but not before grabbing extra tissues. Kacey returned to her seat in the gallery to find Sheila giving her a comforting look…and squeezing her hand. "You did great," she whispered.

"Boy," Kacey whispered back, "I didn't expect all those emotions to come out like that. Wow," she said, wiping her reddened nose and still-tearing and reddened eyes. Sheila patted her leg in response.

"So," Sheila continued, "should I call you 'Miss Miller,' or 'Mrs. Burnett'?"

"Sorry!" Kacey said, whispering.

Sheila winked back. "Don't worry about it," she whispered, squeezing her hand.

Morning transitioned into afternoon, as witnesses and police testified to the brutality of the crimes at the Safe Harbor Retirement Community and their role in it. From the residents' friends and family who escaped all harm, to Detective Fisher and P.I. Banner. All in grisly, exquisite detail. And, above all, Kacey was somewhat taken aback by the judge's apparent impassive demeanor throughout the testimony. Had he seen that much violence that it no longer affected him? The jury and audience were the ones who'd exhibited emotion, sometimes out-and-out gasps and tears at the details. Kacey scribbled pages of notes, but also doodled a cart, pears and onions, and lonely barren landscapes before the day was over.

Throughout most of the day Sheila had secretly from the rest of the world held her hand. And Kacey had liked it.

Liked it very much.

Chapter Twenty

1

Ronda Ettbauer continued talking to her fourth-grade West Cheyenne Middle School class as she drew her marker across cell walls. She left behind deftly drawn, strange, angular characters that looked a mixture of Tolkien and Arabic, and spoke the language associated with the script unhesitatingly, though in a part of her damaged consciousness, way, way back in her darkest, most recessed corners, she knew she didn't know the language. Ronda's mind, however, was quite clear and lucid on this matter, as flooded as it was with scenes of battle and history in faraway lands she'd never been to, and never would, at least in this lifetime.

Did one really need to travel to faraway places if you'd already been there?

Outwardly, Ronda may have been mumbling to herself, but in her mind she was projecting clearly and succinctly to her attentive class, as she properly enunciated this new language, her class dutifully taking notes. My, she thought, what wonderful, hardworking, and diligent students! No one made jokes, giggled, or passed notes behind her back, which seemed vaguely odd to her. They were all focused on her with rapt attention, taking in all she taught. Sure, they asked questions, but that's what classes and teaching were all about.

Another class member raised a hand, and Ronda turned to address her. The nonexistent child asked her nonexistent question in this new language, and Ronda answered back in perfect diction and grammar. The child nodded, satisfied with Ronda's answer. Ronda returned to her task on the wall before her, just as the end-of-day bell sounded, so she dismissed her last class for the day. Wonderful! Now she could spend the rest of her day totally focused on her own work, and not have to answer any more questions. She loved teaching, loved the children, but she'd also found something else that was equally as important. Like her parents always used to say: *Your chores first, then you can play.* She had done her chores, now it was *her* time.

Through her mind the images flew…they'd started with something about a blue-gray wolf and a fallow deer giving birth to a powerful blacksmith with a fire in his eyes…birthed along a river on the other side of the world. There was much violence and deceit, but there was also much wisdom and spirituality…and incredible *power*.…

2

Sheila paid the several-dollar-per-car toll, and she and Kacey made their way through the Sanibel Causeway onto the first spit of land.

"Wow," Kacey exclaimed, "this is absolutely *gorgeous.*"

"I told you you'd love it," Sheila said, alternately looking to Kacey and the causeway. "Even the hurricanes couldn't erase the beauty of the place."

Kacey stared out her opened window, amazed at lazy and fluffy cumulonimbus clouds hanging low over the deep-blue waters of San Carlos Bay. Pelicans, herons, seagulls and more filled the skies above. She inhaled fresh sea air and allowed its balmy breezes to blow through her hair.

"Oh…this is utterly…*beautiful!* I've lived here over half a year and hadn't yet gotten down this way—I didn't even know it existed!"

"I've vacationed here a couple times before, had a couple of assignments. I know of this great restaurant. It has a great view of the bay, and, where we'll be sitting—I made reservations—we'll be able to see porpoises—"

"Porpoises! How wonderful!"

"They jump right out of the water. The restaurant's actually on Captiva Island, a sister island farther up at the end of this road."

As they drove up and over the raised causeway, Kacey again looked to Sheila. She didn't say anything, just took her in. Smiling, Sheila returned the gesture. Kacey turned back to her opened window.

"Wow…what kind of bird is that!" Kacey asked, excitedly pointing out the bird as it flew high across their path.

Sheila leaned forward. "I'm not positive, but I think it could be an osprey. I get some of those birds-of-prey mixed up."

"Man, there are so many beautiful places on earth…I wish I could visit them all—*oh!* Pull over!" Kacey said, pointing to a small beach just up ahead. "I want to get out and check this place out! Get into the water!"

Sheila pulled over onto the white, sandy areas of one of the many roadside beach turnouts. This one was slightly shaded with both Sabal palms and Norfolk Island Pine, underneath which was a picnic table. A man in waders was out in the water, fishing. Kacey was out of the car before Sheila'd applied the parking brake.

Laughing and giddy with childlike amusement, Kacey kicked off her shoes, rolled up her Capri pants, and immediately waded out into the water.

"Oh, this is *paradise!*" she exclaimed, splashing about in it. The fisherman glared at her. She caught his evil-eye and apologized, calming down. Staring out into the bay, Kacey's tone changed. "Sheila," she said.

"Yes?"

"There's something I haven't told anybody about what happened to the Hockers, out on the Interstate."

"Oh, please don't tell me you perjured yourself."

"I'd found a ring."

Kacey closed her eyes, allowing the stiff sea breezes to caress her body and soul.

"So, you did perjure—"

Kacey sighed. "Well, maybe a little—but there's something about it—and it's probably not even related to the murder—"

"Kacey, you don't know that—"

Kacey faced Sheila. She produced the ring from her pocket, slowly uncurling her fingers. It rested in her palm.

Sheila looked to it. "Oh, my God...."

"What?"

Sheila reached out to it, but didn't touch it. "I've...I've *seen* this—"

Kacey closed her hand snatching it back.

"You *what?* How could you?"

Sheila again reached out to Kacey.

"I...I don't know—I only know that I have seen that ring before. Maybe in a dream, I'm not sure...but...I *know* I've seen it before...and there was more...could I...could I please see it?"

I will be with you...

Kacey slowly opened her hand and allowed Sheila to take it. As soon as she'd taken hold of it, Sheila's knees grew weak. Kacey helped her over to the picnic table in the shade. She eased her to the bench, studying her.

"What's going on?"

Sheila stared at the ring.

"Kacey...this is really weird, and I don't pretend to know how else to explain it, but somehow—*in some way*—I *know* this ring. This is *sooo* creepy...it's almost like you and me...I know how much you don't want to hear this, but I can't explain how *right* we are together, and this...this *ring*...is somehow connected to us, to everything—"

Sheila brought a hand to her head and closed her eyes. "Oh...there it is again—"

"*What?* There's 'what' again?"

"Images...a couple...traveling across a barren steppe. Just the two of them," she went on, eyes closed, hand to her head. "They're *attacked.*"

Kacey backed away.

Sheila opened her eyes.

"Now what's the matter?"

Kacey stood before her, mouth open, hair streaming in the wind and seagulls screeching above. She inhaled the sea breeze and suddenly felt incredibly distant from this place—yet as if she were wrapped within Sheila's warm, loving embrace.

"How did you know that! How...did you know about those people?"

Sheila stared at her blankly.

"I've had these same dreams," Kacey said, "images, scenes— whatever you call them. *I've had the same dreams you've had!*"

3

The officer accompanied Detective Fisher into the Punta Gorda detention center.

"You're not going to believe this. I swear, I've never seen anything like it before."

"What the hell is it, for God's sake?" Fisher again asked.

The officer grunted. "I really can't tell ya...you're just gonna have to see it for yourself. It's the craziest thing I've ever seen."

Fisher was led through the detention center's entrance, and taken directly into the rear of the jail, to Ronda Ettbauer's cell.

"This is Ronda Ettbauer," the uniformed officer informed, unlocking the cell door. "Take a peek." The officer stood back, a look of amused amazement on his face.

Fisher looked to the officer, then entered the cell.

Covering every inch of wall, floor—and most of the ceiling—were creepily written characters Fisher had never seen before. Drawings. In black permanent marker.

Thousands of them.

Kacey and Sheila were seated at their table in the restaurant facing Pine Island Sound. Kacey wore her mysterious ring up against her wedding band.

"I can't believe we've had the same images. This is...I don't *know* what this is."

Sheila settled in across from her. "I know. I knew I felt something about you when we met, but this...this is incredible. Surreal. Made-for-TV."

"Do you think it really means anything?" Kacey asked, "you know, like we're really twins, separated at birth kinda thing?"

Sheila shook her head. "I doubt it—and hope not; don't want to add 'incestuous' to my list of qualities," she said, smirking. "What I'm wondering is if all this—the ring, those murders, *us*—are all tied together in some crazy metaphysical knot. There's just a strange feeling about it. Don't you feel it?"

Kacey nodded.

"It wasn't until those murders that I began having those weird dreams...those nasty nightmares. And there was meeting you, and all my guilt—"

"I *knooow*," Sheila said, touching her hand, gently. "You don't have to go into it. But I really feel there's something beaucoup strange going on, here. I don't usually have weird things like this happen to me, I just report and produce them. And your dreams...they're so vicious."

The two sat silently.

"I'm glad you told me about them, though," Sheila added, "but I'm sorry I've been so nasty in them."

"Oh, it has nothing to do with you, I'm sure—"

"I'm not so sure," Sheila said, "I believe that when we dream of another there's an unconscious acceptance on the part of the person we're dreaming about. At least that's what I've been told by some of my more enlightened friends. Of course, it could also just be some Freudian or Jungian imagery on your part, as well. I mean, really, who knows?"

Kacey looked to her.

"We did a piece on dreams and dreaming a year or two ago. Anyway, why I've chosen to take on such vicious symbolism—because that's what I believe it really is, not literal, just symbolic—I can't explain. Unless our mutual desert images are somehow involved. And who knows—with all this violence and research on violence you've been immersed in, it might just be as simple as an unconscious projection, or whatever the official term is."

Kacey again nodded.

"But how does this ring have any meaning to me? To *you?* I mean, I just happened upon it on the Interstate—it might even have been there long before Jack and Hedda even found their way there. If I hadn't been there—if the paper hadn't even hired me—*I* wouldn't have been there—"

"But you *were*, and that's the key. The paper *did* hire you, we *did* meet, and you *did* find it. See what I mean? There's a certain synchronicity to everything. A serendipity. Things like this—I really believe—just don't happen for no reason. It's too weak an argument for such an incredible array of circumstances.

"Could I see the ring again, please?"

Kacey handed it over to Sheila, who took her hand first, tenderly examining it, then the ring. Kacey again found herself excited by the warmth of Sheila's touch. *What was it about her and her touch that no other woman had so similarly effected?* Were they linked? Were they—

"Oh, my God," Kacey suddenly blurted.

Sheila looked up, still holding her hand.

"What if—and I don't know that I necessarily dismiss the idea entirely—but what *if*," Kacey said, looking to Sheila, and focusing in on her deep, dark, eyes, "we both really are tied through some past life?"

A server appeared at their table, depositing water and iced tea. Kacey and Sheila released their hands, smiling uneasily to the server.

"Need more time?" the server, a grinning pimply twenty-year-old asked.

"Yes, please," Sheila answered. The server departed.

"I can't believe I actually said that," Kacey said, looking away, embarrassed.

"That could explain the shared images," Sheila said. "I mean, I always feel a sense of deep, all-pervading nostalgia while around you. I didn't want to say anything for fear of further weirding you out, but I've wondered the same thing. When I first met you…there was a deep—unaccountable—sense we'd met before…or *knew* each other from somewhere."

"Well, since you brought up the dream stuff, and all, I just made the leap. I mean, I've also thought about past lives, but there's no real proof about that sort of thing, is there?"

"We haven't done a piece on past lives," Sheila said, sitting back in her chair, "but I've heard and read the intelligence. Drs. Ian Stevenson and Jim Tucker. Big names. Peter Ramster. Science frowns upon it of course, but I kinda feel that if there's all this overwhelming circumstantial evidence—everybody's talking about it, even if they say they don't believe in it—then there's *got* to be something to it. I mean, how do you explain people swearing they've been places they haven't been before—in *this* life? Or the feeling we blithely dismiss as 'déjà vu'? And anyone interested in this stuff knows about that English lady who went so far as to travel to Ireland to actually put her nagging questions to the test…to find out if she'd actually lived before in that coastal town—*then actually found the remaining members of her children from that life.*"

"No way!"

"She actually *found* them, Kacey, told them stuff only a mother—*their mother*—could have known. How do you explain that? There's got to be something to it. Maybe you—me—we're all tied to this image we keep seeing. Of those men chasing off that other one, leaving that woman behind to be captured. Maybe —"

"Here comes the server again—I think we better order," Kacey said, and opened her menu.

"This is just goddamned weird—hey, get off those things!" Fisher shouted to an officer who started walking over what Ronda had written all over the floor. "Throw some plastic over this stuff—I don't want any of it messed up—and get Pam in here, with her camera."

"Sorry." The officer nodded. "I'll get right on it."

"Then get me a linguistics expert—*pronto.*"

The officer again nodded and left the cell.

Fisher looked to Ronda, as she stood quietly in the corner on the other side of the cell, staring at the floor. She grasped a worn permanent marker in a still-twitching hand.

"What is this stuff? Arabic?"

Ronda said nothing; didn't look up.

"You know what it means?"

The uniformed officer returned with some large sheets of folded-up plastic and a couple other cops.

Ronda shook her head.

"You don't know what this means?"

"I just write it. It fills my head...until I let it out."

"Is it filling your head now?"

Ronda shook her head. "No...but it'll be back."

Fisher motioned for the cops to position the plastic over Ronda's strange script on the floor.

"It will?"

"It's not done."

"It's not? Well, how about you trade me your markers for pen and paper, instead?"

Ronda looked up to him as Fisher held out his hand. Fisher gently removed the marker from Ronda's cold, clammy hand.

"It's not over," she said, "it's never...ever...over."

Mark had rushed home as quickly as possible. While hurriedly setting up Emily for her feeding, he played with the DVR remote and recording menu to find his recording of the past ten hours of *HLN*. As much as he was expecting to see his wife, he was still shocked to actually *see* her. *Hear* her, there, on television. He paused in mid-feeding, hitting the remote's "Pause." He stared at Kacey's image. She sat among the rest of the onlookers, beside a stunning

(*beautiful mommies*)

brunette. They seemed to know each other. It took Emily's wailing to bring Mark back to reality, and realize his pulverized squash had dripped onto the feeding tray instead of making it into Emily's beckoning, hungry little bird-like orifice.

"Oh—sorry, Buckaroo," he said, cleaning up and shoveling a couple quick spoonfuls into her mouth. He turned back to the screen, still paused. "There's your mommy, honey. There she is. Big as life. On TV."

Emily flailed her hands about some more, and tried to say words that vaguely amounted to "ma-ma." Mark faced her, and something knotted in his stomach.

Mommy.

He lowered the spoon and stared at his precious little angel who was busy trying to smear more pulverized squash all over her mouth, again from the feeding tray.

"Oh, my God...you don't even know how to say your own mother's name."

Mark stared at Emily as if truly seeing her for the first time. *My God*, he thought, *what has become of us? How dare we bring another life into this world and not have her know how to call out her own mother's name!*

More pounding by Emily on the feeding tray again broke Mark's train of thought. No more leaving messages. He had to get them back together. Even if she hadn't wanted to be found, she *had* been...it had to have happened for a reason. And he was going to find out that reason, so help them.

Kacey returned to her hotel room without Sheila. As much as she enjoyed her company and the day they'd had, she really needed to be alone for the night...and neither of them had felt up to driving back to Sunset Harbor. Sheila's hotel room was on the first floor, while hers was on the second. Kacey collapsed on the queen-sized bed and closed her eyes.

What was she doing?

It was bad enough she still wasn't sure what she wanted to do about Mark and Emily, but to intentionally complicate matters with another *relationship*...that was a recipe for disaster. Everyone knew the Golden Rule: stay out of relationships for at least a year after divorces—but even that was for *divorces*. She still wasn't sure that was what was in the cards for her and Mark. Though they might be separated (if Mark hadn't served up any papers, that is), they weren't *divorced*. Not yet. Not officially. There was still a chance for reconciliation—

And just why had she left, anyway? She seemed to have forgotten...was it something about dirty diapers? Feeling closed in? A loss of identity?

And did *any* of that matter anymore?

There were people getting murdered in their sleep, and she was worried about changing diapers and being called a—

Kacey bolt upright.

Mommy!

Did Emily even *know* the word? The term? The *emotion?*

Mommy...

Had Mark taught her—

Mommy!

How would she call out to her if she ever returned?

"Oh, what have I *done*...."

Kacey got back to her feet, closed her eyes, and placed a hand to her head. She stood that way for a moment, then opened her eyes. She kicked off her shoes and stripped down, making her way to the bathroom. Putting on her robe, she stared at herself in the mirror.

What had she become?

Was she the same person she'd been a year and a half ago? Could she, really, ever have any kind of a relationship with Sheila? Would Mark take her back? Would *Emily?*

She lowered her head in resignation and cried.

Kacey turned on the TV for company and opened her planner. Dialing her newsroom number, she entered her code, and began to take down her list of messages...when she came to Mark's first message. Her heart stopped. It felt as if her blood had actually reversed in its tracks. Nearly dropped the phone. She'd only heard one word from him, when she'd tried to call him that one time, but now, to hear full *sentences*...she'd thought she'd forgotten what his voice sounded like.

It was all still there, baby...the emotion, the love...the *concern.*

His voice flat-out bowled her over, there was no question about that. It was even a *good* message...not too much emotion, just a "hello, I know where you are" message, and it tugged at her heart. But it was the next one that pissed her off.

He was coming to see her, he'd said.

No!

All her longing and confusion went out the window—how *dare* he! Didn't he get her letter?

Of course not, she'd just mailed it.

Damn him! No...this couldn't be...she wasn't ready!

Son of a *bitch.*

Kacey slammed down the phone and shot to her feet. He simply couldn't do this...he had to stay where he was—let *her* come to *him.* This couldn't be forced...he had to allow her her time, he—

Kacey went back for the phone. Dialed the outside line, then the number that would take her back a million years to her previous life…her life with Mark and Emily and diapers and full-on motherhood and responsibilities. She closed her eyes, trying to calm herself—spewing to him at full-tilt wasn't going to do anyone any good—but he had to be told to back off. He had to let her make up her mind, and come back when *she* was ready. Nobody was going to swoop down out of the sky and steal her off and away, again. *Nobody.* Not ever again, goddammit. *Never.* She would *die* first. *Die…*

When a sudden scary thought entered her mind: *not ever again?*
What "again"?
And where had all that anger come from?

4

Ronda Ettbauer sat naked and huddled in the far corner of her new cell. Her cell mate was a young Mediterranean woman who huddled in a corner opposite to her, silently but emotionally watching her with bloodshot eyes as she calmly, methodically, tore off tiny strips from her orange jumpsuit and lay them out neatly upon her thighs, perfectly spaced and parallel to each other. When Ronda had six narrow strips, she calmly began ripping wider ones, some four-to-six inches in width, and also began setting those calmly and perfectly beside each other on her thighs. Her eyes were wide and pained, and thick tear stains carved down her cheeks. Her mouth was taunt, her chin clenched.

When she'd gotten what she thought were enough, Ronda carefully set the remains of her jumpsuit on the floor beside her, then picked up some of the smaller strips, rolled them up tightly, very tightly. When the first one was complete, she brought it up to her right ear and carefully, forcefully, screwed it into her ear canal as far as it would go. Then she picked up the next strip and began rolling it up, and when she was done, turned her head and jammed that narrow wad into her left ear. Working her jaw, she managed to clear her ears and force both wads in a few extra centimeters more.

Satisfied, Ronda then took up a couple of the wider strips and began to roll those into a slightly elongated ball the size of a small tangerine. She looked to it, compressing it a couple time in her hands, then compressed it once more and crammed it in its entirety into her mouth. She gagged at first, feeling immediately panicked, but, Strong

Soul that she was, closed her eyes and willed the gag reflex and panic to depart. Her cell mate had jumped when she gagged. Once calmed, Ronda reopened her eyes and tried to inhale through her mouth and found she couldn't. The Mediterranean woman began to fidget, whimpering and pacing like a frightened dog as she watched Ronda in her corner. She began to cry, trying to hide her face in the corner, but was unable to *not* watch.

Again satisfied, Ronda now picked up the narrowest remaining strips and rolled those up into tiny, tight, wads. When she had two of them ready, she carefully inserted them up her right nostril as far as they would go. One right after the other. It hurt, but she kept at it. No pain, no gain. Then she picked up the other two strips, and, with her cell mate quietly weeping from her corner, finished the job....

Chapter Twenty-One

1

Tiger sat before the lawyers in the tiny, Spartan, interrogation room. He scratched his bushy heard with fingers that were still not quite clean under the nails, no matter how many times he'd scrubbed them. He sat in his jumpsuit, they in their prim and proper business suits. This was the moment he knew'd been coming. It'd been put off by time, ant attacks, a murder or two, his spa stay in the local hospital, and his jail time, but there would be no more delays. Like his journey here, there was no stopping it. His time on earth would now have a definite end date…a last meal.

Tiger blankly stared at those before him out of pure, unadulterated exhaustion. He was tired…tired of the nightmares, the images, the constant, *constant* wind blasting through his consciousness. It had long since become more than just noises in his head. He actually felt the winds and screams in his bones. He just wanted it all over, as quickly as possible. No matter how things were to get screwed around into knots in the court room, he knew what had happened. What he—and all the others—had done. Whether or not anyone could put it into words, or allow themselves to admit, consciously or unconsciously, there was no controlling what had happened. At least not in any way he knew. And with this knowledge came a peace, one that only someone in his position could ever truly understand.

Tiger gradually tuned back into the men and women sitting before him. How long had they been talking to him?

"…are you listening to us?" Gordon again asked. "Do you understand what we're telling you?"

Tiger looked into Harry's grim face and set jaw as if he'd just awoken from a deep sleep.

"I'm not stupid, sir," Tiger said.

It took such an effort to talk anymore.

Gordon looked to Benét and his companions. "Well, that's good to know. You understand the gravity of your situation? That we're calling you to the stand? Now would be a real good time to come clean."

Tiger stared back at Harry with weary, bloodshot eyes. "I know you don't believe me, but I didn't lead anyone into anything. At least not that I know. I've already been through this with you folks, the cops—everyone. I have nothing more to say. I'm just...."

Tiger paused. He could see his interrogators were annoyed, confused. One side wanted him up there, the other didn't. Can't please everyone.

Tiger sighed, dropped his head into his hands, then ran his hands through his matted hair.

"...I'm just...*tired*. I want it all to just be *over*. Whether or not I die, doesn't matter. I just want to be done with this...thing...this...*life*."

"Why do you say that?" Benét asked.

Tiger looked up to her, incredulous. "Why, so I can start over, again," he said, "do things right for a change."

The suits chuckled among themselves.

"Mr. Tiger," Harry said, "or whatever your—"

"That is my real name."

"When this is over...there'll be no starting over for you. It'll be the death penalty."

Now it was Tiger's turn to chuckle as Gordon and Benét set to arguing. Tiger stared at Harry, allowing the wind to wash over him, through him—grow stronger, for it was still there, echoing hollowly in the recesses of his mind.

Waiting...

"Mr. Gordon," Tiger said, smiling, "and I really don't mean to be disrespectful, believe me, but you know as well as I about what I'm saying, don't you? *Hai? Harry Gordon san? Dore kurai kakarimasu ka? Mata itsuka o-ai dekiru desho.*"

Gordon, who'd been leaning across the interrogation table at Tiger, ready to no doubt lay into him again, suddenly shot back to an erect position, a mixture of fear and incredulity on his face.

2

Kacey once more found herself sitting in the gallery beside Sheila as the trial continued. She looked to the disparate group of people gathered here. What had brought them all to this one place and time? Were they the equivalent of ambulance chasers? Nothing to do at home, so, hey, let's go on down to the courthouse and see us a *hangin?* Kacey's gaze met Banner's, and they nodded to each other. Banner. Genuine tough guy. Vietnam vet turned P.I. Must have had an interesting life. Now, he was just a quiet guy living the quiet, small-town existence—until one of his best friends met the wrong end of an angry blade.

And to her left, Detective Tom Fisher. Now, this was interesting…how could she find him physically attractive, yet also be attracted to the woman she was presently holding hands with? *Bisexual?* As Sheila left her hand for her Blackberry, Kacey looked to her hand. She'd been holding another woman's hand while her husband and daughter were up north wondering about her. None of this made any sense. None of it. And a ring from nowhere that seemed to have an emotional importance to both her *and* Sheila? A mass murder that involved a bunch of seemingly unrelated suspects? What the hell was going on, and how did she find herself in the middle of it?

Then there were Mark's voice mails. He never would have found her had she had her wits about her and kept her name out of the paper—or better yet, used a pseudonym. How stupid was that? Had she *wanted* to get caught?

And now Mark was all hot on the trail to come on down to

(*see us a* hangin)

see her. Great. She was hoping he'd gotten her letter by now, but more importantly…she'd left *him* a message. That had been hard to do. She'd hung up on the first attempt. Her mouth'd opened but nothing'd come out. She'd froze. But he hadn't been there to pick up, anyway, so she'd again tried, after she'd let her anger drain out of her—an anger with which she was quite surprised by its intensity—this time left a message. Calm—a little shaky, perhaps—but calm and collected. She said "hello" to her daughter, told her how much she missed her, apologized profusely, and then left a little white lie: that mommy was on a reporting assignment, and when things had worked themselves out ("worked themselves out," that had been the phrase she'd used), she'd come home.

What a laugh.

And she was far from making any decisions about returning home. She had to make up her mind one way or the other. Sheila…or Mark and Emily…

So, she'd left Mark a message. *Honey*, she'd started, closing her eyes and realizing she'd use the endearing familiar by habit, *Honey, I'm not right yet. I'm still…confused. As much as I may want to return, I haven't straightened things out in my head, yet, and I can't return until I do—do you understand? I can't have you and Emily coming down here in search of me—that won't make anything better and might actually make things* worse—*do you want that? I'm so volatile right now, I'm not sure how I'd react, and I really don't want to make things worse. Please*, please, *stay there; don't come down. Give me my space…I need to do this, to see it to completion. I promise, once I make up my mind, I'll let you know. I'll be open and honest, one way or the other, and if I choose to return, I know we'll need to do some serious talking, counseling, but…just not* now—*okay?*

That had been her message before she'd been decapitated by the beep. Once she'd started talking she found she'd wanted to *keep* talking…to spill her guts. And the familiar emotion did begin to weasel its way back in. When she realized she was talking into a machine she'd help Mark buy, in a house they'd both bought, in the kitchen they both made dinners and love in, well, the tears just didn't stop—*after* she'd hung up.

Why was life so damned hard?

Why couldn't answers to problems be easier? Problems are what they are, but shouldn't the answers be *easy?*

And, most of all—where had Mark been?

It was late at night, why hadn't he been home? Why hadn't he picked up the phone? True, when she'd initially called, she'd dreaded him being there, but once she got into the call, she'd hoped—*prayed*—he'd pick up, so she could hear his voice and actually get real-time responses, maybe even put her daughter (*Emily*, use her name, dammit!) on the phone so she could wail and cry and tell them both she would be on the next plane home…

"This ought to be interesting," Sheila whispered to Kacey, bringing her back to reality. Without looking to her, Shelia added, "You okay?" She turned to her, regrasping her hand. "What's the matter?"

"I'm fine," Kacey whispered back. *Just fucking fine….*

3

Mark had taken the day off to sit before their TV and watch the

Safe Harbor murder trials live on *HLN*. Kacey's call had been too much for him to deal with. He'd been in the bathroom when she'd called, and when he'd rushed out and heard her voice…realized it was *her* talking…he just couldn't bring himself to pick up the phone.

Would it have done them any good?

Would he just be a babbling idiot on the line and ball his brains out without getting in a word edgewise? Or would he unleash a fury of pent-up rage upon her? He didn't know, and his body didn't give him a chance to find out. He just stood there, Emily sleeping soundly in bed, unknown to her, her mommy on the phone. But what probably more than likely kept him from answering was her pleading with him to *not* come find her. To stay put. To *not* come. To allow her her space.

Good God, *how much more frigging space did she need?*

So, as much as a part of him wanted to pick up that phone, the emotional pleading for him to *stay away* (again, the words "*not* come," "*not*" this, "*not*" that), and the ensuing verbiage that offered possible resolution to this whole, damned mess, all kept him at bay.

And maybe just the pure, unexpected shock of having her on their phone late at night had also paralyzed him.

He'd frickin' woosed out.

Perhaps a greater man would have been able to pick up the phone and bitch her out…but not him. He always did the right thing; was the one who gave up personal fun and excitement to change diapers and take on a desk job. *He* was the one who did what was necessary to change his lifestyle into that of a *family*. *He* was the one who'd caved while his wife had not. She'd kept the adventure…and maybe that was part of what kept him from answering. *She* had guts. The guts to not give in, to not sell out. To stand up for what she believed in whether or not it was right or hurt other people's feelings.

He wasn't like that.

He actually cared about what others thought. Always did the right thing. When skydiving, did so conservatively. Scuba dived well within dive limits. Did everything by the book. Even when they had Emily. He'd read all the books, did all the research. Changed his mindset. *For them*. The family. It was no longer about him or her. It was about *family*.

But Kacey had been able, however angry it made him, to stick to her guns in the face of adversity…of pissing him—and their families—off, and do what *she* wanted to do…and that was gutsy, and maybe, just maybe, that's what really kept him from answering the phone: *he was afraid of facing her.*

Of facing all the guts she'd had that he hadn't.

4

"Your Honor," Defense Attorney Frenchie Benét said, "We call Billy Williams to the stand."

Billy Williams glanced nervously about him as he came to the stand. Sworn in, he was directed into the box. He continued glancing nervously about him as Benét approached.

"Mr. Williams, would you kindly state your full name and occupation for the record?"

Billy shifted uneasily in his seat, cleared his throat, and answered, "Billy Raymond Williams. I'm—I was—a software engineer."

"Your first name is not 'William'?"

Billy shook his head. "No, ma'am, it's 'Billy.'"

Defense attorney Frenchie Benét nodded pensively approaching the jury box. "And what do you mean by 'software engineer'?"

"I design complex operations systems for military space applications."

"Could you be more specific?"

"No ma'am, I cannot. It's classified."

"And you hold the proper security clearances and need-to-know?"

"Yes, ma'am."

"What is that clearance?"

"Top secret."

"I see. And is it safe to say that the government performed a detailed and thorough background investigation on you before granting you your clearance?"

A little more at ease, Billy nodded. "Yes, ma'am. These clearances are very expensive and thorough. They don't just hand them out to anybody."

"I see. So you're telling this court that the government—our Federal Government—deemed you a low-to-nonexistent security risk?"

"Yes."

"Thank you. Now, Mr. Williams, what can you tell us about the events of March 10th, at approximately one a.m.?"

Here, Billy again grew nervous, fidgeting in the box. "Not much." He looked down to his hands.

"Excuse me?"

"I mean that it's largely a blur to me. Foggy." Billy shifted and twitched. "I...I don't recall how I got here...or anything about entering that community. I-I have...vague images of entering homes, but all I really remember is being arrested."

"You have absolutely no recollection of your actions—of committing any crime?"

He shook his head. "No."

"Objection!" Harry Gordon said, shooting to his feet. "We are not trying Mr. Williams on his memory, but on his actions."

"Overruled," Stoker said.

"Were you read your rights?" Benét continued.

"I was."

"Did the police tell you what you were charged with?"

"Murder."

"How did you respond?"

"I was in shock—still am. I couldn't believe I'd committed *any* kind of murder."

"Why is that, Mr. Williams?"

"I'm what might still be called a conscientious objector."

As Kacey scribbled notes, she gave a surprised look to Sheila, who also looked to her.

"I see." Benét let the words hang in the air. "So...you've never hurt nor killed anyone?"

"My parents were both heavy into the peace movement and raised us accordingly. I even hate killing ants or bugs."

"Thank you, Mr. Williams."

Benét returned to her seat. Prosecutor Harry Gordon got up from his table and approached Billy, who grew increasingly agitated, finding it hard to look Harry directly in the eyes.

"Mr. Williams, it is true you work for the military?"

"I'm subcontracted to the government, yes."

"Does your work find its way into satellites and other applications."

"I can say that my work has many applications, most of which I cannot discuss." Billy again shifted in his seat.

"Is it safe to say that your work finds its way into battlefield conditions, where men and women—possibly children—are killed?"

"I create software, sir—"

"There're no software packages in fighter and bomber aircraft? Spy satellites? Equipment used to gather intelligence, to kill and maim? To allow others to do the same?"

Billy grew silent. Looked to his feet. "I design *software*, not bombs—"

"Answer the question, please."

"Yes."

"So, as a conscientious objector—a pacifist—your work is, in essence, more than likely used, all or in part, to help hurt or kill...whether or not it is in the defense of our country."

Billy gritted his teeth. "It could be."

"Now, were you or were you not found inside the home of Fran and Jeffrey Hubble, on March 10th of this year, at approximately one-twenty-five a.m., in the Safe Harbor retirement community, covered in blood, and holding a bloodied—"

"Objection!" Benét argued. "This information is already a matter of record!"

"Overruled," Stoker replied.

Billy nodded. "That's what I've been told."

"Oh, right...because you can't remember," Harry said, spinning around and returning to his table. "But, correct me if I'm wrong," he said, grabbing a folder, which he waved before the witness stand as he returned to him, "don't you have a good memory? I mean a *really* good memory?"

"Objection! Your Honor, Mr. Gordon has already pointed out we're not trying my client's memory!"

"Mr. Gordon?" Stoker asked.

"Your Honor, I am merely pointing out Mr. Williams' own words. My direction will shortly come to light, if your Honor will allow."

Stoker nodded.

Gordon placed a sheet of paper before Billy on the witness stand railing. "I have here Exhibit D. Mr. Williams, do you recognize this?"

Billy winced as he leaned over to examine the document.

"What is it?"

"My résumé."

"Could you turn it over and read for us—"

"I know what it says."

"Could you please enlighten this court as to what it says, then...verbatim?"

Billy shifted in his seat like a cornered animal.

"It says...'I possess a unique trait that would greatly benefit the company and national security.'"

"And what would that trait be, Mr. Williams?"

"A photographic memory."

"A photographic memory.

"Let the record show Mr. Williams correctly recalled the phrase in question—to the word."

Harry retrieved the résumé and returned to his seat.

5

"Mister Magruder," D.A. Benét began, "do you consider yourself a good man?"

"Yes."

"A kind man?"

"Yes."

"An honest one?"

"I do."

"And," Benét said, turning to the jury and smiling, "even though not gifted with a photographic memory, a fairly decent one?"

Nervously, Paul Magruder answered, "Ah, yeah, pretty good. I guess."

"Now, can you explain to us where you were and what happened in the early morning hours of March 10th?"

Paul Magruder shifted in his seat on the witness stand. "Well, I can't exactly say where I was up to a certain point—"

"Why is that, Mr. Magruder?"

"Because…I don't recall it all."

"Why not?"

Magruder paused before answering, fidgeting. "I…I don't know. It's like it was all…a haze—until I ended up here."

"In Sunset Harbor?"

"In jail."

"And do you know why?"

"No."

"Does it scare you?"

Magruder nodded. "Yes." He glanced toward the jury.

Benét stood directly in front of Mr. Magruder.

"Mr. Magruder, in your estimation, did you commit the crimes attributed to you on that aforementioned night in March?"

At this point Magruder grew highly agitated.

"*No!* I did not! I am absolutely *not* a murderer!"

Benét raised her hands in a calming gesture. "Please, Mr. Magruder, it's okay. Relax."

Magruder calmed down, but remained obviously edgy.

"There's no way I could have done any of those...things. I'm just not the killing kind."

Benét nodded. "So, you're telling us that you don't feel you'd committed these murders, you don't know how you got there, or what you were doing there—just that you found yourself in jail at the end of the night—morning, early morning?"

"Yes, ma'am."

"Mr. Magruder, were you administered a polygraph—"

"Objection!" Harry said, "inadmissible except by stipulation! I've heard no such—"

"Overruled, Mr. Gordon." Judge Stoker said, "whether or not they are, in this particular case I am quite interested in the outcome. Proceed, Ms. Benét."

Benét nodded. "Again, Mr. Magruder, have you been issued a poly?"

He nodded. "Yes."

"The results?"

"I was exonerated."

The court room erupted into agitated commotion. Kacey and Sheila exchanged looks.

"Order in the court!" Stoker demanded, slamming his gavel. "*Order!*"

"Thank you, sir. I have no further questions."

Harry approached Magruder.

"Mr. Magruder...what's the 'killin kind?'"

"Excuse me?"

"You're telling us that even though you were caught, literally red-handed...covered in blood and gore, in the actual throes of committing yet *another* murder...that you took a polygraph saying you were innocent—*and passed?*"

Magruder nodded, nervously. "Y-yes."

Gordon chuckled in confusion. "Mr. Magruder...could you please explain that to me? How can that be? Either you did it or you didn't. It can't be both. Maybe you have a certain mental prowess that enables you to evade these tests?"

Magruder cast the court room an anxious look. "As I told the Miss Benét, I can't explain it. All I know is that I know I couldn't *possibly* have committed any murder—"

"Mr. Magruder—the human condition has proven itself time and again that once-thought peaceful men and women can and do, indeed, commit the most heinous of acts, given the proper circumstances."

"I did not kill those people!"

"Mr. Magruder—"

"Look, I don't know who did—but it wasn't *me!*"

"Mr. Magruder, if you can't control your outbursts, I will be forced to remove you from this court," Stoker admonished.

"You did kill, shoot, then brutally bludgeon to death eighty-six-year-old Matilda Jenkowicz?"

"No, I did not!"

"Roll her up in a carpet, then tenderize the hell out of her with a number 34 Rawlings baseball bat?"

Harry tossed pictures of her battered and brutally deformed corpse on the stand's railing before him.

"No!"

"Mr. Magruder, I am warning you—" the judge reminded.

"Or seventy-three-year-old Henna Pearlman? Tying her dead-or-dying corpse between a post and her car—" Gordon continued, also tossing her mutilated corpse pictures before Magruder. Magruder shoved them all off the stand, onto the floor.

"I did *not!*"

"Brutally ripping her apart—"

"Lies! All *lies!*" Magruder shouted, his voice cracking as he shot to his feet. He stood in the witness box, visibly shaking, tears streaming down his face. "I don't know who did these things, or why you think *I* did—but I *didn't! I didn't!* Why won't anyone believe me!"

Before Stoker could utter the command, three bailiffs were on him, but Magruder fought them off. Stoker pounded his gavel trying to restore order to the court room, as those in the gallery again grew agitated. Benét tried to shout above the din that her client's testimony be stricken from the record, as Harry Gordon calmly returned to his seat, a faint smile across his face. He cast Benét a triumphant look.

"Mr. Gordon!" Judge Stoker admonished, "if I find you resorting to such theatrics in my court room, again, I will consider you in *contempt.* Do you understand me?"

Gordon nodded. "Sorry, your Honor. I didn't realize how agitated Mr. Magruder would get."

"I don't believe that for a moment."

"Your Honor—" Benét continued, but was interrupted by the Stoker.

"Ms. Benét, I am leaving the last witness's testimony intact. We will recess until tomorrow morning." Stoker banged his gavel. "This court is in recess until eight-fifteen a.m., tomorrow."

Chapter Twenty-Two

1

"Dr. Preston," Harry Gordon said, "would you kindly tell the court your profession and why you are here?"

"I am a state psychologist and was ordered to examine each of the defendants for mental competency to stand trial."

"Dr. Preston, with your indulgence, I'd like to revisit some of our facts, if you would."

Preston nodded.

"Could you please, again, tell the court your findings?"

Preston sighed. "I found them all, without exception, fit to stand trial."

"What about Mrs. Roberts? Was she not catatonic?"

"Later, I was able to get through to her and get her to communicate."

"And by what means did you ascertain this judgment?" Harry asked, facing the jury.

"All the standard battery of tests, direct and indirect interrogation, passive observation, and so on."

"So, in your professional opinion, these defendants are psychologically and emotionally fit—capable of undergoing these proceedings?"

"In my professional opinion, yes, they were all quite aware and cognizant of who they were, and why they were arrested and incarcerated, however…a few did deny their actions—"

"Yet denial is not a prerequisite to insanity nor murder?"

Preston nodded. "No, sir, it is not. Just because someone denies a crime—or an alleged crime—doesn't mean they didn't do it."

"So, in your concerted, expert, opinion, each of the defendants are sane enough to stand trial. Our defendant, there, is sane to stand trial."

"Yes, they are. He is."

Gordon nodded, returning to his seat.

"Counselor," Stoker said, looking to D.A. Benét, "do you wish to cross?"

Benét got to her feet, slowly and pensively approaching the witness stand.

"Dr. Preston—do you believe in past lives?"

"Excuse me?"

"Did you or did you not discuss the topic of past lives with your patients?"

Dr. Preston remained calm, but paused before answering. "We only discussed what my patients wanted to discuss."

Benét quickly returned to her table and grabbed a thick folder, flipping it open.

"And did you discuss with Mr. Billy Williams, and our defendant, Tiger, here—or anyone else—just such topics?"

"Yes."

"Why?"

"During the course of my examination these patients all brought up the subject—so we discussed it."

"In what way?"

"Well…during the course of my observation of Mr. Williams, for example, I found him doodling barren landscapes and ancient warriors. He talked of…being attacked, and killed in a sand storm…in a desert. When I pressed him on this, he refused answers, insisting I wouldn't understand."

"He just started talking about this to you, out of the blue? Just like that?"

"Yes."

"And the others? The defendant?"

Dr. Preston looked to Tiger, who unnervingly stared back at her.

"Tiger, as he calls himself, was a bit more vocal about the whole thing—"

"How so?"

"At first…he talked about hearing all this wind when there really wasn't any."

"Wind?"

"Yes, like Mr. Williams described earlier. Apparently, since he first became homeless, he said it had all started with this hollow wind screaming through his head—curiously, this is a common link between all the suspects I am unable to explain. Tiger also told me of a warrior on horseback he'd met in the middle of winter in New York City."

Benét snickered.

"You're telling us that a *ghost* warrior appeared to a homeless man in the middle of New York City, in the middle of the winter—and you believed him?"

"Ms. Benét, I believe *he* believed it."

"Is there anything else?"

"Yes." She again looked to Tiger, who, this time, just stared straight ahead into space.

"Go on."

"Tiger and the others believed this aberration compelled them to commit these crimes. That the wind, horses, and voices inside their heads had forced them on. Niggled them—"

"They hear voices in their heads, telling them to kill, yet you still declare them sane?"

"How do you interact with your own mind, ma'am? We all have some form of a 'voice' in our heads…we just don't always act out what we're thinking. In every other manner of my investigation they are all, as unequivocally as anyone in my position can determine, sane."

"Go on."

"When I left the suspects alone in the observation room, they all doodled out depictions of ancient warriors. Battles."

"How did you know they were ancient?"

"Well, in Tiger's case, for example, they looked it. He's an extremely accomplished artist for someone in his situation. But both Mr. Williams and Tiger—as well as others—told me so. When I asked who they were drawing, they all—even Tiger—became fearful of these images…angry even."

"Dr. Preston, I must insist—the subjects are on trial for murdering seventy-two individuals, talk of past lives—yet you continue to deem them mentally competent?"

"As I've said, despite traditional methodology, my findings show they exhibit no psychological disorders during my investigation of them. All subjects know their position in time and space, where they are, what they're charged with, and—"

"Doctor, they believe wind and long-dead warriors made them kill!"

"That is their belief."

"Do you believe in them, Doctor?"

"I believe they believe it…"

"Do *you* believe in reincarnation?"

"I do…but, whatever the reason—"

"Do you believe these murders are past-life related?"

"Objection!" Harry shouted. "Past lives? Hocus-pocus…Ms. Benét already stated—"

"Overruled," Stoker said.

"In your professional opinion," Benét continued, "do you believe the voices, wind, and drawings indicate my clients were exacting past-life vengeance?"

Preston inhaled, then answered, "Yes," sending the court room into a blizzard of whispers and chuckles.

"Order, people!" Stoker shouted.

"Thank you, Doctor," Benét said, returning to her seat.

"Mr. Gordon?" Stoker asked.

Prosecutor Harry Gordon returned to the stand.

"Reincarnation? Past lives? With the court's indulgence—and at the risk of going all Juan-Martinez-and-the-seven-dwarfs—I'd like to examine this for but a moment, if I may?"

Stoker nodded.

"Doctor…do you think murderers should be freed because they're just getting even from other lives, since—using reincarnational theory—we all never really die, anyway, so what's the point, right?"

"We're all responsible for our actions. Events from one life do not justify murder in another."

"But, we all know how fallible memories are…well, most of us, anyway. Do people with photographic memory ever recall past lives?"

"I have no data on this—"

"Then who's to say our suspect's memories are accurate? Do you remember what you ate three weeks ago? What you wrote in your diary when you were six?"

Preston remained stoic; looked back to Harry without supplying an answer.

"The witness would be testifying to somebody *else's* life…this person testifying wasn't there…or may have been, but certainly not in the subject's present body. It would be hearsay—inadmissible in court."

"That certainly sounds logical—"

"Normally, when a witness testifies, we cross-examine, redirect, as we're doing now. Call other witnesses…but how could we find witnesses from other lives…," Harry smirked as he turned to the jury, "unless we're all part of the same 'Past-Life Mystery Club' and hang out together across our various lives?" He turned back to the court. "And even if no other witnesses exist—in or out of our time—we always have physical evidence, can investigate sensory abilities…did they wear glasses? Are they deaf? The jury can evaluate how he or she appears. But, if he or she's testifying about a past life, can we really pursue any of this?"

"Counselor," Stoker admonished, "get to the point."

"Your Honor, I'm trying to put this past-life fable to bed."

Stoker impatiently waved him on.

"Doctor…does our present-day defendant know whether his memory is accurate or edited? What if it is part of reincarnation to reset—distort—any so-called past-life memories?"

"I can't answer that. You've thrown a lot at me, but until this is studied further—"

"Studied *further?* I don't think so! As much as I've rattled on we're not here to study past-life theory, Doctor. We're here to solve a murder. A *mass* murder. Thank you."

"I think you've said quite enough for several lifetimes, counselor," Stoker said. Muted chuckles filled the court room. "Ms. Benét, redirection?"

D. A. Benét smiled and rubbed her hands as she came to her feet. "I'm not sure I could follow such a stunning display of legal soliloquy, your Honor, however, in any case—no redirection."

As Preston departed the stand, Banner, who'd been checking a text message on his cell phone, got up and whispered into Harry's ear. Harry nodded, then got to his feet.

"Counselor? Is there a problem?" Stoker asked.

"May we approach the bench?" Harry asked, looking to Benét. The judge motioned Benét and Harry forward.

"Your Honor," Harry began, "I've just been informed that another of our suspects has committed suicide, exposing new evidence that may directly impact this trial. I request a recess."

"Who is this person and what is the nature of this evidence?" Stoker asked.

"Ronda Ettbauer, your Honor, she was in the Punta Gorda facility, and was found…well, suffocated…with an as-yet unidentifiable script covering her cell walls. Once translated and analyzed it may affect the outcome of this case."

"Very well." Stoker pounded the gavel. "Court is adjourned until eight-fifteen a.m., Monday, so that counsel may incorporate new evidence."

Chapter Twenty-Three

1

Fisher, Gordon, Benét, and a uniformed officer entered what had been Ronda Ettbauer's Punta Gorda detention center cell before her transfer and subsequent suicide. Large sheets of semi-transparent plastic covered the entire floor, and in the center of the cell stood an older, professorish-looking man adjusting his glasses and studying the walls. A camera was slung over one of his shoulders. On nearly every inch of available jail cell space—including most of the ceiling—were strange, vertically scripted characters.

"Oh…my God…this is…*incredible*," Harry said, mesmerized.

Equally awestruck, Benét was speechless.

"This is Dr. Arty Ofo," Fisher said, introducing them to the man in the center of the cell. "He's a linguistics expert from Tampa."

Ofo placed his face up against a wall, better repositioning his bifocals. "Fascinating," he said, "every stroke…meticulous; *perfect*. From the same direction. Written by someone who looked as if they'd been scripting this their entire life." Ofo turned to the group. "Who did this? Are they still here?"

"No," Fisher said. "She took her life this morning."

"Most distressing, most…unfortunate," he said, absentmindedly returning to the wall. "I would have loved to have met her. And you say she'd never written this before?"

"Unknown, sir, but highly doubtful—she'd been a grade-school teacher from Wyoming."

"What do you make of it?," Harry asked.

"Uighur Script, Middle Period Mongolian, thirteenth century—"

"Mongolian?" Harry asked.

"Yes—why? You expected something else?"

"It just looked…Arabic, I guess…."

"Oh, no, Arabic—to the untrained eye, anyway—is smoother in construction, written horizontally," Ofo said, gesturing before the wall. "This is all vertically constructed. Arabic also uses a small circle, or *sukuun*. You see all these little dots? Mongol, or Uighur Script, doesn't have—"

"We'll take your word on it. Thanks, doctor," Harry said.

"Forgive me. Suffice it to say this is definitely Mongolian. Adapted from the Sogdian, or present-day Iranians. So Arabic was a good guess, actually," Ofo said, momentarily turning back to Harry. "Sogdian was derived from older Aramaic. The Uighurs and Mongols are now thought to have coincidentally developed their language from the Sogdians, versus the Mongols borrowing the thirteenth-century Uighur tongue, as had been previously considered. This script was popularly used only up until 1941 when Cyrillic became the standard. But it's still called 'Uighur Script' in—"

"Ah, thanks," Harry said, chuckling, "I only understood—well, not even half of what you just said. What does it say?"

"Again, Forgive me. It'll take me a little while to translate it all."

"How long?" Harry asked.

"A couple a days...."

"Can we get something by Sunday? We return to trial Monday."

Ofo nodded, pensively. "I suppose so."

Ofo unslung his camera, took a light reading, then began snapping pictures. Harry and the others stood back out of the way. Harry turned to Fisher.

"She'd stuffed rags into her nose, mouth, and *ears*? The nose and mouth I can understand—but *ears*?"

Fisher shrugged. "Maybe she just wanted some quiet time."

2

Mark dumped his bag on the floor, the mail on the counter, and set Emily down in the living room. He removed his jacket and flicked on the TV with the remote, immediately changing the channel to *HLN*. Sitting on the edge of the couch, Mark began to separate Emily from her jacket. The TV came to life with a court scene already in progress. The Safe Harbor Murder trial.

"Laddle-laddle-laddle," Emily merrily intoned, now free from her jacket, tongue dancing between her lips. She stalked off toward her toy pile, rocking her elbows and shoulders in that mock-marching-band parade across the living-room floor. On the televised *HLN In Session* replay, Judge Stoker declared court recessed until Monday.

"*Damn!*" Mark said, getting to his feet. He tossed the remote onto the coffee table and snatched up a giggling Emily up from the floor.

"You silly little Buckaroo!" he said, playfully rubbing his nose into her belly, blowing raspberries. "You hungry?" He swung her through the air and deftly inserted her into her highchair.

Emily giggled wildly, also continuing to sing her "laddle-laddle-laddle," then opened her mouth in her wide birdlike fashion.

"Guess so!"

Mark strapped her in, then went about preparing Emily's dinner of strained peas and turkey, and a sippy cup of apple juice. Grabbing a beer for himself, he sat down and began feeding her…when one of the envelopes from the mail pile caught his eye. It was just a plain white (creased) number-ten envelope, but it somehow called out to him. He gave Emily another spoonful of peas, then reached across to the envelope.

It was from Kacey.

Mark stared at the envelope until Emily's short chirps and open-mouthed pleading reminded him of his need to continue feeding her. Giving her another mouthful of turkey he carefully, nervously, opened the missive.

"*Dear Mark and Emily, I have no idea where to begin, so I might as well just start writing and see where it takes me….*" was as far as he got before Emily again protested for lack of nourishment. As he fed her, thoughts of "can't we just be friends," and "I've found another" shot through his mind, as well as the last time they'd made love. Feeding Emily with one hand, he read the letter with the other. Phrases like "*I really tried to make things work…but something inside me just snapped…*" and "*I'm really messed up, and I can't come back until I find out what's the matter…*" hit hard, and he repeatedly ended up missing Emily's mouth with an unsteady hand until he had to stop altogether.

He couldn't believe she'd actually, *finally*, made contact after all this time. *Her.* Kacey—his wife—Emily's mother.

She'd finally made contact. A phone call and now this letter. This letter had been in *her* hands, scribbled with ink that had issued forth from a pen that had known *her* touch. These words represented thoughts that had originated within *her* head, and with which she had taken the time to put to paper—to *communicate*. To *them*. This was the closest they'd gotten to her since her infamous and ignoble departure.

Why the hell had she left, dammit? Why wasn't she coming back? What the hell was going on, and wasn't this all just a dream—a frigging nightmare?

It was all here, in this little south-Florida communiqué, and in it she'd pleaded, just like her voice mail, that they—*he*—not come down. Not hunt her down (there was the flurry of those "not" words again). That they (*he*) leave her be and allow *her* to come to them. On *her* own terms. She was eternally sorry for all the hurt she'd caused (he saw what he swore were tear stains all over the letter)—and was still causing—but that she didn't know how else to deal with it. She said she felt "close" to figuring it all out, but it was still a tenuous thread, at best, one that could easily snap, should he come running…

Yet, through all this letter had to say, one thing surfaced through the haze as he put it down, Emily screaming in the background: *all this assumed he'd take her back.*

Would he?

Should he?

If she'd done this once, what was to prevent her from doing it again? Would another catastrophic event again elicit the same flight response? Could he risk raising their child in a family like that? Could *he* risk getting emotionally reinvolved?

And what did he really feel toward her?

Mark stared at his daughter, suddenly conscious of the fact he hadn't fed her in several minutes and that she'd been wailing away, hands hanging uselessly, palms up, on her high-chair tray. Mark realized, with perhaps the greatest clarity of his entire life, how much he really, *really* loved his daughter, and would never, *ever*, allow anything—or anyone—to *ever* hurt her, again.…

3

Harry sat behind his desk back in his Sunset Harbor office, studying documents at just the other side of nine p.m. He leaned forward into a pensive steeple with his fingers pressed against his lips. These people—to the man and woman—*had* committed the crime, there was precious little doubt of that—but there was something distinctly odd to the entire case. And now this latest development of the Mongolian characters scrawled across an entire jail cell's floor, walls, and ceiling (how had she done *that?*), by a another suspect who'd also taken her life. What was it with all the languages? *What was it with him understanding the Japanese Tiger had spoken to him?*

Had he imagined it?

Had it really *happened?*

He hadn't the time for this shit!

He had a trial to win. And how the hell did his so-called "Japanese experience" fit into any of this?

Did it?

Or was it just a case of repressed imagination suddenly set free? An ill-timed coincidence? Japanese…Chinese. Were there any so-called facts tying the two together? He was seeing a shrink because of sleep and stress problems, while Ronda had committed murder, been confined to a jail cell, and just seemed to spontaneously begin writing a no-longer-used Asian language she knew nothing about. Yes, she'd been a teacher, but her background professed absolutely zero knowledge of anything Asian, let alone *Mongolian.*

And that had been an interesting and unexpected tack Benét had taken—*past lives?* Jesus, what'd possessed her? Okay, so Benét was obviously playing the insanity card, but…as much as he'd argued against it—for he didn't want any insanity pleas to win this case—he really wasn't as confident as his rebuttals presented. Past lives? How could something like that really exist? He supposed anything was possible, when you got right down to it. If there really was a Supreme Being, One so all-powerful, he supposed He/She/It *could* create a world where past lives existed. Exist.

What *would* be the tense?

But, short of that documented lady who went off to Ireland in search of her then-seventy-year-old "kids," and that little "WWII pilot boy," where was the proof? Even all that could be explained away. Nobody knew better than a lawyer how easily and convincingly arguments could be made for either side of a coin. *Who's payin ya, baby…*

Harry's head suddenly drooped forward…then snapped back awake. Man…he needed some serious sleep. A year off. He'd had a long day, a long week, and now he had to do some serious research into what to do next…

As Harry's eyes closed, he swore that there were more plants in here than he remembered…tall, tree-like things…the scent of an ocean, and who was—

* * *

Harry wasn't just watching a movie, he was actually participating in it.

But how had he ended up in a theater—he was supposed to be home...in bed?

And he actually smelled trees...a briny *sea?*...felt the energetic wash of sea breeze across his face...

Watched as foreign warships approached.

Good God, they just kept *coming!* Filling the ocean before them; noticed how one man in particular (he wasn't sure how he knew it, he just did) a samurai, oversaw some kind of...*bakufu* (the word just popped into his head) operation.

Samurai?

He was the one from his experience with Arnot.

The very same guy...and he stood on a shore...no, it was more than that...he stood on a beach before some sort of fortification...a wall...*ishitsuiji* was the word...

Thousands upon thousands of ships...it was mind boggling...the most he had ever seen in his entire life, and, most likely, he—or anyone else—would ever see...they stretched from horizon to horizon. It was *unimaginable* the amount of ships he saw on the ocean, and a new emotion began to fill him, one with which he wasn't familiar...an abysmal sense of impending dread. Battle was near, and they all might very well perish...

The entire flotilla lay anchored out just beyond the island...ships full of horse and men. Harry not only inhaled the smell of air and sea, now, but of camphor.

Camphor trees.

Already they had repelled the advancing horde twice: once at the north end of their *ishitsuiji*, and the other at another beachhead elsewhere. The samurai's—*his*—pulse quickened. They were ready for a new plan, a *daring* plan...

Under the cover of night, Harry gave the go ahead, and hundreds of *Kamakura bakufu* samurai loaded up hundreds of skiffs and fishing boats and took to the water. They commenced hit-and-run attacks—

slaying the invaders and burning their ships. Night and day they did this. The fear that he'd felt earlier had quickly dissipated, as he and his warriors turned the siege into a *bakufu* victory.

But what was fear?

Samurai knew not that word, nor the concept, as much as *he* might. Was *he* feeling it—or the samurai? Was there a difference? Samurai were built for fighting.

Not fleeing.

Gripping the railing of his seat, Harry watched as ships burned in the night.

Railing? There were no railings attached to theater seats…

Standing in the boat, Harry looked behind him. They were all there, right where they should be. His men. Pikes and swords at the ready. Quiet. Focused. Harry looked to himself. To his samurai general garb. Looked to his hand as he gripped his sword—not too tight, not too loose. He looked up. They were closing in fast on their target—

No thinking was involved. Harry boarded the ship.

He saw from the light of their flames and closer proximity that what they'd boarded was actually three ships lashed together. He smiled. So much easier to complete their task. Harry led his troops against the foreigners amidst a blur of steel and smoke and blood. Harry worked his way through the carnage like a scythe through wheat. Every opponent before him met death, swift and bitter. Their other ships worked their way around their foes, brutally decimating them in like manner. The enemy fought bravely, but they were no match.

And their ships stank; they were doing them a favor—so many *horses.*

Into the sea, they poured…

Suddenly, Harry turned to himself in the midst of battle, and stared into his own hot, severe gaze. The battle faded away into a distant background…but Harry felt something about a massive storm…a *typhoon*…brewing.

The two stood before each other, alone, on an empty deck, sails snapping above. They remained so for what seemed an eternity. Harry couldn't turn away. Didn't want to. There was something in those eyes. Determined, willful—pleading. Harry studied those eyes. Their message. He sat down behind his desk, as the battle-weary general stood before his desk and spoke:

"Nani wo mananda no? Nani wo mananda no?"

Harry shot wide awake. Stood before his desk. His eyes were wide open, his hands outstretched. His clock ticked softly in the background. Before him stood no samurai. No ocean. No battle. He stood alone, all nerves afire. He slowly sat back down.

Kare ha nani wo mananda no?

As Harry mentally said the words, he physically spoke the translation: *What had he learned?*

Again, he spoke the words. *"Kare ha nani wo mananda no?"*

Where was this coming from? How was he able to speak and understand *Japanese?*

He shot back to his feet. *He actually understood each and every word—* he'd been asking himself *what had he* learned!

Harry looked to the vase on the pedestal over by the entrance to his office, and thought: *Mukou ni aru watashi no doa no yoko de, dai no ue ni aru kabin wo mite iru.*

He translated the thought with ease: *I am looking at a vase on a pedestal, over by my door!*

Harry collapsed back into his chair.

He knew no Japanese. He knew nothing about Asian languages. But here he was thinking and speaking this language as if he'd grown up with it—when he realized he was thinking about all *this* in Japanese.

Ittai nani wo yatte iru no....

4

Tiger, was, in all honesty having great difficulty in sorting out reality from fantasy, from the sounds and visions that continued to fill his head in increasing volume.

It was starting all over again.

The ghostly images were parading before him in greater and greater number. He lay on his cot, all lights off, everyone secure from the first round of cell checks, and stared into the darkness above. The sound of the wind had grown more insistent since his move from the hospital, and the images...he wasn't sure *where* he was. Was he on some wind-blown desert steppe, in south Florida, or back in New York City?

Was he in an office building, punching a clock, or slogging down through Georgia?

It was all so dizzying, and it didn't matter if his eyes were open or closed, because his mind was a-ragin, pure and simple—

Now, he was hoofin it down a stairwell amid horrendous screams and confusion.

Had there been an earthquake?

He was flying down the stairs as fast as he could, hordes of similarly impressed people on his heels. One false step and he'd tumble to his death, trampled down stairs that never seemed to end, heart beating wildly, deathly afraid of *something*...

Or was he really back in the recesses of an alley in North Carolina, behind a dumpster, ravaging for food?

But none of this could be, because he was really in the midst of unfathomable carnage...his family dead and dying about his feet. Everywhere he looked, death and destruction, death and destruction!

He'd just been daydreaming to get away from the unspeakable reality he lived.

He was a young man, and it always ended the same way...first there was the arrow that screamed through his body, piercing his chest, but continuing on through to the wall behind him (he saw that it actually stuck into the crude mud-brick wall for a moment before crumbling away from loosened chips), then came another warrior riding toward him, arm outstretched. Stunned, he looked to the man, whom he saw lower a hand toward him. Choking on blood, and trying to inhale through the new hole in his chest, he clutched at the arrow shaft and tried to reach out for the hand—but this warrior was not trying to help...he was delivering the *coup de grace* of a beheading stroke...

For but a moment, he's looking up at his body as it slowly crumpled to the dirt where (*confused!*) the rest of him (*what* rest of him?) lay. As the blood gushed out from his neck and his vision faded, he found himself feeling extremely tired, staring at his body at an angle that made no sense. He remembered asking himself...*how can this be?* How can he see his entire body on the ground before him like that...

Tiger bolted upright in his cot. Felt for his neck.
Still there.
Attached.
But he didn't feel all there. Something was wrong...skewed...he

might be laying on a cot in a Florida jail cell, but he knew damned well that that wasn't necessarily where he *was*. Something was coming…was very near…and it was ripping his reality apart. He closed his eyes and felt his neck; rolled his head about.

Yeah, still attached.

Chapter Twenty-Four

1

Harry jerked awake to the blaring noise of an explosion going off inside his head. Jolting upright, he found he'd fallen asleep alongside his office phone.

He was still at his office.

Shaking his head, he also saw the sun had come up and found out how stiff a body can get after having slept the entire night hunched over one's desk.

Harry grabbed the phone, immediately trying to speak as if he hadn't just been sleeping at his desk, but his vocal cords weren't cooperating. What initially came out, instead, was an embarrassing half-squeak, as his dulled and dry cords tried their best to perform. Clearing his throat, he again tried.

"Hullo?"

"Mr. Gordon?"

Harry again cleared his throat. "Yes?"

"This is Arty Ofo, from—"

"Oh, yes, professor, good morning—what'd you find?"

"Well, this is really strange, but this lady had written—and it utterly baffles me—an almost page-by-page rendition of sections of an ancient text, called *The Secret History*, about Chinggis"

(*Chin Gas*)

"Khan and his rise to power."

"Chinggis what?"

"Yes—well, I'm sorry, but most in our western world know him as 'Genghis,' with a 'G.' 'Chinggis,' though not literally translatable, is thought to mean 'body of water,' or something like that. 'Oceanic,' or 'all-powerful ruler'—"

"Genghis Khan? Why would a Wyoming elementary school teacher write about a Mongol warrior hundreds of years old—"

"Almost eight-hundred, actually—"

"Let alone in ancient Mongolian?"

"That I can't answer…but the script does contain portions of *The Secret History*."

Dr. Ofo paused and Harry could hear a rustling of paper across the phone lines.

"She even writes about other stuff that doesn't appear in any known texts of that period, though has been greatly speculated. Some of it in minute detail. She also devotes a fair amount of her writing to the more spiritual aspects of the ruler and his people…in the first person, I might add. It's really creepy. As I read the stuff, I kept checking over my shoulder. Swore I was being watched. Some of this stuff we have absolutely no records of—and though it has been greatly speculated, especially in numerous texts and websites I've researched, this actually spells it all out."

"Huh."

"I'd write it off as fantasy from a delusional mind, were it not for the corroborative detail she includes…stuff only scholars—or someone who's actually *been* there, *lived* there—would know."

"You're kidding."

Ofo chuckled. "It's like…she was actually there, experiencing all this stuff first hand, then writing it down. She talks of their *Koko Mongke Tengri* concept, for instance, or 'The Eternal Blue Sky'…"

(*Coco*)

"…it was long thought to be more of a western, monotheistic deity, but she spells it out in no uncertain terms that it was more than that…that it was, indeed, more of a *representation* of the all-encompassing nature of so-called ultimate Cosmic laws and pantheism. Soul transmigration, or reincarnation, also figured heavily in their lives, which, perhaps, explains their sheer ferocity and determination in battle. And their creative and skilled use of water to both deny and drown adversaries during sieges is rather ironic, considering Chinggis's name. Perhaps a morbid irony not entirely lost on the minds and souls of his victims. His signature exploit, if you will. His original name, before he was declared Chinggis Khan, ruler of all the Central Asian tribes during a great assembly, or *kuriltai*, was 'Temujin,' which meant 'blacksmith.' That was in 1206—or the year of the Tiger, in Chinese. I thought that interesting, given the defendant's name, you know, in your trial? On the whole, a curious choice of names, all around, don't you think? The whole thing is simply…uncanny…*fascinating*…for all that lady's disturbing accuracy—"

"I'll say," Harry said, absentmindedly, as he flipped through an "Important—Rush" folder on his desk. "And you say that you've never heard of anything like this before?"

Ofo again chuckled. "Are you *kidding*? Never. I mean, this is *history*, the Mongolian Holy Grail we're talking, here. Little is known of their daily life, really, their spirituality or shamanhood—it's not like they wrote all this stuff down—or if they did, we haven't found it. They were a nomadic, warrior clan—or clans—they weren't into diaries; it was the succeeding generations that wrote all this stuff down—"

"Thank you, Doctor, you've been most informative…insightful."

"My pleasure. Um, can I…do I have your permission to use any of this? Publish it, I mean—my findings?"

"For that you'll have to get back with us after the trial, since it's currently evidence—but I don't see any problems once we're done."

"Thank you…you have no idea how important this is to Mongolian scholars like myself. It's literally like she'd actually *lived* that life, then came back to tell us about it. I can't find enough adjectives to describe this find. *Thank you*."

"Thank *you*, professor. I wish you all the best."

"Good bye."

"Bye, professor."

Harry hung up.

Mongolians?

What the hell had this to do with the murders? Ronda Ettbauer? Harry pushed aside the paper on his desk, and grabbed Ronda's folder; flipped it open. Scanning her fact sheets, he found absolutely no mention of any data indicating familial mental illness—though her parents were a bit on the strict, religious, side. And she also had no knowledge of Chinese, ancient, Mongolian, or otherwise. She was an elementary school teacher, that was all. No Asian specialization of any kind. Zip. Yet…here she was, caught red-handed at a crime scene with a handful of others, most of whom were awaiting a trial's outcome to forever determine how the rest of their lives would be spent. She'd been the lucky one. The others would more than likely spend their remaining life behind bars. He doubted the death penalty would be imposed…but one could always hope…

And where the hell had her words come from? How had she been able to write in "*Oygur*," or whatever it was the professor had called it?

2

Kacey entered her apartment, soaking in the air-conditioning after a humid, muggy day outside. Though it felt great to be back, her return ride with Sheila had largely been a silent, uncomfortable one. The trial had put a new spin on things…a new perspective…and it shook her world. She realized that not all things were nice and good for others. Intellectually, she'd supposed she'd always known this, but now she'd seen firsthand just how nasty other lives have had it. Her life had been pretty good…except for deserting Mark and Emily, that is. She never realized just how great she'd had it until hearing all the gruesome testimony and detail. It seemed different when it was all written down on paper, in her articles, but when it was vocalized—actually spoken into the air and hit the old tympanic membranes—it seemed to take on a much more intense, personal impact she found hard to deal with.

And she'd been holding hands with a *woman*.

This had to stop—all of it—and she had to get back to reality. Maybe that's why she'd been having the nightmares…it had all been unconsciously stewing around inside, and she'd been too busy, too…misdirected…to deal with any of it.

Sheila…was a great woman, and she'd had a great time with her, but she wasn't for her. Journalism was a fun, exciting life…but she missed her family. Maybe this was what she needed. Time alone. She picked up drafts of articles and glanced over them. Such nasty details. Murders. The Hockers. She glanced out the window toward her beat-up car, the driver's-side window still covered in plastic mat and duct tape; looked to the clock. There was still time.

Still…*time*…

Putting down the papers, she pulled out a phonebook and looked for a mobile windshield repair company. Finding one, she made an appointment—for today. Those murdered were unable to do things like this, just like the suspects. Yes, she had it pretty darned good. Do what she wanted, when she wanted. She sat down and closed her eyes, laying her head back against the couch-back and wall.

Still time…

The ring

Always on her mind. There was just something about it…she *knew* it…and somehow, Sheila and her were tied to it…but how was that even a *remote* possibili…

Chim-a acha ghuyu, minu tölüge yabughad ögügechi!

Kacey bolt upright. Two people…attacked on a barren steppeland…

Odu, yag odu yabu, busighu!

The images hit swift and powerfully…a woman's *pleas*…dire peril…

She grabbed the couch; her heart raced.

Tede chim-a yi alakhu bar jabduju baiina. Chi odu yabu, türgen yabu! Tede nar masi olaghula baiin-a. Chim-a acha ghuyu, minu tölüge yabughad ögügechi!

As Kacey, the vision blasted through her like a divine wind, she once again found herself understanding the strange language.

…as long as there is a sun and the wind, I will be with you, but if you stand to fight them, you will surely be killed! Now, go, *my love!* Go!

Kacey stood, but swooned, overtaken by an overwhelming flood of imagery…of a far-off land swept by wind. Instead of her apartment, she sat in a crude wagon—actually a smaller cart—a man on horseback beside her. She wasn't just viewing this—she was…she was…*there*; *was* the woman. They were young, bundled in nomadic clothing, the both of them. Off in the distance she spotted three men on horseback racing toward them. There was an incredible sense of urgency—*fear*—and she knew her new husband would be killed.

Go! Kacey urged with all her heart and soul, *you* must leave! *As long as we both shall live, there is a chance we shall again meet! Here, take my shirt!* she said, pulling it off, *take this! Remember me—my scent! Now go, my love!* Quickly!

Kacey-as-nomad watched her new husband speed off toward the distant hills without her, felt her heart leap into her throat. She looked back to the attacking riders. When she thought her husband should now live, survive the attack, she felt a kernel of joy…*but should she kill herself or allow herself to be taken?*

She had pledged her vow to her husband on the promise that they should meet again, and had to honor that vow.

The riders were upon her amid a flurry of thundering hooves and dust, one immediately ripping the reins to their

(*my love!*)

cart from her hands. Of the other two, one positioned before her, and the other on the other side of the cart. No one said a word, though Kacey felt as if she were, again, living a nightmare—but she knew *this* was real. Real *life*. It was no dream…*it was reality.*

As all four rode on, the bleakness of her situation impressed upon

Kacey an incredible, unspeakable despair. The nomad that she now was burst into the most grievous howl. Wailing, she cried, *"My husband has never turned his back in dishonor, nor run from battle, yet you had made me send him away on my honor! He will find you and send you back to before you were born! We will be together!"*

One of the men riding beside her sharply backhanded her.

"You are ours, now," he commanded, *"your husband is no more! We will cut him up into little pieces and feed him to you if you ever speak of him again—or he comes riding into our tents! No more of this!*

Kacey came to as the doorbell turned into a manual rapping at the door.

"Hello! *Harbor Glass and Mirror! Hello?"*

Kacey shot to instant wakefulness and immediately darted for the door.

"I'm so sorry," she apologized, opening it and swiping away lose hair from her face. Rubbing her eyes, she said, "I dozed off."

The Harbor Glass guy smiled. "No problem, ma'am. I just got here. Didn't know if the doorbell worked. You called for a car window replacement?"

"Yes. You probably already saw it's the one with the plastic mat for a driver-side window?"

"I did," he said, smiling.

"Need me?"

"Nope. I'll get back to ya when I'm done." The man scribbled something on his clipboard and departed.

Kacey closed the door and sat back on the couch, staring at the ring.

...as long as there is a sun and the wind...

She held it up against her wedding band.

She'd made a mistake. A huge one. It was time to grow up, sister, move on. Make a decision one way or the other and quit leading others on. Screwing up *other* lives.

Kacey grabbed the cordless and dialed a number from a piece of paper in her pocket. No one picked up, but the voice mail for the room did kick in.

"Sheila...this is Kacey. I don't quite know how to say this, so I'm glad you're not there. It makes this that much easier, though I probably don't deserve it. Look, I'm getting my car fixed, so I'm gonna drive down Friday by myself. I think…I think we need to stop seeing each other. I know you won't believe me, but it's really nothing against you. I hope you understand…someday. I have to get things back in order, and I can't do that with you there. I'm sorry…I'm not mad, really I'm not, and I treasure the time we've had together, but I just need to do this, need to be by myself. Get back into who and what I am—only better—you know? Please, don't take this personally—you're a wonderful…*beautiful*…person. But I have to be alone. Thank you for helping me, I really mean that…for being there. Both times. You don't know how important you've been—and are—to me. Or maybe you *do….*"

Kacey reverently replaced the phone back into its cradle. She sat back down at her table and dumped her head into her hands, feeling more alone than when everything first happened.

As long as there is the sun and the wind, I will be with you….

3

Prosecutor Harry Gordon, sporting an upset stomach, approached Tiger, who sat relaxed but nervous in the witness box. Tiger's hair was neatly combed and detangled, his beard cleaned up but not shaved, and he wore a meager, powder-blue, state-provided dress shirt, neutral trousers, dress shoes, and a tie. Harry bet he hadn't looked this good in years. As he approached the stand, though, Harry slipped on what seemed to be sand. He paused, momentarily dizzy…off balance.

Sea-sick, if he hadn't known any better.

He cast a slightly surprised look to where he'd slipped. Regaining his composure, he continued.

"Tiger…are we to understand that to be your real name?"

Tiger looked to Harry, then the jury, and nodded. "It is."

Winds gently rustled in Tiger's head.

"Can you tell us where you were in the early morning hours of March 10, just after one a.m.?"

Tiger shifted nervously in his seat. "I was walking down a road—"

"Tamiami Trial Boulevard?"

Tiger blinked, wincing. "I don't know the name…it's just a street, a road, like any other."

"So, you were walking down this road…"

Tiger again winced. "I was, ah, *walking*, as I said…not knowing where I was going, or why…just…walking. It was warm…and the ants…the ants were hungry."

"Ants?"

"They just kept coming…attacking me…wouldn't leave me alone."

"What'd you do?"

"Kept walking. It was all I could do. Nothing else mattered."

"Where'd you come from?"

"Up north…somewhere."

"You don't remember where you came from? Where you were born? Please, sir—"

Tiger shook his head.

"Okay…we've established you walked in to Safe Harbor from parts unknown. You do know that was where we found you?"

Tiger shrugged. "If you say so."

Gordon scoffed. "I say so. That's where we found you with the others—"

"Objection!" Benét sounded. "There has been no basis for tying this man to the rest of the suspects!"

"Your Honor," Gordon interjected, "that's precisely what I'm attempting to do. He was arrested with the other suspects, in the same location, doing the exact same thing as everyone else we apprehended there."

"Overruled," Stoker said.

"We picked you up along with the others, in the Safe Harbor Retirement Community, in Sunset Harbor, Florida, on the night of March 10th, at about two in the morning. You, along with everyone else, were found knee-deep in an apparent murder spree that left an entire retirement community dead. Now, we ask, why, sir, were you there? What was your purpose?"

Tiger blinked, the noise in his head partially drowning out Gordon's words. Tiger's words came out measured and pained.

"I…don't…*know*. I really…*don't*. All I know is what you tell me. I have no memory or knowledge of any of this. I don't even know these people—"

"You don't know the people you were there with?"

"I don't know any of them."

"You acted solely on your own?"

Tiger flinched, turned his head slightly.

"Are you all right?" Stoker asked.

"I have…headaches."

"Are you having one now?" Stoker asked.

"Yes."

"Bailiff—please get the defendant aspirin and water," Stoker directed.

"Thank you," Tiger said, nodding to the judge.

"Tiger, I repeat the question," Harry said, "are you saying you acted on your own?"

"I'm saying I don't know *what* I did, *how* I did it, nor *why*."

Frustrated, Harry turned to the judge and threw his hands into the air. "No further questions."

"Miss Benét?" Stoker asked.

D.A. Benét approached the witness stand.

"Tiger…were you read your rights?"

A Bailiff brought Tiger Excedrin and water.

"Yes."

Tiger took the pills and drank deeply of the water, eyeing it uneasily as it went down.

"Did anyone test you once you were incarcerated, use the term 'fit' to stand trial?"

"Yes…I talked with that psychiatrist."

"You mean psychologist?"

"Whomever."

Benét nodded, eyeing him. She turned away from the witness, a thoughtful hand to her chin; looked back to him.

"Sir, did you plan to murder those people—whether or not you remember the actual act? To your conscious mind—*now*—at this very moment, did you ever plan, or otherwise consciously intend to harm, the residents of the Safe Harbor Retirement Community?"

Tiger shook his head, "No, ma'am, I did not."

"To your current, conscious state of mind, did you know those you were arrested with, or are part of a group, cult, or otherwise, whose intention it was to murder or otherwise harm those people at that retirement home?"

"No, ma'am. No." Tiger fidgeted inside the witness stand.

"Did you know, or in any way were you associated or have contact with, at any time in your life, those you are being accused of murdering?"

Before Tiger could answer, however, the sounds in his head again ratcheted up in volume, and he yelped out in pain. Brought a hand to his head.

"Sir? Are you all right?" Stoker again queried.

"I...uh...oh, God...."

Benét looked uncertainly to Stoker and the jury, but not Gordon. "Please, sir, I need your answer."

"*No*, I do *not* know those people!"

"Are you sure you don't? Think, hard, sir, to both of those questions. Or do you answer to another name of...*Wallace T. Bryce?*"

Kacey sat on the other side of the public gallery from Sheila, Banner, and the rest of the group she'd been sitting with up to this point. She set her notepad on the bench, beside her, brushing away stray grains of sand. She looked up to find Sheila staring at her and tried to look busy taking notes. Most of the time Sheila quickly looked away, but once or twice she held her gaze. She was sure there were tears—restrained emotion—in her eyes, on her face, but tried not to think about it. It had to be this way. She had no choice. She really wasn't interested in her that way, she knew that now.

And there was a strange atmosphere to the day, the trial.

Things felt...thicker. Heavier.

Not so much in an oppressive way, but in a...an *expectant?*...way. She pulled out her ChapStick and applied some to her lips...when it dawned on her this was the first time she'd used the stuff since moving here (though always continued to carry it). And that was the other thing...it felt surprisingly *dry* in the courtroom.

Since when was any location in Florida *dry?*

Searching in her purse, she found an old tube of lotion and applied some. As Kacey returned the lotion to her purse, she moved her head to one side somewhat quicker than normal and grew dizzy.

What was wrong with her?

She felt decidedly beside herself. Something was different about today, peculiar, and it felt as if it was quickly becoming...*weirder.*

Kacey looked down to her hand. To the two rings she wore. Stared at them. Her vision blurred, and she thought...just for a moment...she saw two hands where there should only be one. She tried to shake it off, shook her hand, and tried to concentrate back on the trial.

There seemed a definite shift in the tone of the court proceedings. Kacey picked up her notepad. Heard a high-pitched ringing *way* in the back of her head, almost unimaginably so. She scribbled a note or two, still trying to shake off her blurriness, and, now, this internal ringing.

When all this was over, she was going to need some serious recuperation time, then thought…

Wasn't this how everything started?

Tiger wasn't the only one in need of Excedrin. Banner wasn't quite himself. He wasn't sure *who* he was, but he felt…different. Had a high-pitched ringing in his head and a headache. There was also something bothering him "upstairs," like a sinus problem, but of the *mind*.

And he kept seeing…shapes…he kept seeing things at the edge of his vision, but each time he turned…gone. Nothing there. And one moment he swore he'd heard the snort and stomp of a horse (as silly as that sounded in a *courtroom*), but when he turned toward the sound found a guard had merely scuffed a chair across the floor.

When this trial was over he was seriously considering retirement.

Sheila simply could not concentrate. She knew it was bound to happen…but what troubled her most was that it'd happened so quickly. One day they were doing great—and the next?

History.

Had it been something she'd done, something she'd said?

No, Kacey'd insisted, it had just been that she needed to sort out her life, once and for all. It hadn't been about anything she'd done.

But, had she, in all truth, moved too fast and Kacey was just being polite?

Or maybe it really wasn't about her at all. After all, she *had* left her family—child and *husband* (key word: *husband*, not *wife*). There were other dynamics going on, she was sure, of which she simply wasn't a consideration. This wasn't about her…it was about *Kacey*.

Sheila looked to her hands. They were shaking—her whole body trembled—and she didn't know how long she could stand it. She'd been dumped before, but this time was different. Every time she looked over to her, she tried not to show her hurt, her *love*, but failed every time. The tears…she could cry an ocean of tears if she allowed herself…but no, she couldn't have that. She was a professional. But, this was pure torture, sitting in the same room with her, living in the same *universe* with her, yet no longer feeling the warmth of her skin…the warmth and tenderness of her palm wrapped within hers, the kiss of her lips. They were meant to be together, but now they were, once again (and why did this one thought, above all else, feel like such a death sentence?...*departing.*

Splitting up.

That one thought brought on such intense, soul-killing feelings of abandonment and she wasn't sure she could handle it.

They were meant to be together, yet Kacey just didn't seem to feel the same way about it—or was doing a great job in hiding it. She had to *know*...had expressed similar feelings when they'd been together...touring the islands...in the restaurant—*how could she so abruptly and totally turn everything off like that?*

Cast it all away, like giving away the shirt off her back?

Sheila brought a tissue to her eyes, lightly dabbing around her mascara.

How could she do this to her again?

Again?

"Answer the court, please, sir," D.A. Benét asked, "Are you also known by another name?"

"Answer the question, Mr. Tiger, and I remind you you are under oath," Stoker warned.

Tiger wiggled nervously in the stand. "I don't know what you're talking about."

Benét held up the documents. "Does not the name Susan Sibley mean anything to you?"

Tiger stared back at her, jaw clenched.

"Or how about the offices of Meyers Financial," Benét continued, checking her documentation, "on the thirty-seventh floor of the Pall Meadows building?"

"I don't know what you're talking about—"

Tiger had difficulty breathing. Gripped the chair. His mind reeled as the wind in his head wailed to sirocco proportions. His *sister? Here?* How had she been—

"I don't believe you...I've had no contact with her, since—"

"Are you not, Mr. Tiger—or should I say...Mr. *Wallace T. Bryce*—brother to Susan Sibley, one of the suspects who'd also been arrested—"

"Counselor," Stoker said, "I remind you you are this man's *defense.*"

"Your Honor, I ask the court to bear with me. I'm trying to establish Mr. Bryce's state of mind, that there is no cult nor conspiracy on the part of my clients."

"Tread carefully, counselor."

Benét nodded to Judge Stoker in acknowledgement. She turned back to Tiger.

"Tiger…is it fair characterization that you'd fallen upon hard times?"

"Yes," Tiger said.

"Wanted—needed—to get away from all the stress of having been a successful broker?"

"Yes."

"Tiger…you still hear voices and other noises in your head?"

Tiger paused, then said, "Yes."

"Daily? Throughout the day?"

"Yes, every minute; they never leave me alone. They're there now."

Benét nodded. "And you emphatically state that, aside from your sister, you do not know any of the victims?"

"N-no, I do not know any of the victims."

"No more questions, your Honor," said, returning to her seat.

"Mr. Gordon?" Stoker asked.

"Mr. Bryce, is it? Well, how very interesting, though not entirely correct," Prosecutor Harry Gordon said. Tiger sat visibly flustered in his witness stand. "I have it on good authority that you also knew a Stephen Acres, who'd been one of your managers. One of the many with whom you'd beaten and cut up with your bottle that night in Safe Harbor."

"Objection, your Honor!" Benét said. "I saw no such reference in the documentation!"

"Your Honor, perhaps Ms. Benét missed it, but that name *is* among the victim list," he said, holding up a document with the name on it in one hand, the "Important—Rush" folder in the other. He brought it up to Stoker.

"Overruled," Stoker declared.

Benét sat back down, flipping through her documentation.

"Sir, whatever your name, why did you skip out on life during that Pall Meadows plane crash? With all the missing and dead who had no choice—paid for it with their lives—you chose to sneak out. Why was that, Mr. Bryce? Did you have something to hide? People to kill?"

"Your Honor, move to strike!" Benét said, getting to her feet.

"Withdrawn," Harry said, turning away from Tiger. "Tell us, Mr. Bryce, why did you run away…and why commit murder…leading your sister and the others to our quiet little harbor town, which will now forever carry the stain of your carnage?"

Harry turned back to Tiger.

Tiger was no longer listening to Gordon's pleas for culpability. Inside Tiger, aka Wallace Theodore Bryce's mind, was a flurry of confusion…wind…thundering hooves…murder…

His *sister?*

How had she possibly gotten involved?

And she'd *killed* herself? *Taken her own life?*

Why *had* he killed those people?

Had his sister—whom he hadn't had any contact with since the crash—really also been a part of it—only to later have the guts to take her own life rather than face the inevitable? Why couldn't *he* have killed himself?

What had become of him?

Of the successful man he'd once been? Of the amount of power he'd once wielded? Of the *battles* he'd fought…

Harry stood before the witness box, folder in hand.

"Mr. Bryce…I submit the following: in 2010 you had an affair with Mr. Acres' young wife, Terri. I submit Mr. Acres become aware of the affair and was poised to ax you from the company. When Mrs. Acres was confronted with this knowledge by her husband, she'd told you to take a hike. I…."

Tiger sat dumb and numb, nervously twitching as Harry read off the litany of acts he'd committed in a whole nother—*different*—life, one to which he was no longer attached. He no longer knew that man any longer, that *him*. Tiger slid his feet around on the floor of the box among the sand…piles of it that were spread around at the foot of the witness box and accumulated in its corners. There was sand in his shoes. Grass also grew down there, beneath his feet…

The noises were too much, the questions…too much.

"*Don't you hear it?*" Tiger blurted out, his voice strained with fear. He leaned forward, grabbing the witness box's wooden handrail. "Don't you *hear* them?"

Gordon looked to Tiger.

"Hear what, Mr. Bryce?"

Harry snorted and coughed, tried to clear his sinuses; caught scent of an odd smell to the air.

Camphor?

"The *wind!* Oh, my God, the *wind,*" Tiger said. "And the

thunder…the-the pounding *hooves*. They're coming…all of them…they're coming again, and there's nothing we can do about it! We tried, oh, Lord, how we tried, but there's really no way to stop them, I see that, now…"

"Please, if this is some insanity—"

Tiger shot to his feet, wild-eyed, and grabbed at his clothing.

"I-I need to get out of here…they're going to kill us…I can't let that happen—not *again!*"

Bailiffs were already closing in on Tiger before Stoker called for them. Stoker went for his gavel, when he, too, became confused, gavel poised in mid air. His eyes glazed over as he stared out across the court room. Sand blew across his bench, and the smell of ancient lands permeated the courtroom…

A strange, sparse grass had sprung up across the entire floor. Drifts of dirt and sand piled up against benches, tables, and doorjambs. A bitter, desiccating wind cut through the room, evaporating all humidity.

And a gigantic presence descended upon the court like a heavy cloak.

Stoker slowly came to his feet behind the bench…arms to his sides…his mouth open in an expression of truncated bewilderment. What he felt was curiously familiar…familiar-like-*E*noch-familiar…but it wasn't Enoch. This was a far different entity that had taken up residence inside him…someone far more…*earthy*. Coarse. Someone…some*thing*…more commanding…imposing…*intimidating*.

Stoker felt no threat. He searched out the presence, and before he knew it—

"*I HAVE RETURNED.*"

The voice that issued forth from Stoker thundered in a booming, authoritative, tone. A voice vastly unlike his own filled the room. Stoker was no longer Stoker. Stoker had become something much, much, *more*…

Legs spread powerfully apart, the entity-as-Stoker planted his fists firmly into his hips and took up a new, confident stance behind the bench. The entity-as-Stoker surveyed the once-court room as if it were his empire. He glared at all present, not only those in the jury box, but the man in the witness stand, the men and women of the gallery. He sneered and narrowed his eyes. Recognized each and every face that stared back at him.

Chuckling mightily, he declared, "*I SEE I STILL COMMAND FEAR IN ALL OF YOU—THAT IS* GOOD!" and broke into uproarious laughter that shook the mortal foundations of all present....

Chapter Twenty-Five

1

Out of the mists of Time had emerged a land of sand and grass, steppe and mountain. And from its desolate, windswept barrens had come a blue-gray wolf and a fallow deer. Together they had traveled across an inland sea and camped upon the source of the Onon River, whereupon their first son was born. Dynasties had come and gone…empires won and lost. The eternal struggle for that which one did not have continued to rage among clans and tribes that roamed the endless pastoral and desert steppes…

…a brave warrior hunting with his falcon along the Onon had spied a couple traveling alone on the steppe. Seeing the woman beautiful, the warrior had ridden back to his tribe, beseeching his two brothers to accompany him…

And from this history had been birthed another from a stolen wife and a brave warrior. A child with a fire in his eyes, a clot of blood the size of a knucklebone die clutched in his right hand, and the destiny of Heaven's Will imprinted upon his soul. He had been given the name Temujin, and had risen to a power and grandeur not seen then nor since. A reluctant warrior king, later enthroned as Genghis Khan, he had united the Mongol people under one identity. Ruthless and wise, genius and mighty, he had commanded a land from Yellow to Aral Sea. With wisdom and purpose, and no thought to greed he did reign. A man of his time possessed of great energy and method. And upon his death, a thousand horsemen had he ordered to trample asunder his burial site until it could no longer be found…where it still eludes all who seek it to this very day…

2

The entity-as-Stoker stood before the court that was no longer a court. There no longer resided familiar marble flooring, nor rich mahogany paneling. Now were dun-colored Mongolian grasses and drifts of sand piled up against bench and table legs. Along walls and behind Stoker's bench now clustered Scots, Siberian pines, and larches whispering in hot, desiccating winds that swept throughout the room-that-was-no-longer-a-room. What had been benches, tables, and seats, had become hillocks, rocks, and open grassland steppe...a river running through it, above which shone a brilliant, deep blue sky. The musty scents of dirt and grasses filled the air.

Yet each person knew that...in some dimension...they still resided in a *court* room...

The entity-as-Stoker stood before them, nodding and silently smiling ear to ear as if overseeing troops. Tiger, the jury, lawyers, and those in the gallery still saw Stoker as the judge in chamber robes—but also in the leather accoutrements of a mighty Mongol warrior. On his left arm was strapped a dagger and small shield, and to his side a saber and quiver of arrows, a bow slung across his back. His gaze penetrated all, his presence beside each person in the court room-turned-steppe, and in their minds burst images of an ancient land and a powerful warrior's rise to unparalleled distinction. They experienced his father stealing his mother from another. His mother birthing him into the world. Experienced one of his brothers as he stole from Temujin, and how Temujin had later killed him for that. Experienced Temujin's strength...*his* marriage, and his own wife's history-repeating kidnapping and her subsequent rescue by Temujin; were with him at his *kuriltai*, when he was proclaimed *Genghis Khan*, master of all Mongolia...and lived with him though each and every one of his conquests. Discovered that Genghis's actions were the results of insults and wrongs against his people, rather than mere efforts at primal and materialistic expansion and exploitation...

Hogelun Ujin, late of the *Olkhunugud* people, dustily rattled along in her cart, unexpectedly jarred back to waking consciousness. She'd daydreamed of a people—tall and round-eyed—who lived in a far-off land and were arguing about one who sat on a bench before them. She shot her hands out of the loose-fitting folds of her garments, grabbing the sides of the cart.

It had all been so *real!*

She'd really felt as if she'd grown up and lived among those people—herself tall and round-eyed—and lightly stroked her face with the backs of her fingertips.

It was actually quite frightening, now that she looked back on it. She shivered; tried to remember other details from the dream, like her name (she actually remembered it). It was something like Kurashi…Kraiji—no…*Ka-cey!* She'd remembered it! It was the most real dream she'd ever had. She'd had a family—a husband and one child—and there was something about another woman. There was something very familiar about her. These people lived in a hazy, indistinct land, surrounded by vast quantities of water, and they'd all gathered together in a *kuriltai*, in a very large *ger*. She'd never seen anything like it before—it was truly massive, as tall as a mountain and filled with many, many, people-filled layers…

Shaking it off, Hogelun looked to Yeke Chiledu, her new husband, a nobleman from the *Merkid*. She smiled. He rode just ahead on horseback. He was a fine man, and would make a good husband. Maybe her vision foretold of good things to come—she had had a child, in her dream…

Regrasping her reins, Hogelun lightly tapped the horse. On one of her fingers she wore a ring her new husband had given her, and remembered there had even been something about that in her vision, too.

But as she settled her mind back into her present, and looked out over the steppes before them, there was something else…something dreadfully ominous lurking in the background of her dream…something that she intuitively felt had a connection to her—Hogelun (why did her name suddenly sound so funny to her?)—*here*. She wrinkled her face. She would ask *Tengri* for guidance…

Harry-as-Kioshu peered out across the water as he stood fast in the heavily tossed-about fishing boat. There were many of them, and they'd all just left Takashima. The weather was quickly worsening, but they must not let the invaders triumph!

As Kioshu looked out across the expanse of dark, roiling water that seemed at once familiar yet make-believe, he couldn't shake the nagging images of that faraway land. Again. He must remain focused in his duty to Japan. He shook his head.

But wasn't he supposed to be in a trial? *Wasn't he a law-yer? A…law-yer…?*

If he was supposed to be at a trial (a *murder* trial), how could he be standing in a tossed-about fishing boat, inhaling salty air and fighting stiff, storm-driven winds? Battling an invading force? Never had he seen so many ships at one time…

What was *law-yer?*

The term "Armani" entered his mind, and he felt it had to do with attire. He fingered his metal and leather armor. Chided himself for behaving as a child. He was *here*, in the ocean, standing in the belly of a commandeered fishing boat preparing to do battle…

Fisher-as-Bogorchu milked his mares, when out from the distance rode a lone stranger. Bogorchu stood to meet the man, who asked, "Have you seen any silver-white geldings come this way?" The young man on horseback, powerfully built and imposing, had a fire in his eyes hard to ignore.

"Yes," Bogorchu replied, feeling a strangeness to his voice. "This morning I saw men ride through here…eight horses that sound like the ones you seek. Come."

Bogorchu walked the stranger to the tracks. He felt a familiarity with what he was doing…something called *plice* and *invest'gichon.*

"Come," Bogorchu said, "Let me give you a rested horse and together we will get your horses back…."

*Why did his words feel so strange…*different *sounding? He felt as if someone were inside him, having difficulty communicating.* Bogorchu suddenly had an urge to fish…to "detect fish"…but had no idea what that meant.

No matter! He must help this man with the fire in his eyes…

Sheila-as-Yeke Chiledu sat upright on his horse, scanning the wind-blown steppes along the Onon River. Something wasn't right. Up ahead. The river to their left was deserted, except for a young goat drinking from its waters. His recent wedding to Hogelun Ujin was still forefront in his mind, but something was wrong…*terribly* wrong…

Then he saw them. Three of them…galloping toward them at frantic speed.

Yeke looked to Hogelun, who was already looking to him with fearful eyes. They exchanged quick, emotional words, before Chiledu kicked his horse, and broke off toward a nearby hill at full bore. He would attempt to draw their attack. Riding hard, he whipped and kicked his horse into full speed, hoping to double back and return to his bride—

When the thought of him passionately kissing Hogelun, one last time, entered his mind—but as a *woman*...

Banner-as-Subetei had just sent a hail of arrows into the air against the Russians, while simultaneously ordering the lighting of dung and naphtha behind his troops. The battle was brutal and frenzied along the Kalka River, north of the Caspian Sea. The Russians, as was fully expected, charged. Subetei turned, catching glimpses of their standard

(*Banner?*)

banners flapping above their armies. He ordered his archers to retreat into the now heavily smoked rear. The Russians blundered right on through the smoke screen in pursuit...and were met not by lightly armed archers, but his heavily armed cavalry, wielding swords, mace, and lances. Subetei's victory was swift and brutal as they routed the enemy...

Tiger-as-Şakir Istikbal's eyes were wide with fear, his mind still filled with the painful echoes of screams and wails. His vision, fading fast on the one hand, grew clearer in another way he couldn't comprehend. Ants ran across his face, but he couldn't swipe them away for some, quite disturbing, reason, though he swore he felt his arm move...

Ants. Everywhere.

And he had crazy images of sitting at a bench before a group of people who all silently stared back at him. As he looked around, he saw his body—his *full* body—before him, separated by space from the him *viewing* it. He tried to scream, but nothing came out of his mouth...open and closed...open and closed...

Tiger-as-Şakir sat beside his head, staring at his body. Everywhere were dismembered corpses. He couldn't comprehend—he knew he'd been slain—but why wasn't he *dead?* Where was he? *What* was he—

Tiger-as-Şakir's attention was suddenly diverted to a body next to him. He didn't recognize who it was, but seemed to suddenly focus on the moaning the man continued to emit. He still *lived?* How unfortunate. How unfortunate for the lot of those not lucky enough to have been killed on this blood-soaked battlefield of what was left of their home, south of the Aral Sea...

A growing "whoosh" of noise built off in the distance, accompanied by a mounting rumble through the earth. It sounded like—but it couldn't be, couldn't *possibly* be—they were nowhere near the sea...yet what he heard was definitely the onrush of something that made no sense...

Water?

It sounded and felt as if the sea itself was—

The waters of the Amu Darya did not normally flow through the streets of Urgench, but today they did, and as their on-rushing torrents overtook him and those around him, Şakir watched as his severed head was kicked about like a bouncing, rolling ball ahead of the churning, angry waters of the diverted river, as it wiped clean the slaughtered town of his, and his people...

Kacey-as-Hogelun sat upright in her cart as she watched Yeke ride off without her into the hills. The three riders diverted after him at full gallop, and her heart leapt into her throat.

No!

Though she did not scream out, inside she screamed with all the fear and rage of a loved one for the life of their lover.

She must not lose Chiledu!

NO! Oh, blessed *Tengri*, this must not *be!*

She stopped the cart and jumped to the ground, watching as her husband valiantly tried to outrun them. There were three of them and they meant to have her—and at the death of her beloved. *If she had to live a thousand lifetimes, she would find Yeke...*

Banner-as-Subetei sat in an after-battle feast where he and another general laughed it up, enjoying the spoils of their victory over the Russians. As Banner's point of view pulled back, he saw them dining atop a huge, crude, wooden box, sealed with mud and dung and straw in all its cracks, including its union with the earth. As he and his fellow commander dined, another portion of his mind entered the mud-and-dung-sealed box to find three captured Russian princes suffocating within. The after-battle fate of respected enemy among the Mongol required their blood be not spilled where they stood. Banner-as-Subetei was sure they didn't quite appreciate the honor they were given...

* * *

Harry-as-Kioshu looked to a sky filled with literally *screaming* arrows.

Harry tried to flinch, to run away, but the samurai warrior he was also stood his ground. The first volley of arrows rained down upon them, and he watched as they buried their shafts deeply into their boats, though some bounced harmlessly off the sides and deck. He saw that the arrows that did not stick into the planking were dull. Picking one up, he found round, blunt heads with six holes drilled into them. He whipped it back and forth until he heard a slight whistling sound. Clever. Arrows that did, indeed, *scream*. Tossing it away, he looked to those samurai who remained. Many had taken hits, but many were restless to engage. This enemy would be stopped, or they would die trying.

Another volley, that same whistling scream filling the air, and, again, their boat, and those around them, were struck. But this time they returned fire. Harry felt that familiar

(what *"familiar?"*)

rush of adrenaline as he prepared for battle. But he also saw that the seas were quickly turning rough. They would have to strike hard and fast, before the storm…

Harry-as-Kioshu fast forwarded the experience and saw that the storm had finally hit full force. He and his men had taken shelter on the island, but the ships had not been so lucky. He watched as they smashed against each other and sank to the bottom of the sea…

The entity-as-Stoker, as if standing beside each person, in each person's *mind*, spoke, while images of Mongolian history flashed through their minds.

I am he who was once known as Kokochu and Teb Tengri…shaman to the Khongkhotad clan, defeated by Odchigin, brother to Temujin, Chinggis Khan. I come with him, for we are no longer separated, and I help Chinggis speak through the one called Stoker, who is yet part of me in another place and time. We do this in an effort to, once and for all, conclude old wrongs that have been wrought upon those whom have not yet accepted the necessary conclusion.

All individual images within each person merged and flowed from a single gestalt. Teb-as-Stoker no longer *spoke*, as *presented* lives…lives that directly permeated each person's consciousness. Each individual experienced, in exquisitely refined detail, all the lineages of their multiple lives across Time. Each had, in some way, been involved in the great and bloody warring of the Mongol empire, either under Genghis, or another khan's rule...as well as many *other* lives, across *other* countries and times...

Images of captured, respected warriors, flew past...of these respected warriors having been rolled up into carpets and beat to death...of having been boiled alive...suffocated...other images of respected Mongols having been laid to rest in places of honor atop mountains...

Kacey saw how the aged and polite Jack and Hedda Hocker had been fierce warriors under Genghis.

Billy Williams and Ronda Ettbauer had been brutally dismembered on the eastern fringes of the advancing Mongol hordes' kingdom, as was Tiger.

Harry...Harry had been one of many defending samurai against a later generation of Mongol attacks under Kublai Khan, across the Sea of Japan's Korea Strait. Each and every person on trial for murder, on that distant, future, Florida peninsula, had been at the business end of swords, lances, and violence wielded by the great and mighty ruler Genghis Khan. Each realized, in their distant future, that what they had done was unconscionable, and had been the result of their inability to come to terms with their own deaths. Realized how they'd been distanced from themselves—and the Truth—by their blind, seething obsession with revenge. They had been unable to feel a final, fully exacted sense of revenge for their brutal deaths across many lifetimes. Felt that—though they had repeatedly, *individually*, killed *their* killers in other lives—this time would be different. They had constructed an ensemble attack, one their killers would least expect. It would be in the waning years of their *most-comfortable* existences, when they were least expecting any further reincarnational retribution. The remaining past-life Mongol victims would rise up and give their past-life butchers what *they'd* experienced, on a much more personal, hand-to-hand level. And it would never end...was still going on in *other* lives...

They...were the last of the dead...the rest of whom had already made peace with their past. But now they saw their futility, their ignorance, and hung their heads in shame.

None of this had been needed...but had been needed to be worked through. Each saw their relation, and how they were all *one*. But, now, each also saw that they needed to take full responsibility for their actions. No act is punished, though each lesson is experienced until learned.

Teb-as-Stoker smiled and bowed his head. He metaphorically stepped aside to again allow Genghis to reenter Stoker. Genghis's entity was a far more powerful, all-pervading presence, and when he spoke, he shook the consciousnesses of each soul.

"*DO NOT FEAR ME, MY PEOPLE!*" the entity-as-Genghis-through-Stoker tried to whisper. "*There is no need to any longer fear who I once was—or who you once were. As much as I am every bit of who I once was, I am no longer, in those terms, that personality. I am the slayer…and the slain…*

Each person experienced Genghis in his different incarnations…as a knight killed during the Crusades, as a Russian killed in future Mongol raids, and as a samurai killed during the invasion of Takashima.

"*Everything you are, I, too, have been. We learn both sides of the coins we live and are never immune from that which we do to others. That is the lesson, my friends.*"

Everyone experienced Genghis talking with shamans, performing his *own* rituals…conversing with the Taoist sage, Changchun…and was with Genghis during his 1227 Yinchuan campaign…

Genghis came through to each person in both word and image. Through the souls of all present whirled the imagery of his death, the thousands of cavalry that had trampled his burial site into historical obscurity…

"*Since my death, I have come to appreciate different aspects of existence as I had never known. Largely ignored, and not much is talked about in your histories, was my spiritual nature. In my later years, I sought to better understand it. Yes, I had, indeed, been described as a man of my times, but, with few exceptions, what has been overlooked is that I tried to better the times for those over which I reigned. In certain terms, and for my own purposes, it was—in your terms—merely the price of admission that I was as violent as I was…not unlike your current need to be…connected…through your current lives' technologies. I cannot vouch for all my troops and their actions—they have their own responsibilities—but I did try to rise above it. I was physical. So, at times did indulge in certain physical aspects better left unexplored. However…I must insist my motives were honorable. To be honest? It was a shame I died when I did, for little of my good intentions or aspirations were carried on by those succeeding me!*"

Genghis broke into tumultuous laughter.

"*Much has been incorrectly and inappropriately attributed to me. I never consciously intended to be a conqueror, and personally cared little for material gain in and of itself, other than as the spoils of war for my people…a means to an end.*

When you lead warriors, again, in your terms and your terms alone, *you need to speak their tongue, and theirs was a tongue of violence and riches. And none of this even* touches *upon the distortions?"*

As Genghis imparted this information, all experienced events blasting through them like scorching winds…each became part of the thoughts, emotions, and *intentions* Genghis had had throughout his lifetime…each experienced firsthand everything Genghis had done…and *why*. They were with him as he prayed…as he distributed herds of goats among his people…as he rode alone across the steppe, staring pensively out across its vast grasslands…

"I needed to know how others *lived, and needed those better off than us to help my people become better off than them. I knew we had not the needed skills to bring our empire to great levels, so I…imported…it. I did what any parent would do for their family. It is not under my control that those fearful and weak of mind or body attribute and focus only upon that which they lack, resultantly giving to certain conditions exalted, distorted, statuses. I lacked for nothing and tried to learn within the framework of my existence then. So, to* that *end, myself and my people complimented each other. If I am guilty of anything, that is it. There will always be distortions, for many did, especially following my death, greatly distort my efforts…or, at the very least, misunderstood them.*

"All is cyclical, my friends, and though not in any way a good and valid enough reason, but what I did to you, you have all done to me, and those I commanded, in other incarnations. You have, finally, discovered your obsession…now grow beyond it, and with it. Take my blessings and eternal request for forgiveness, and forever be the better for it—learn the deeper truths and joys to your own incarnations!

"Once again, I apologize for my part in your lessons, and I will continue to do so until all is learned. In my killing you, price of admission or not, I also killed portions of myself.

"Each of you must now move on…to other systems…at the completion of your current existences. Take that knowledge with you to look back upon your journeys as a parent does a child who had made mistakes—but learned *from them. What we do in our infancies allows us adult growth, and to develop in these other systems in which we now find ourselves. Learn from it, grow from it…*then move on.

"But, before we go, one more thing…"

Here, Genghis radiated a light so bright not one could look directly into it.

"As much destruction as I've wrought upon this existence, I am returning—in your future's future—to wield a different form of power! I am not yet done with your world?"

Genghis again broke off into profound, boisterous, laughter, fists thrust into his hips and head thrown back.

"My second coming, as it were, had been timed, in your current focus's futures, with the re-entrances of other personalities to bring about a greater global facilitation of the Human Condition…in ways that will shake the very foundations of any Koko Mongke Tengri!"

"I look forward to our final kuriltai, in this system's incarnations, with great anticipation and joy—for we will and have already brought about a greater expansion of consciousness that will, and has forever, changed how Humanity conducts itself—and which contributes to all *systems of existence.*

"We leave you now."

As Genghis and Teb departed, all felt as if their souls had been knocked from their purchases. Tiger, Billy Williams, Pete Cooper, Margrit Malotki, Paul Magruder, and the others all saw, with stunning clarity, how, throughout their lives, they'd been constantly and tirelessly reliving, in one way or the other, the apparent righting of what had been their deaths at the hands of Genghis and his army—though they'd conveniently forgotten the other lives wherein which *they'd* been the killers…as Sumerians, Assyrians, Romans, Celts, Egyptians, Bosnians, Arabs—even Canadians and Americans. Slayers had, indeed, also been the slain.

All returned to the familiar court room, in Gulf Coast Florida. Each, from gallery onlooker to Stoker himself, sat in muted contemplation of their experiences—including those still in their jail cells, scattered from Sunset Harbor to Punta Gorda. No one talked, moved, nor sneezed…but all sat quietly, listening to their breathing…contemplating their multiple existences, their multiple *lessons…*

Howard Stoker sat quietly, hands folded in his lap, and contemplated his gavel for a thousand years…

Harry Gordon still stood before Tiger, both hands clasped before him, and stared at a spot of court-room floor for a thousand years…

Kacey Miller stared at her two rings, while Sheila Petrova stared at her hands. Both did so for a thousand years…

Banner returned to his thousand-yard stare for a thousand years…

And Tiger remained on the witness stand, staring at the richly finished wood of the stand before him for a thousand years…

When time again kicked in for the south Florida microcosm of that

Lee County court room, each silently went where they needed to go. Each suspect knew their part, and played out their roles to their needed conclusions, under the laws governing not only the state of Florida, but the physical existence in which they had all accepted their roles.

Because, what comes around does, indeed, *go* around....

Epilogue

The funny thing about life, Kacey Burnett mused (besides how good it felt to again use her married name), as she walked toward the awaiting, red, white, and blue *Greyhound* bus, was that it constantly changed. No matter what you thought you *might* be doing, or where you thought you *might* be headed, it could, and almost always did, change on you in an instant. Never say never, and never burn your bridges…if at all possible. You never knew when you might need to double-back over that very same bridge on a return trip.

Had all this *really* happened?

Sheila and Kacey had cried torrents as they'd hugged each other all night in her apartment. They'd finally made their peace. Why she'd chosen to desert her like that during her abduction by the three charging Mongolians on those desert steppes all those lifetimes ago, became brutally apparent when she remembered that Sheila had had an affair on *her*, when she'd been her consulate husband in the early 1900's, in Pakistan. That, in turn, led to a host of other emotions and memories that simply overtook both and turned them into blubbering fools as they fell asleep in each other's arms. The love they'd felt for each other ran deep, and, obviously, across lifetimes, but now that they both understood their part in each other's lives, there was no need for embarrassment—nor avoidance. They promised to see each other again, and to forever stay in contact. Sheila really wanted to meet her husband and daughter, and Kacey promised she would.

Sheila, on the other hand, had packed up and was ready to continue on with her own life. She'd made some mistakes along the way, but was ready to move on. No, she wouldn't go back to her ex-husband…that was another experience she was going to leave for another existence…but now she *understood*. Life was looking brand new to her and she was, finally, ready for it…to allow it to unfold and create itself; whatever the terms were, she was ready for it, and eternally grateful for a chance to finally understand and right things between her and Kacey.

Life was indeed funny, she said to Kacey, as she left her apartment that morning, packed her things, and left for New York.

Funny, indeed.

So, Kacey stood before the bus's open door and took in the last of Sunset Harbor, Florida. A glorious rising sun glinted its golden-red rays over the terminal and across her face. She closed her eyes and soaked it in.

Yes, life was great.

Life was a *journey*.

Things were going to be far from perfect upon her return. There would be a lot of work needed to repair all that had been undone—on both their parts—to...reintegrate her back into Mark and Emily's lives. But she was willing to do whatever was needed. She wanted her life back. Wanted her husband and daughter back. She looked down to the picture of her twenty-month-old Emily, which had come in the letter Mark had sent, and had been waiting for her on her return from the Fort Meyers. She clutched it to her chest, and the tears ran freely down her face.

"Are you all right, honey?" a lady of easily seventy years asked, reaching out to her. She stood before Kacey and the door, one small, overnight bag clutched in her other hand. She reminded her of Hedda Hocker.

Kacey laughed, choking back tears.

"Oh, yes, ma'am, thank you—I'm actually better than I've been in years."

Kacey smiled, then turned around, and took her first

(*steppes...*)

back into her new life....

About the Author

F. P. (Frank) Dorchak began writing at the age of six. He writes gritty, realistic paranormal fiction that delves into the realms of the supernatural, the unexplained, and the metaphysical to explore who we are and why we exist. Frank is published in the U.S., Canada, and the Czech Republic with short stories, non-fiction articles, three novels, *Sleepwalkers*, *The Uninvited*, *ERO*, and the story "Tail Gunner," in *The You Belong Collection – Writings And Illustrations By Longmont Area Residents* regional anthology.

http://www.fpdorchak.com

www.ingramcontent.com/pod-product-compliance
Lightning Source LLC
Chambersburg PA
CBHW021516240626
47154CB00002B/659